RUNNING DARK

RUNNING DARK

JOSEPH HEYWOOD

Guilford, Connecticut

An imprint of The Rowman & Littlefield Publishing Group, Inc.
4501 Forbes Blvd., Ste. 200
Lanham, MD 20706
www.rowman.com

Distributed by NATIONAL BOOK NETWORK

British Library Cataloguing in Publication Information available

Library of Congress Cataloging-in-Publication Data available

ISBN 978-1-4930-4197-8 (paperback)
ISBN 978-1-4930-4719-2 (e-book)

∞™ The paper used in this publication meets the minimum requirements of
American National Standard for Information Sciences—Permanence of Paper
for Printed Library Materials, ANSI/NISO Z39.48-1992.

Printed in the United States of America

To the late Rick Asher, Chief of Law Enforcement,
Michigan Department of Natural Resources.
As Shakespeare wrote,
"For courage mounteth with occasion."

RUNNING DARK

PART I
THE UPPER PECULIAR

1

NEWBERRY, NOVEMBER 11, 1974

"Dey're dirtier den dirt."

Eldon "Shuck" Gorley was in the Newberry DNR office for the last official time—to turn in his badge and state-owned equipment. Grady Service, within three days of going out on his own as a conservation officer, was guzzling black coffee and studying a report from Lansing while he waited for a meeting with the district law supervisor. Gorley, carrying a severely dented thermos, sat down across from Service and poked through a box of donuts that someone had left on the table. "Be da first deer season I ha'n't worked in twenty-seven years," the retiring officer said in his raspy voice. He was unshaven, had wavy white hair, leathery skin, and bushy salt-and-pepper eyebrows.

"Your first in da Upper Peculiar," he added, looking at Service.

Service chuckled. The Upper Peninsula surely was peculiar, especially for conservation officers. Gorley was not a gregarious man and had just spoken more words than Service had heard from him since he'd arrived from training downstate. Gorley's nickname came from his ability to "out-stupid stupids" with a well-honed and effective "aw shucks" routine.

"Treat each season like a gift, eh," Gorley said. "We only get so many."

"I will," Service said, not sure what the older man wanted. Gorley rarely talked or showed emotion, but was respected as an aggressive and thoughtful officer.

"You get da chance," Gorley continued, "youse might wanta be sittin' up on da Gutpile Ridge Grade Road night 'fore da opener. Dose Ketola brothers, dey like ta slow-roll da clear-cuts out dat way. I dogged 'em da past twenty years and always come up empty, but dey're dirtier den dirt, and dey'll be out dere, bet on dat. Dey buy old twenty-twos, use 'em once, and chuck 'em. You get 'em, trow da book at 'em for me, eh?"

"The Ketola brothers," Service said.

Gorley nodded and grinned. "Dirtier 'n dirt, an' I made sure da whole town knows I'm retirin' 'fore da opener and a green-butt rookie's takin' my place. Good huntin.'"

Service shook the man's hand. He had a powerful grip and clear blue eyes. Gorley placed his thermos in front of Service. "Little beat-up, like me, but I won't be needin' 'er anymore." The name SHUCK was etched crudely on the metal thermos. Gorley paused and added, "I knew yer old man. He was a warden's warden, and if he hadn't loved his hooch . . . "

Gorley didn't finish the sentence. Grady Service's father had served in World War II in the Marine Corps and had joined the DNR when he returned. He had been drunk when he'd stepped in front of a truck at night and was killed. Service had been sixteen years old, and though father and son had never been close, the loss hit the boy hard, causing him to withdraw into himself and trust few people. Service likewise had served as a marine—in Vietnam—and now he was in the U.P. as a conservation officer, history repeating itself. He had sworn he would not be like his father, but so far he was following the old man step for step and he found it unsettling. At six foot four and two hundred and twenty pounds, he didn't look much like his old man—and he certainly didn't want to be like him—yet this was the only job he had ever wanted.

"We all got stren'ts an' weaknesses," Gorley said. "Back when your old man and me got dese jobs, dey wanted toughs. Chances of gettin' convictions in da courts was so low, was our job ta rough up da poachers and put da fear of da DNR inta dem. Back den we used our saps first, talked later. But now da law's changed and we have ta use our brains a lot more den our fists, and dis is how she ought to be. You can't enforce da law by out-gooning da jerks. I heard you got stone dukes just like your old man, but you been ta college. Use dat noggin. Dat's all I gotta say."

They nodded at each other as Gorley left the room, one finishing a long, difficult career, the other just starting out.

There had been a hardness and an edge to Shuck Gorley's voice that reminded him of his father and all the men who had served with him, the old-timers now known as horseblankets because of the knee-length heavy wool coats they had worn back then. He had inherited his old man's stained and frayed coat. His father had always worn outer clothes two or three sizes too large to allow him to pack layers underneath in cold weather. It had always hung on his father like a loose sack, but it fit Grady Service almost perfectly, and he liked wearing it, though he wasn't sure why. *Stop thinking about the old man,* he cautioned himself. *This is your career, your future.* When he finished his cup of coffee he said aloud, "Ketola brothers," and shifted his attention to his first solo patrol.

Service was rooting through file cabinets when Sergeant "Sugar Sam" Surrey, the area law supervisor, came looking for him.

Surrey had so far proven to be a helpful and supportive supervisor. Service was to ride two more days with him and then be on his own.

"Little early in the career to be trollin' files," Surrey said, grinning.

"I was looking at the file on the Ketola brothers."

Surrey chuckled. "Shuck never could get those boys and it's stuck in his craw his whole career. Think a green-butt rookie like you can do what he couldn't?"

"Just getting to know the territory," Service answered, putting the folder back in the cabinet drawer. There had not been much to learn. The file was filled with reports and notes from Gorley, mostly speculative and accusatory; the reality was that he had never been able to catch the brothers doing anything illegal. Service wrote down their address and made a note to check his county plat book later.

2

GUTPILE RIDGE, NOVEMBER 14–15, 1974

"Shouldn't youse be oot in da woods?"

It was the night before rifle season for whitetail, and Grady Service's first solo patrol as a conservation officer. He sat in his Plymouth Fury 444, engine off so he could hear. All the lights were off, inside and outside. He got out and stood beside the vehicle, smoking and cupping the butt in his hand to hide the glowing ember, half listening, parked beside a massive jack pine blowdown at the edge of a clear-cut adjacent to the Gutpile Ridge Grade Road. The area had been logged over two years before and now bristled with new growth and sprouts of plants, rough grasses, and trees. In some ways it reminded Service of areas that had been carpet-bombed in Vietnam. At night deer would drift into the area from adjacent cedar and tamarack swamps, and poachers would slow-roll the logging roads and rutted two-tracks looking for animals to freeze with their spotlights so they could shoot them.

Many COs insisted poachers seldom worked after 1 a.m. or so, especially the night before the state's firearms opener, but Service had tried to put himself in a poacher's mindset and decided the best time to be out would be only a few hours before the season officially opened at first light—a time when most hunters, and presumably lawmen, would be fast asleep. Service knew that at night the animals would be deep into their feeding routine and presumably more interested in food than danger as they got ready to drift back to their day cover.

It had been colder for the last ten days, in the low teens at night, with daytime highs barely above freezing, and tonight, finally, it was snowing. Feeling the small icy flakes on his face, he was glad he had gotten the Fury tucked away before the snow started. His tracks would soon be hidden from anyone cruising the logging road.

Just after 3:30 a.m. he heard a vehicle trying to negotiate the frozen two-track. He could hear it sliding and bumping around on frozen grooves so deep and solid they could rip steering out of the driver's control.

There were not a lot of deer near his position. The real concentration was a half-mile south, farther into the clear-cut. He knew that poachers would look for large herds and pick off animals closest to their vehicles. Typically they would use their headlights or a handheld spotlight to mesmerize an animal and knock it down with a single shot. Some would gut the animal and haul it out immediately; others would gut it and leave it where it fell, coming back later to pick it up. With this snow and cold, Service figured they would leave this one. In summer and early fall, the weather was too warm and would quickly cause the meat to spoil, but it was well below freezing tonight and spoilage would not be an issue.

It was a poacher's dream: black night, no moon, no stars, just soft waves of wet snowflakes fluttering gently in the darkness. Snow cover would mute sound and make tracking easier.

When the vehicle appeared, only its parking lights were lit, and they seemed to have been half taped to further reduce light.

Even with poor visibility he could see that it was a pickup, and as soon as it passed, he got into the Fury, started his engine, and pulled out to follow, closing steadily until he was seventy-five feet behind it. Some officers would run without lights only if they had a sneak light to help them see the way. Such devices were cannibalized from military-surplus jeeps and jury-rigged to DNR patrol units. Service preferred to run with no light of any kind. Even as a boy he had been comfortable in complete darkness, and now he was driving in darkness so intense it might be the devil's belly. But darkness was not his foe; it was his ally and his edge. As a boy his old man had never let him use a flashlight. At night he was expected to get comfortable with the black and use his eyes. The old man's bizarre rules had always pissed him off and frustrated him, but when he got to Vietnam, his ability to deal with darkness had not only made him a better marine than most who were with him—it had probably saved his life. Now on his first patrol, he felt in total harmony with the blackness that surrounded him.

As the truck moved into the area where there were herds of deer milling around, Service maintained his interval and kept his window down so he could hear. Snow swirled through the window onto his sleeve and neck, but he felt no cold—only anticipation for what the people ahead of him might do. Training done, he was finally alone, hunting poachers.

After fifteen minutes the truck stopped. Service did the same, immediately turning off his motor. A light flashed over the roof of the truck into the field to the east, and Service got a glimpse of a deer in the light, followed by a tiny muzzle flash and the snap of a small-caliber rifle. The light then went out and it was dark again. *Driver's the shooter,* Service told himself, *passenger the spotter.*

Service watched the men get out of the truck and ease their doors shut without latching them. He got out when the men disappeared into the stump-filled field and quickly moved over to the pickup, carefully staying in the truck's tracks to obscure his boot prints. He saw a rifle on the front seat and backed away, using his hat to brush away any sign of his boots, memorized the license plate number, and returned to the Fury, wishing he had parked farther back in case they decided to check behind them with flashlights.

A few minutes later, the men got into the truck without checking their rear and pulled away. Service started his engine and followed. When the pickup got out to Broken Heart Road, the driver of the vehicle switched on his headlights and aimed west on the hardtop. Service followed, his Fury still dark, hanging back more than he'd done on the two-track in case another vehicle came along from either direction to light him up.

No vehicle came and the truck made its way steadily, never exceeding the speed limit. The vehicle left the hardtop several times to take short jaunts down snow-covered dirt roads and once pulled over to the shoulder, turned off its lights, and sat for more than four minutes before moving on. Service made a mental note of a couple of visual landmarks and the mileage on his odometer, and continued to follow.

Eventually they turned down an improved gravel road and from that, cut up a short two-track driveway, where they stopped at a large pole barn. Service watched one of the men get out and open the door. The vehicle disappeared inside, the door closed, and it was dark again.

It took less than ten minutes to find a rifle where the men had briefly parked to discard it. Service checked the weapon to make sure it was unloaded and smelled the barrel. It had been fired. He assumed it had been wiped clean, but made sure to handle it with his gloves just in case.

Rifle in possession, he returned to the clear-cut, parked a quarter-mile from the area where he had seen them shoot the deer, and trudged a half-mile through fresh wet snow, weaving his way around stumps and debris until he found faint footprints with his penlight. The tracks led to a deer, still warm. A steaming pile of viscera lay nearby.

Service knelt beside the carcass, where he made two tiny incisions in the deer's hide to conceal his markers, and carved a small mark on the hoof of the right foreleg. It was an eight-point buck, not a monster by any measure, but a nice deer with a tight basket rack, probably a two-year-old animal.

When he got back to the Fury he used his penlight to check his plat book. The truck he had followed had turned into a forty-acre parcel owned by Stanley and Leo Ketola. Gorley had called this one, he thought, then corrected himself. No, the old CO had set it up—for him. He could have made the arrest when the men shot at the deer, but something held him back—his first patrol, maybe—or something else he couldn't quite peg. Maybe it was the desire to have his first arrest be unassailable in court. In training he had heard over and over that officers needed to think through what they were doing or risk spending a lot of time in court in front of juries that often sided more with the scumbags than a sense of justice. When you were tied up in court, you couldn't cover your territory. He had decided early on to do his best to make his cases ironclad.

Having located the kill and the rifle, he returned to the house where the truck had disappeared into the pole barn, made his way through an aspen stand to a woodpile that had obviously not seen recent use, and tucked the rifle between some logs in the stack.

He spent the rest of the early morning patrolling back roads, noting where tent camps were located and where tracks led down entry roads to hunting camps. Just before first light he was in Brown's Hotel in Newberry ordering scrambled eggs and Swedish pancakes, the waitress giving him a questioning look.

"Shouldn't youse be oot in da woods?"

"Plenty of time," he said, nursing his coffee. He assumed the poachers would get to the carcass barely after first light, tag it to make it look legal, and keep hunting until later. If they were as good as Shuck Gorley claimed, he assumed they would find the quarters he had inserted in the belly incisions, and the external hoof marking.

"Youse're da new game warden," the waitress said, bringing his breakfast.

"Grady Service," he said.

"Nikki-Jo Jokola," she said. "Youse want coffee for da t'ermos?"

"Thanks," he said, handing it to her.

When he tried to pay for the coffee, she refused and held up her hands. "Shuck, he found my twins when dey got lost one time. Dose two scamps wandered down to da river and were gone all night, but Shuck, he found 'em, made sure dey was safe, and chewed dere butts out." She smiled at the memory. "You take care of folks da way he did and we'll call 'er even, eh."

After his leisurely breakfast, Service drove over to the Luce County sheriff's office and made arrangements for backup. He had a handheld radio in his Fury, the sort COs called "brick" radios. He would call the deputies when and if he needed them, presumably later in the morning.

Shuck Gorley looked befuddled when he stepped out onto the porch of his house in his green long johns. "What're you doing here?" the retired officer asked Grady Service.

"Using my head. You want to take a ride with me?"

Gorley considered the invitation. "I'm sure not goin' hunting openin' day wit' so many downstate sound-shooters skulkin' around out dere," he said.

"Okay with your wife?"

"She give up on me an' life a long time ago," Gorley said matter-of-factly. "Let me get some duds on."

At 8 A.M. Service dropped the retired officer a half-mile short of the Ketola property, and drove past the entrance to the driveway, hiding his truck in some trees farther down the gravel road that passed in front of the property.

As it often did when the sun began to rise, the air temperature seemed to drop. Service took his thermos and cut through gnarled jack pines to the house, found a scrub oak tree to lean against and began his wait, shifting from one foot to the other to keep the cold from creeping up his legs. He was less than thirty feet from the pole barn.

The pickup truck pulled in just before ten. Two men got out, each with an open beer in hand. They looked to be in their late sixties or early seventies.

"I guess we had da luck," the passenger said.

"No talkin'," the driver shot back.

The exchange suggested the driver took the lead in things, and that the man knew his business. Professional poachers never talked in public about what they did. Keeping their mouths shut was what made them successful. His old man used to say that big egos were what got lawbreakers caught. The ideal poacher would be a tongueless mute.

Service waited for them to go to the back of the truck to pull the deer out of the bed before he made his move. The passenger had a hold on the back legs of the animal. Service grabbed the man's arm, making him spin and stagger backward.

"DNR!" Service said. "Conservation officer." When he stepped toward the pole barn door, the driver bumped him with his shoulder, but Service deftly kicked the heel of the man's support foot and he collapsed. Service grabbed the deer by the antlers, wrenched it away from them, and said, "On your knees. *Now!*"

"*Holy Je-Moley!* What's da bloody deal!" the driver shouted with alarm. Service looked at the tag affixed to the antler. The animal was legally tagged.

Service glanced in the truck, saw two rifle cases, took them out, unzipped the cases, and made sure they were unloaded. One was a Model 94 Winchester .30–30, the other a pump-action Remington with a short barrel, probably a .30–06. Both were empty; only the .30–30 smelled like it had been fired recently.

Service saw right away that the mark on the right forehoof had been shaved away. The two men knelt impassively in the snow as the conservation officer poked around until he found the first of the two slits he had made in the deer's skin earlier that morning. He inserted his finger. The first quarter he'd put inside was gone; same with the second quarter in the second incision.

"Lose somepin'?" one of the men asked.

"You got names?" Service said.

"Stanley Ketola," the driver said. "My brudder Leo," he added with a nod.

Service asked in a nonthreatening voice, "Where's the twenty-two, Stanley?"

The brothers looked at each other. "We don't got no twenty-two," Stanley said. "Right, Leo?"

"Ketolas don't hunt deer wit' no plinker," Leo added with an affirming nod.

Service said, "I was behind you fellas last night, followed you, saw you shoot the deer, followed you back here, witnessed the whole deal, start to finish."

Stanley Ketola grunted. "Me and Leo never liked no DNR fairy tales."

Service examined the carcass. The .22 wound was separate from a larger hole. "You two stay right where you are," Service said. He walked back to his watch spot, got his thermos and set it down so both men could see the inscription on it, and filled his cup. He saw them exchange glances.

Service took a swig of coffee and let out a sigh. "You boys been around and you know how this goes, right?"

"Yeah," Stanley said. "Da easy way or da hard way. Dat's a fairy tale, too, *bub*."

Leo grinned and nodded at his brother.

"How about we look in the pole barn?" Service said. "That okay with you fellas?"

"You got a warrant?" Leo asked.

"Do I need one?"

Leo blinked and Stanley glared at his brother. "Dat buck dere's legal. Guess you'll be movin' on, eh?" Stanley said. "You don't got reasonable suspension to be pokin' around da property."

Service sighed: reasonable suspension? "Tell you what," he said. "Anything I find in the barn I won't hold against you unless I can prove this buck is illegal."

Neither man showed any emotion, but both obviously were trying to analyze the unorthodox challenge.

"What's da deal?" Stanley asked warily.

"You shot this deer just after three-thirty this morning and you both just drove in here with open containers of alcohol," Service said, fingering the tag on the antler. "But we'll forget the open containers, just to show you fellas I'm not tryin' to be chickenshit here."

"We got dat buck dis mornin'," Stanley said emphatically. Service felt certain that Stanley had been driving last night and that he had done the shooting, but Leo had tagged the animal. He had no idea why.

"We?" Service said.

Leo laughed. "Brudders, we always say we, eh?"

The two men were stone-faced.

"So you fellas are telling me you both shot this buck before first light, right, one of you with a twenty-two, the other with a bigger caliber? Is that your story?"

"Holy moley, we din't say dat," Stanley said.

"You shot the deer," he told Stanley. "This morning."

Leo stammered, "Hey, dat's my buck. I shot 'im dis mornin', maybe seven-t'irty. Da buck's legal and no bloody way youse can prove udderwise, eh?"

Service said, "I'll take that as a yes."

"Yes to *what?*" Stanley said, his voice rising slightly. "We din't agree to nuttin'."

"What I hear you saying is that you got dirt in the barn and dirt out here," Service said.

"Dis is baloney," Stanley said, his eyes showing stress. "Youse're loony."

"Look, guys. I know you've been at this a long time," Service said. "You're professionals and I'm a professional. I say I've got you cold, you say I don't. How about we show our cards?"

The two men looked at each other and stared at him. "We want our lawyer," Stanley said.

"What do you need a lawyer for? You got a legal deer, right?"

Leo said, "Get off'n da property."

Service said, "I thought you guys were pros, but all I see is a joke."

Stanley bristled. "We don't gotta put up wit' dis crap from no rookie woods cop."

Service knelt and dramatically poked his finger into the second hole in the deer hide and wiggled it around, probing deeply.

The men watched his hand.

"You lookin' for change?" Leo asked, laughing out loud.

"Shut yer pasty hole, Leo," the other Ketola snapped.

Service eased out a tiny swatch of blood-soaked red cloth and held it up. "The human mind is predictable, boys," he said. "People always think in series of threes—in this case, marked hoof, two quarters in the hide—and you fellas were feeling pretty good about finding three markers and eliminating all the evidence." Service waggled the red patch. "This is number four. I put it there last night—ahead of the second quarter."

The two men studied each other. Stanley said, "Dat s'posed to prove somepin'?"

Shuck Gorley suddenly walked around the back of the pickup with the .22 rifle in hand, yelled, "Catch!" and flipped the rifle at Leo, who caught it awkwardly.

Service looked at the men. "Nice grab," Service said. "Let's summarize where we are: I saw you shine and shoot. I followed you here, I went back and fetched the twenty-two from where I saw you ditch it, I marked your deer, and now the twenty-two has your fingerprints on it, Leo. I think Stanley shot the animal, but since you claim it, you get the brunt of the charges."

Leo Ketola dropped the rifle on the ground.

Service used his brick radio to call the county and within ten minutes they pulled up the driveway. The sullen brothers stared off into the distance while they waited. Service poured coffee for Shuck Gorley.

"Carcass, rifle, lies—now we have a reason to go into the pole barn," Service chanted, walking past the kneeling brothers.

There were twelve deer suspended from stainless steel hooks in a cooler in back, and parts of birds and a couple hundred pounds of lake trout and walleye fillets in a commercial freezer.

"You fellas been busy," Service said to the brothers as the Luce County deputies put them in their patrol cars.

Stanley Ketola looked out at Gorley and grinned. "Well, you never got us, eh Shuck."

Service wiggled the thermos in front of the older brother. "Who do you think sent me out there to wait for you two, and who do you think spread it all over town that he wouldn't be working anymore? He knew you boys would be cocky with a rookie on the job."

The patrol cars backed down the driveway with their prisoners and headed for Newberry.

Shuck Gorley stuck out his hand and grinned. "Thanks for including me."

"This was yours all the way," Grady Service said. "You called in the order. I just made the pickup."

Gorley stared at him. "I think you got a heap more brains than your old man had," he said. "You stay safe out here."

Service continued his patrol until nearly 10 P.M. that night, and when he got home his wife Bathsheba was already in bed. He looked for leftovers in the fridge and found none, showered, and crawled into bed beside her.

"You decided to come home," his wife said coolly with her back to him. When he put his hand on her hip, she pulled away.

"I had a lot to do." He briefly explained the arrest of the brothers and how Gorley had been after them for years and always came up short.

"Like little boys," she said. "They cheat, you try to catch them, and for what—a bunch of stupid animals? Good God, Grady, is this any way for a grown man to live?"

She could not have found more destructive words.

PART II

WAR IN THE GARDEN

3

GARDEN PATROL, NOVEMBER 20, 1975

The hunters had suddenly become the hunted.

Grady Service had no idea what was happening. Sergeant Holloman had
called the trailer at 2:30 A.M. and told him to report to Sergeant Blake Garwood at the Fishdam boat launch at noon.

Grady Service was less than eight months into his responsibility for the
Mosquito Wilderness Tract, the same area his CO father had patrolled before
him. His wife, Bathsheba, was gone, having abruptly departed six months ago
for Nevada to file for divorce. She had lasted less than a year trying to adapt to
life as a CO's spouse before throwing in the towel. Service felt that some of it
was his fault, but he was still angry, and sometimes he even missed her when
he crawled into bed alone at night. But since his transfer from the Newberry
district to the Mosquito Wilderness he had focused all his energy on his new
responsibilities, and thoughts of Bathsheba were fewer.

He protested because it was the second week of his second deer season
as a CO—and first in his new territory—and he didn't want to leave the
Mosquito Wilderness unprotected.

"Just meet Garwood at the launch," was Holloman's clipped response.
"And don't be late."

"It's not my territory," Service argued.

"As I recall, our patches say *Michigan* Department of Natural Resources,"
Holloman said. "Which means we go where we're needed. Blake's partner
came down with the flu; he needs help and you're it. This takes priority over
deer hunters in the Mosquito."

Service didn't try to argue about his lack of knowledge and dislike of
boats. He knew from some of the other officers that the Fishdam River launch

site was used for patrols down Big Bay de Noc along the Garden Peninsula. During his time in Newberry he had participated in some Lake Superior marine patrols during salmon and steelhead runs, but he had never done a patrol in northern Lake Michigan, and from what other officers had said, duty in the Garden could range from deadly boring to just plain deadly. He didn't relish either alternative.

The Garden Peninsula was a twenty-one-mile-long, shark-tooth-shaped, cove-pocked neck of land between Escanaba and Manistique. It was part of what geologists called the Niagaran Escarpment, limestone, dolomite, and shale-gypsum formations that snaked south from the Garden across a string of rocky, barren islands that eventually led like a geological arrow to Wisconsin's Door Peninsula. When the first whites arrived in the area they found Noquet and Menominee Indians using the area's rich soils for gardens, giving the area its name, which persisted to this day.

The western extremities of the peninsula were largely untillable, with limestone sometimes found within inches of the surface, and though some people still farmed the center and east of the peninsula, few except the occasional fruit grower and small dairyman could earn any semblance of a living. The primary economic focus of the peninsula had been and remained one thing: fish. Since the establishment of Fayette State Park, locals were happy to take dollars from tourists, even though tourists were a nuisance and sportfishermen not particularly welcome. Fish in the Garden were about money, not recreation.

Fayette had risen during the Civil War, when the North needed iron for its armies. The smelting operation had closed in 1891, leaving intact ruins and a ghost town that had been turned into a campground, state park, and historic site. Fayette, Service thought, was like the rest of the Garden Peninsula. When there was no more money to be made, the village had been abandoned.

Fewer than a thousand people lived on the peninsula, which had two villages, Garden and Fairport. The DNR had reason to know both of them well. Fairport had been a commercial fishing center since 1880, and nearly all of its residents still fished—a few of them legally, a lot more of them illegally. In 1969 DNR fish biologists had finished studies of Lake Michigan yellow perch, whitefish, walleyes, and lake trout, and decided that heavy pressure on fish stocks had to be reduced. Commercial licenses that lapsed would no longer be renewed. Unlike the past, if you didn't fish every year, you couldn't just jump back in and start up another year because it looked like there were big runs and money to be made. You had to keep fishing every year in order to keep your license, and if you let it lapse for a single season, you couldn't renew. And no new licenses would be issued until biologists judged the fish populations could handle it. "Order Seventeen" became an instant bone of contention.

Garden fishermen immediately donned sweatshirts that said DNR = DAMN NEAR RUSSIAN, and rebelled. Since 1969 there had been repeated confrontations between the DNR and the fishermen who were harvesting illegally. Locals had used long guns and pistols to take potshots at officers, mostly to scare them away; they also had rained rocks on them, vandalized and stolen their vehicles, assaulted and threatened them with knives and scissors and clubs, sometimes with large groups surrounding one or two uniformed game wardens. So far there had been no serious injuries, but everyone knew that the clock was ticking as long as the dispute continued.

After a confrontation a few months back, the Delta County prosecutor had declared to the state that he would no longer allow county deputies to assist conservation officers until such time that the state beefed up its force, its equipment, and its training. The U.P.'s law boss had simultaneously reduced the frequency of CO patrols down the peninsula for nearly two months, a decision that had many officers angry and ashamed, and had Gardenites crowing with delight.

Service had never been called in to assist in the Garden, but the decision to cut back the DNR presence there had rankled him because he saw it as just the sort of gutless decision imposed by some spineless bureaucrat in Lansing. It never occurred to him that Lansing might not have had anything to do with the curtailment.

Blake Garwood was a tall, stooped man with black hair and a full mustache that drooped over the corners of his mouth. The marine safety sergeant's duties involved regular lake patrols, and Service had met him only once, and then just to be introduced.

The sergeant arrived fifteen minutes after Service, but earlier than their meeting time.

"Lend a hand," Garwood said, tossing an orange life jacket to Service. The two men moved boxes of gear from the trunk of the patrol car to the dark green eighteen-foot Glastron on the trailer. Some of the boxes held various lengths of nylon rope and some homemade welded grapples. Empty green plastic fish bins were already lashed securely into the boat. Loading done, Garwood backed the trailer down the ramp until its wheels were in the water. The two men unlashed the craft, pushed it off the trailer, and Service held a line to the boat while the sergeant parked the vehicle and trailer against the trees at the landing. They both pushed the boat away from shore and hopped aboard. Service looked at his watch. It was noon, straight up.

The sky was gunmetal gray, but there was no snow and visibility was good.

"Your partner's sick?" Service asked.

Garwood was fiddling with a battery cable. "Garden flu," the sergeant said glumly. "It can hit anyone at any time."

The outboard motor gurgled and rumbled as they worked their way out of the sinewy river mouth, curving left, passing jutting boulders as they moved toward the open water of Big Bay de Noc.

"Your first time out here?" the sergeant asked, yelling over the straining motor as he tightened his life preserver.

Service nodded. The boat was bouncing and bucking against three-foot swells.

"You got green gills?" Garwood asked.

Service shook his head. He had never been seasick, but he also knew that motion sickness, like flu, could strike at any moment. Garwood patted the bench seat behind the console where he sat, indicating that Service should join him.

"We got shit for power. Putting the weight back here will help us get onto a plane," he yelled as he pushed up the throttle. The boat's nose rose up and the motor howled and groaned as the boat drove through the surface resistance and began to skip over the water, dislodging a fine spray that soaked both of them. Service used his hand to brace himself on the console as the boat raced along, slapping the waves beneath them.

"We're running south toward Round Island," the sergeant shouted. "We got a tip last night from a tourist that some rat fishermen out of Fairport and Garden are working whitefish spawners. No way to tell if this will amount to anything, but we have to check it out. Keep your eyes open and do what I tell you."

Service nodded, uncased his binoculars, and began scanning ahead.

Twenty-five minutes later Round Island appeared over the bow, and Garwood was pointing with his binoculars. Service saw a white boat with a horizontal red stripe and a huge outboard motor. Two men seemed to be scrambling to pull in nets.

The sergeant shoved the throttle forward and Service glanced at the instruments, which showed 32 mph, the tachometer at 5,000 rpm, and near its red line. "This is all we have!" Garwood yelped.

Service saw the striped white boat's motor come to life, its nose lift, and bubbles erupt from the stern. One of the two crewmen was dumping something out of white boxes over the back.

"How many boxes?" Garwood asked.

"Four," Service called out. "So far."

Despite having speed and the angle coming in, the white boat began to steadily pull away from them. As they passed the area where the boxes had been dumped, Service caught a glimpse of fish floating in the water. "Whitefish, I think," he yelled as they raced past them, knowing they could have been anything.

The sergeant nodded, picked up the ship-to-shore radio microphone, and requested ground units be dispatched to Fairport. Service had no idea why Garwood thought the boat was headed to Fairport instead of Garden, but he kept his mouth shut and let the sergeant do his job.

"ETA, thirty minutes," Garwood said, concluding his transmission. "Marine Patrol One clear."

At 12:40 P.M. Service saw the two-hundred-foot-high multicolored limestone cliffs of Burn't Bluff looming ahead. The white boat continued to steadily pull away.

"This bloody equipment—" the sergeant griped, not finishing his thought. Service saw him pushing the throttle so hard that it looked like he'd risk breaking it off if it would have produced more power.

Service saw another boat appear in front of them and run parallel to the white boat, keeping up with it. Both boats were two hundred and fifty yards ahead, but he could see that the second craft's motor was a huge red Evinrude.

As the two boats rounded Burn't Bluff heading southeast, the two craft separated, the new arrival veering northeast toward Sac Bay and the white boat cutting due west toward open water. After four or five minutes the white boat angled sharply back to the southeast and accelerated, raising a gaudy roostertail.

"Fairport for sure," the marine safety sergeant called out.

Just before 1 P.M. Service saw through his binoculars what looked to be a pier on the west end of the village. Beyond it were at least two more, one of which led to a commercial fish house, the other cluttered with moored commercial fishing tugs. The piers looked crude, made of nothing more than large black boulders held together by aged gray railroad ties, laid horizontally. As they passed three hundred yards offshore, Service saw four vehicles pull up to the westernmost pier and discharge eight people. Two men from a lime-green pickup with a white camper cap brandished rifles.

"Guns," he reported to Garwood, who didn't alter course.

Service heard the report of a rifle followed almost immediately by a splash not five feet from their port side. A second shot was not as close, but in the same general midship area, and Service hunched slightly as the bullet ricocheted off the water and zipped over their heads.

Garwood didn't flinch.

The white boat stopped at the pier cluttered with larger cigar-shaped commercial fish tugs, but nobody got off, and as the Glastron closed the gap, the back of the white boat erupted in froth and bubbles as it took off racing west. Garwood cut his wheel to get in behind the white boat and shorten the distance between them, playing the angle. As they zoomed back past the western pier in pursuit, the white boat cut sharply to starboard and reversed direction back to the east.

"They're trying to suck us in!" the sergeant yelled as they headed back for the tug dock. Garwood didn't alter course.

Service heard another shot and saw a water spout twenty feet directly in front of them. A second shot stitched the water twenty feet to their port side, and Service shouted, "More shots fired!"

Garwood was immediately on the radio, profanely wanting to know where their "goddamn land units" were, but the radio was silent.

They were beginning to close on the tug dock when the white boat turned sharply, its bow coming up out of the water, pivoted, steadied, and came roaring directly back at them. Service immediately saw somebody on the bow with a rifle. Four shots sounded in close order, but Service didn't see where the rounds hit because the Glastron swerved sharply as Garwood began to zigzag in evasive maneuvers. The hunters had suddenly become the hunted.

"Drop line!" Garwood screamed. "Throw the line!" he said, gesticulating at an equipment box. Service grabbed handfuls of nylon coils and began flinging them over the stern.

"Cocksuckers!" Garwood cursed, aiming the Glastron for shoals between Summer and Little Summer islands. Once into the shallows, he retarded the throttle to idle and cut the wheel hard, causing the boat to yaw sideways in a lazy circle. "Line?" Service asked as the motor idled.

"To foul their props," the sergeant replied. "Sometimes it works."

The white boat immediately turned back toward Fairport and Garwood slammed the throttle forward and renewed pursuit.

As they passed the north tip of Summer Island, Service saw a small aluminum boat near shore. It had a large blue motor and two men in red hunting clothes, both with rifles aimed at the DNR boat. He tapped the sergeant's shoulder and pointed. "More long guns."

"This is how Custer felt!" Garwood said with a distressed laugh as he pushed the throttle to red line, and veered northwest to keep out of rifle range.

In the process of avoiding the potential ambush they lost sight of the white boat, but as they approached the Fairport fish house dock they saw a CO patrol car parked near it and three more DNR vehicles quickly roll in behind it, spilling their passengers. Garwood roared toward the end of the dock and cut the throttle. As they drifted past, a stocky blond man with a scoped, high-powered rifle jumped on board, unslung a second rifle, and thrust it at Service.

"How many shots fired?" the man asked.

Service thought for a moment. "Eight—four we saw hit the water."

"Damage?"

Garwood shook his head. "Service threw line."

"You get their prop?"

Garwood shook his head again. "Did the white boat pull in?"

The new man said no. Garwood headed west, and they began to poke into every bay and inlet north of Fairport toward Garden. During the search the new man introduced himself as Len Stone. He wore the three stripes of a sergeant on his jacket sleeve.

Later Garwood picked up the mike and radioed Fayette State Park.

"This is Marine Patrol One. We're low on fuel; can we top off with you?"

"Affirmative," came the reply from the park, which was between Fairport and Garden.

As they motored into Snail Shell Harbor, the small bay in front of the park, the radio crackled. "This is Air Four, Blake. I've got a white boat in a slip in Fairport."

"We'll head down that way as soon as refueling is complete," Garwood radioed.

"Thanks, Pranger."

Service asked, "Is that Joe Flap?"

Garwood nodded.

Joe Flap had been a contemporary of his father's. Flap had been a DNR pilot, but when the department came under budget constraints, he had become a CO; when budgets were healthy again, he resumed flying for the DNR. The pilot had flown combat in Korea with the marines and for the U.S. Forest Service out west after that. He had come to Michigan after a stint of bush flying in Alaska and northwest Canada, and had crashed so many times he was nicknamed Pranger. Service had always assumed that Flap would leave Michigan and head back west or to Alaska. He was surprised to hear his voice.

Heading south, the radio came to life again. It was one of the shore units. "Where are you right now, Marine Patrol One?"

"Sac Bay headed southeast," the marine safety sergeant reported.

"Hold your position. We've got a Troop unit with us and we'll go down to the docks and check out Air Four's report."

"Marine Patrol One is clear," Garwood said, cutting the throttle to idle and allowing the boat to wallow into the rocky confines of the small bay. There was no sign of the boat with the Evinrude motor that had ducked into the bay during the earlier pursuit of the white craft.

Thirty minutes later they got word that the boat in the slip did not have a red stripe and that all seemed quiet in Fairport.

"Okay," Garwood said to Stone and Service, "let's pack it in for today."

It took two hours to get back to the Fishdam River launch, and while they pulled the boat, a mud-spattered blue pickup did a donut in the lot and sped away too quickly to get a license plate. Service saw only that the driver was a dark-haired male and his passenger, a woman with long, unkempt blond hair.

As they prepared to leave, the same vehicle came by twice on US 2, the last time racing east toward the Garden Peninsula.

Garwood walked with Service to his patrol unit. "This was a good tip, and if our equipment was equal to theirs we could have had them," he said wistfully.

"Is this a normal patrol down here?" Service asked.

The sergeant shrugged. "What's normal? If we don't change our tactics or upgrade our equipment soon, we're gonna keep sucking hind tit with these rats."

Stone said with a hiss, "Dis is so much *bullshit,*" and drove off with Garwood.

Service drove around the perimeter of the Mosquito Wilderness on the way to his 1953 Airstream trailer, thinking about the frustration of the day's mission and the intensity he'd seen in Garwood and Stone. He didn't really think much about getting shot at, because he had been in that position before and this time the firepower was limited. He got into his bunk just after 10 P.M. and rolled around, trying to get comfortable. His last thought before falling asleep was that he needed to build a damn cabin and stop living like a damn gypsy.

4

ESCANABA, DECEMBER 15, 1975

". . . Only a fool pokes a stick into a hornet's nest."

The small conference room in the Escanaba DNR office was smothered in attitude, expressed mainly in body language. There were twenty conservation officers jammed into the room, all of them from the two law enforcement districts that spanned the north shore of Lake Michigan. The room was as quiet as the aftermath of a fatal accident, in part because the officers were only a couple of weeks out of the fifteen-day-long firearms deer season and nearly worn out from long days and nights, dealing with every imaginable human behavior. Service felt a mixture of gloom and anger in the air. He found a seat behind the other officers and sat quietly. Several of the men nodded to acknowledge his presence, but nothing was said. Even the usually ebullient Colton Homes looked glum. Homes was in his early thirties, a six-foot Sumo with chipmunk cheeks, a military haircut, a perpetual smile that implied that he was up to something, and black horn-rim glasses that made him look like a hungry owl.

They waited ten minutes before two unsmiling lieutenants and Captain Cosmo Metrovich sashayed into the room. Metrovich was the Upper Peninsula's regional law enforcement supervisor; his officers called him the law boss, and in the U.P. he was the penultimate authority for game wardens. Service had been in the U.P. nearly a year and a half, and whenever Metrovich's name came up, even over beers, nothing was said about the man, good or bad. Maybe the silence was because he was new to the force, Service thought, but in the Marine Corps, and even in the Michigan State Police, gossip and carping about supervision was a refined art. He had expected much the same from COs, but so far had not seen it and wondered what this signified. His company commander in Vietnam had always insisted a bitching grunt was a happy grunt.

"All right, men," Metrovich began. "I've asked both districts here today to review the strategy for the Garden Peninsula."

Sergeant Lennox Stone from Menominee thrust his hand in the air and waved it like a tomahawk.

Service's only exposure to Stone had been the one bizarre and frustrating marine patrol on Big Bay de Noc, and that day Stone had not bothered with small talk. All Service knew was that Stone, like himself, was a native Yooper, and that he was reputed to have started with the DNR when he was fourteen, sitting in fire towers, and later working as a state hunter, trapping, poisoning, shooting, and removing problem animals before taking a game warden's position. Stone, in his mid-forties, was short and barrel-chested with piercing blue eyes and a shock of blond hair overrun with cowlicks.

"Far as we know," Stone said, "dere ain't no strategy down dere to da Garden."

Service saw Homes and a couple of other officers nod in agreement, and based on his one-time experience down there, he had to agree that unlike the marines, where every action was thought out in advance, it was difficult to see any strategy in effect in the Garden.

The captain showed a tight-lipped grin. "It's good to have a man willing to speak up," Metrovich said. "We're a team, and I expect all of you men to speak your minds," he added.

"Maybe da boys is full-up saying how dey feel and gettin' ignored," Stone said, putting his hand just under his chin. "Dose outlaws down to da Garden do as dey damn well please, Cap'n."

"Not everyone in the Garden Peninsula is an outlaw," Metrovich said, sharply correcting his sergeant.

Stone ignored the rebuke. "We know da ones in da cemeteries sure ain't—at least no more, Cap'n—but all da rest of dem we got our doubts about, eh?"

More nodding heads and a few smiles.

"You cannot paint all residents with the same brush," the captain said.

"Like to paint 'em wit' tar and feathers is what," Stone mumbled.

The captain slapped the table. "*This* is the problem!" he said forcefully. "You men have to look at the big picture . . . and at history. These people have lived off fish for generations, and we have to expect—and try to *understand*—that it will take time for them to adjust to the new rules and regulations."

Stone didn't back down. "Cap'n, dat buncha rats has never followed rules or laws, and even if you don't wanta see it, dey've declared war on us. We got good officers don't want to go down dere because dey know dey won't get no support. Even county and Troops don't go down dere unless dey got to. Dis Order Seventeen's got no teeth."

Service saw that Captain Metrovich looked uneasy and heard a shift in his voice. "All right, while it's accurate that Order Seventeen does not carry criminal penalties, I will remind all of us that there are license revocation procedures clearly outlined, and these *will* be adhered to, understood?" the captain said. "Due process, gentlemen, due process."

Stone grimaced. "No offense, but you call dat strategy, Cap'n, to act like gentlemen wit' a buncha rats?"

The supercilious Metrovich glared at the sergeant. "We do not have to become the animals we hunt," the captain said haughtily. "This is not the good old days when game wardens did their talking with their fists."

Stone said, "Wit' all due respect, Cap'n, whatever it is we're doin', it ain't workin'. Maybe it's time to go back to da old ways, or give da boys somepin' different."

Service saw that even Lieutenant Dean Attalienti nodded at this. The other lieutenant, Cooper Edey, showed no reaction. Edey was responsible for the district that contained the Garden Peninsula, but he was retiring soon, seldom showed emotion, pretty much went along with what Metrovich wanted in order to get along with him, and, Service had heard, never went on risky patrols with his men. Technically, Edey was his boss, and so far, with the single exception of his one unscheduled Garden run, Edey and his sergeant had left him alone in the Mosquito, which suited Service just fine.

"The strategy," Metrovich said, "is stated thusly: Only a fool pokes a stick into a hornet's nest."

Stone huffed audibly. "Dis ting's about money, Cap'n, and I say if it's about money, den we need to make some dents in dere bloody wallets."

Attalienti stepped up beside the captain. "What have you got in mind, Len?"

"Order Seventeen is administrative wit' no criminal penalties, and only if da bad guys repeatedly violate da rule, can we start proceedin's to revoke dere licenses. But all dis takes a long time, and meanwhile da bastards keep dere stuff and dey're out dere still takin' fish and makin' good money. Dose rats down dere tell da newspapers dey take fish to keep off welfare, which is a buncha hooey, eh. Dose rats got fifty-t'ousand-dollar houses, got new trucks, got new snow machines, and dey got new boats wid two-hunnert-horse motors dat leave us suckin' wind. Seventeen says where and when dey can fish and what dey can fish for, so I say we see anyting even suggests dey're violatin', we move in, seize dere nets, take dere boats, grab dere motors, secure dere snowmobiles, seize *anyting* dey need to fish and impound da whole stinkin' bloody lot and immediately start condemnation proceedings."

Captain Metrovich was shaking his head, trying to reason with Stone. "Proceedings take a long time, and what you're suggesting surely would be reversed by the courts. It would undoubtedly be characterized as illegal seizure—and harassment."

"Maybe," Stone said, "but we all know dat dose courts don't move so fast, an' every day we got dere gear, dose assholes down dere to da Garden won't be takin' fish. We don't need no criminal penalties in Order Seventeen. All we gotta do is grab dere stuff an' trow it all inta da courts and make da rats hire lawyers ta get it back."

The room began to buzz and Captain Metrovich had to hold up his hands to reassert control. "We *have* a policy," he repeated. "We will make our patrols and enforce the laws we have and, if there are violations of Order Seventeen, we will follow the extant process. Am I being clear?"

Even Stone took this declaration stoically.

"One final item," Metrovich said. "Chief Nill is stepping down, and I have been asked to deploy to Lansing for six months to serve as acting chief. In my absence Lt. Attalienti will be acting captain."

"Why's the chief steppin' down?" Colt Homes asked.

"He has a health problem," Metrovich said, not expanding.

None of the men congratulated Metrovich on his assignment and none of them stuck around to talk. They got up en masse and quickly left the building.

Service was walking to his vehicle to head for home when Attalienti pulled him aside.

"You know where the Beer Barrel is?"

"The bar in Rock?"

"Be there tonight at seven-thirty. Wear civvies and drive your personal vehicle. Park behind the house with the barber pole out front, hoof it over to the bar, and don't be late."

"I'm supposed to work tonight," Service protested, his mind already back in the Mosquito Wilderness on things he needed to do there.

"This *will* be work," the new acting captain said, walking away.

Now what the hell was going on? Service wondered. Since he'd gotten into the Garden mess, nothing made sense, and he was beginning to feel frustrations that reminded him of those he thought he had left behind in Vietnam.

5

ROCK, DECEMBER 15, 1975

"I'd rather get stung in the face than in the ass."

Service found it mildly ironic that he couldn't remember the last time he'd seen a train run the railroad tracks that paralleled Rock. It was a town settled by railroad workers and known as Malton Spur and Maple Ridge before being named Rock by a long-forgotten postmaster. The area was well named: Glaciers had left a deep layer of drift rock that had to be turned over before any planting could be done, and as far as Service knew, the only reliable crop remained rocks and some small, hard potatoes and stunted sugar beets, equally hard. Rock was a town without flair, and it was appropriate that the Beer Barrel was a two-fisted drinker's bar that made no pretense of being anything other than what it was.

Service was dressed in jeans, a red plaid wool shirt, and a black down vest. He parked his black ten-year-old Ford pickup behind a white shotgun house with an ancient and faded barber pole out front, and walked a hundred yards over an icy gravel parking lot to the bar. The interior was dark, the floor and furniture nicked, and he and the acting captain appeared to be the only ones there. Attalienti led him upstairs to a small office, opened a small door in the floor beside an old oak desk, and said, "Sit here and keep quiet. Your job is to listen." Service nodded and sat down, wondering if the acting captain had all his marbles.

The meeting in the room below didn't start for another hour, and over that time a dozen officers filtered in to be greeted by Attalienti and Sergeants Garwood and Stone.

Service's viewpoint was directly above tables pushed together in the main bar. Attalienti sat among the men, Stone and Garwood on either side of him. "I called you here because I think Len is right about this Garden money angle," Attalienti began. "I think our lawyers in Lansing may get their assholes tight, but the Garden deal is about money, so we're gonna put some bodies on this and poke the stick into the hornet's nest." The acting captain paused to let the words sink in, and added, "I'd rather get stung in the face than in the ass."

Service saw all the men grin.

Attalienti continued, "You men are here because you're going to be the core team, even if you're in different districts. I don't mean to disparage anyone, but we have some officers who're not crazy about patrolling the Garden. You men may not be crazy about it either, but knowing what I know about each of you, I think you'll go. You've been handpicked for this."

Service saw more nodding and sensed an unspoken swell of determination in the room below.

"Edey has decided to retire in January. As acting captain, I will appoint Len Stone to be acting lieutenant in Edey's stead. Len will spearhead this effort," Attalienti said.

Eddie Moody, a new officer from Manistique, leaned forward. "Do we put the hammer on the rats right away?"

"No," Attalienti said. "The big push will start in April after the ice goes out and the walleye and perch spawns begin. Between now and then we will conduct routine road and snowmobile patrols."

Colt Homes spoke up. "How is dat different?"

"Nobody goes solo into the Garden," Attalienti said. "No exceptions."

Stone spoke up. "We never go down dere wit' fewer den two vehicles and four men. I'll always be one of da four. We'll conduct no patrols without having county and Troop resources on standby. Between now and April we'll go down dere, varying our days an' times. Dey've been outnumbering us down dere, but we're gonna try to rectify dat, and when April comes we'll start going in with *real* force."

"You'll be on *every* patrol?" Moody asked Stone.

The blond sergeant said, "Can't let you boys have all da fun, can I?"

This lightened the mood in the room, and for more than an hour, Service listened and made notes while the officers and supervisors talked about rendezvous points, communications and backup procedures, and other technical matters.

After the men were gone, Attalienti walked with Service to his truck.

"You hear okay?"

Service nodded.

"That seem like work enough for you?"

"Yessir," Service said.

"You're probably wondering why I had you stashed upstairs, and I'll answer that. You were a recon marine in Vietnam, and I know you keep your cool and use your brain. Garwood said you didn't flinch during your patrol with him, and Shuck Gorley made a special point of calling me to talk about you—and I can tell you, Shuck is real picky about endorsing people. When I was an officer working with him, it took five years for him to decide I could be trusted. I have a job I'd like for you to do, but if you accept, what you're doing will be strictly between us, understood?"

Service nodded.

Attalienti continued. "I understand how Len Stone feels, but Metrovich also has a valid point: Not everybody who lives on the Garden is a rat. Our main focus there has been the major commercial operations out of Garden and Fairport, the ones with the tugs, paid crews, and wholesale fish houses, but they already feel our presence. The guys I want to put the heat on now are the rat fishermen, the greedy little bastards with fast boats who flaunt the law and do whatever they please. We're gonna put a dent in them."

"But?" Service said.

"You can't dent something you can't identify. I've been contacted by a Garden resident who's fed up with behavior down there and wants to help us. Frankly, I don't know if this is legit, a provocation, or hooey. But if it's real, it means I need to send somebody into the Garden alone to work with the contact."

"How do we beat the crow line?" The Garden was famous for its early warning system—a series of homes with lookouts who immediately used their telephones to report the appearance of any marked police vehicle on Garden Road, the main route down the peninsula.

"That will be your problem to solve," the acting captain said.

"Me?"

"I want you to go down there. Chances of one of the rats recognizing you is minimal, and you haven't been involved in this mess long enough to be affected by the confusion and lack of direction. If you volunteer, you'll report to me directly until you can authenticate the veracity of the volunteer informant. If you develop doubts—and I mean the *slightest* tickle in your gut—we're gonna drop this. But if you think it feels right, I want you to go undercover to observe and gather information. You will be there strictly for surveillance. You will *not* be enforcing laws. Your job will be to stay invisible until you can gather what we need and get the hell out. *Capisce?*"

"What about the Mosquito?"

"Others will cover your area for you, and you're going to be out at a time when there won't be much going on anyway. Are you in?"

Service said, "Who's my contact?"

"It's good you volunteered," Attalienti said with a grin. "You were asked for by name." He had a twinkle in his eye. "The contact is a prominent personality in the Garden and is concerned about maintaining confidentiality. They'll come to you."

"When?"

"Soon, I'd think," the acting captain said. "Come see me afterwards."

Service asked, "How will Lansing react to this?"

Attalienti grinned, "Hell of a lot easier to ask for forgiveness than permission. I want to know who the rats are, who leads them, how they stage operations, their land-side tactics, meeting and gathering places—everything you can learn that will help us to understand who and what we're dealing with. Observe and learn—do not act. Understood?"

Service nodded, but he wasn't really paying attention. Why had he been asked for by name, and why the hell did this feel more and more like Vietnam?

6

SLIPPERY CREEK, DECEMBER 17, 1975

. . . he wondered if having one leg halved discomfort, or doubled it . . .

It had been two days since the meeting in Rock, two days of routine patrols in the Mosquito. Conservation Officer Grady Service arrived home at Slippery Creek the way he had departed the night before—running dark, no interior lights, no headlights. It had begun to snow the previous afternoon, and overnight the storm had left six fluffy inches on the ground.

There were tracks leading up his road, and next to the trailer he saw a small dark pickup still sweating snow off its metal skin. The tracks told him it had arrived not long before him.

He parked behind the truck and approached it cautiously. He had spent last night's patrol alone, and the sudden appearance of another human being always put him on alert.

The driver's window slid down. "Officer Service?" He nodded. "We need to talk." The voice came from a face cocooned in a parka hood pulled tight around a gaunt face.

He nodded, opened the cabin door, and left it open as he shed his own parka and boots.

"Sorry to barge in on you like this," the voice said from the doorway.

"Coffee?" he asked, glancing over and seeing that she had no left leg and a metal crutch attached to her left wrist.

"Could use it," the woman said, closing the door. She took off her parka and unzipped her knee-high boot, which folded over. It had a feminine contour and a low heel.

"Fixings or black?" Service asked over his shoulder.

"Natural," she said.

The woman sat silently while Service began to boil coffee. His father had always boiled coffee and though it was too strong for most people, it was what Service preferred.

"Am I interrupting something?" she asked when he turned back to the table with cups and saucers that didn't match.

"No." He was used to being called on at all hours.

He brought the pot to the table, filled two cups, and sat down. His feet felt cold from a night in boots and snow, and he wondered if having one leg halved discomfort, or doubled it, from winter cold.

She grinned slyly. "One leg is like half a glass of water. Am I half empty or half full?"

"What can I do for you?" he asked, cursing himself for fixating on the one leg. *Dope,* he told himself.

She sipped the strong coffee and showed no reaction. "Your Captain Attalienti said I could talk to you, so the real question is what can I do for you people—not vice versa. I'm Cecilia Lasurm," she said with a formal air. She had a low, gravelly voice, jet-black hair cut short, a long neck poking out of a thick black turtleneck, no makeup or jewelry. Her eyes were huge and engaging, a faded blue color with green streaks.

"I teach in the Garden," she said. "Born there, went to school up to Northern, and came back to live and teach."

"Garden or Fairport?" Service asked.

"This shows how little you people know," she said. "I live in between," she said, "but the only *school* is north of Garden and it's called Big Bay de Noc. The Garden, Cooks, and Nahma school districts consolidated years ago."

"I'm sure the officers who are down there regularly know this," he said.

"Granted," she said, "but there are a number of obvious things they don't see or understand. I'm not a particularly subtle woman," his guest announced. "The Garden is controlled by a bunch of thugs and punks. Most people there don't want it that way, but if you go against them, your barn burns, your tires get cut, and windows start breaking."

Service understood. The lawless had always harassed the law-abiding into deaf- and dumbness in some reaches of the U.P.

"I've spent nearly a year trying to find the right man, asking around, talking to people, trying to find the most competent game warden I could. Word is you're new and cut no slack for scofflaws. I don't need a knuckle-dragger. I want a thinker," she added.

"There are a lot more experienced people than me," he said. "The Garden isn't my turf."

"I want you, and Attalienti says you're my contact. I also know that the DNR brings men in from all over the U.P. to handle jobs in the Garden. Right now your officers are not there as often as they used to be, and the local jerks think they've driven you out. I came to trade."

Service leaned forward.

Lasurm continued. "There's only one main road in and out, and the outlaws have lookouts and a CB-radio and telephone system for passing the word when the law comes down Garden Road. They probably have the back way covered too, but that road's narrow and too easy to cut off and trap a lawman, so you're forced to use the western route to go south, or come in by water; either way, you can't exactly sneak in. What you people lack is information—a scorecard, who does what to whom. I can give you that."

"How?"

"I teach at the elementary school, and I am also the district's so-called visiting teacher—which means I go to houses to take lessons to shut-in kids. I have the kids and relatives of all the troublemakers in my classroom, and have for the past few years. Some of those kids are in high school or just out. When you have a job like mine, you hear and see things others don't. For example, I can tell when the fish runs start and the rats go to work because their kids help unload fish, and the spines of the walleyes and perch puncture their hands. I see it every year. It's like being a priest."

"A priest can't break the confidence of the confessional."

"Don't be literal. I said *like* a priest." She frowned. "If somebody doesn't start talking and teaching you people what in blazes is going on, we're going to be at war for a long time, and sooner or later one of those potshots is going to hit somebody and all hell will break loose."

Interesting, Service thought. "What do you get out of this?" he asked.

For the next hour she explained, and though he didn't agree with some of her assumptions and theories, he realized that if she knew as much as she claimed, she could be the key that would finally open the Garden Peninsula to the law. All she wanted in return for her cooperation was that the Garden normalize for a few years so the kids now in elementary school could grow up in an environment where locals were not always pitted against all outsiders—DNR, trolls, sportfishermen—anyone "not from the Garden." Her intensity was palpable. "You realize if they catch you down there alone, they might kill you," she concluded.

She had given him enough tidbits to convince him she was worth the risk. "I can't promise anything," he said, knowing the go, no-go decision was his.

"You just take the offer where you have to and when you're ready, put an ad in the Manistique classifieds." She handed him a piece of paper that read MATTHEW 7:7.

"You run this and a date, time, and place, and I'll be there to talk," she said.

"Matthew seven-seven?" he asked.

"Ask, and it shall be given you; seek, and ye shall find; knock, and it shall be opened unto you."

"I thought you weren't subtle."

Cecilia Lasurm smiled.

7

MARQUETTE, DECEMBER 19, 1975

" . . . you're well suited for this secret squirrel stuff."

Attalienti had moved to Cosmo Metrovich's office in the Marquette DNR building adjacent to Marquette Prison, which had been built before the turn of the century and housed some of the state's most dangerous criminals. The architecture of the regional office featured a strange roof with hooked ends that resembled the beaks of birds of prey. Officers referred to the regional office as The Roof.

It was almost closing time and Fern LeBlanc, Metrovich's long-legged secretary, gave Service the once-over before ushering him to the captain's office, which looked out toward Lake Superior a few hundred yards away.

Service closed the door and stood in front of the captain's desk at parade rest.

"Relax," Attalienti said. "Coffee?"

"Had my daily ten-cup ration," Service said, sitting down.

"Make your contact?"

"Yessir," Service said, quickly relating the specifics of the visit from Cecilia Lasurm.

The acting captain listened impassively, his hands on the blotter in front of him, and when Service had finished, asked, "What do you think?"

"I think we've never had an opportunity like this before and maybe we won't have another one."

"How do you want to proceed?"

"I spend time with her, pick her brain, and look over the area."

"How will you beat the crow line?"

"I don't know yet," Service said, "but to maintain secrecy once I have a plan, I don't think I should reveal it, even to you."

Attalienti grinned. "I think maybe you're well suited for this secret squirrel stuff."

"I want to take two weeks, longer if needed."

The acting captain looked surprised. "Two weeks is a heckuva long time to arrange coverage for your area."

"This is either worth doing right or not doing at all. We have time now, and you said we won't start the real operation until April. If I'm going down there, I don't want to waste my time."

"If you can take the pulse of that place, you won't be wasting your time, but operating alone carries inherent risks."

"Understood," Service said.

"Not just the risks to you, but to the woman as well. You have to get in and out of there without footprints. We can't implicate her."

"She wants to do this, and so do I. My gut says it's the right thing to do."

"Do you always trust your gut, Grady?"

"Yessir."

"Good," Attalienti said. "All I ask is that you let me know the timing so I can arrange coverage. We're going to say you are on leave for a family emergency."

"Thank you." He didn't bother to point out that he had no family.

"When you take out the ad in the Manistique paper, use an intermediary to place it."

"Sir?"

"Let's not underestimate that Garden crowd. At times it seems like they have our playbook."

"I didn't think we had one," Service said.

"We don't, but we're trying to develop one, and this is the sort of paranoia those assholes can create. The best way to cover a trail is to not have one in the first place," the acting captain said.

8

SLIPPERY CREEK, DECEMBER 24, 1975

Naked Skydivers Go Down Faster.

Grady Service pulled into the clearing where his Airstream was tucked away and saw a red pickup that was both vaguely familiar and out of place. He used his radio to report out of service, and sat wondering what this was about. He took out his notebook and leafed through the pages.

On the opening day of deer season Service had found a red Ford pickup parked in the lower Mosquito River area. That night he had monitored the truck until after dark, waiting for the hunter to come out. When it got to be an hour after shooting hours, he began to wonder if the truck had been dropped off and the hunter gone elsewhere with friends. It had snowed steadily since midday, and there were no tracks into the dense line of naked tamaracks that served as a natural windbreak for the massive cedar swamp beyond.

He had called in the license number for warrants and wants and come up empty. The license number in his notebook matched the plate on the truck now parked near his trailer. His notes showed that the truck was registered to a Brigid Mehegen of Harvey, which was just south of Marquette. She had been born in 1947, which made her twenty-eight. That night he had just about decided to drive on when he saw a flashlight bobbing through the trees. He walked over to the truck, keeping the cab between the approaching light and him, and waited.

There were audible grunts interspersed with muted curses, and when he stepped out to identify himself, a woman chirped, "You got a broken back?" She had a rifle slung over her shoulder and looked tired.

"Pardon?"

"I hauled a damn buck all the way to the tamaracks. Least you could do is offer to help."

"Let's go," he said.

The deer was just inside the tree line. Service illuminated it with his penlight. It was a huge, black ten-point animal. The tag was correctly affixed to an antler.

"Swamp buck," he said.

"Here," she said, working the lever to show him the rifle was unloaded, and handing him a beat-up Winchester 94. She pulled off her hat and ran her hand through medium-length brown hair. "I thought I hit 'im pretty good, but it took me till mid-afternoon to find the sonuvagun. He swam the river and crawled under a blowdown. Funny how wounded deer head for water," she added. "You think people have the same inclination?"

Service didn't know and didn't care. Mid-afternoon: How far back had she been? The river was more than a mile from where they stood. "What time did you shoot it?"

"A little after nine this morning. I took an hour to drink half my coffee to give the big bugger time to lay down, but when I went after him all I found was some hair and a little blood and I figured it was damn gut-shot. I had a partial trail for about two hundred yards, then nothing. Thank God he went to the river and started bleeding more."

"You crossed the river?"

"Yeah, twice, but it wasn't too bad because the old adrenaline was pumping, eh. Now I'm *freezing*," she said, her teeth chattering.

He was not sure whether to be impressed at her determination or her foolishness. The thermometer was almost down to twenty, under a bitter and stiffening northwest wind. Being wet in such conditions invited exposure and hypothermia. He grabbed the deer's antlers, but she pushed his hand away and dragged the deer to her truck alone. She let him help her heave it into the bed and he let her get in the cab, start the engine, and turn on the heater. She took off her gloves and put her hands over the vents, waiting for the warm air to come.

She handed him her hunting license and driver's license without him having to ask.

"I've been dogging this big boy since July," she said. "My own fault I made a lousy shot, but I wasn't going to lose him to jerks or brush wolves."

Brush wolf was the Yooper term for a coyote. "Been hunting long?" he asked. A woman hunting was unusual. Alone was unprecedented, even in the U.P. where women were famous for going their own way.

"My grandfather started taking me with him when I was ten, and I went on my own as soon as I was sixteen. I've gotten a buck every single year, but this is the best one so far. I used to hunt the high country west of Cliff's Ridge, but the damn ski resort crowd got to be too much to deal with. Bampy used to hunt down this way and he told me where to come." She paused for a second and added, "Sorry I jumped you for not helping. I can get a tad cranky when I get tired and cold."

"It's okay," he said, handing her licenses back to her. Bathsheba had gotten more than cranky when she was cold, and nearly as often when she was warm.

"You're Service," she said, and added, "I'm Brigid Mehegen, a Troop dispatcher out of Negaunee," she said. "It's my job to keep track of new law enforcement personnel in the area."

"Grady," he said.

"Thanks again," she said, closing her door and rolling down her window. "With all the deer you guys confiscate, you probably eat venison year-round," she said with a gleam in her eye. This myth—that they allegedly took home all the illegal game they confiscated—irritated all game wardens.

"Not that often," he said defensively. In fact, all the illegal game that officers confiscated went to families and shut-ins who needed food.

She laughed out loud. "I'm puttin' you on, guy! I know you're all a buncha Boy Scouts."

"That old buck is likely to be tough," he said. Who *was* this woman?

"Not the way I'll cook it," she said. "See you around sometime," she said, putting the truck into gear and driving away.

Three or four times since deer season she had been the on-duty dispatcher when he was on the radio, and she had given him a bump and made wisecracks about the cushy life of game wardens and how he'd better be nice if he wanted Santa Claus to come. He had smiled and shook his head when he heard her on the radio, but didn't think much more about it. He met a lot of peculiar people in the woods, and she was just one of many. The dispatcher was totally unlike his ex-wife who had dispatched their marriage.

He had not seen her in six weeks, but as he got out of his patrol unit, Brigid Mehegen popped out of her truck. She was wearing a red parka and beat-up Sorels.

"I hope you have an oven in that little bitty rig," she greeted him.

"A small one."

"Size doesn't count as long as it gets hot," she said with a wink.

He stood staring at her as she opened the passenger door of her truck. "Help?" she said.

They carried two large cardboard boxes and a smaller one into the trailer. He turned up the heat and helped her take off her coat.

"Beer's in the bed of my truck," she said, taking something in aluminum foil out of a box and putting it on the tiny counter in the area that served as his kitchen and dining room.

There were two six-packs of Strohs long-neckers in a paper bag in the truck bed, and when he came back inside, Mehegen had shed her sweater. She wore a T-shirt that proclaimed NAKED SKYDIVERS GO DOWN FASTER. It was clear she wore nothing underneath.

She took two bottles of Strohs from one of the six-packs and a church key out of one of her cardboard boxes, popped the caps, and handed a beer to Service. She tapped her bottle against his and said, "*Slainte.* I cooked the roast this afternoon; now let me get it warming and boil some water for the potatoes. I brought plastic plates. I figure why waste time doing dishes when we can toss them, right? My environmentalist friends would throw an eco-freaky hissy-fit, but what the hey—what they don't know can't sour their stomachs, right? You like garlic in your mashed spuds?"

He nodded, and she said in a husky voice, "Okay, drink your beer and get outta that monkey suit while I do some woman's work."

Service opened the bathroom door to serve as a wall, shed his uniform, and put on sweatpants, wool socks, slip-on logger boots, and a plaid wool shirt.

Mehegen was sitting down when he stepped back to the other end of the Airstream. She held up her bottle like a pointer. "It's Christmas Eve and neither of us has another to fuss over, but I don't want you jumping to the conclusion that I came here to get laid," she said.

He had no idea how to respond.

"Unless *you* think that's a good idea," she added. "Do you?"

He felt his face reddening and she laughed. "Okay, I can see the Boy Scout game warden's not all that comfortable with a direct female. No sweat. Let's just enjoy this dinner and get to know each other. But no cop-shop talk. I talk to cops all day, every day, and while I appreciate what all you guys do, I get sick of the yammer. Okay by you?"

He found himself dumbly nodding.

She got up when the water boiled and dropped small red potatoes into the pot. Then she took something out of the smallest box and put it on the table.

"You know about *Luciadagen?*"

"Is that like Sadie Hawkins Day?"

She laughed so hard that tears formed in her eyes. "It's a Swedish deal, ya big lug, 'Saint Lucia's Day.' The Swedelanders in the old country used to celebrate it around December thirteenth, and considered it the first day of winter—never mind that they were a good week ahead of the actual solstice. They'd crown a young girl as the *Luciadagen* queen, and the women would start cooking around midnight. In the morning there'd be a feast, and afterwards they'd all go out skiing, maybe the men would shoot their rifles a bit, then they'd all jump in the sauna."

He stared at the glistening concoction on the table. It was shaped like a cat that had been hit by lightning.

"*Lussiketbröd*," she explained. "It's part of the festival. Saffron dough brushed with egg whites, filled with sugar, cinnamon, chopped nuts, and raisins. Go ahead and knock off a piece," she said with a wink, handing him a small jackknife.

"Isn't this dessert?" he asked.

"Hey guy, it's Christmas Eve and we're celebrating. We don't have to stick to the rules, eh? Time for you to eat some of my cat," she added, lowering her eyes and smirking.

He did as she ordered and tasted the bread, which was light and sweet. "Good," he said.

"My cat tastes good?" she asked as he chewed.

"A little dry," he said.

She laughed and said, "That's the spirit!" She touched his arm. "She gets wetter as the meal goes on."

"Mehegen isn't a Swedish name," he said, awkwardly changing the subject.

"Yoopers, we're all a buncha mongrels, eh? We take what we like from all the cultures around us."

She took several garlic cloves, smashed them with the flat of a knife, took off their skins, snipped off their tops, wrapped them in aluminum foil with a little butter and chopped fresh chives, and put them into a warm oven.

When the potatoes boiled, Service tested them with a fork, drained them in a colander over the small sink, transferred them back to the pot, and mashed them for her. She insisted on adding the salt, pepper, garlic, and butter, and stuck the batch back on the burner.

She took his empty beer bottle, set it aside, and opened another for him. "Your wife left you over to Newberry," Mehegen said, opening another bottle for herself. "She couldn't cut it," she added.

Before he could react, she said, "Hey, I'm *not* snooping. Every cop in the Yoop makes it a point to know everything about every other cop up here."

He didn't bother to point out that she was a dispatcher, not a road officer, and as far as he was concerned, his private life was none of her business. Not that he had much of a private life anymore.

When the roast and potatoes were done to her satisfaction, she sent him out to her truck to fetch two bottles of wine from a warm sack in the backseat.

She let him open both bottles to let them breathe. "Red wine should be room temp, right? I bought that warming sack over to Green Bay. Cost me way too much, but up here with so much bloody cold, how do you carry wine around and drink it properly if you don't keep it warm? Be damned if I'll stoop to screwtop wine."

"Right," he said as she filled two plastic wineglasses with dark red liquid, handing him one as she sat down. "You want to say a prayer?" she asked.

"No, but you can."

"I don't pray," she said. "I plan." She held her glass up and touched it to his. "Dig in."

Service expected the roast to be tough, but it was tender and flavored with slices of onion, garlic, basil, and rosemary. Over dinner and wine she gave him her life's story. Age twenty-eight, divorced twice, not planning to trouble herself with marriage again. No boyfriend at the moment. She was working for the Michigan State Police, taking law enforcement classes at Northern. She had applied for the Troop Academy in Lansing even though the Troops had never hired a woman. She said her post commander assured her that it was being "seriously pursued at the senior command level," and in a couple of years would happen. Meanwhile, she would finish school and, if necessary, take a county job where she could find one.

"You're a skydiver?" he asked, looking at her T-shirt.

She smiled. "I thought you'd never ask." She pulled on her boots, clomped outside to her truck, brought in a diminutive eight-millimeter movie projector, plugged it in, and threaded on a spool of film. "This isn't all that long, but you might get a hoot out of it."

She refilled her wineglass. "Keep your yap zipped till it's done, okay?"

The film was amateurish, with the camera bouncing and jerking all over. Obviously the camera operator had jumped first, and then captured two people plummeting from the side door of a Beechcraft Bonanza. Service watched as the two spread their arms in free flight and flew toward each other. As the camera zoomed tighter he saw that it was a man and woman and they were wearing helmets and boots and nothing else, and when they got to each other, they somehow maneuvered and tried to copulate as they fell toward the ground. "Just like eagles," Mehegen said. "We jumped at twelve thousand. I had the camera."

The camera angle went from a view of the upcoming ground to actually being on the ground, watching the naked couple land and do their parachute landing falls, just as Service had learned to do in the marines.

The two were kissing and laughing and brushing off leaves and ground detritus. Then the camera was focused on a single woman, equally naked and bowing for the camera. It was Mehegen.

The film ran out and clicked as it spun on the spool. "Well?" she said.

"Art film, not a movie," he said.

She giggled. "I know *that* definition. Bare tits and ass make it art." She poured more wine for herself. "My friends had more fun than I did," she said. "That was my third jump and their fiftieth. I thought I'd wet myself waiting to go out the door."

"Did you?"

"No," she said as she took scoops of melted ice cream and put it on slices of *lussiketbröd*.

Service didn't like to drink a lot, especially if there was any chance of a duty call.

"Is there room in that bed of yours for two?" she asked.

He said, "I think it's designed to sleep one."

She laughed. "You know what they say: What sleeps one will lay two."

"New math. I haven't tried that," he said.

She smiled. "Well, that's both a damn shame and fandamntastic news," she said digging into the bread and ice cream with a spoon. She took one small bite, put the spoon down, stood up, and leaned over and kissed him on the forehead before moving down to his lips.

"Christmas Eve," she said. "We can take turns playing Santa."

Service awoke to two gunshots. A naked, sleeping Brigid Mehegen was draped over his shoulder. He pushed her aside and rolled off the bed, grabbed his sweats, went to the other end of the trailer to find his boots, and stumbled around trying to get them on.

Two more shots sounded outside. He grabbed his four-cell flashlight, unsnapped his .357 revolver, pulled it free of the holster on his gunbelt, and stepped onto the porch. His light illuminated a gigantic animal that snorted and startled Service, who slipped on the icy porch and fell hard.

"Turn that bloody light off—you're scarin' the bejeezus outta my reindeer!" a stentorian voice roared.

Prone in the snow, Service rolled onto his side, shone his light toward the voice, and saw two of the biggest horses he had ever seen. They were light-colored and their rear haunches were spackled with even lighter spots. "Those *aren't* reindeer," he said.

The animals appeared to be harnessed to a van. The voice on top said, "I'm Santa Claus, and I decide what reindeer look like."

The van suddenly lit up. It was decorated with Christmas lights outlining the windows, including the windshield. "You done boning my granddaughter?"

Service heard Brigid Mehegen's voice behind him and it was anything but pleased.

"Jesus, Perry, what the hell are you doing here?"

"Came for my Christmas prezzie," the man shouted at her. "I don't see that a hormonally driven hornycane should change tradition. You know your Bampy likes getting his presents Christmas Eve, and here it is already by-God Christmas morning!"

"Dammit, Perry, act your age and go home! I'll be there tomorrow."

"It's already tomorrow," the man pointed out. "And I'm already here!"

"You don't deserve a present," Mehegen snapped at him.

"I'm your beloved Bampy."

"Where's the gun?" Service demanded as he got to his feet.

"Right here in my holster," the old man said, patting his hip.

"Well, leave it right there."

"I just wanted to get my granddaughter's attention," the man said.

"You're a stubborn, self-centered old man. I never should have told you where I was going," Mehegen said. "Who'd you steal the horses from?"

"They're reindeer," he insisted. "And I didn't steal them. They sort of followed me."

Mehegan stepped beside Service and poked him lightly in the ribs. "They still hang horse thieves, right?"

"Uh, I believe so," he said.

"Hokum," the old man grumbled.

"He's a cop," Mehegen said, touching Service's arm.

"Not a real cop, just a game warden," the man said.

"Horses are animals," she countered. "So are reindeer. That makes it his business."

"Why do you always have to go and ruin my surprises?" the old man complained.

"Because you never think anything through," she said, her rage barely contained.

"You are going to return those horses right now and hope the owner hasn't called the county."

"There's no reason for that tone of voice," he complained. "I'm your grandfather, father of your beloved mother."

"Not tonight you're not," she said sternly. "And mom was Bitchzilla on her best day. Where do these horses belong, Perry?" One of the animals turned and nudged Mehegen with its nose and she stroked it gently. In a mock whisper she said, "Don't worry, we'll save you from this madman." Turning to her grandfather she demanded to know if his "rig" was running.

"Would run good enough if I turned the key," he said from his rooftop perch.

"Get your scrawny ass down here," she said. In an aside to Service, she added, "Let's unhitch the horses. Do you ride?"

"Not if I can help it," he said.

"You can't help it tonight," she said, looking at her grandfather. "He'll drive and we'll ride behind him. How far?" she asked with a growl as the old man slid off the roof of the van, bounced off the hood, and landed on his behind in the snow.

"I wasn't counting," he grumbled, brushing himself off. They went into the trailer to put on more clothes and socks and get their coats.

The ride took close to an hour, and by the time they approached a farm with open fields several miles from Service's property, dawn was breaking. They were greeted by a cheery voice. "You found my kids, eh? Dey're always runnin' off. Dose two Percherons is smart horses, and no matter how I lock 'em in, dey always find a way out. Dey act up on youse?"

"No," Mehegen replied.

"Dey're s'posed to be workin' animals, but I can't find a job dey like. More like t'ousand-pound puppies."

Service and Mehegen dismounted and the old man whispered to the animals, who stepped toward him, nickering and nuzzling him while he slipped them some sugar cubes. The animals were twice as tall as the man, but obediently did what he asked, bumping him gently with their noses, their tails swishing the early morning air.

"Merry Christmas," the man called as he walked down the road between the animals.

"See, it worked out fine," Mehegen's grandfather muttered as he got out of the van.

"Keys," she demanded, holding out her hand.

"I got a license to drive," he countered.

"Not with me you don't," she said, snatching the keys away from him and ordering him into the back through the sliding side door.

Service got into the passenger seat and Mehegen started the engine. When the Christmas lights came on, she screamed, "How do you turn these fucking things off?"

"Toggle on the left dash," her grandfather said. "Potty mouth."

"Shut up," she commanded, turning the lights off. "How do you like my grandfather?" she asked as they pulled away. Service had no reply.

"Hey, a little respect," Perry said. "Where's my present?"

She didn't answer, and when they got back to Service's trailer she got out, opened her truck door, pulled out a gun case, and thrust it at him. "Merry Christmas. Now get the hell out of here."

"You don't have a nip and a taste of *lussiketbröd* for your Bampy?"

"Git," she said harshly. "I mean it, Perry!"

The old man opened the gun case and gulped. "A new scattergun!"

"Sixteen-gauge, your favorite," she said. "Don't shoot your foot off."

"I had my scattergun stolen," Perry said in Service's direction. "Some Philistines from down below copped it."

"You walked out of the woods and left the damn thing," Mehegen snarled. "You try to blame everything on people from below the bridge."

"Only because they deserve it," he said resolutely.

She handed the old man's keys to him, took Service's hand, and led him to the porch.

"We're going back to bed," she said, tugging Service's sleeve.

"*Lussiketbröd?*" the old man said in a pleading, almost pathetic tone.

"Next year—if you're still alive," she said, pulling Service inside and slamming the door. She immediately put her arms around his neck and said, "Memorable Christmas, eh?"

"Is he always like this?" he asked.

She laughed. "He's a pip, and he's got the world convinced he's sane, but I know he's totally nutso." She pulled out a chair. "Sit. Still, you gotta admit, he knows how to capture attention." She added, "This isn't done yet."

Service sat down as Mehegen got out a plastic plate, cut a large piece of the bread, uncapped a beer, and sat down beside him.

Seconds later there was a rapping on the door. "Sugarpie, it's snowing out here."

"Come in," she shouted at the door.

Perry stepped inside carrying his new gun case.

"*That* stays outside," she said.

"A flatlander will steal it," he protested, clutching the case to his chest.

"It's okay," Service said, trying to play peacemaker.

"No it's not," Mehegen insisted. "He's not allowed to have firearms in the house."

"This isn't his house," Service reminded her. "It's mine, and I have firearms in here."

"I left my pistol in the van," Perry offered.

Mehegen threw up her hands and rolled her eyes. "Close the door! You're letting the snow in."

Perry saw the bread and immediately grabbed at it, but Mehegen lightly slapped his hand. "Act civilized," she said. "You remember how, right?"

"Was me taught you manners," he said, sitting down, the gun case propped against his leg. "And I don't like that tone of voice."

The man devoured the bread and cut himself a second helping before grabbing at the beer, which he didn't quite get and knocked over the edge of the table. It hit with a pop, spewing foam across the floor.

Service grabbed a sponge and immediately got on his knees to soak up the beer. "Paper towels," he told Mehegen, who stepped past him just as there was an explosion from the table. Service felt her collapse heavily on top of him.

"Goddamn it, Perry! *Goddamn it!*" she began shrieking as she scrambled off Service.

He looked up to see the end of the gun case tattered and burned, and a hole in the ceiling. Snow was wafting gently through the hole, landing on the bread and table.

Mehegen began to shout at her grandfather, but Service grabbed her arm and began laughing, until all three of them were laughing and unable to speak.

It was late morning before they could get Perry on his way and the roof hole patched.

Work done, they immediately went back to bed. "I warned you not to invite him in with that damn shotgun!" she said.

"Where did he get the ammo?"

"From his van. He's been carrying it ever since he lost the other one. Merry Christmas," she said, kissing him lightly.

They tried to make love, but kept breaking into laughter and finally gave up. Mehegen went to sleep in the crook of Grady Service's arm as he lay there wondering if his ride on the Percheron had permanently removed a layer of his skin.

9

TRENARY, DECEMBER 28, 1975

"I watched da whole sad parade."

It had taken several telephone calls to track down Joe Flap's current address. Apparently the pilot didn't stay put too long in any one place and moved from rental to rental. For the moment he was living in Alger County on a farm northeast of Trenary on Trout Lake Road.

Christmas Eve with Brigid Mehegen and her daffy grandfather had been memorable to say the least, but what stuck in Service's mind most was her T-shirt and homemade movie: NAKED SKYDIVERS GO DOWN FASTER. Late Christmas Day he'd begun trying to track down Joe Flap.

Service grinned when he saw an airplane tail poking out of a barn-turned-hangar. There was a faded yellow windsock on the silo attached to the barn. A flatbed truck with a snowplow was parked next to the two-storied house, half of which was unpainted with exposed pink insulation. The other half was painted aquamarine blue, and not recently by the looks of it.

Another five inches of snow had fallen, and the temperature had dropped nearly to zero for the third consecutive night. Lake surfaces had gone from skiff ice to the real thing, and if it remained cold it wouldn't be long before ice-fishing fanatics would be hauling their shanties onto lakes.

There were fresh footprints from the house to the barn.

Service found Joe Flap sitting on a bar stool. He wore a sleeveless gray sweatshirt streaked with grease, military flight coveralls turned down to the waist, a green John Deere ball cap, and his traditional Errol Flynn pencil 'stache. His old horseblanket coat was hung from a peg and it was as greasy and stained as everything else around the man. Service saw that the engine cowling was open and the pilot had some sort of device with protruding wires held in his lap. Flap was a short, wiry man who shaved his head and had a scar that ran from the center of his skull down to his left eyebrow, a memento of one of his numerous crashes. Service had never known the man's age; he hadn't seen him in years, and now he looked a lot younger than he remembered.

Service plopped a case of Old Milwaukee on a workbench.

The pilot stared at the beer, then at Service. "You got youse a pretty good memory," he said. "Heard you joined da green," the pilot added, "and got da Mosquito, too."

"I haven't been there that long," Service said.

"Long enough ta make some of da dirtballs whine."

Flap got up, opened two cans of beer, and handed one to Service.

"Glad you made it home in one piece," he said with a crooked grin. "Dat Vietnam was one serious clusterfuck."

Service raised a can in salute. "There it is."

They both lit cigarettes.

"You've been flying the Garden," Service said.

"When dey need me."

"Is there an airfield down there?"

"Skis out on da ice," Flap said.

"An inland strip?"

"If dere was, da ratfucks down dere would turn it into a flak trap."

"No place to let down?"

"Couple places, mebbe in an emergency, but only if I was plumb-out-of-IOUs-desperate—and even den I'd have second thoughts." Flap studied him. "You got somepin' in mind?" he asked, arching an eyebrow.

Thoughts too amorphous to share yet, Service reminded himself. "I heard you on the radio last month."

Flap looked at him. "You know," he said, "our people never went to da slip where I spotted dat white boat."

"No?"

"Dis time our guys were willing, but da Troops wit' dem were new and a little shaky, which isn't unusual, eh. Dey made one ceremonial loop and bugged out. I watched da whole sad parade."

"You never said anything on the radio."

Joe Flap shrugged. "What would be da point? If our so-called leadership don't have da balls to get in da dirt wit' da grunts, why should grunts hang out dere *cajones?*"

"You're saying this isn't the first time?"

"Depends on who goes. Get da wrong mix and dey settle for a symbolic drive-through. Problem den is dat all da locals see a bunch of game wardens wit' dere tails between dere legs. Dis sure ain't da same outfit your old man and me signed on wit."

Service had heard similar lamentations from a couple of people, but he had ignored them. "Do the locals down there monitor your radios?"

"I s'pect so, but I usually run radio-silent an' open my mouth only when I have to. Why?"

"I had that one patrol down there and I didn't much care for what I saw," Service said.

Flap nodded solemnly. "You're not alone, son. Your old man was still alive, he'd get some of da boys together and dey'd go down dere one night wit' saps and brass knuckles."

"Times change," Service said.

"Mebbe," Flap said, "but assholes are forever assholes, and dere was a time not dat long ago when a warden wouldn't back down from anyone. You did, you might as well turn in your badge."

Flap was right, but this tight-jawed attitude had also caused several men to be killed in the line of duty over the nearly ninety years that the state had employed uniformed game wardens. "You think we've backed down?"

"How many shots fired at your patrol dat day—seven, eight?"

"Eight," Service said.

"You return fire, defend yourselves?"

In fact, they had swerved and run when the attacks became direct. Until Stone boarded the boat, they had had only handguns for defense.

"Don't feel bad," Flap said. "Da boys ain't never shot back at dose ratfucks. Da Garden's startin' to put a stink on green uniforms. You just visitin', or you got an official reason for droppin' in?"

"I didn't realize you were still flying for the department."

Joe Flap grunted. "I'm fifty-two: Guys my age make a hundred grand wit' da airlines, and all da stews they can screw."

"You regret not joining the airlines?"

Flap sneered. "I ain't no bloody bus driver."

"I always thought you'd head west again," Service said. "Or up to Alaska."

"Used ta say that, an' I almost did. But when dis Garden mess kicked up, I decided ta see 'er through. I ain't much for walkin' away from a scrap."

The two men made small talk for a while and Service asked his father's old friend about aircraft procedures and capabilities, but kept his other thoughts to himself.

Joe Flap walked him out to his patrol car. "Sorry you had ta join dis sorry outfit," he said. "Your old man—"

Service cut him off. "My old man's dead, Joe. Let's leave him that way. I'm not him—I'm me."

The pilot looked at him quizzically. "I guess we'll see about dat. Bear scat don't never fall far from da bear."

10

SHOW-TITTIES POND, DECEMBER 31, 1975

"Do they expect you guys to live like this for twenty-five years?"

Once again Brigid Mehegen had shown up unannounced, pounding on Grady Service's trailer door just after dark. He opened up to find her with a bottle of Cold Duck in one hand and a package of meat in reddish-brown butcher paper in the other. "Just so we're clear on this," she said, extending the gifts to him. "Fuck buddies, nothing more."

Service laughed and let her in, put the sparkling wine in a bucket of snow outside the door on the stoop, stashed the package in the fridge, and opened beers for them. "Does Perry have a New Year's Eve act?" he asked. He liked Mehegen, but this was all a bit too fast, and there was an aura around her. She was attractive and engaging, but was she a flake or a free spirit? He wasn't at all sure.

"I told him if he shows up, I will put two in his hat and gut him."

Ten minutes later the telephone rang, and Service groped around for a pen to make notes. "You're sure they're there now?" he said, reaching for his boots as he hung up.

Mehegen handed his gunbelt to him. "Where are we going?"

"We?"

"I came to spend the night with you—as in one plus one equals one. You got a problem with women riding along?"

He was in too much of a hurry to argue, and he had to admit it would be nice to spend another night with her.

Walking to the patrol car he explained, "The woman on the phone wouldn't give her name, but she claims two guys up on STP shot two deer with a crossbow last night. They're driving a blue pickup, make unknown. She said their names are Ivan Rhino and Eugene Chomsky."

Mehegen got into the passenger seat and buckled her safety belt. "The caller saw them do it?"

Service said, "One of them's been yapping about it." He looked over at her. "You stay out of the way."

Mehegen saluted with her left hand and smiled. "STP?"

"It's a summer hangout for local teens and occasionally the biker crowd. Most years it barely qualifies as a pond, and it's not named on maps. The name is strictly local."

She laughed. "You talked right around that one."

"Show-Titties Pond," he said.

She laughed even louder. "You take your honeys out there in your day?"

"I was busy with other things," he said. From age twelve through college he had played hockey virtually year-round.

"I can't believe you were celibate," she said.

"I wasn't," he said.

After a few minutes she asked, "Do you know you haven't turned on your lights?"

"Yep."

"Do you always drive around at night without lights?"

"Usually," he said.

"The DNR endorses this?"

"There's no written policy," he said. He had been told during training that there once had been, but department lawyers ordered it rescinded, feeling they could work better from ambiguity than specificity. Officers were never ordered to run dark and many didn't. In the U.P., where there were more two-tracks and logging trails than hardtop roads, the practice tended to be a standard operating procedure.

"I'm surprised the Lansing lawyers allow it."

"Nobody asks."

"And if you plow into somebody?"

"They'll have to ask."

She braced both hands on the dashboard.

He braked suddenly, stopping the vehicle in the road, and took out his plat book and penlight. The caller told him there were two camps owned by flatlanders from the Port Huron area. Service looked up the Floating Rose Township maps, found STP, and saw there was state land all the way around the pond except for the northwest corner, where two twenty-acre parcels showed the owners as August and Angie Agosti. He turned off the penlight, dropped the book on the back floor, and accelerated.

Most back roads had stayed fairly mushy until mid-December when it got cold; now all the two-tracks and gravel roads were snow-covered, pitted and frozen. They would likely stay frozen into late April or early May. He kept both hands on the steering wheel as the ruts yanked violently at his tires.

He knew that a tote road-driveway led north up the west side of the pond to where the private parcel was, but he stopped in a logging area west of the STP entry road, parked the Plymouth, left the motor running, and started to get out.

"Are we going for a walk?" Mehegen asked.

"One of us is."

"Don't pull this," she said.

"You're gonna be a cop, right?"

"That's the plan."

"I've got my brick," he said, showing her the handheld radio. He held up two microphones for his vehicle radios. "You know radios, right? County on one, DNR on the other."

She sighed. "I know."

"I'm gonna walk in and scout the place. When I call, bring the car up to the camps. Can you do that?"

"I guess."

He gripped her upper arm. "This is important: You're my backup. When you come, no gumball flashing and no siren unless I tell you to light it up and play your music. Understand?" He showed her the toggles for the overhead gumball and siren. He didn't mention the stupidity of game wardens having gumball lights. In the woods you needed to be as nondescript as possible, and a big light on your roof made you stand out, even if it wasn't lit. Obviously somebody in Lansing wanted COs to look like the Michigan State Police. Having done both jobs, he could tell the originator of the idea that the only similarities in the jobs were wearing a badge and being armed.

He eased open his door and took out the ruck, which he kept filled with emergency gear. The ruck still smelled new, and he shook his head when he thought about how he came to have it.

He had been in Newberry three weeks before starting official solo duty in the district when his sergeant told him to report to the garage where the district's fire-fighting equipment was stored.

There he found an elongated green panel truck with a DNR emblem on the side. A man was sitting behind a sewing machine in back. The truck was filled with racks of shirts and trousers and coats and hats, and bins of boots. The man had medium-length gray hair, a jowled round face, and thick black-rimmed glasses that made his eyes look bigger than they were. He also wore a green felt cap with a pin sprouting colorful feathers, and a well-tailored and crisply pressed dark green jaeger jacket. His face was flushed, his nose bulbous.

"I am Vilhelm, quartermeister, just like za Wehrmacht," the man said imperiously. "Ve haff only so much time, so you vill now please to stend on line and poot out arms, *ja*." The man stepped forward, pointed to a piece of tape on the floor of the truck, and demonstrated with his arms. "Like zis, *ja*."

Service stepped up and extended his arms.

"*Sehr gut,*" the man said extending his measuring tape. "You haff important new job, *ja*." When he finished measuring he wrote down some numbers and said, "You are beak fellow."

The man went back to a rack, rattled some hangers, and brought out a long-sleeved gray DNR uniform shirt for Service. "Try on."

It felt a little snug. The man poked at Service's back with a sliver of chalk. "We tuck here, *unt* here, *ja*." When the man reached for Service's pants, he took a step back and the man's reaction was immediate. "You vill not moof, *ja*." The man measured his waist and inseam. "Off!" he said, tugging at Service's pants and went to another rack, coming back with a pair. "You try."

They were a little tight in the waist. "Okay, *ja*, I let zis out, no problem," he said.

"You were in the German army?" Service asked.

"*Ja wohl.* Ve lose. I am conscripted. How old am I?"

Service thought the man looked to be mid- to late seventies. "I'm not good at guessing ages."

"Zixty. Ve are trapped by Ivan from za East, Americans and Tommies in Vest. I lose leg on za Oder. I am zixteen by one month, ja. Za surgeon, he cleans and cauterizes za stump, makes bandage, and ve all retreat. Ve vill not surrender to Ivans. I valk mitt crutch and carry Mauser more zen one hundred kilometers so I can raise my hands to American GIs. Zey put me in hospital, giff me gut care, zen I am POW for more zen one year until zey investigate to make sure I am not Nazi. Ven Wehrmacht took me, I was apprentice to tailor in Munich. America welcomes Germans with a trade, unt zey let me come to America."

Service didn't ask how he ended up in Michigan working for the DNR.

"You fought in Vietnam," the man said, staring at Service.

"Yes." How had he known?

"You haff za eyes," the man said, patting his arm. "Velcome home, velcome to DNR. You haff important job, *ja*? Now, you smoke, *unt* I vork."

Service lit up on the back of the truck while the man sewed. After awhile the tailor had him try on the shirt again. It fit perfectly, and the man smiled and nodded. "*Ja, sehr gut!* I come back one year, you need fix, I fix, you need new, I get or make." The man reached into a box and dumped a green rucksack and equipment bag on the ground behind the truck. "I make from GI zurplus canvas tent. Two dollars each. Zey vill last forever. Za uniforms all ready in three days, *ja?*" Service dug out the money and paid.

"Hey, Willie," another CO said, coming up to the truck. "Your Kraut pension come through yet?"

"Zere iss no pension for losers," Wilhelm answered with a pained grin. "Stend on line, arms out, *ja.*"

Another officer grabbed Service as he was putting the ruck and bag in his patrol car. "Experience counts with Willie. The older guys get all the good stuff and the best service. If you want an extra good fit, you offer him booze, venison, beer, or fresh fish. That's why Willie comes to this district every year—for venison and wild game, just like back home in Germany."

"Thanks," Service said, feeling for a moment like he was back in the marines, learning to work the system.

Ruck on, he made sure his shotgun was unlocked behind the seat and looked at Mehegen. "All you have to do is this," he said, taking her hand and showing her how to pull the weapon loose. "It's Remington, twelve-gauge, semiautomatic, slug in the boiler, four more slugs behind that."

She got out and felt her way around to his side as he tightened the straps of his ruck. He checked his watch as she slid into his seat. "Give me at least ninety minutes to get back there and snoop around, but when I call, come fast."

"What if I don't hear from you in ninety minutes?"

"Call the county for backup."

He walked into the cedar swamp, angling northeast.

There was no moon. Snow was coming and going in varying intensity, the temperature around thirty and falling. Little snow made it through the canopy filter, most of it piling up overhead. When the sun came out, it would be a frigid rain in the understory.

He moved steadily, not hurrying. The roots of the cedars were a tangle, some of them sticking up nearly a foot, threatening to twist an ankle or break a leg. In cedars, you learned to take your time, even if you had good night vision, which he did.

It took twenty minutes before he saw a tiny halo of light in the distance and guessed it came from the camps. He always carried a compass, but rarely needed it. If he was on course, he should be seeing the lower of the two camps. He slid more to the north to approach the upper camp first. Behind the cabin in the trees he found a trailered boat with an outboard, two Ski-Doo snowmobiles, and a vintage Indian motorcycle, all of the vehicles draped with snow-covered canvas tarps. Indians were antiques and worth a fortune to certain collectors. His old man had once owned one and used it for patrol until he fell off it and broke an arm; his supervision told him to stick to four wheels. Service wondered what happened to the old motorcycle. It had been red, and a beauty.

The cabin was dark and there were no vehicles nearby. He moved behind the cabin and into thick willows for cover. He could see a light on the corner of the other camp, and as he moved south he saw light coming from behind the other cabin. He crouched to make a low profile and advanced steadily, stopping often to listen. When he got to the edge of a clearing, he squatted and watched. There was a sliver of glow in the clearing, and suddenly embers rose into the night and something screamed and metal slammed and he could hear pounding. *What the hell?* His first thought was a burn barrel.

"Hold that fucker down," a voice growled.

"Damn bandit," another voice said.

Service saw two figures near the sliver of fire, and there was just enough light to see the silhouette of the barrel.

Somebody began to pound the metal barrel, bellowing, "There, there, *there!*"

Now what? Service thought.

He could hear something thrashing frantically inside the barrel, but the sounds had faded from screams to moans and hisses. He snapped on his four-cell flashlight.

"Conservation officer!" he announced. "What's going on here?"

"Got Bandit!" a voice said excitedly.

"Shut up, Eugene!"

"*Gumby!*" the other voice said. "Not Eugene. Gumby—not Eugene!" The tone was something between frustrated and pissed.

Service said, "What's in the barrel, guys?"

"Not your business," one of the voices said.

"Bandit," the first voice said. "Got 'im good!"

"Can I see?" Service asked.

"You got a warrant?" one of them challenged.

"Yeah, got weren't?" the other voice chimed in.

"Shut up, Eugene."

"Gumby!" the other voice insisted.

Service looked them over. Two males, one of them six-five with a cherubic face and an extra wide body of muscle and baby fat. The other was shorter, lean and feral in appearance, furtive in movement, with long hair hanging loose and wild.

"Stay right there, boys," Service said. He stepped forward and used the end of his flashlight to slide the lid off the barrel. Sparks exploded into the night and showered him as something leaped out of the barrel and began to run circles in the clearing, falling, getting up, and plunging on through the snow, its fur singed, the snow causing a hiss that blended with the animal's keening.

"Got *Bandit!*" the larger of the two men said. "Got 'im good!"

"Step over here by the barrel," Service said.

"We don't got to," the long-haired one said.

"Got badge?" the bigger one asked.

Service had his radio on a strap. He kept the light on the two men and toggled his radio. "Two-one-thirty, move up, no lights no music." Should he call for county backup? His mind was torn between keeping an eye on the two men and knowing he had to put the animal out of its misery. He glanced

68

in the barrel and saw charred and stinking remains of other animals. The stench pinched his nostrils. *Sickos*, he told himself.

"Okay guys, we're gonna walk around the cabin to the road. Stay in front of me." The larger man walked backward looking back at Service. "Gumby see badge?"

The larger man was Gumby. "Ivan Rhino?" Service asked the other man.

"Gumby," the big man insisted. He looked to be late teens at the oldest.

"Shut up, Eugene," the other man said, ignoring Service.

They had just reached the east side of the cabin when Gumby smacked the other man so hard he went down on his face and immediately scissored Gumby's legs out from under him, dumping him in the snow and pummeling his face.

Service saw vehicle lights coming up the tote road. He stepped over to the two men on the ground and jabbed the smaller one away with his boot.

Gumby immediately clamped onto his leg and started clawing at his holster, shouting, "*Get gun! Get gun!*"

Service bopped him once on the head with the butt of his flashlight and the man collapsed on his side in the snow.

"Fucking retard," the other man grumbled.

Mehegen pulled up in the squad. Service had the smaller man help his partner to his feet and guided them roughly toward the vehicle. "Call the county," he said. "Two prisoners to transport."

"What for?" she asked.

"Make the call," he said with a growl. "There're extra cuffs on the parking brake. Toss them to me." Mehegen did as ordered, stared at him.

"Sit," he told the skinny one. He cuffed the small man's leg to the big man's wrist, took the second set, attached it to the larger man's wrist and the smaller man's wrist. He could hear Mehegen on the radio, knew the county wanted a ten-code beyond a request for transport in order to assign a priority, but he still didn't know exactly what he had. He stepped over to the patrol car and whispered, "Just say yessir to whatever I say, okay?"

"Yessir," she said.

"Okay, Officer Mehegen. You've got the shotgun, right?"

"Yessir."

"If these two don't behave, if they try to get up or cause any trouble, shoot them."

"You can't do that!" the smaller man said.

"Yessir," Mehegen said.

Service went out into the clearing and found the animal. It had collapsed next to a fallen log on the edge. Heat rose into the night air, blended with the stench of burned hair. Service put the light on the animal. The raccoon was still breathing shallowly. He took his backup piece, a .38 snub, out of his pocket and put one round in the animal's head. He used a stick to knock the top off the glowing barrel and wedged two more coon carcasses out of the hot coals and went back to the patrol car.

"County in twenty minutes," Mehegen said.

"Good."

Service undid the cuff from the little man's leg and told both men to get up. He snapped the cuff on the little man's other arm and led them around the patrol car. "In here," he told the smaller man. He opened the passenger seat door, put his hand on the top of the man's head, and pushed down, helping him to get in. The big man remained docile.

"Shoot him if he even sneezes," Service said.

He heard Mehegen say, "Yessir."

He led the larger man to the steps that led onto the porch of the small cabin.

"You're Gumby, right?"

"Yeah, Gumby."

"Your partner's Ivan Rhino, right?"

"Yeah, Ivan."

"Gumby, how about we go inside and look around your place."

"Got weren't?"

"Why would I need a warrant?"

"Ivan said."

"I don't need a warrant if you invite me in. You want me to see your place, right?"

The man thought for a moment. "Okay, yeah."

Service reached for the door, but the boy balked. "What?"

"Him-her inside?"

"Somebody's inside?"

"Him-her?" Gumby said, his head nodding rapidly.

"Did you guys shoot some deer, Gumby?"

"So's him-her can eat 'em," he said, smacking his lips.

"It's good to eat deer," Service said. "You like to eat deer?"

"Him-her does," he said with a nod at the door.

"Your mother?"

"*Her.*"

"Got a name?"

"Cunt."

"The woman's name is Cunt?"

"Ivan says," Eugene said.

"You want to tell her we're coming inside?"

Gumby opened the door a crack. "Comin' in, Cunt!"

"Turn on the lights," Service told the boy.

"Turnin' on light!" Gumby shouted before reaching gingerly inside the door.

"*Retard!*" a muted female voice bellowed from somewhere in the cabin.

Gumby tried to go in, but Service restrained him and eased through the door first, into a messy living area.

"Ma'am, this is the DNR. Please step out here so we can see you."

No answer. "Where are the deer, Gumby?" Service asked the boy.

They walked into a dining area off a small kitchen. There were four deer heads on the floor, several severed legs on a table covered with newspaper, ragged haunches, blood and deer hair all over the floor, piles of guts overflowing buckets, the place an abattoir.

"Deer," the boy announced.

"You use a gun to kill them?"

"Robin Hood," the boy said.

Robin Hood? "A bow and arrow?"

"Yeah, Robin Hood."

"Can we talk to the woman you live with?"

"Her-him? Got weren't?"

"I'm inside now; I don't need one, remember? You invited me in."

"Oh yeah."

"I've been nice, haven't I?"

"Hit Gumby's head."

"Because you tried to grab my gun."

"Yeah," the boy said.

Service toggled his brick radio. "Two-one-thirty, let me know when you see lights from the county boys."

"Ten-four."

"Ma'am?" Service called out.

"She's not here," a female voice called back.

"How are the Agostis?" Service asked the boy.

He shrugged.

"They own this place."

"We found," the boy said, shaking his head.

"What the hell are you doing out there, Eugene?" the woman yelled from a darkened room at the end of the cabin.

"Gumby!" Eugene shouted. "*Not* Eugene!"

He stepped toward the room with Service behind him.

"Turn on the light, ma'am," Service said.

"Him got badge!" Gumby shouted.

"Dummy," the woman shot back with disgust.

"Show Robin Hood," Eugene said, stepping gingerly into the darkness before Service could stop him.

"Get the light on, Gumby."

Service heard movement and what sounded like a scuffle. The boy stepped out of the room, looked back, said, "Her-him *hurt* me!"

He took one step forward and fell on his face. Service saw a knife handle sticking out of the lower right side of the boy's back.

"County's coming," Mehegen announced over the radio.

"Call an ambulance," Service told her.

"Are you okay in there?" she asked.

"Get an ambulance!"

Where was the woman? He looked at the boy, knew the wound was serious, but he couldn't do anything to help him until he knew where the woman was. The boy looked like he had gone right, so Service crawled on his knees to the door, reached inside with his left hand, groped for the light switch, flipped on the light, and stayed outside the door to the room.

Two deputies came through the living room, guns drawn. One of them reached for the knife in the boy's back. "Don't touch him," Service said.

"He'll bleed out."

"Let the medics handle it!" Service said forcefully. He had seen knife wounds in Vietnam.

Service peeked in the door. A woman sat on the bed holding a sheet up to her chin. There was an unassembled double-barrel shotgun on the foot of the bed and a crossbow and brass lamp on a side table. "Where are the bolts, ma'am?"

The woman had long stringy blond hair, didn't answer.

"Ma'am, if you're armed and you try something, you are going to be shot dead—do you understand what I am telling you?"

She looked at Service and smiled fecklessly. One of the deputies stood on the other side of the door opening, his revolver drawn.

"Ma'am, please lower the covers."

The woman leered. "You wanna see my titties!"

"No, ma'am."

"Why not? I got *real* nice titties," she said, crestfallen.

"Cunt got *big* ole titties," Gumby mumbled from the floor.

The woman lowered the sheet to reveal pendulous breasts hanging off an emaciated frame.

The deputy pointed his pistol at her. Service stepped gingerly inside and snapped the covers off the bed. There were two crossbow bolts by the woman's left leg.

The deputy handed Service a pair of cuffs. Service handcuffed the woman, got her up, and draped a blanket around her shoulders.

The other deputy was still staring at the knife lodged in Eugene's back.

"You okay, Gumby?" Service asked, trying to soothe the boy.

"Her-him punch," he said.

Service knew what a stabbing felt like initially. "Just once?"

"Two, three times. Her-him don't punch hard. How come hurts?"

Service knelt beside the boy, asked the deputy to help him. They tilted the boy slightly, got his shirt untucked. In addition to the knife stuck in him, there was a stab wound and a slash. The slash wasn't bleeding much. The stab wound was bleeding steadily, but not spurting. Artery intact, he told himself, and steady but not heavy flow from the protruding knife, which looked to be in deep. Was there organ damage? No way to tell. Most vital organs were buried deep inside the body and not easily reached by anything other than cataclysmic force. In Vietnam a chaplain once proclaimed this was by God's design. If so, Service told the man, God must have planned on people wreaking violence on each other, which made humanity's flaw either a screw-up on the part of humankind's creator, or a matter of malevolence, neither of which he thought much about. The chaplain called him a blasphemer. So be it, Service thought: To live you had to deal with life as it came to you, which meant bumping heads with assholes and understanding you were mortal.

Mehegen was suddenly kneeling beside Service, her hand on Eugene Chomsky's face. "Don't move. It's gonna be okay."

The boy stared up at her with wide eyes as she continued to talk softly to him. Mehegen glanced at Service and gave him a look that chilled his blood.

"Where's the fucking medevac!" Service screamed.

Mehegen took his arm and led him out to his Plymouth. The ambulance was coming up the road, bumping and sliding, lights flashing. Service leaned against the grille while Mehegen poked in his pockets until she found his cigarettes. She lit one for each of them.

The ambulance attendants moved quickly, and Service half-listened to them barking orders at each other and the deputies as they brought Eugene out of the cabin, loaded him, and raced away.

"Medevac?" Mehegen asked. "Did Scotty beam us elsewhere?" Service had no idea what she was talking about. "Captain Kirk, Mr. Spock, *Star Trek* . . . on TV?" she prompted.

He shrugged. He didn't own a television. He walked over to the sheriff's cruiser where Ivan Rhino sat glowering in the backseat, and then moved on to the next vehicle where the woman was in custody, the blanket still draped over her.

A deputy interrupted him. "You'd better step back inside," he said.

A second bedroom in the cabin was littered with firearms, fishing rods, a couple of salmon nets, boxes of ammo stacked up, two chain saws, and piles of tools. Service studied the mess, said, "There's a boat on a trailer, a couple of snowmobiles, and an Indian motorcycle under tarps in the wood line behind the next camp."

He went back outside and opened the door of the car where the woman sat. "Ma'am, what's your name?"

The woman turned her head away and he turned to a nearby deputy. "Find any ID?"

"Not yet."

No ID, and where was their truck? How did the caller know the men's names, and identify the truck, but not mention the woman? Was she a late arrival? If so, how did she fit in?

Service told the deputies he would drive up to Marquette later and write up his report. They discussed charges and decided they would start with stolen property, illegal deer, and the raccoons. Once they got more on the stabbing, that would become primary.

Not thirty minutes later another deputy, a sergeant, came up to him. "The boat and motorcycle in the woods match the descriptions of stuff stolen from some lake camps this summer. We've had camp break-ins since last June, more than thirty of them, and probably a bunch not yet reported because the owners are down below and don't know. Just last week an old guy over in Carlshend got the shit beaten out of him and ended up in the hospital—broken arm, jaw, lost some teeth, broken rib. The descriptions he gave us were pretty discombobulated, but we'll put together a lineup and see what he says. You should have waited for backup," the sergeant added.

Service grunted and shrugged. The man was right, but it had been his call to go in alone, and you did what you thought you had to.

He went back into the building with evidence bags and began bagging animal parts. Mehegen worked alongside him. The sergeant and his deputy concentrated on the bedroom where the stabbing had taken place. Service examined each piece of meat and saw that one of them had a hole near the shoulder joint. He took out his pocketknife, dug around in the hole, and, using gentle leverage, pried out a slug.

Mehegen said, "What's that?"

"Slug. Let's check all the meat again."

They eventually located a second slug about the same size as the first one. Service slid both into plastic envelopes and they hauled all the evidence, including the crossbow and bolts, out to the Plymouth. Service also bagged the raccoon carcasses from behind the cabin.

The sergeant and his men were still working when Service and Mehegen began an external search.

Two hours later they were still traipsing around the woods and swamps that abutted the pond and camps. "What the hell are we supposed to be doing?" Mehegen demanded to know.

"Looking for their truck," he said.

"Shouldn't we be looking near a road?"

"My God!" he said, bumping his forehead with the heel of his hand. "I never thought of that."

"Dial down the sarcasm," she said.

"The tip I got told me about a truck. The camp was filled with contraband, and they didn't exactly go to great lengths to hide any of it, so where is their ride?"

"Are you always so suspicious?"

"It's in my wiring."

"My feet hurt," she said. "Can we like . . . you know?"

"Not yet," he said. "I have to get up to Marquette to do the paperwork, and drop evidence at the district office in Escanaba. You want me to drop you back at the Airstream? This will be a rest-of-the-night deal."

"Not a chance," she said. "In for a dime, in for a dollar."

"What exactly does that mean?" he asked.

She shrugged and grinned. "It's a cliché. When I'm tired, clichés pop out. Aren't you tired?"

"Sure," he said.

"Then show it," she said. "It will make me feel better to know I'm not the only one dragging."

Mehegen remained in the patrol car while he put the evidence in the district office locker, and she slept on the drive to Marquette and while he went into the county building, wrote his report, checked on Eugene Chomsky's condition, and talked to deputies. Chomsky had already undergone a transfusion and almost two hours of surgery. The knife had not touched vital organs, but there had been heavy internal bleeding and he had gone into shock. He was listed as critical but stable.

Service asked that Ivan Rhino be brought into an interrogation room. Rhino looked even more cadaverous and disheveled than he had looked at the camp, his eyes sunk in his head, his skin yellow. Service offered the prisoner a cigarette, which he accepted. Service lit it for him.

"What was the deal with the raccoons?"

"Ask the dummy."

"Burning them alive was Chomsky's idea?"

"Everything was his idea," Ivan Rhino said.

Service looked at the man. "Eugene's not going to die," he said. "What about the woman?"

"What woman?" Rhino said, exhaling a cloud of smoke.

"I suppose you don't know anything about a pickup truck?"

"I don't know squat, man, and I don't talk unless there's a lawyer sitting here holding my swinging dick."

Rhino had not asked how Eugene was. If Eugene died, everything would be dumped on his shoulders.

Service left the prisoner and went to find one of the deputies who had been at the camp. He found one huddled with a detective named Kobera, who looked like he'd been jerked out of bed and dropped into the room. The deputy said, "Everything we found out there is on a list from the camp break-ins. There's other stuff too, not on the list, which says they've been busy again."

"Arraignment?" Service asked.

"Gotta get lawyers for them and give the old man a look at Rhino. We'll arraign tomorrow afternoon, late," he said. "Rhino says he has no money for a lawyer."

Service mashed out his cigarette. "The woman talking?"

"Total lockjaw."

"Anything in the system on Chomsky and Rhino?"

"Not yet. We'll give you a bump when we get our shit more together," Kobera said. They exchanged phone numbers.

Mehegen slept until they were ten minutes from his place. She didn't snore, but cooed like a pigeon. When she woke up she asked, "What time is it?"

He had no idea. "The sun's up," he offered.

Back in the trailer he poured a glass of champagne for each of them. They toasted the new year, got undressed, ignored the shower, and crawled into bed. Sometime later she put her head on his shoulder. "Do they expect you guys to live like this for twenty-five years?"

He smiled, but his mind was back in the camp. They had a crossbow, so why the bullets? And how the hell could they interview Gumby? His language was awkward, his thoughts jumped around, and he seemed to have the emotional stability of a child. The boy's jumbling of pronouns left Service wondering if he had missed something. Service thought, the boy seemed to have gotten my gender right when he talked about my badge, so why the other confusion? The case had looked cut and dried last night. It didn't feel that way this morning.

11

GARDEN PATROL, JANUARY 8, 1976

"Dat ain't no confetti!"

Just like last time, Service was alerted in the middle of the night for a Garden patrol, but this time the caller was Acting Captain Attalienti. Despite webs of sleep-induced fugue, he questioned the advisability of showing his face—given the pending recon.

"Don't sweat it," the acting captain said. "Meet Stone at the Fishdam boat launch. Be there at zero-nine hundred."

"I take it we're not checking nets," Service said. He had heard that snowmobile patrols generally met well before daylight.

"Think of it as a parade," Attalienti said. "No snowmobiles."

Service arrived at 8 A.M. and waited. Colt Homes was first to pull in; he parked next to him and got in. "Heard you pinched some camp raiders," he said.

"I got a tip that a couple of guys whacked some deer with crossbows." He didn't mention the recovered slugs because he still hadn't worked out what had actually happened.

"Don't you *love* dis shit!" Homes chirped. "You never know where it will lead. I heard da value of da recovered goods is around forty grand."

Service hadn't heard this. What he had heard was that the old man who'd been beaten up had positively identified Ivan Rhino in a lineup, and Eugene Chomsky by photograph. Neither man had a record. Rhino was twenty-two, from Peru, Indiana; Chomsky not yet sixteen, from Milwaukee—a juvenile runaway. Rhino had a court-appointed attorney and was not talking. Chomsky was still in the hospital, his condition raised from critical and stable to just stable. He would live.

Because the robbery and break-in charges were far in excess of what the men would get from illegally killing deer, or even for burning raccoons alive, Service had not attended the arraignment. He was glad the Chomsky boy would live. The only lingering question for him was the identity of the woman. So far, she remained in jail, unidentified, and facing charges of attempted murder and felonious assault.

"Here's da kicker," Homes said. "Da broad from dat night hired Odd Hegstrom. Can you believe *dat*?"

"*Ode*, like in poem?"

"No, man. It's spelled O-d-d and pronounced *Ode*. He's an Icelander, Greenlander—somepin' like dat."

Service shrugged; the name meant nothing.

Homes said, "He's a lawyer out of Ironwood. When Order Seventeen come down, da Garden fish house boys hired him ta fight da DNR. He's a very tough operator."

"And he took the woman's case?"

"Everybody's shaking dere heads, but at least she'll have ta identify herself now."

Service immediately wondered if she was a Garden woman, but shoved the thought aside. The potential for other connections was too large to dwell on. Still . . .

Eddie Moody was the next to arrive, then Budge Kangas, a veteran CO from Menominee County, and, finally, acting lieutenant Lennox Stone.

The four men stood in the morning air drinking coffee and smoking as snow continued to fall. Stone handed them dark green ski masks. "We're gonna take a little ride this morning," he explained. "I'll lead, followed by Kangas, Moody, Homes, and Service. Keep a close interval, say, three car lengths."

"What're these for?" Moody asked, holding up a mask.

"Psychological warfare," Stone said with a grin.

"Garden Road?" Homes asked.

"Yep, right down da gut, all da way ta Fairport."

"Why?" Kangas asked.

"We need to test da crow line."

"What's to test? We know it's there."

"We'll talk about it after we're done," Stone said.

They pulled out and headed east precisely at zero-nine hundred. It was five or six miles east to Garden Road. Light snow continued to fall. Garden Road began at a spot called Garden Corners, the main landmark a nondescript gas station called Foxy's Den; the road stretched the length of the peninsula. The patrol drove the speed limit, lined up like spring goslings, and passed through the village without incident. It struck Service as odd (if not ominous) that they had not seen a single northbound or southbound vehicle during the run down to the village, and there had been nobody on the streets when they passed through.

The convoy continued south for eight miles, past Fayette State Park.

The park was the former site of a pig-iron and smelting operation that grew out of the need for iron spawned during the Civil War. In its heyday it had been a stinking hellhole someone had once compared to Cleveland's worst slums. Service had never been into the park and had little interest in seeing the ghostly remains of a town; the U.P. was filled with them, most of them the detritus of companies scarfing up the state's natural resources and moving on.

Their destination was Fairport, a village seven miles below the park, and the terminus of the twenty-one-mile-long peninsula. The snow had stopped as they left Garden, and they were bathed in morning sunshine as a few illuminated flakes swirled off the trees.

They were approaching a sharp turn with a cedar forest on both sides of the road, when Service was startled by something striking his hood and skipping off his windshield, quickly followed by more impacts. Ahead he saw things raining out of the cedars toward the other vehicles, and wondered how Stone would play it.

They went less than a hundred yards when Stone radioed, "Dat ain't no confetti! Hang a one-eighty, boys!"

Service cut sharply to the left, stopped, backed up, jerked his wheels to the right, stopped and shifted to drive, steered sharply left, and headed back to the north. Missiles continued to bounce off the Plymouth, but as soon as he got up the road away from the cedars, the assault stopped. He watched in his rearview mirror as the others turned and began to follow.

Coming into Garden he saw a crowd of twenty or more men on the porch of Roadie's Bar on the east side of the road, and as he got closer, he saw they were wearing black ski masks. They began to heave softball-size rocks and bottles at him. A brick or something as heavy smacked his passenger window with a popping sound and spidered it, but did not break it out.

"Service, you're too far out front," Homes yelped on the radio, and Service executed a quick U-turn in front of the bar. The rock throwers immediately fled, some of them through the front door, others down the sides of the building.

When the other vehicles got closer, he did another U-turn into the lead and they drove out of the village and off the peninsula without seeing another vehicle.

Out on US 2, Stone accelerated and passed Service, settling into the lead position, and led them to the Ogontz boat launch, which was five miles south of US 2 and located on the west shore of Ogontz Bay.

Four other DNR vehicles were already parked in the lot, officers milling around outside.

Dean Attalienti nodded at him as he got out of his squad with his thermos and joined the group.

The acting captain said, "While you men went down Garden Road we went down Harbor Road on the east side. We got eight miles in and got cut off by trees dropped across the road, so we turned around, and a mile back they had dropped more trees. It took us thirty minutes with a chain saw to clear the barricade."

"Dey rain rocks on youse?" Stone asked.

"Just the tree barriers, but now we know that they have enough people for the crow line to cover both sides, and we have to assume some of the middle roads and trails, too. They obviously don't want us down there without knowing about it, and they've put enough resources on it to get what they want. All this business today was to let us know it's their turf."

Service considered telling them that the rock throwers at Roadie's had fled when he'd made his sudden U-turn in front of the bar, but he kept his mouth shut. Mobs acted like mobs as long as they felt in control. The slightest threat to such a group usually shifted psychology to every man for himself.

"We got stoned north of Fairport," Stone said.

"I got hit in Garden when I was in front of you," Service added. By the time the patrol caught up to him, his attackers had disappeared.

"I seen da rocks and stuff on da street," Stone said.

"We need unmarked vehicles," Homes offered.

"Not just unmarked," Attalienti corrected him, "but blenders—vehicles that look like they belong down there—trucks, vans, that sort of thing."

"So what was the point of today?" Moody asked.

"A probe in force," Attalienti said.

"But we turned tail an' ran!" Homes said angrily. "Now dey tink dey've won another round."

"Winning a round isn't winning the fight," the acting captain said. "You men did fine today."

"I'm sick of being a target," Homes groused.

Ninety minutes later, Service was back in the Mosquito looking for snowmobile tracks; the machines were banned from operating in the wilderness tract, but this didn't keep a few idiots from trying it. While he drove around he thought about the excursion onto the Garden, and decided it had not been a total waste of time. Now they knew the crow line covered the entire peninsula, and whoever organized it had enough manpower not only to put together simple assaults, but to drop trees behind the eastern patrol—a clear message that they could cut off and isolate officers whenever they chose.

It was also interesting how the crowd at the tavern had split so quickly. This suggested they didn't want one-on-one confrontations, which meant they were in total group-think down there. Marines were taught to fight alone and in groups, but in all circumstances to keep fighting until ordered otherwise. Attalienti was right: The Garden crowd seemed to have considerable manpower at their disposal, and some sense of tactics. But it was still not much more than a mob, probably held together by beer as much as fidelity to a real cause.

The sniping tactics around the peninsula suggested recklessness and a desire to harass rather than homicidal intent. If they had wanted to kill officers, today would have been the day—but there had been no gunshots, just rocks and projectiles. The Garden people weren't looking so much to kill their rivals as to simply keep them at bay while they took fish illegally and made their money. This wasn't about philosophy or politics—it was about money. And if Cecilia Lasurm could point them to the leaders, there was a chance the DNR could focus pressure and gain some control.

Attalienti was on the phone with him around 8 P.M. "I'm having second thoughts about your recon. It seems to me that the only way to beat the crow line is to go in on foot at night and hope there's no snow to give you away. Have you got a plan in mind?"

"I thought we agreed that whatever I work out will remain with me."

"Yup, you're right; I guess I'm just a little edgy. You'll let me know when you get the timing worked out?"

"That's what we decided."

He liked Attalienti, but he'd begun to wonder if he was one of those managers who had to have his hand in everything, delegating nothing. On the plus side, the acting captain was showing a distinct interest in the welfare of his men.

12

HARVEY, JANUARY 10, 1976

"Are you serious?"

Mehegen's house was a small bungalow with Cherry Creek meandering through the back yard. As soon as Service pulled into the driveway, Perry came out of the house and stood on the front stoop.

"She's not home," the old man announced gruffly. He was wearing a red plaid wool shirt, suspenders, and black pants tucked into knee-high leather logging boots.

"Steal any more reindeer?" Service asked.

Perry said, "How much did it cost to fix your roof?"

"Nothing. The fix we put on it will last." Sooner or later he had to build a permanent cabin on his Slippery Creek property. "I'll just wait for Brigid."

"So you can bone her?" Perry said.

"Jesus," Service said.

The old man grinned and held up his hands. "Don't take it personally. She bones everybody. Got it in her genes, no pun intended."

"You should watch your mouth," Service said.

Perry shot back, "I didn't say anything to you I wouldn't say to her."

"Are you going to invite me in?"

"What the hell for? You're not here to see me."

Service was opening the door of the Plymouth as Mehegen pulled into the driveway and jumped out. "Sorry I'm late," she said breathlessly. She skipped over to Perry and pecked him on the cheek. "You didn't invite him in, offer him coffee or a beer?" she asked, her hands on her hips.

The old man shrugged. "What do I care if he has a beer?"

Mehegen rolled her eyes, waved at Service. "C'mon."

They sat in the kitchen at a small table with a yellowing formica top. She put out two cups and reached for the coffee.

Perry stood in the doorway. "What, nothing for your old granddad?"

"What do I care if you have coffee, old man?" Mehegen said.

Perry swore softly and made a show of stomping upstairs.

"Well," she said, "our New Year's Eve was the most interesting one I've ever had. I'm glad you called me," she added. "I was beginning to think I was going to have to take the reins on this. Should I be encouraged?"

"Where do you get your parachutes?"

"This is about *parachutes?*" she asked incredulously.

"It's a simple question," he said.

"Asked by a cement-head," she said. "I thought this was about a different recreational activity."

He remained silent, waiting for her to get it sorted out in her mind.

"Wildcat Jump Club," she finally said. "All of our purchasing is done through the club, and we store our stuff out at Marquette County Airport. We've got a building out there."

"Is there a way to borrow a chute?"

"What the hell for?"

"Something," he said evasively.

"Open your eyes! This is the season for jumping into a bed, not out of a goddamn airplane."

"I need to borrow a chute," he repeated.

"For you?"

"No details," he said. "Sorry."

She studied him briefly and sighed. "These days the harnesses are custom-built to fit each jumper; chute size reflects experience and the kind of jump being attempted. You can't just borrow a generic size."

"For discussion purposes, say somebody about my size," he said.

She laughed. "Are you serious?"

"I'd appreciate the favor," he said.

She raised an eyebrow and smiled. "With a quid pro quo, right?"

"As long as you don't ask for details and set me up to talk to your guy."

"When?"

"As quick as you can arrange it."

"People are funny about loaning their gear," she cautioned.

"Just get me someone to talk to."

"You're certainly not your happy-go-lucky self today," she said.

Perry huffed through the foyer and slammed the front door.

"I have to get going," he said.

"You're gonna owe me, pal."

Perry was chipping ice off the edge of the driveway when Service went outside.

"That was fast," the old man said.

"That's why it's called a quickie," Service said, getting into his patrol unit.

13

GARDEN PATROL, JANUARY 21, 1976

"Three patrols and you're bitching like an old-timer."

It was nine degrees Fahrenheit when Service left the Airstream, bound for the old Indian cemetery on the Stonington Peninsula. This time he had two days' advance notice to get ready. He was told to bring along his snowmobile and make sure it was in working condition. He had spent a good portion of yesterday changing plugs and oil, and doing other routine maintenance. It was not quite 6 A.M. when he towed the trailer with the Rupp into the gathering area. A weathered picket fence peeked out of the snow, marking an old grave, he guessed. The group would not assemble for another forty-five minutes, but he hated to be late; he spent the time worrying about how well he had packed for the patrol. Group activity irritated him; he preferred working alone in his own territory.

Last week he'd acquired a second thermos in Rapid River, and today he had both filled with coffee, laced with sugar and cream. He poured a small cup and sat as other vehicles began to pull in and jockey around to park. He stayed in the Plymouth, smoking. It was too damn cold to be out shooting the shit.

Eventually Colt Homes wandered over, rapped lightly on his window, and gestured for him to get out. Service refilled his cup and got out, twisting his head to stretch his neck and back. He had so many layers of clothing on, he felt like an overstuffed sausage: wool long johns, two pairs of knee-high wool socks inside Bean arctic felt liners and military-surplus white Mickey Mouse boots, heavy wool uniform pants, a wool undershirt, his winter-weight uniform shirt, a black wool sweater, and military-surplus gauntlet-style mittens that reached up to his elbows, and all of this under one-piece insulated coveralls that were too tight with everything crammed underneath.

Homes had taken up a spot in the center of the vehicles and was crunching an apple as he waited for the men to gather around him. The others shuffled toward the center, their boots making the Rice Krispie snow crackle and pop in the frigid air. The men all wore the same black coveralls and stomped their feet to keep circulation going.

"She's a fine mornin', boys," Homes proclaimed.

"Cram the bull, Homes, we're freezing our balls off out here," Budge Kangas complained.

"Dere's no wind," Homes countered. "It could be a lot worse."

"It *will* be a lot worse when we get on the sleds," someone pointed out.

"Exactly," Homes said, "and den we'll stop and it will feel warm!"

Service counted seven men, including himself: Homes, Moody, Kangas, Shaw from Mackinac County, and Stevenson and Larry Jakeway, both from Menominee County.

Budge Kangas said, "I'm at a hundred and twelve hours for this pay period. Are those Lansing assholes ever going to kick in overtime? These Garden shindigs are always twelve hours, *minimum.*"

"That's what override's for, right?" Eddie Moody asked. Like Service, he was relatively new to the job.

"Override is eighty-nine point two hours," Kangas said. "That's a bit short of one-twelve by my math, and I've got two ex-wives and five kids to support."

"Try using rubbers," Homes quipped, and all the men laughed, even Kangas.

Service thought about the pay situation the men were talking about. Each man was paid for 89.2 hours, every two weeks. Some periods they might work 80 hours, others more than that, and the differential, in the officer's favor, was designed to give them control over their schedules and make up for night calls, holiday work, and other disruptions, not to mention investigations that could eat a lot of an officer's time. You couldn't be effective in the woods with one eye on a clock. So far, Service decided, he was probably working close to ninety hours and he didn't mind. He hadn't joined the DNR for money; he'd made more as a Troop. And he liked being busy.

"Fucking override," Kangas said. "How long is that even gonna last?"

Homes said, "Okay, enough jaw jockeying, let's get down ta business. I'm takin' seven this morning."

"Yer outta your mind, Homes. Gimme four," Moody said.

"Where's Stone?" asked Stevenson, one of the officers from Menominee County.

"In a vehicle. He'll meet up with us at Fayette. Joe Flap's been upstairs watching the rats put in a gang of nets over the past few days."

"How do we know it's rats?" Kangas challenged.

"We don't," Homes said. "It could be tribals, but we won't know dat until we look."

Kangas pressed his point. "It's legal for tribals to net north of Sac Bay after November first."

Homes grinned. "But rats can't, and some of 'em are counterfeiting tribal permits an' some are hiring on wit' da Indians, taking pay or a percent of da haul, and all three of dese practices are illegal. Plus, da tribals have ta be using da proper-size mesh on dere nets—so we've gotta go look, get it?" Then he added, "I've got seven, Eddie's got four. Who's next?"

Shaw, the officer from Mackinac County, whose first name Service couldn't remember, said, "Give me six."

Stevenson chimed in, "Two."

"Jesus," Homes said. "Are you trying ta shit on our patrol?"

"These patrols turn to shit on their own, no matter what we do," Budge Kangas piped up.

Service asked, "What are we doing?"

"Buck each, guessing how many of our machines will start," Homes said.

"I'll pass," Service said. Why would the men bet against themselves and the outcome of the mission?

"You can't pass," Homes said. "We'll give you five."

Bets made, Homes announced it was time to get the vehicles off the trailers and get them cranked up.

Service's snowmobile started up right away and Homes yelped that this was a good omen, because Service was driving the worst pile of shit in the entire Yoop.

Stevenson and Shaw could not start their machines. Service and Moody had both taken turns pulling the starter rope for Shaw, but it was no use. Homes told the two men to reload their sleds and take their patrol units over to a location off US 2, just north of Garden Corners. They were to wait there until the mission was completed, or until they were called in as reserves, in which case they would dump their trailers and race down Garden Road in their trucks.

"How far across?" Service shouted at Homes over the popping of the surging motors.

"Eight miles, more or less, due east. It'll take us about an hour."

"On flat ice?" Service asked. He had limited snowmobile experience.

Homes laughed. "Since when is Bay de Noc ice flat?"

Service pulled a black balaclava down over his face, jammed his helmet over it, and pulled his goggles into place. He looked around. None of the helmets or machines were the same. A couple of men had newer model Rupps. There was a Ski-Doo and an elderly Polaris, none of them the top of the line power-wise, but all of them with better suspension than his machine.

The patrol pulled out with Homes immediately gunning his throttle and surging ahead, bouncing and yawing across the ragged ice of Big Bay de Noc. Service was last in line and struggling to maintain a steady speed, even with the others pulling ahead of him. Most of the time he rode standing on the machine, bending down to the handlebars and keeping his eyes glued ahead as he steered around moguls and ice chunks the size of refrigerators, popping tentatively over various pressure ridges created by alternate freezing and thawing. His posture was like riding a horse English-style, letting his knees rather than his back take the pounding from the ice as they surged eastward, their machines screaming and straining, leaving blue plumes of oil fumes hanging in their wakes. The ice ahead of him looked like a boulder-strewn wasteland rendered in white and gray, with hints of dirty blue and pale green.

Homes halted a mile west of Snail Shell Harbor and scanned ahead with his binoculars, waiting for the others to catch up.

"Stone said he'd mark net stakes wit' red patches," he yelled at them over idling engines as he continued to look at the area ahead. "He come out here on foot before first light. Spread out, an' when you find a stake, yell so we can figure out the layout."

Service had no idea what what was going on, but puttered slowly eastward with the other officers.

Moody found the first stake, and by then Homes announced he could see a lifting shack that was eight feet or so long, and two or three feet wide—shaped like a big Popsicle. Inside it the rats would place a space heater to protect the men pulling the nets from beneath the ice while they harvested their take. It took a while for Service to see what Homes was pointing to. The shed had been painted white and pale blue-gray to make it less visible. It was damn effective camouflage, Service noted, not the work of an amateur.

Homes sent Kangas north to try to locate the northernmost stake, and when that was found they reconvened at the first stake where Homes used an ice spud to clear the hole in the ice and hook the net line. The net line was connected to a crude wooden superstructure made of two-by-fours that the fishermen slid under the ice through a series of holes. The nets were attached to the superstructure, with weights to hold them down on the rocky bottom where the fish schooled. Homes probed in the hole with a long pole tipped with a hook until he caught something and pulled it up. The net was green nylon and began to ice as soon as it hit the open air, making it heavier and harder to move and manipulate. A few fish were stuck in the net. Homes took one look and said, "Large mesh. Let's look for net registrations. Dis one is naked," he added.

Kangas said, "The one on the north end said SSM one-twenty-two. It's red."

"Sault Saint Marie tribe," Homes said. "One of dem might be licensed for large mesh—if it's theirs. But are we dealing with tribals, or rats trying to act like tribals?"

Homes used the radio to contact Stone. He explained the situation, and Stone said he would make a call and find out who held license SSM 122.

The men used the time to find the rest of the marker stakes and to clear holes. An hour later Stone called back and said no license number 122 was assigned to the Soo Tribe, and told Homes he and the men should commence pulling the nets.

They eventually located nine nets connected in a series called a gang, and began the process of pulling them, taking turns in the lifting shack. While some men hauled, others removed illegal whitefish from the nets and stacked them on the ice like firewood.

They had been at it for more than three hours and had six of the nine nets piled on the ice. Stone came driving out in an unmarked green Ford pickup just as they were loading the unwieldy nets into a sled to be hauled back to the Stonington by one of the snowmobiles. They immediately transferred the icy, stinky nets and illegal fish into the bed of Stone's truck. Later they would move the nets into the evidence locker in the Escanaba office across from the U.P. State Fairgrounds, and let the legal process work. The fish would be frozen for later distribution to the needy.

"Dis will hurt da rats," Stone said, appraising the day's work. "Each net costs dose bastards eight grand new." Service blinked several times: The value of the gang was more than fifty *thousand* dollars? Suddenly the economic underpinnings of the seizure strategy made sense to him. Hobby fishermen didn't invest fifty grand in equipment. The rats who told reporters they fished illegally to stay off welfare were bullshitting; this was about money, big money by U.P. standards.

"Surprised we haven't had visitors," Homes said to Stone.

"I expect we will," the acting lieutenant said, staring south toward Burn't Bluff. "Air Four's got his eyes on da Port Bar up near da park. Dere's a heap a machines dere, an' if da rats get liquored up and come lookin' for trouble, Pranger will give us a call." Stone turned to Service. "You want to help Moody in da lift shack?"

Service went inside and found a perspiring, red-faced Moody. "I'll take over," Service said after watching for a minute or so. Moody stepped back and lit a cigar. He crossed his arms and pulled on his elbows to stretch his muscles. "Be nice to have a winch," Moody said wistfully.

Service, who lifted weights and ran every day to stay in condition, soon found his neck, back, and arms burning from the effort of pulling the net, but he eventually got into a rhythm. He was paying attention only to what he was doing when there was a loud crunch and he was bounced off the wall of the shack and dropped hard to one knee, dazed but still clutching the net he had been recovering.

Moody grunted, "Fuck!" and shouldered the door open.

Service heard someone screaming, "Youse Nazi bastards have pulled your last fuckin' nets!" and Moody was yelling something about a truck.

Service tried to get out the door, but someone came crashing in and began punching and clubbing him. Service ducked, slid on wet ice, and sank a leg into the hole in the ice as the man landed on top, flailing at him with a board or a stick, an attack that was more emotion and testosterone than effect. Outside Service heard men shouting and the roar of unmuffled snowmobiles and knew that whatever was happening was larger than his attacker in the shack. He wrestled the man to the side, got a hand free, and jabbed him in the throat with the heel of his hand. The attacker immediately rolled off and started gagging. Service got to his feet, but the man was persistent, and although still gagging audibly, he clawed fruitlessly and furiously at Service's legs, trying to tackle him. Service took a half step, pivoted, and drove a fist into the man's temple, stopping him where he was.

Service shouldered his way through the door looking for Moody, but found the hood of a truck against the shack. All around him snowmobiles were racing around, and men in twos and threes were fighting and wrestling and swearing and grunting, and as he tried to figure it all out, his attacker again came at him from behind and tried to put him in a bear hug. Service pivoted away and smashed the man's collarbone with a short, hard chop. The assailant bellowed in pain and dropped to his knees as Service drove his hand into the man's throat again, and looked up to see another pickup truck coming directly at the lift shack.

He was too tired to think clearly, and before he could decide how to evade, the truck slid sideways and stopped about five feet away from him. Stone, hanging out the driver's window, shouted, "Jump in!"

"My machine!" Service protested.

"Da rats got it!" Stone said. "Get your ass *in!*"

Service got a foot on the back bumper and rolled into the bed of the truck, landing on a pile of slimy, icy green nylon that reeked of fish.

A man with a black ski mask was trying to run toward Stone's truck, a rifle in hand, but the truck began to fishtail and bounce wildly, its tires burning the ice as Stone tried to get purchase and accelerate. As soon as he had a little momentum he headed west, away from shore onto the bay ice.

From the rear of the truck Service watched snowmobiles turning to pursue, but it was hard to stay focused as the truck bounced and slid and yawed over the ice. Service managed to find a strip of metal welded to the side of the bed and took hold, feeling the cold sear his bare hand.

The wind blowing against him was freezing the leg he had dunked to mid-thigh and his face and hands, but he had no choice but to hold on. He managed to wrap some net mesh around his hand to keep his skin from direct contact with metal.

Eventually most of the snowmobiles broke off the chase and turned back to the east. Only a few continued to follow; Service counted four. It took several seconds to realize these were the other officers, and the machine that was missing was his. It also dawned on him that both thermoses, his helmet, goggles, gauntlets, binoculars, and flashlight were still on the Rupp.

As they approached the Stonington, Stone slowed considerably and began a deliberate and careful meandering course to the southwest, paralleling an eight-foot-high pressure ridge built up between the shore and the water's edge. After a while Stone stopped the truck and told Service to get out and walk. As soon as he was over the side Stone gunned the engine and the nose of the truck shot up the pressure ridge like a sounding whale, and crashed down hard on the other side, still on four wheels, but leaving the confiscated fishing nets draped over the cab and tailgate. Service scrambled over the ice berm, pushed the nets back into the bed, and got into the passenger seat.

"Okay?" Stone asked, driving north and weaving between icy boulders sculpted by wind on the snow-covered barrens.

Service put his hands on the heater. "My stuff's on my machine."

"We'll get you more. You see da boys?"

"They're coming. The rats ran with them for a while."

"Dat's typical. Dey had dere attack. Typically dey chase for a bit, an' den retreat."

The marines had used similar tactics in Vietnam, Service remembered; only when they chased their enemies, they meant to kill them.

The other officers were still a couple of hundred yards out on the ice when Stone found a relatively clear path through the barrier cedars and followed it to the unplowed two-track road that led into the area where the squads and trailers were parked at the cemetery. He left the engine running, and handed Service his thermos. He groped under his seat and pulled out a flat pint of brandy, uncapped it, and set it between them. "Drink."

The officers pulled up on their snowmobiles as Stone got on the radio. He called Air Four several times, got no response, and finally reached Shaw on the radio.

"Where are youse?" Shaw asked.

"Back where you guys started dis morning," Stone said.

"On our way."

"You guys hear what happened out dere?" Stone asked.

"Sort of. Air Four called us and said you needed backup. We ran hard but got only to the parking lot before we got pelted with rocks and bottles."

"Air Four called *you*?"

"He said he couldn't raise any of youse."

"Okay, see you in a few."

Service got out. All the men were wide-eyed. Moody had a nasty cut on his ear. Homes had a cheek that was swelling fast, and Kangas was carrying his left arm like it had been broken.

"What happened?" Service asked.

"Asshole with an ice spud," Kangas said. "Fuckers were on us before we could react."

Service lit a cigarette and watched Homes scoop snow to hold against his face. Air Four had reached backup, but not the group under assault. Had their radios failed? Communications failures had been a way of life and had cost lives in Vietnam.

Stone got out of his truck and handed Service another cup of coffee.

"Who won?" Homes asked with a stupid grin.

"We got six of dere nine nets," Stone said. "Right now dat's da only score we care about, boys. Budge, I'm gonna follow youse over ta da hospital in Escanaba."

"I don't need a babysitter," Kangas complained.

"Dat shoulder needs attention."

Homes grinned. "It was like a joust out dere."

"What that was," Kangas said, "was a clusterfuck."

Moody joined in. "Why didn't somebody warn us we were about to get rammed?"

"She happened too fast," Stone said. "Air Four called Shaw and Stevenson for backup, but Joe couldn't reach us."

"Our equipment is shit," Kangas said. "We can't chase when we need to, and we were damn lucky to get outta there with the rats hot on our asses."

Shaw and Stevenson pulled in and got out. Shaw's windshield was broken out; he had jammed cardboard in the opening to help disrupt the wind flow. Stone walked around the two patrol cars and stopped behind Stevenson's. "You got a bullet hole back here—small caliber. You see da shooter?"

"Never knew anything was fired until now," Stevenson said, looking shaky.

The eight men slowly began to relax and exchange bits and pieces of the action, but Stone cut them off, insisting that Kangas and Moody get to the hospital, and the others pack it in and write their action reports.

Service and Homes were the last to leave. "What forms do I use for lost equipment?" Service asked.

Homes poked around in his Plymouth, but came up empty-handed. "Stop at the office in Escanaba tomorrow and draw what you need. Connie will handle it."

As a marine, Service had been accustomed to debriefings fairly soon after actions; the informality and apparent disorder of this aftermath left him confused and shaking his head. You couldn't learn from mistakes if you didn't catalog and dissect them.

"If we don't get our shit together," Service said, "somebody's gonna get killed."

Homes grinned and patted the larger man on the back. "Three patrols and you're already bitchin' like an old-timer. Do you realize dat's da first time we ever run a truck all da way across da ice from Garden ta Stonington?"

Service looked at the other man's beaming, swelling face. "You'd think an old-timer would learn to duck."

"You'd think," Homes said, as if nothing had happened, and handed Service five one-dollar bills. "Beginner's luck," he carped as he got into his patrol car and pulled away, towing his snowmobile.

The attackers had come in from the west. With air cover and workable communications, the tactic shouldn't have mattered, but commo had failed and the rats had gained tactical surprise. This, more than anything else he had seen, convinced Service the rat leaders knew what they were doing. He also thought about the man with the rifle out on the ice. Once again, if the rats had been intent on killing, they had both surprise and superior numbers today, and yet the only shot fired had been a small caliber into the trunk of a car up in the state park's parking lot. The leaders not only knew what they were doing—they were also exerting powerful discipline over their people. Service was impressed, and felt a cold rage growing inside him. The rats were beginning to look like a formidable enemy.

14

ESCANABA, JANUARY 22, 1976

"I mean, none of you guys want that duty, right?"

The adrenaline and scrap of the previous day had more lingering effects than Service had expected, and he was increasingly pissed that the rats had gotten the thermos Shuck Gorley had given him. He pulled into the parking lot of the Escanaba DNR office, cursed the continuing snow, and glanced at the sign across the street, which read U.P. STATE FAIRGROUNDS. He shook his head. The actual state fair was held downstate, but that didn't keep Yoopers from declaring their own state above the bridge.

Connie Leppo was the effervescent dispatcher-secretary for the law enforcement district. She smiled when she looked up and saw him. "Heard youse guys went another round wit' da rats yesterday."

"You hear anything about Moody, Kangas, and Homes?"

"Looks like youse're da only one didn't get a mark out of it."

"Mine are hidden," he said.

She said, "Budge has a slight separation of da shoulder, Eddie took four stitches in his ear, and Colt you couldn't damage if you hit 'im in da head wit' an anvil shot out of a cannon."

"I lost some of my equipment. Homes said I need to fill out some forms."

"I heard," she said, setting a manila folder on the counter. "Just one form, and it's in dere."

"Thanks," he said.

"Len broke two fingers," she said.

"How?"

"On a rat jaw."

"He never said anything." When had Stone been out of his truck?

"He wouldn't," she said with a combination of admiration and disapproval. "He's old-school, like your dad."

What had Shuck told him—that times had changed and brains counted more than clubs? His old man would have gone ballistic yesterday, and Stone may have lost it temporarily during the melee, but he had kept enough presence of mind to get the nets into the truck and get them out of there. Confiscating nets had been the whole point of the patrol.

Service sat at the long table in the conference room and took care of his paperwork, including his handwritten report on the previous day's action. Leppo brought him two cinnamon rolls and coffee. "Mum made da bakery fresh dis morning," she said, "and she's got a little side business. You like 'em and want more, let me know, eh. She needs about twenty-four hours for special orders."

"Thanks," he said, peeling off a chunk of a roll.

She continued, "I'll ship your paperwork up to da regional office." Marquette will take care of getting youse a replacement machine. One thing: It won't be new."

He nodded, said facetiously, "I'm shocked."

She grinned. "I bet. The rest of da stuff you get locally. You pay for it and submit da receipts. Stone will cut a check to reimburse you."

"That sounds simple enough." And inconvenient.

"Except dat you have ta shop at an approved state facility, which means Delta Sporting Goods, or you go up ta Marquette, ta Lindstrom's."

"What about the gauntlets? They're military surplus."

"Da state doesn't buy directly from da feds. All surplus stuff we get from local dealers, but we don't have a good one up here, so za quartermeister, he leafs us za extras," she said, switching to a rough German accent. "Unt I haff za key to za zhtorage roomp. Finish your bakery, give a zhout, and I'll open it for you, *ja?*"

He put his report on Leppo's counter and she led him to the storage room and let him pick out a new set of gauntlets. "Da good news is, you can't very well pull snowmobile duty in da Garden if you don't have a machine ta ride, eh?"

"What's good about that?" he asked, looking at her.

"I mean, none of youse guys want dat duty, right?"

As he walked out to his patrol car, a green garbage truck pulled into the lot and a man got out and began carrying trash barrels to dump into the back of the behemoth.

The sign on the truck said BAY DE NOC TRASH HAULING: LOWEST RATES IN THE COUNTY. There was a local telephone number under the company name. The DNR office was almost in the middle of town. Why wasn't the city picking up the state's trash, and why wasn't the state buying surplus equipment directly from the feds? He put both questions out of his mind and headed back to the Mosquito, squinting through his spidered windshield and making a mental note to ask Leppo about the procedure for getting it fixed.

15

SLIPPERY CREEK, JANUARY 29, 1976

Only one thing was certain: He'd hit a nerve.

Cecilia Lasurm leaned her crutch against the wall inside the door, hopped over to a chair, sat down, took off her gloves and hat, which she dropped on the floor, draped her coat and purse on the back of the chair, lifted her leg, and unzipped her boot. Service had been up to Marquette earlier in the day, after an uneventful morning patrol. He'd returned minutes before she drove up. The last time he had seen her, she had worn black trousers and a black turtleneck. Tonight she wore a knee-length pleated blue wool skirt, her face glowed with makeup, and pearl teardrop earrings dangled from her earlobes. When she lifted her leg to shed the boot, he had been shocked by its length and shape and had looked away, telling himself such feelings were not only unprofessional, but also weird.

"I believe this snow will never stop," she said.

Waves of Alberta clippers had been skidding across the upper Great Lakes, leaving two to four inches a day since the New Year began, and long-range forecasts called for the assault to continue. "There won't be any on the ground in August," he said.

Lasurm didn't react to his lame joke. "We've got a lot more than usual," she said, "but not as much as here."

"Garden, the epicenter of the Yooper Riviera," he said, attempting another joke and wondering why.

Lasurm smiled. "I must admit that the DNR's presence has been reestablished, but you people are still taking a licking down there. The way to break a bully's hold is to erode people's fear of him. You have to expose him to his followers."

"I see," Service said unenthusiastically. Two days ago another patrol, this one attempting to pull nets off Burn't Bluff, had been fired at by a sniper. Homes had been there and called that night to vent. With Metrovich gone to Lansing, and Attalienti and Stone running the show, officers were expecting a change in approach and results. So far they were not seeing either, and he knew that potentially, a lot depended on his recon.

"Coffee?" he asked.

"Thank you," she said. "That four-car stunt a few weeks back," she said. "What was that supposed to accomplish?"

Service filled their cups and sat down. "Our deal is that you have to convince me that you've got something worthwhile."

Lasurm raised an eyebrow. "All business, eh?"

"If I come down there, I'll need to be in the area at least ten days, and maybe two full weeks."

She nodded resolutely. "You'll stay with me."

"Too risky for both of us," he immediately countered.

"You let me assess my own risk," she said. "As I tried to explain before, I'm everywhere and nowhere. People don't really notice me. Besides, are you expecting to check into a no-tell motel, or live rough in the woods? One sighting and that will be that. You're already on their list."

"What list?"

"You people have your list and they have theirs. They make a note of each one of you they see and then try to identify you. They've even sent people up to other counties to check you guys out."

"Where do they get the names and addresses?"

"I don't know, but I know they have your name. You've been down there at least twice, and maybe you were part of the four-car run when you guys all wore masks. That whole deal got their sphincters tight. Why did the DNR come down in four cars and why were they wearing masks?" Lasurm laughed softly. "You shoulda heard them whine about that!"

Stone had told them the masks were for psychological purposes, and apparently they had actually had some effect. This surprised him.

"They got your Rupp, and at first they thought your name was Shuck."

"That was the name on one of my thermoses," he said.

"They were able to determine that Officer Gorley is retired up to Newberry, but eventually they got your name."

"How?"

She shrugged. "I don't know everything."

"Do they know where I live?"

"Don't Yoopers always know where the game warden lives?"

"Then why are we meeting here?" He was flabbergasted.

"Because tonight they're putting down nets," she said, "and they don't have the people or the time to be sitting around watching you and your little trailer. If they weren't busy tonight, I would have cancelled. Next time, we'll select another place. You should assume they know where you live, but that doesn't mean they are watching around the clock. So," she went on, sucking in a deep breath, "you're to have ten days to two weeks with me on the Yooper Riviera. When?"

"I haven't decided yet."

"You need to decide and give me some warning so I can do what I have to do. Do you think you can get in undetected?"

"I'd better," he said.

Lasurm sipped her coffee. "The incident at Burn't Bluff the day before yesterday? One shooter," she said.

"You saw what happened?"

"No, I heard the shots and saw someone, but I couldn't see who. I can only attest to number."

"But that you're sure of."

"Absolutely. Four shots were fired in close order, and then I saw him about fifteen minutes later."

"Where were you?"

"Trying to carry something from my truck to the house."

"You live near Burn't Bluff?"

"Technically I live on it, though in reality I'm about three hundred yards east. The shooter came out through my west wood line to meet a vehicle. When they do these things, they usually drop off the miscreants and pick them up afterwards. And no, I did not see the pickup vehicle."

He had wondered about this, but he wanted more information on the list. "You claim they have a list."

"They have a list—it's not a claim. And how do they manage it? I don't know. There are sympathizers everywhere. Perhaps some of them even wear green?"

It was unthinkable that a CO would knowingly confirm information for the rats. "You said you would provide us with names," he said.

Lasurm opened her purse and took out a small piece of notebook paper. "The leaders," she said, "in order of importance."

He read the names: Peletier, Groleau, Renard, St. Cyr, Troscair, Gagnon.

"All French," he said, tapping the list, "but Gascoyne and Metcalf aren't here." Gascoyne owned the commercial fish house in Fairport, Metcalf the Garden establishment.

"Gascoyne and Metcalf hired Odd Hegstrom," she said. "Some of the rats, as you and your comrades so colorfully characterize them, work for Gascoyne and Metcalf and have their own fishing interests on the side. The big fellows would like to see the so-called rat operations out of business because they cut into fish stocks, which means their profits, but the same people who compete with them illegally also work for them at times and, in some cases, sell fish to them, which puts the fish houses between a rock and a hard place."

"The fish houses buy from the rats?"

"Sometimes it's cheaper than sending out your own boats and crews, especially those times of year when it's illegal to lay your hands on the fish you need for business. Better to let others risk their boats, nets, and so forth, yes? You people need to understand how interconnected everything is in the Garden, blended by business interests, intermarriage, and money. The word down there is that Hegstrom convinced Gascoyne and Metcalf he could get them ten more years of fishing before the ax falls."

"Based on what—and why ten years?" Service wondered if the state had tried to subpoena the fish houses' financial records, and if not, why not?

"I don't know," she said.

Stone and Attalienti had made similar observations about the Garden, and it was becoming clearer to Service that his two supervisors had more than a rudimentary idea of what was really happening. Still, why had Hegstrom promised ten years, and why had that been a selling point for the fish house operators?

"Peletier is the lead rat," he said, looking at the list and refocusing the conversation.

"When Pete talks, the rest of them listen."

"What does he do for a living?" Service asked.

Lasurm said, "Like most people down there he can do a lot of things, legally and illegally. Officially he's a carpenter."

"Does he lead from the front or the rear?"

"I don't know," she said, "but you can assume if he's not involved on a particular day, he knows about it and has given it his blessing. Most of his people know to keep their mouths shut. As evidence, have you had a single informant other than me?"

"Mouths shut, or else?"

"Your words, not mine," she said. "All of them on the list can trace ancestors back to the original settlers of the peninsula. Most of them came up from Beaver and St. Martin islands. A few came down from Quebec." Lasurm paused for a second and continued. "Pete is married to Ranse Renard's sister. Renard is married to St. Cyr's eldest daughter, and so forth. Interconnected: They're all part of one thing and of a single mind about the DNR and its rules." She made direct eye contact and said quietly, "They *really* don't care for you fellows, and with good reason if you look at it from their perspective."

Lasurm studied him for a moment before continuing. "I wonder if you know your own department's history? In the 1880s fish harvests were down and the state banned fishing with nets for certain species in some locations around Beaver Island. The fishermen objected, and said the state could not tell them what to do," she said. "In 1897 the state sent a game warden out to the island and he ended up shooting at a boat and confiscating a fisherman's gear. The locals hyperbolized this as the Beaver Island War. The result was that some of the fishermen migrated north to the U.P. where they expected they could pretty much do as they pleased," she said, drawing in another breath. "And here we are nearly eighty years later, and the state and the fishermen are doing precisely the same damn thing: Fighting over fish. How's that for irony?"

Could she be right about this? He also wondered why no one had ever written an in-depth history of the department. A marine wore the Corps' history as a second skin. "What about the differences between farmers and fishermen?" She had mentioned this during their first meeting.

"The fruit growers are a separate branch of the farming community. They raise about fifty varieties of apples and do okay. The other farmers—even those claiming to live hand to mouth—as well as some of the rats have started cultivating dope as a side business. They're calling it Garden Green."

"Dope?"

"Marijuana. It's not what you'd call a developed crop yet, but it's under way, and those who use it swear it's among the most potent around. The real legit farmers resent the rats and dope growers because they scare away customers."

Dope? He'd seen some drug use in Vietnam, especially among rear echelon motherfuckers, and it was obviously a problem throughout much of the United States, but here in the U.P.? After a second he decided it made sense. If the rest of the country was rife with drugs, why not here? He reached for the envelope he'd picked up in Marquette, put it on the table in front of Lasurm, and slid out the photograph. He wasn't sure why he was showing it to her, except that if Lasurm was as knowledgeable and connected as she claimed, and the woman in jail was from the Garden, she might provide an ID and help move the case along.

Lasurm stared for a long time and he noticed that she spread out her fingers and placed them on the surface of the photograph—to cover it or draw it closer, he couldn't tell.

When she finally looked up at him she said, "Is this what you people call a mug shot?"

"Yes."

She drew in a deep breath, lifted her hand as if it had suddenly quintupled in weight, bent down, picked up her boot, and slid her foot into it. "I have to leave now," she said with a flat voice.

"Do you recognize the person in the photo?" he asked.

"I have to go now," she repeated, hopping to the door and attaching her crutch to her wrist. "It's a long drive."

"She's in the Marquette County Jail charged with attempted homicide and felonious assault, and probably some counts of grand theft. Odd Hegstrom is her lawyer."

She ignored this as she walked out the door. Her departure was so abrupt that he wasn't sure what to think. Only one thing was certain: He'd hit a nerve. He immediately began to question the jailed woman's Garden connection and Cecilia Lasurm's motives. She was their sole informant so far. Or was she? What if she was working for the other side? He refilled his coffee cup and took off his boots. Even if it was a setup, he knew he had to go to the Garden.

16

GARDEN PATROL (AIR RECON), JANUARY 31, 1976

" . . . look for shadows on da snow."

Joe Flap tended to the controls of his single-engine Beaver with a disinterest that had Grady Service in a cold sweat. They had taken off from Escanaba at 11 A.M., headed northeast, and looped south to run down the west coast of the Garden Peninsula. For the first time in weeks they had seen a cloudless, snowless sunrise, and though a bluebird sky surrounded them, the flight was anything but smooth. It was vaguely reminiscent of the *chop-chop-chop* of running a snowmobile across the ice of Big Bay de Noc.

Joe Flap said, "Toivo-da-Yooper's down Detroit for da Red Wings game, eh. It bein' Detroit, dere's flatlanders in da row behind 'im, and dis guy's yackety-yack and says real loud, 'Only two tings come down Canada: hockey players and hookers.'"

Flap looked to see if Service was listening before continuing. "Toivo, he turns around real slow, eyeballs da jerk, and says, 'Da wifey's from Canada.' Da flatlander's eyes get real big an' he says, 'Yeah, what position does she play?'"

Service let the pilot laugh himself out and said, "Three things come from Canada."

Flap scrunched up his face. "Eh?"

"They send us snow, too."

The pilot clucked and shook his head. "Was a joke."

Service stared out at the Garden Peninsula as they cruised at 120 miles per hour. There was no wind at ground level, and not much at two thousand feet—when Flap cared enough to keep the altimeter needle steady. Service saw fields and farm sections and pastures, snow-covered roads, woodlots and rolling hills, the whole thing looking idyllic and benign, the picture of serenity from above; he pictured hardy people in their houses, fires crackling in their fireplaces and wood burners. Blue-gray plumes of wood smoke wafted from chimneys and corkscrewed straight up until the surrounding air skinned the heat out of the rising air.

"What're we lookin' for?" Flap asked.

"Nothing in particular. Just give me the Joe Flap special look at the Garden."

Flap considered this. "Well, I ain't pranged here," the pilot said, adding, "yet."

They crossed US 2 west of Garden Corners and headed south along the peninsula's jagged western shoreline. Service had a map in his lap and traced their route: the wide half-moon arc of Jack's Bluff and the insinuation of Valentine Point and Kates Bay, which barely jutted in from Big Bay de Noc; Ansels Point; the two-mile-long Garden Bay; Puffy Bay next; then the massif of Garden Bluff, and off to the west in the bay, Round and St.Vital islands. Ahead were South River Bay, Snake Island, and Middle Bluff, which marked the location of Snail Shell Harbor in the lap of Fayette State Park; Sand Bay lay south of the park; the jagged cliffs of Burn't Bluff next, and Sac Bay tucked politely beneath the towering bluff's southern bulge. Then, on down to Fairport with Rocky, Little Summer, and Summer islands off to the south, and farther out, the purple-gray silhouettes of Poverty, Gravelly, Gull, and St. Martin islands.

Service used his binoculars to scan for nets or lift shacks on the ice, but saw nothing.

Joe Flap braced the stick between his knees and flew with both hands on his own binoculars. "Sometimes you don't see da lift shacks if dey got da good camo, so youse look for shadows on da snow. An' look for foot trails packed down where dey move from hole to hole."

He added, "Dere at eleven o'clock, see the shadow?" They were near Ansels Point. Service looked and finally located the structure, which, like the one they had encountered on the patrol, was painted to blend in.

"Can you land anywhere down there?" Service asked.

"Almost," Flap said, nosing the aircraft down.

From two thousand feet the ice had looked smooth and smoky gray-blue. As they descended Service could begin to see the jagged rises, severe moguls, and precipitous pressure ridges that characterized the chaotic surface; by the time they were lined up for a landing, he was sure the ice below would shred the bottom of the plane, but Joe Flap eased the bird down onto the aircraft's skis with an assertive *thump*. He let the plane skid and hop for a moment before slamming the throttle forward, jerking the nose of the aircraft into a steep banking climb with the engines screaming their objection. Service thought he was going to lose his stomach.

The ride on the ice had been bumpy, the sound like an ironing board skimming across a rock garden, but the ride was not nearly as harsh as on a snowmobile or in Stone's truck, there being more give in the aircraft's skis and struts. "We'll run up da eastern shore and cut back across da center," Joe Flap said, banking the plane south and twisting the nose back to the northeast as they began to gain altitude.

The one thing Service had seen on the way down was that the various bluffs along the west coast were close to sheer and at least two hundred feet high. Even with snow, he could see that the multihued limestone outcrops were pocked with holes and small caves, offering good places for shooters to hide themselves to ambush lawmen below.

By contrast the east coast of the Garden Peninsula sprawled before them was more wooded and flatter than the west coast, and punctuated by numerous cedar and tamarack swamps that looked like black tumors from above.

On their next run Service asked Flap to descend to five hundred feet and fly along the road that led from Garden down to Fairport as he studied the terrain where the rock-throwing had taken place. He saw two-tracks and snowmobile trails within a third of a mile of the cedar swales where the attackers had hidden. He made notes on his maps as they flew. There was little talk, and most of the time Joe Flap was watching the ground with his binoculars and not paying attention to anything that might be at their altitude.

After nearly three hours of crisscrossing the peninsula, Flap turned the aircraft west toward Escanaba.

"Do you make night runs down here?" Service asked as they flew along.

"When dey ask," Joe Flap said.

"No, I mean do you make *your own* night runs down here?"

"Sometimes I come up and just look around at night. You can see stuff good if dere's a good moon, or if dey use any light at all. If we had enough people on da ground at night, we might make some good pinches, but dey don't seem ta want ta do dat, and I can't blame 'em. Hard enough to deal wit' rats in daylight, eh."

17

GRAYLING, FEBRUARY 1, 1976

"All this over fish?"

He had decided that using Brigid Mehegen to help him get a parachute would not be smart: too close to home, and her grandfather was nosy, eccentric, and unpredictable. Better to get help from someone he knew he could rely on.

Grady Service and Luticious Treebone were about the same height, but Tree was considerably heavier, the difference being a lot more muscle. When the towering black man swaggered through the swinging doors of Spike's Keg o' Nails, all sound stopped—as if all the oxygen had been sucked out of a vacuum jar. The big man smiled, waved a hand regally, and announced, "As you were, people—I ain't Jimmy Hoffa."

The patrons laughed and went back to their conversations.

Treebone took a seat across a small table from his friend. "How come when you need something, I always gotta drive up to some whiteboy redneck roadhouse?"

"Lots of Detroit people have places up here," Service said.

"Not of the brother hue," Tree said. "You see why I couldn't be no woods cop. I ain't got the prejudice, but I gotta see my own people, you know?"

"And Kalina hates small-town living."

Treebone rolled his eyes and nodded solemnly. "There is that."

"You bring it?" Service asked.

"In the trunk. I ever leave you hang?"

Luticious Treebone took reliability as a religion. Service had graduated from Northern Michigan where he had been a fair student and a competent hockey player. Tree had played football and baseball at Wayne State and graduated cum laude. They both had volunteered for duty in the Marine Corps, and met at Parris Island boot camp; they both took the same specialized training, and spent a tour in the same long-range recon unit in Vietnam, both of them coming back with numerous decorations and little desire to talk about what they had seen or done. Both had attended the Michigan State Police Academy in Lansing and spent two years as Troop road patrollers before transferring to the DNR. After just one year as a CO in Oscoda County, Treebone took a job with the Detroit Metropolitan Police. They had been friends for more than twenty years, and were closer than most brothers.

"How's Kalina?" Service asked. Kalina was his friend's wife. It had been because of her he'd taken the job in Detroit.

"Wonderin' how the single life's sittin' with you."

"I haven't bought a leisure suit yet."

Treebone howled. "They got that disco shit up there?"

"Hell, we just learned about some guy named Elvis. You gonna ask what I'm up to?"

Treebone shook his head. "I know you're going outside the envelope and I really don't wanna know more than that, man. You believe they give you your daddy's old territory?"

"I'm not spending a whole lot of time there," Service said, and explained to his friend the situation in the Garden Peninsula. He did not talk about his surveillance assignment.

"All this over *fish?*"

"Fish is money."

"I hear you, but more money in fish than dope? The brothers hear that, there won't be no fish left in the Detroit River or Lake St. Clair!"

"We got dope too," Service said. "Supposed to be a new thing. You want to see what you can find out about it? Street name is Garden Green."

"I heard of that shit, man, but even if they got supply, a buncha Yoopers not gonna be supplyin' Motown, dig?"

"If it turns out to be nothing, so be it."

"Kalina is dying to know if you're dating anybody special."

"Nothing steady."

Treebone laughed. "I told her you'd be married to your job."

"It's not like that."

"Bullshit. You gonna invite me up there this summer to chase some of those pretty little brook trout you don't tell nobody about?"

"You bet." Trout fishing was a passion that both men shared. When they first met, Treebone had been a confirmed worm-dunker, but had since converted to fly fishing and—when he had time, which wasn't often—was learning to tie his own flies.

"From what you say, it sounds like you boys in green don't have your act together up in the Garden."

"We're trying."

"They sendin' you in to do a snoop, am I right?"

Service said nothing.

"I know you'll think it through before you commit," his friend said quietly. "Just remember—this ain't 'Nam, and you are no longer in the business of capping bad guys. It's our job to catch 'em, gather evidence, and let the courts take it from there. End of speech. Now can we eat?"

They were eating cheeseburgers when a young woman in a ski sweater came over to the table and nervously tapped Treebone on the shoulder. "I'm sorry to interrupt your lunch, but do you play for the Lions?"

"No, ma'am; I just got out of the joint."

The woman scrambled away with a red face.

Service looked at his friend and shook his head. "You just have to stir the pot."

"Just reinforcing the stereotype. A big black man's either an ex-con or a jock."

"And everybody north of Detroit is a redneck."

"No man, north from Detroit to the bridge they're rednecks; above the bridge, you motherfuckers are a whole different species—one they don't even have a word for."

Service looked at his friend and saw he was not smiling. "I hope this is not gonna be an armed snoop," Treebone said.

When Service didn't respond, Treebone grimaced.

"Be cool," his friend said as they embraced. "You need somebody to get your back, you call."

18

PREACHER LAKE, FEBRUARY 6, 1976

"Once people take on a deep notion about something,
you can't change their minds."

His old man had driven him to the Mimolov swamp when he was thirteen. They had parked on a jack pine plain and walked nearly a mile through muddy swales and cedar tangles until they got to a single ruined building standing on a hummock of high ground. The building's roof had rotted away, but most of the walls of lime- and fieldstone still stood.

The old man sat on the stone sill where a window had once been, lit a cigarette, popped the cork of his pocket flask, took a long pull, and said, "What do you see?"

Service had no idea what the old man wanted; he rarely did.

"Guess what this place was?" the old man asked with slight irritation.

"A church or a school?"

"Church," the old man said. "Good. Now, what do you see?"

"The roof's gone, windows too. Porkies, probably."

"Okay. What else?"

Service saw nothing and leaned against a wall, wishing the old man wouldn't pull this stuff on him. The stone floor was littered with chunks of stone that had broken off under years of freezing and thawing, and there were holes between the fieldstones, but no sign of nests. He looked along the base of the wall. No spiderwebs, no animal droppings, no tracks in the dust, no sign of animals at all. It was normal for animals to move into abandoned structures almost immediately.

"No animals," Service said.

The old man nodded. "Right. A preacher named Proudfit built a church here, all by himself. Back then the loggers were thicker than mosquitoes. He hired a guy to go round to the logging camps to announce services, and one Sunday the loggers came and found Proudfit hanging. Nobody knew if somebody had hung him, or if he'd done himself in, but the church got marked as dark and people stayed away, and over time it came to be a place where scores got settled. Two men had a beef, they came here and fought it out—sometimes to the death, sometimes with spectators—but usually it was just the two men alone with their hatred. Some say hundreds have died here. More likely it wasn't anything close to that, but people were afraid of this place. At one time there were a thousand people living within a mile of here. They called it Preacher Lake. Within six months of Proudfit's hanging, they were all gone, abandoned their shacks and cabins and moved on. The Indians still claim the place has spirits all around it, which is why animals won't come into it—not a bird, not a snake, not an ant."

"There's no lake," he told his father.

"Never was. Just a string of beaver ponds, and they're long gone."

"Do you believe in spirits?" Grady asked his father.

"Makes more sense to me that Proudfit built this place on bad ground—that there's something here animals can't tolerate. 'Course, porkies ate the wood, so not all the animals are afraid of it, right?" The old man dropped a cigarette on the floor and mashed it with the heel of his boot. "Once people take on a deep notion about something, you can't change their minds. Don't matter if what they believe makes sense or not," his father said.

"Do people still come here?"

"Not to kill each other. Your great-grandfather showed me this place, and I've been comin' since I was a tyke. I've never seen another human being except those I brought. You ever need real privacy, this is your place."

Service had never forgotten that day. He had visited the place regularly over the years and had never seen anyone, which he attributed to the area's isolation and inaccessibility rather than fear of evil spirits.

It was the perfect place to meet Cecilia Lasurm.

During his time in Newberry, he had gotten to know the waitress Nikki-Jo Jokola, pals without romantic involvement. When he was ready to place the ad in the Manistique paper, Nikki-Jo took care of it, and they'd put Nikki-Jo's phone number in; when Lasurm called her, Nikki-Jo told her to dress warm and where and when to meet him.

He had selected the site so that she had to negotiate a long, almost perfect oxbow in the road, and he had placed himself so that he could make sure she wasn't being followed. He had arrived three hours before their meeting to wait for her. When she drove by, slipping and sliding, he could see her talking to herself and fighting the steering wheel, but she was alone. He had quickly trotted back to his vehicle to wait for her to reach him.

When she pulled up, he was waiting on his new Rupp, the motor running. Lasurm looked tired and nervous.

"You mighta picked an easier place to get to."

"We don't want easy," he said.

The snow was knee-deep, the surface crusted over. He had a sled behind the snowmobile, which was loaded with gear. He had already broken trail into the old church, stacked firewood, and arranged an area for their arrival.

He started the snowmobile and held out his hand for her to get on behind him.

"You sure this thing will handle it?" she asked.

"You should have seen my old one," he said.

She smiled. "I have."

His mouth hung open. "You know where the Rupp is?"

She nodded. "They think of it as a trophy. They get drunk and urinate on it."

Service cringed. *Rats.* When they got to the remains of the building, he helped her inside, lit a kerosene lantern, and ignited a fire between some rocks on the stone floor. He put a small iron grill over the fire and put on the coffeepot. He had rigged a tarp to make a lean-to inside the ruins, and set it up so that they and the fire would be protected from snow falling through the open roof.

"This seems extreme," she said.

"Coming into the Garden is extreme. I wanted to make sure that you weren't followed and that we'd have complete privacy."

He had balsam boughs stacked on the floor, covered with a canvas tarp. Two sleeping bags were rolled up on the tarp. He didn't expect to spend the night, but winter weather was fickle and it paid to be prepared.

He had trapped two snowshoe hares the day before in the swamp behind the Airstream, and now he put the meat on a metal grate over the fire and began to grill them.

Lasurm watched him go about his tasks, sipped her coffee, and remained silent.

"You're thinking about living rough in the Garden?" she asked.

"There may be a couple of days when I have to," he said. "There's a lot of territory down there and I've got to cover it on foot. I thought about snowshoes or skis, but I don't want tracks. It's easier to cover footprints."

"There are several places down there where you can hole up," she said. "Did you bring maps?"

She used a pencil to mark the places and described them to him. "You're going to work at night?" she asked.

He nodded.

"This place makes me feel uneasy," Lasurm said, looking around the abandoned, decaying structure.

He related the story his father had told him years before, and after he stopped talking, she said, "I feel what the Indians feel, don't you?"

"No," he said, pouring coffee for her.

"You don't know how to read me," she said as he turned the cooking hares with his knife. She held up her leg and wiggled her boot. "I can't say I miss the other one," she said. "It's more of an inconvenience than anything. Life is about managing inconvenience . . . would you agree?"

"I never thought about it."

"I'm not surprised," she said. "I would think that game wardens prefer to swim in either black or white water. For you people, the ambiguity of gray is the real inconvenience."

"It's not that simple," he said.

"I'm sure you find gray very frustrating," she said.

"What is it that brings out your preachy side?" he asked.

She laughed. "You don't need a church to be spiritual."

"Like the Indians?"

"Anywhere was their church, and I'm not preachy. I'm simply comfortable in my own beliefs."

"Such as?"

"Lots of things churchgoing Christians would not agree with."

He sensed she was pressing him to ask for more, but he had his own agenda. "You're gonna run a lot of risk with me in the Garden," he said.

"I don't fear risks," she said, "but if you're going to be out nights, you're going to have to be in by certain hours, or stay out all the next day. People in the Garden aren't nosy so much as observant, and what they see, they talk about. They say information can move from one end of the peninsula to the other faster than a lightning bolt. We call it Garden speed."

Where was she going with this?

"For all practical purposes, my house is on Burn't Bluff. I'm two and a half miles from Fayette and the Port Bar, which is a short walk from the state park," she said. "It's four miles south to Fairport and seven miles north from my place to Garden." She drew pencil lines on the map to show him. "If you get caught out, there are several places where you can lay over for the day." Again, she marked the places on the map and described each one to him.

If nothing else, Lasurm was thorough.

"Did you kill people in Vietnam?" she asked.

"Vietnam is in the past," he said. Where was she going now?

"We only left there last year and then with our tails between our legs," she said. "How does the U.S. lose a war to rice growers?"

"We didn't lose," he countered.

"Perhaps not on the battlefield," she said. "But there was no true political commitment or mobilization of national will, and wars are not all won and lost on battlefields. They sent you over there and you fought and you were on your own with not a lot of support from back home."

"You're not really talking about Vietnam," he said, watching her eyes and trying to read the tone in her voice.

"What's Lansing's commitment to the Garden?" she said. "They send you people in to enforce what amounts to an administrative rule and give you no tools. Why? Is Lake Michigan more important than Lake Superior or Lake Huron?"

"What are you driving at?" he asked.

"If you check around the government I think you'll find that each salmon or trout taken in state waters by a sportfisherman represents about eighty dollars to the state economy. That same fish from a commercial license brings the state a buck and a quarter."

"Those numbers are news to me." Astonishing news.

"It's news to a lot of people," she said, "and if the numbers aren't a hundred percent accurate, they certainly reflect the magnitude of the ratio. If you're Lansing, why revitalize commercial fishing? There's a lot more money to be made boosting sportfishing."

He couldn't dispute her logic, and wondered why he'd never heard such data before.

"Sportfishing is more important than commercial fishing for the state economy, and tourism is our second-leading business. The DNR planted Pacific salmon to eat the alewives and cut down on the summer die-offs, which stunk up beaches and put off tourists. I doubt they foresaw the economic windfall," Lasurm said. "Do you know about Jondreau?"

He did. "A L'Anse Chippewa," he said. "We were briefed on the case during training. COs busted him ten years ago for not having proper safety equipment on his boat and he fought the ticket."

She nodded. "It happened in 1965," she said. "The lower court dismissed his case, but he took it to the state supreme court, which found in his favor. This had limited impact in terms of tribal rights, but it helped the tribes see that the courts could be useful. More important is Albert 'Big Abe' LeBlanc," she said. "LeBlanc is a Bay Mills Chippewa. He fished in a closed area during a closed period, and when he was arrested, U.P. Legal Services helped him fight it. You know—UPLS?" she said, lifting an eyebrow.

He shrugged; he'd never heard of it before. LeBlanc had been arrested while he was in the Newberry district, and a lot of the officers had bitched that it could lead to Indians fishing and hunting whenever and wherever they wanted. There had also been a lot of national publicity and heated editorials about the case. Attalienti's secretary was named LeBlanc. Was she tribal, a relative of Big Abe?

"Don't they teach you people *anything* in your training? U.P. Legal Services was created by Odd Hegstrom. What we have now is a federal case, *U.S. versus the State of Michigan,* and in all likelihood the feds will uphold treaty rights as they now interpret them. The LeBlanc case started last year, but there's no way it will come to trial for another two or three years, and it could be ten years before it all gets settled."

"And then?" he asked.

"I don't have a crystal ball," she said, "but what if the state eventually buys out all those people who still had valid commercial licenses for Lakes Michigan and Huron and lets only the Indians have all of Superior's waters and certain parts of the other Great Lakes?"

"That seems like a reach," he said. But the fewer licenses in effect when this happened, the less the state would have to pay out, and there was little doubt that Order Seventeen was aimed at reducing the number of licenses.

Everybody in law enforcement had assumed this had been done to revitalize commercial fishing in Lake Michigan, protecting the commercial fishermen from themselves in the short term to improve their long-term interests—but what if they were all missing the real intent?

"Talk to your people and see what they have to say," she said. "It certainly makes for an interesting what-if, eh?"

It did; and ten years fit the time frame Hegstrom was alleged to have given the Garden commercial fishermen. If she was right, Order Seventeen was the preparatory move to boost sportfishing in Lake Michigan and remove white commercial fishermen. If those fishermen had ten years left to make money, they were going to keep violating, and to hell with what Lansing said. After a moment he concluded that if they were going to violate, they'd try to do it in such a way so as to not jeopardize their licenses. This crude analysis also supported Len Stone's contention that the whole Garden situation was driven by money. Lasurm knew one helluva lot, but he couldn't just take her word for it. He needed to probe Lansing and find out what was going on. If he could just figure out how.

When the meat was done, he cut portions and put them on military mess plates and gave Lasurm salt and pepper. They ate quietly.

"There's something about meat grilled outdoors," she said.

After their meal, they talked more about logistics while he was in the Garden, and he told her he was aiming for arrival on February 14, so long as the weather was bad. If not, he'd push it back twenty-four hours, or until a time that it got bad.

"You're coming in bad weather?" she said.

"Anything short of a Big Blue Norther," he said.

"You really *are* an interesting man," she said.

"Last time we met, you walked out when I showed you the mug shot," he said.

"The girl in that photograph is twenty-two. She is my daughter, and she's a junkie."

"She's the real reason you came to us," he said.

"Too bloody late," she said. "For her."

"Who got Hegstrom to take her case?"

"I don't know," she said, "but I can guess. We'll talk more when you come to the Garden."

It was a less than satisfying answer, but he told himself it would have to suffice.

19

LANSING, FEBRUARY 10, 1976

"If the state owns it, Jumping Bill manages it."

A *Detroit Free Press* columnist had once written that finding out what went on inside state government in the capital was akin to going to the moon: a helluva challenging journey to a destination without air, water, logic, or significant gravity. Michigan's elected legislators were notorious paradoxically for ferocious independence and blind party loyalty. But even some of the most popular elected officials were often ignorant of the engine that ultimately drove the governmental machine.

One night Service's old man had come home with a friend, both of them soused and stumbling around like the earth was on gimbals. "Son, this is the most powerful man in Lansing."

Service remembered his first impression of Bill Fahey: five feet tall and equally wide, with a thick red nose and diaphanous gray angel hair that seemed to grow in clumps. The little man had grinned and mumbled, "Geez oh Pete, da game warden speaketh truth!"

"Jumping Bill" Fahey held the official title of state properties manager, a job he had held since 1947. "If the state owns it, Jumping Bill manages it," his father explained. "He's the state's landlord."

Service had thought about this some and never quite understood how someone in such a nondescript position could be so powerful; he wrote it off to his father's sense of hyperbole and too much alcohol in both men.

Jumping Bill came around regularly after that, and Service eventually discovered that they had become pals after his old man wrote the man a ticket for shooting a deer ten minutes after shooting hours had ended, and

Fahey had paid his ticket without bellyaching. Out of this unusual meeting, a friendship was born. Fahey was originally from Gladstone, and still had a hunting camp north of Rapid River. One time Service had queried the old man about his other friends and discovered that his father had written tickets on every one of them, usually after they had become friends.

One morning Service got out of bed to find his father and Fahey drunk on the kitchen floor, a stringer of gutted and dessicated brook trout between them. Service had washed the trout, rolled them in cornmeal, and fried them. The smell brought the drunks back to life, and when they crawled into chairs, he served them trout for breakfast, setting a bottle of Jack Daniel's between them.

When his father died, the governor had attended the funeral and had heaped praise on the officer who had been drinking on duty and stepped in front of a truck. Service never doubted that Bill Fahey had somehow engineered the governor's appearance, and it was then that he began to suspect that Fahey's power was something more than mere drunk-talk.

When Service graduated from the Michigan State Police Academy, Fahey showed up for the ceremony, red-faced and mumbling, stinking of gin, food stains on his twenty-year-old tie. He'd not seen or talked to Fahey since his father's funeral, and was surprised to see him. He was even more surprised to see Colonel Edgar Browning Proctor, the top Troop in the state, fawn all over the little Yooper, who rarely uttered a complete—much less coherent—sentence.

Fahey pumped his hand, grinning and slurring, "Geez oh Pete."

After the ceremony, Proctor (who was called EBP behind his back—for "extra big prick") had pulled Service aside.

"You're a friend of Fahey's?"

"My dad was."

"Your father?"

"Frank Service."

Proctor had gaped at him. "You're Ironfist Service's son? I didn't know," the state police commander said. "I was post commander in Iron Mountain, and I knew your dad. If you're half the cop your father was, I'm glad we've got you in the Troops."

Fahey told him after the graduation party to look him up if he ever needed anything.

Until now there had been no reason.

Fahey answered his own phone. "Properties, Fahey."

"Mister Fahey, it's Grady Service."

"Geez oh Pete," Fahey said. "How does it feel to ramrod the Mosquito?"

"Good," Service said. Had his father's friend been keeping track of him?

"Geez, you sound good," Fahey said. "What can I do youse for?"

"I'd like to talk to you about something," Service said.

"Not on the phone," Fahey said. "Face-to-face. You comin' down to Lansing soon?"

"Nossir."

"Geez oh Pete, I'd better fix dat, eh? You'll get a call, okay?"

Two hours later Attalienti telephoned. "You're going to Lansing tomorrow," the acting captain said.

"I am?"

"Metrovich just called me. The director has requested you as our liaison with SPO on a special project."

"SPO?"

"State Properties Office."

The current director of the DNR was John "Jungle Jack" Curry, who had come to Lansing in 1967 from Alaska where he had been the number-two man with Alaska Fish & Game. The Michigan salmon program was attributed to the director, and officers told Service that even Curry was caught by surprise at the program's success. The salmon had been planted with no firm idea of whether they would survive or not. The program's main goal was to reduce alewife overpopulation. It was also common knowledge that Curry had not shown a lot of concern about the Garden situation.

"Why me?"

"SPO has decided to conduct some kind of real estate and asset audit, and the director wants someone to run interference. Metrovich got the impression that State Property asked for you by name, and, if so, Jungle Jack's not one to buck the flow, so you're going. The request is highly irregular and Cosmo and Curry both have their antennae quivering with suspicion. I'm sure Curry doesn't want some dirt-boot CO dealing with another agency, but he's too savvy to cross swords with the property kingpin. You're to meet a man named Fahey at Lou Coomes restaurant in north Lansing at noon tomorrow. Fahey's the director of State Properties. I were you, I'd head down there tonight. The weather from the bridge down to Grayling can get ugly. After your meeting you are to report to Curry and Metrovich."

Service started to laugh and stopped when he realized that Fahey's little exercise in muscle might just have earned him a couple of enemies in his own department. "Goddamn Lansing," he said out loud.

The restaurant was not far off US 127 and had a towering neon sign that looked like the gaudy trail of a comet. The restaurant was filled with men in dark suits.

The maître d' eyed Service's uniform and said, "This way, Officer."

She led him to a private dining room where Fahey was already seated, a napkin—already stained—tucked in over his tie. He had a drink in front of him and a large bowl of olives stuck with green and white toothpicks.

"Geez oh Pete!" Fahey greeted him. "You made it."

"You made it happen," Service said.

"Easy enough when you've been around as long as me. In your dad's honor we're gonna have an old-fashioned U.P. lunch—cudighi on Finnish rye, smothered in onions and hot Italian mustard. The cudighi comes from an old Finn up to Lake Linden. People back home are always sendin' me stuff. I get a box of Trenary Toast once a month, but one of my staff members broke a tooth so that gets tossed soon as it arrives."

Fahey handed him an envelope. "This is a memo from me to your director. It apologizes for any inconvenience and explains that the audit is postponed until a later date. 'Course, I don't suggest when, because it's good to keep others on edge. State bureaucrats hate unscheduled audits, so he'll be relieved when he gets this—at least for a while. How about a drink?"

"Just coffee," Service said. "I'm on duty."

"Geez oh Pete, not a chip off the old block—but hey, it's the smart thing to do. You remember that trout breakfast you made for the old man and me?"

Service remembered. He said, "Do you know Acting Chief Metrovich?"

When Fahey transitioned from small talk to business, his fool's mask evaporated. "Acting's all he'll ever be. Cosmo's all shine, no metal. Wouldn't say it's raining until somebody above him says it's so. When Cosmo's six months are up, he'll retire and a man named Grant will get the captain's job. He's new to the DNR, but he's a man with depth. He came to Lansing from the federal government in Washington, D.C. The U.P. needs a captain with the kind of pluck you fellas have."

"The men never talk about Metrovich," Service said.

"People don't talk about air, either. It's just there. Cosmo isn't heavy enough to leave footprints if he walked across a swimming pool filled with Jell-O. Attalienti may make a good captain down the road, but not in the U.P. They're taking a good look at him now. He might do well in one of the southern law zones. Deano's a good man." Fahey didn't say who "they" was.

Fahey had surprisingly incisive insight into the law enforcement division, and Service decided to test it. "Len Stone?"

"Yooper-tough and right out of the old school. He'll get the permanent lieutenant's job and, if he wanted to, he could move downstate for a captain's job—but they'll never get Len out of the U.P. Besides, he can retire in eight or nine years."

A waiter brought their lunches and they tried to eat while three different men "popped in" to pay homage to Fahey. They all had jokes for him, and Fahey had a quick comeback for each of them. The well-spoken and thoughtful man of minutes before immediately backslid to ridge-running bumbler when people came into the room. Their last visitor was a long-legged woman with black hair and green eyes who talked to Fahey but stared the whole while at Service. Fahey introduced her as "Shay-the-Lay," and she laughed and corrected him. "It's Shay da Leigh."

"Never was good wit' names," Fahey said with a chuckle.

"Except when you want to be," she said, excusing herself for interrupting.

"Good girl," Fahey said when she was gone. "And a crack lawyer in the Legislative Services Branch. You're a senator or a rep and you want to draft a bill, you call in LS and they help you to write it and put it in the appropriate capitolese. Shay's the best they've got, great brain and an even greater wild streak. She was raised over to Bessemer. You can trust her."

They finished eating in privacy and Fahey had two more vodka tonics. "So, what was it you wanted to talk about?" his father's pal finally asked.

"The Garden."

Fahey nodded solemnly. "Those boys sure didn't take to Order Seventeen. Still taking potshots at you fellas, I hear."

"Somebody's going to get killed," Service said.

Fahey pondered this as he took a drink. "Smart boys down there. They see the handwriting on the wall."

"Such as the end of commercial fishing in Lake Michigan?"

Fahey raised an eyebrow and cracked a grin. "Just like your old man. I don't know how, but that sonuvagun always knew what was going on," he said. "The fur trappers came first, then the mining companies and the loggers, and now the oil companies are coming in. The fact is that commercial fishermen aren't important enough to have the power to get what they want. See, in Lansing, clout and power count. Companies have pretty much always gotten what they wanted as long as the state got a good cut. Money speaks, eh?"

"There's more money in sportfishing than commercial fishing," Service said.

"Geez oh Pete, this salmon thing's bigger than anybody dreamed, even Curry. The commercial net boys keep at it, they'll kill the salmon. You know what brought down our fish stocks more than any other factor?"

"Lampreys."

"Nylon," Fahey said. "With nylon fishermen no longer had to make their own nets out of linen or know how to repair them, which they did all the time. Nylon's lighter, cheaper, stronger, and requires a lot less upkeep. Capital and costs down, profits up. Nylon changed Great Lakes commercial fishing."

Service decided to push a little. "I heard the Indians might get to keep their nets."

Fahey straightened his shoulders and took another drink. "Well, all that's in the federal court system and there's no way to predict those buggers, but if I were a betting man, I'd bet the Indians will come out of this winners."

"And white commercial fishermen will get bought out?"

"You've got good sources," Fahey said, raising his glass in salute. "The few who've been able to hang on to their licenses would get bought out."

"Do you know Odd Hegstrom?" Service asked.

"Since the old days. Smart fella—and cagey as they come."

"He created U.P. Legal Services."

"Not with a lot of support from the state bar or Lansing. People think Odd's addicted to fighting windmills, but that's malarkey. He just doesn't like to see people pushed around, and when he goes into a fight, he likes to win. Usually he does."

"Political ambition?"

"What does a man need political office for if he's already got power? Odd's not all pro bono. He's got one helluva law practice, and though he's got the tribes pro bono now, I'd expect that down the road they'll become real billable hours and a cash cow. Why the interest in all this?"

"I'm just trying to figure out the Garden."

Fahey laughed. "When you do, let me know. I've never figured those buggers out. The situation there's not all that complicated, eh. People up there know the end's in sight and they're gonna milk it all the way."

"Lansing knows this?"

"Some do, some don't. Most who know don't really give a bloody hoot. The Garden is a skirmish in a small war to get the state to where it wants to be economically. The Garden ain't Gettysburg. Hell, it ain't even the Toledo War!" Michigan and Ohio had taken up arms because both wanted the strip of land that contained Toledo. The compromise gave Toledo to Ohio and the Upper Peninsula to Michigan, and hard feelings still lingered above the bridge. The U.P. had been incorporated into the state's territory without having a say in it, and then its resources had been taken away by mining and logging companies, all with Lansing's blessing.

"And if the Garden gets bloody?"

"Some might like that. Be a good excuse for the governor to call in the National Guard the way it happened during the Detroit riots. The Garden boys know this, so they have to walk a fine line between fighting the inevitable and keeping doing what they want to do to make their dough. They can't let it get out of hand or they've got no chance, eh."

"They've got no chance anyway," Service said.

"They don't know that."

Service was impressed not only with Fahey's knowledge, but also with his crisp and simple explanations of history and political realities.

A waiter brought them a six-inch-square cinnamon roll and put it between them as he poured coffee.

"Coffee's boiled," Fahey said. "Bakery's from L'Anse. Lou has it delivered daily just for Yoopers working in Lansing. You going back this afternoon?"

"If I can."

"Hard to predict those guys, but Curry and Metrovich will be suspicious of why I asked for you. They'll be trying to figure out what the heck I'm up to, and how you fit in. When they ask why, just tell 'em the truth. Your old man and me were pals."

Which meant he should tell a half-truth. If he hadn't asked for information from Fahey, he would not be in this position.

"Anything else?" Fahey asked.

"I always wondered how you got your name."

Fahey laughed with a mouth full of cinnamon roll. "Never mattered to me I was the size of a popcorn fart. I been a competitive little shit my whole life. I played baseball at Michigan Agricultural College—that was State before it got renamed. I wasn't the most talented player on the team, not even close, but I love baseball. It's the only game that stops after every play and gives every player the chance to think through all the possibilities for the next play. Baseball's a thinking man's game, and I always managed to stay several jumps ahead of the other guys."

And still did, Service knew. Fahey's unimpressive physical appearance would make him easy to underestimate. "How'd you get your job?"

"The college got me a summer job in properties, and after I graduated I went off to law school."

"Where?"

"Harvard," Fahey said with a little grin, watching for Service's reaction. "I finished law school at age twenty. Pearl Harbor came along and I volunteered for the U.S. Marines and they sent me out to the Pacific. I got discharged in 'forty-five as a sergeant, and came back to Lansing and got into properties part-time while I studied for the state bar. When I passed the bar, they offered me the manager's job and I took it. I don't mind Lansing, and it isn't all that far from home, especially with the bridge. They gave me a bigger title since then."

The Mackinac Bridge had opened in 1957. Before that travelers were forced to cross the straits by ferry, and at certain times the delay could be hours for one of the five boats, and sometimes weather prevented any crossings at all. The bridge had opened a flow of tourists and newcomers that some Yoopers still resented. Like Brigid Mehegen's grandfather, for one.

Service did a quick calculation. Fahey was fifty-seven or fifty-eight now. He looked a lot older. *Harvard?*

Service drove to downtown Lansing, parked in a public lot, and walked over to the Mason Building. He signed in at the central registration desk on the ground floor and sat down to have a smoke while the uniformed receptionist called upstairs. Did they think he stole the green uniform and badge? The message was clear: Stay out unless you belong here.

Jungle Jack himself came down on the elevator to fetch him and escorted him up several floors to his office. He'd seen Curry at graduation but had never talked to him. The director was a tall, gaunt man with long, graying red hair. He wore a houndstooth sport coat instead of a suit and had a smear of blue ink on his left hand.

The director had a corner office that lacked fancy appointments. There were three framed sheepskins on the wall: a PhD and an MS from the University of Minnesota, and a BS from Montana State. There was also a color photograph of Curry, an equally tall, thin woman, and two ectomorphic boys, probably the wife and sons. None of them were smiling. A stuffed gray wolf was on a pedestal in the corner, and on the wall behind the director's cluttered desk, a stuffed four-foot-long Chinook salmon, at least a fifty-pounder by the looks of it.

Curry walked behind his desk and Service stood in front of it, handed him the envelope from Fahey, and watched him rip it open and read.

"Postponed until when?" the director asked, looking up from the memorandum.

"Mr. Fahey didn't say."

"And why a postponement?" Curry pressed.

"He didn't give a reason."

Curry did not invite him to sit. "He asked for you by name."

"He was a friend of my father's," Service explained.

"And a friend of yours? I'm told you Yoopers all stick together."

"First time I've seen him since I graduated from training," Service said.

"But he asked for you. Did you talk about the audit?"

"Nossir, we just made small talk, and he apologized for me having to drive down here for nothing. We had lunch and I came here as directed."

"Bureaucrats," Curry groused. "I'm sorry you had to waste your time," he said, a statement made out of convention, not conviction.

"You've got the Mosquito," the director said.

Not a question. "My father had it too."

Curry ignored the reference to his father. "Fahey was the big mover in getting the wilderness designation."

"I didn't know that."

"Not many people down here have actually seen it, but those who have swear it's one of the state's natural jewels."

"It is."

"Might be worth my time to take a tour." This was also convention absent conviction.

"Any time, sir."

The director let the memo flutter to his desktop. "Postponed," he said. "I'd like to know what Jumping Bill is up to. He's a slippery one."

Curry led him down a corridor to Metrovich's office and walked away without another word.

Metrovich waved him in. "Take a seat," the acting chief said. "How'd the meeting go?"

"The audit's been postponed. I delivered a memo to the director from Mr. Fahey."

"Did you read it?"

"Nossir. The director told me what was in it."

"I see," Metrovich said. "You're sure you didn't read it?"

"I saw it was a single page, typewritten."

"Okay then," Metrovich said. "I guess that's it."

Service wasn't sure he'd been dismissed because the acting chief was staring past him. "Shall I go, sir?"

The acting chief did not respond, and Service walked alone out to the elevator. When the door opened, he found himself alone with Shay da Leigh, her hand poised next to the buttons. "Sporting goods or housewares?"

"Lobby," he said.

"Me, too."

The door shushed closed.

"Fahey's one of a kind," she said.

"I'm learning that," he said.

"You know, of course, that a junior conservation officer meeting alone with one of the state's most powerful people has triggered a wave of paranoia in the department."

He smelled flowers and citrus wafting off her. Her skirt swished when she shifted her weight. It had been a long time since he'd heard a woman's skirt make such a sound. "I got that feeling," he said.

"People here fight for face time," she said. "It's an unspoken currency."

He nodded. Why was she talking to him? "You have business with the DNR?" he asked.

"One of my clients," she said.

"You write legislation for the department?"

"Not exactly. The director insists on writing first drafts. I get called in to clean them up. Mostly I edit for clarity and style. Have you seen the ink on Curry's hand?"

Service nodded.

"I doubt he ever washes it," she said. "The ink is his way of showing the department he's a working director, not a paper-pushing figurehead. He's angling for bigger things. I give him a year until he moves on."

The elevator bounced when it stopped. "Let a girl buy you a drink?" she asked. Her skirt whispered when she asked him.

"I have to head north."

"A drink and a talk about the Garden?" she pressed, one eyebrow raised.

"I guess I have time."

"Jumping Bill thought you might," she said. "This meeting isn't serendipity."

20

HASLETT, FEBRUARY 10, 1976

"You cops are all missing the gene for trust."

On the way out of the Mason Building, da Leigh suggested they meet in Haslett at a bar called Pagan's Place, "across from the amusement park."

He parked across the street under a row of leafless elms and changed from his uniform to jeans and a sweater. A sign above him said LAKE LANSING AMUSEMENT PARK: CLOSED UNTIL SUMMER. He glanced at the sign and went inside and saw her on a stool at the bar. Despite the time he'd spent in Lansing as a state cop, he had never gotten familiar with the fastest routes; he'd never cared to, knowing his time in the capital was temporary. By contrast, Bathsheba loved the city, knew the shops and restaurants, and never tired of going out and feeling the whirl and smug superiority of government employees.

Da Leigh sat so that her legs stretched out in front of her.

"I like the way you walk," she said when he sat down. "Self-confident, not quite cocky. Most men can't pull that off."

He ordered a draft beer from the barmaid, but da Leigh amended the request. "Two aquavits," she said. "Linie."

He protested mildly. "I have a long drive tonight."

"It's true," she said. "You people really are Boy Scouts."

"It's common sense," he said, "not moral high ground."

She laughed and clucked appreciatively. "So," she said. "The Garden."

He waited for her to take the lead. The aquavits were delivered in tall shot glasses. The woman lifted hers, held it out to him, and clicked his glass, saying "Skoal." She swallowed hers in one gulp, set the glass down, and ordered two more.

He drank as she drank, felt the aquavit explode in his belly like a plume of rolling napalm.

"I write a lot of administrative rules," she said. "And believe it or not, it's an art."

"I'll take your word for it."

"My hand was on Order Seventeen," she said. "Start to finish."

"For whom?"

"Curry was the driver, but the governor's people were aware of it and saw a couple of drafts."

"Why not write it as law?" he asked.

"Too slow. If the legislature gets involved, it becomes a political football, and U.P. legislators have purchase in both houses. Yoopers elect their people over and over; they understand the principles of paleopolitics, and how seniority leads to rewards. An administrative order avoids the morass so that the department can get something into play immediately, and others can start getting used to the idea. It's expedient."

"But the order gets shifted into law later."

"Sometimes, but not always. It's not a given."

"Curry wants to boost sportfishing," he said.

She smiled. "He actually has sympathy for commercial operators, but the state budget is under fire, and the DNR budget is always among the first things attacked. Sportfishing will bring in a lot of revenue and he can't ignore that. He didn't come all the way from Alaska to fail. Are you sympathetic to people in the Garden?"

Two more aquavits were delivered and consumed after another chorus of "Skoal."

"I just want to understand what we're dealing with," he said.

"Curry fancies himself an intellectual, a steward of state treasures. He barely tolerates law enforcement."

"We enforce the law. We don't look for the director's approval."

"He allows questions and input from a select few pets, and he has a wet finger up in the air continuously."

"Order Seventeen is a process. It carries no penalties."

"Licenses can be revoked," she said defensively.

"It's a lugubrious process that requires multiple infractions. I don't understand why we don't subpoena the offenders' financial records," he said.

"People and companies are guaranteed privacy, remember? Due process?"

"It makes our work difficult."

Another round of drinks came and went. Service felt hot and rolled up his sleeves.

"Laws and administrative orders are not written to facilitate ease of enforcement," she said.

"Officers are being shot at," he pointed out.

"I've heard," she said. "You?"

He nodded, and she asked, "What are you people doing about it?"

"About Order Seventeen or being shot at?"

"Do you think I'm the enemy?"

"No comment," he said.

"It was Jumping Bill's idea that I 'bump' into you. Do you think *he's* the enemy?"

"No," but he also understood that Fahey had not survived so long without being a trader and compromiser. "The LeBlanc case is a shadow over everything," he said.

She licked her lips. "You bet. The state has to play this right or the sportfishing plan could get shredded. The feds have deep pockets; we don't. What we really need is a Republican in the White House to tell the states that it's our right and responsibility to manage our own environmental concerns and resources."

"Jerry Ford is a Michigan Man."

"He's been caretaking and cleaning up since Nixon waved bye-bye. It's not clear Jerry can win if he runs on his own. Seriously," she added, "how are you handling the Garden?"

"Following the letter of the law and practicing ducking."

She laughed out loud and touched his forearm, the warmth of her fingers searing him.

"You cops are all missing the gene for trust," she said. "Is that part of your selection process?"

"No more than for lawyers," he shot back.

"Touché," she said.

"I like to deal with what I can see." What had Lasurm said—that he wanted a world in black and white? She wasn't far off.

"Rocks and trees and guns," she said. "This thing down here is just as real. We even get shot at."

"Words don't splatter brains," he said.

She paused and looked at him, patted his hand. "You're right. It's not the same, and I wasn't trying to demean the risks you guys run. But this world has multiple realities, each with its own rules. Some of them are not nice."

Her apology took him by surprise. "I didn't mean that as a put-down," he said.

"I deserved it," she said. "I get criticized for being shrill when I think I'm just being direct and passionate. The Pill and the sixties have begun to liberate us in the bedroom, but it's not the same when we have our clothes on. Curry's being pushed to hire women in law enforcement," she said. "The state police are considering it, and the Natural Resources Commission doesn't want the DNR to be second to the Troops. How does that grab you?"

"I don't have a problem with it."

"Will your wife feel the same way?"

"Divorced," he said.

She ordered two more drinks, doubles this time, which they drank down. Service felt the napalm cooking his brain.

"Women don't threaten your view of the world order?"

"No."

"How do you separate long legs and sex appeal from professional competence?"

"Ask her politely."

Da Leigh poked him in the arm, threw her head back, and laughed out loud. "We're getting drunk."

"Getting?"

"You don't like to think?"

"I think about things I can do something about," he said.

"Trees and rocks and guns," she said.

"Sometimes long legs," he added.

She tucked her chin down and looked at him. "How long since the divorce?"

"A while."

"You seeing someone?"

The napalm had coated his brain, its heat making the tissue swell. "A fuck buddy," he said.

She blinked and giggled. "That's a new one," she said.

"Was for me too," he admitted.

"It sounds liberated."

"Or two losers looking for justification."

She shrugged, grinned and held up her shot glass. "Linie: The Swedes make it and send it on a ship around the world before they sell it. Can you imagine going around the world like that?" she asked with a leer.

"We confiscate their gear," he said, trying to get the conversation back to business, "and ask the courts for condemnation proceedings."

She studied him and grinned. "That takes a lot of time, and the courts don't make it easy or automatic."

"But while the court decides, they don't have their gear. No gear, no poaching."

"That's outside the spirit of Order Seventeen."

"It's expedient," he said, playing back her own logic.

"No wonder they're using guns."

"They were using guns *before* we started this."

"You think this is the right thing to do?"

"Doing something is more important than being pushed around right now." Even with the aquavit in him, it was clear after today that conservation officers were risking their lives as part of a larger political strategy: The powers in Lansing did not give a damn whether they stopped the poaching or not.

They each had one more aquavit and when the drinks were gone, da Leigh looked at her watch. "My house is ten minutes from here." She rested her hand on his arm and insisted on paying the bill. "Expense account," she explained. "Don't worry, your name won't appear."

On the sidewalk she threw her arms around him and kissed him for a long time. "You're not a Boy Scout in all things, are you?"

"Nope," he said.

"Thank God," she said.

She kissed him at the front door in the morning. "Jumping Bill's finagling to get you down here the way he did has put you in a tough position," she said.

"He arranged it knowing that," he said.

"Bill doesn't do anything without purpose. Your being here was his game and his decision, but *you* be careful, Boy Scout. Don't go get yourself shot by one of those goddamn Gardenians."

21

NEWBERRY, FEBRUARY 11, 1976

"Sometimes the flaw's so visible it's invisible."

On the way out of Lansing he swung by the Capital City Airport and spent an hour with a meteorologist from the National Weather Service.

Nikki-Jo Jokola smiled and winked when Service sat down in a booth in the bar of Brown's Hotel. "Youse're a bit late for breakfast today," she said. "And we had a nice meat loaf for lunch."

"No thanks." He gave her a piece of paper with information for the next newspaper ad. "For the thirteenth," he said.

"I'll drive down to Manistique tomorrow morning," she said. "Shuck's sick."

"With what?"

"The out-of-da-action blues. If you have time, stop by an' see him."

It took a long time for the retired officer to come to the door, but his hang-dog face lit up when he saw Service. "Your replacement's thicker'n lead," Shuck Gorley said. "Name's Parker. He transferred up from Ingham County to 'get inta da action.'"

"I didn't pick him," Service said. He didn't even know him.

"Roars like a lion, brains of a spruce grouse," Gorley said.

Service laughed. The spruce grouse was so low on avian intelligence that it was in danger of consignment to Darwin's dustbin. "This Parker stop in to pick your brains?"

"Dat one couldn't pick a hot dog wit' a fork. He don't need ta talk to me. He knows it all."

"Nikki-Jo's worried about you," Service said.

"Dat woman worries if she don't got worries," Gorley said disgustedly.

"She cares about you."

"Dere ain't a problem. Just dis Parker yayhoo. How's da Garden?"

"Pretty damn confusing."

"*Dat* mess, it don't never change," Gorley said. "Get inside, youse're lettin' my heat out. I got coffee on."

Service followed the man into his kitchen. The house was clean and orderly. "I lost your thermos."

"Your thermos," Gorley corrected him, "not mine. How'd you lose 'er?"

"The Garden," he said, and then he related his Garden patrols, everything he'd seen and experienced and had been thinking. Gorley listened attentively until he was finished.

"Dean told me he might use youse down dere."

"Based on what you told him," Service said.

"We need good officers dere. Da Garden's always been lawless, eh. We always had trouble gettin' guys to serve down dere. An' dat crow line dey got now, dat ain't new, but back when I done patrols down dere, da line wasn't dere first line a' defense."

"It wasn't?"

"Nope. Dey had inside dope, always seemed ta know when we were comin' down dere. We never figured out why or how, but da old captain, Cortney Denu, he made da officers handwrite all dere reports and send 'em direct to him, an' he personally sent 'em on to Lansing. Only he opened 'em—same wit' plans. And when an op was bein' put together, we never met in Escanaba. We met somewhere outside Delta County. Once we started dis, we managed to get in on dem and make a few pinches."

"But now everything is running out of Escanaba again."

"Dat was Cosmo's doin'. Da people down to da Escanaba office whined, said dey was insulted by Cap'n Denu, said it hurt dere feelings; so Cosmo, he put tings back da way dey were when dey weren't workin'."

Service didn't know what to say. A probable security leak had been identified, and now it was being ignored? Did Attalienti know about this?

"We had security problems here too," Gorley went on. "Some years back we had a poacher named Jepson, tall, baby-faced sonuvagun, and we worked like hell tryin' ta nab 'im, but he was always one step ahead. I had west Chippewa County back den, and George Zuchow had eastern Luce, where dis Jepson character lived, and George and I tried like da dickens to nail 'im. After close to a year, I said ta hell wit' it—all da bloody time I spent on dat case was lettin' other stuff go. You can't get 'em all."

Service understood.

"Den I got in a wreck and busted my leg and dey put me on restricted duty. I had to go inta da office every day and help do dispatch and run errands for da lieutenant and junk like dat. Seemed like Zuchow come in every day ta bitch and moan about Jepson and how he'd eluded him again and what he was gonna try next. I mean, every day. 'Course, da whole office started following da war between dose two. And every day about da same time, George showed up, da bakery guy come to da canteen and brought new donuts and took da old stuff away, and I watched him and noticed he sorta hung around, not doin' anyting couldn't be done in one minute. So I went to da LT and I asked who da bakery jamoke was, and he said talk ta da secretaries. Da secretaries said dey t'ought da LT was havin' it brought in for everybody. Next day da bakery guy comes in jabbering with George, and I put my hand on 'is chest and I tell 'im to show me some ID, and he rabbits, but I grab 'im and put 'is nose on da floor and we got out 'is wallet. Da jerk's name is Jepson! He's da brudder of da bloody poacher. Nobody ordered no fresh bakery. Dis guy's been bringing it in on 'is own and listenin' ta what's going on and passing da word on. Dey *bot'* went to jail."

"Sometimes the flaw's so visible it's invisible," Service said.

"Routine can be as good as pokin' your eyes out," Gorley said.

22

MARQUETTE-HARVEY-TRENARY, FEBRUARY 11, 1976

"Even your old man wasn't dis crazy."

Attalienti leaned back in his chair and listened to what Service had to say about security in the Escanaba office.

"That happened years ago; it was thoroughly investigated, and written off to coincidence," the acting captain said. "What was the Lansing thing about?"

Service guessed Attalienti suffered the same paranoia that existed downstate, local supervision being an extension of Lansing. He considered telling him everything, but held back. "I don't know. I showed up for the meeting and Fahey said the audit was postponed, and he apologized for making me drive all that way."

"You talked to the director and Cosmo?"

"I told them exactly what I told you."

"Why did Fahey ask for you?"

"He was a friend of my father's."

"I don't think I buy that," Attalienti said.

"We had a lunch in honor of my old man and talked."

"Cosmo's in a twitter. He's called me three times and says Curry's all over him. Both of them are certain there's more to the meeting with Fahey than your just being the son of his friend."

Service had to take a deep breath so that he could say quietly, "I had lunch. The audit's postponed. Fahey gave me a memo for Curry and I delivered the memo to the director. I met with Metrovich—end of story."

"Careers can get destroyed by people who dabble in politics," Attalienti said.

"I'm *not* dabbling in anything," Service said forcefully to the acting captain. "*You* sent me down there," he added.

Attalienti stared at him. "Okay, sorry. They're just rattling my cage and I had to rattle yours. Don't sweat it."

"There's nothing to sweat," Service said. "I'm going into the Garden the night of the fourteenth," he added.

"Why then?"

"The weather window's what I want."

Attalienti looked at him like he was unbalanced. "They're predicting a blizzard."

"Exactly," Service said.

"I don't like this at all," the acting captain said, frowning.

"You said it was my call."

"But in a blizzard?"

He called Brigid Mehegen at home and asked if he could drop by.

There was no sign of Perry. "Got Valentine plans for us?" she asked coyly.

"I'm not going to be around," he said.

"What does that mean, 'not around'?" she asked.

"Family emergency."

"Where?" she said, her voice demanding and suspicious.

"Far away," he said.

She gave him an annoyed look. "I arranged that meeting you wanted. My guy said reluctantly he'd talk to the 'whuffo.'"

"Whuffo?" Service said.

"Jumper talk for straight-legs," she said. "You know: Whuffo you want to jump out of a perfectly good airplane?"

"Thanks," he said, "but I thought about what you said. Borrowing wasn't the smartest idea."

He could see her weighing his words, measuring him. "Is there anything I can do to help with your family emergency?" she asked.

"Thanks, but it's something I have to take care of on my own," he said.

"I was hoping we could get some time together," she said.

"Rain check?" he said.

"It's snowing, in case you haven't noticed. Have you heard the weather forecast?"

"Been too busy," he lied. "Where's your grandfather?"

"Snowshoe hunting with a couple of his pals," she said disgustedly. "What is it about old men and hunting?" she asked. "Do you want something to eat?"

"I had a big lunch," he said.

"The bedroom's available," she said, "or did you have a big one of those too?"

He laughed, but didn't answer.

She hugged him politely before he left, and gave him a searing look that let him know she knew he was bullshitting her.

So much for the fuck-buddy concept, he thought as he backed out of her driveway.

Joe Flap was waiting at his house near Trenary.

"I want you to fly me to the Garden the night of the fourteenth," Service said.

"Have you seen da weather forecast?"

"It's what I want."

"Fly you ta da Garden for what?" the pilot asked.

Service lifted his hand, opened his fingers, and made a downward fluttering motion toward a tabletop. The pilot shut his eyes and said, "Oh shit."

"Yes or no?"

"Even your old man wasn't dis crazy," Joe Flap said. "I'm in."

The pilot got two beers from the fridge and the two men sat down at the table and spread maps out and began discussing what Service had in mind. At one point, Flap asked, "How youse gonna gauge da wind?"

"I'm not. You're the pilot."

Joe Flap looked at the map and shook his head. "You got balls, kid. But da jury's out on your brains."

23

MARQUETTE, FEBRUARY 14, 1976

"She'll pop up like a butterfly in a hurricane."

The noise inside the single-engine DHC-2 Beaver was nearly unbearable, but Service wore a headset with an interphone connection, and he tried to ignore the ear-shattering roar as he checked his gear for the umpteenth time.

Joe Flap had taxied into position for a northeast takeoff into a heavy wind that made the aircraft shake as they sat waiting for clearance. Six inches of fresh snow had fallen in Marquette during the day, with up to another twenty inches being called for tonight. The snowfall in the Garden was less, as it normally was, but even down there forecasts called for ten to twelve inches over the next twenty-four hours. Service was pleased. The worse the weather, he reasoned, the fewer the people who would be out.

Service knew his pilot was less than pleased about his plan, but he had committed to helping; now he sat in uncharacteristic silence, fiddling with the choke, leaning the mixture of the engine and constantly exercising the ailerons to make sure they weren't icing up.

"Can we get off in this wind?" Service asked over the intercom.

"She'll pop up like a butterfly in a hurricane," the pilot said. "I filed VFR, and Minneapolis Center is pissed and Green Bay is pissed and da tower people here are in a snit, and da snowplow drivers are bent outta shape, but VFR is my bloody call, not a buncha scope-dopes and ground-pounders, eh." VFR meant Visual Flight Rules, the term for a pilot operating independent of ground-based radar control. "I can see my prop, eh? Dat makes 'er visual."

"Can you get back?" Service asked.

"I piss more gas den it takes ta get youse down to da Garden. I got a good eight hundred miles range. If dey close da field here, I'll take 'er downstate to

Traverse City or even Grand Rapids. You don't gotta worry about Joe Flap. Youse keep your mind on youse," the pilot concluded sharply.

The tower called on the radio. "DNR Air Four, the plows are clear of the runway. You're cleared on to the active, contact Green Bay at . . . " Service listened as Flap wrote the frequency on his leg pad. "Wind, zero four zero at thirty-two knots, gusting to forty. You sure you wanna do this tonight, Air Four?"

"Wind's right in our snoots—tanks for da info, DNR Air Four."

Flap released the brakes, which vibrated and made a clunking sound, and pulled onto the runway facing into the wind. He pushed the throttle up slightly, let the engine rumble, and shoved it further forward. The bulky aircraft began to vibrate more violently and to move slowly forward. Service sat in a seat behind the pilot and looked out a large triangular window on either side. He could not see the sides of the runway, and when he looked forward all he could see was a sea of snow flooding the windscreen. "DNR Air Four is rolling," Joe Flap reported to the tower.

The engine strained and roared and the gear chattered, barked, and vibrated under the strain of moving. Service thought it would take a long time to get airborne, but suddenly the nose came sharply up and they were aloft, bouncing around in uneven air. He looked at the instruments and saw they were climbing at a rate of just over a thousand feet per minute.

Joe Flap was on his radio, "Green Bay, DNR Air Four is airborne, VFR, requesting angels two."

"Roger, DNR, squawk three one four four, you are cleared to two thousand, maintain heading of zero four five. You're all alone up there tonight, Air Four."

"Roger, Green Bay, tanks for da help. Level at two thou, steady on zero four five. Youse have a good night."

Service felt the aircraft turning to the right as the pilot altered course to the southeast for the twenty-five minute flight to the Garden Peninsula.

He used the time to go over their plan again. The highest terrain in the

U.P. was seven hundred and forty-six feet. In the marines he had jumped numerous times at six hundred feet above the ground elevation; tonight, for safety, he would step out at seven hundred and fifty feet, which would provide adequate time to deploy his chute and equipment bag. Treebone had used his connections to get the chute from someone at the Air Guard unit at Selfridge Field in Mt. Clemens. Probably Joe Flap would cheat up a little, thinking he was helping, and there was no way to stop the pilot from doing this; if he was a little higher, he'd be in the air a little longer, but not all that much. Flap had argued vehemently for him to jump at two thousand feet, but Service figured there was too much potential for windage and getting too far off his drop zone. He'd rather go out low and get it over with fast. Because there would be no time for a second chance at such a low altitude, he had not bothered with a reserve chute, knowing if he had a problem, he'd end up as brush wolf chow. He had discussed the jump at length with Tree, who agreed that the simpler, the better. Tree didn't lecture him on the advisability of jumping; his friend had stuck to details, making sure he had covered everything he needed to address.

The temperature at Marquette had been minus eighteen at takeoff. Manistique and the Garden were eight or nine degrees warmer, but with the Beaver flying at a hundred miles an hour, the wind would be blasting him when he got outside, and the wind chill would be brutal. The trick was to minimize exposure and get on the ground as quickly as possible.

"Heading into da Garden," Flap said over the interphone.

"How's the wind?"

"Pretty steady at about twenty, right out of da northeast."

"Okay."

The plan was to drop him over farm fields northeast of Cecilia Lasurm's house and let the wind carry him down to a field about a mile north of her place. If Joe put him in the right field and if he got down without breaking a leg, getting to her place should be easy. Not the time to dwell on "ifs," he chastised himself. He needed to focus on those things he could control. Getting him to the drop zone was the pilot's job. Sweat the stuff you can control, he told himself.

Their indicated airspeed was just under one hundred and ten knots. The wind was banging them around from time to time, but the old Beaver, built in 1954, was Joe Flap's favorite, and the pilot quickly recovered from each burble.

Service was dressed heavily. He wore the same long johns and socks he'd worn during the snowmobile patrol, but this time he had no uniform and no badge, and wore insulated sweatpants over his long johns, and a wool sweater and heavy white parka over his snowmobile suit, which he had streaked with white paint. He also had a lightweight white parka with olive-charcoal camo patterns, but this was in his equipment bag, and he would use it as an outer layer after he was on the ground. The top layer would provide no warmth, but it would make him hard to see against snowy terrain.

Joe Flap announced, "Youse got eight minutes."

Service said, "Removing hatch." He unlatched the door and stowed it against the starboard bulkhead with a strap. Flap said it wouldn't affect his flight profile or comfort to have the door out; he could always crank up his heat to compensate. Service wrestled his gear bag over to the door and checked that the zipper was secure. The bag was white and had two straps so it could be attached to either side of his parachute harness at the waist. Once his chute was open, he would release the equipment bag, which would drop away and ride down ahead of him on a thirty-foot-long lanyard. There was a risk of landing on the bag or having the lanyard get tangled in trees, but he was jumping into an open field and hoped there would be no complications like telephone wires or fences. Don't think about it, he told himself. Focus on what you're doing and keep your head in the game. Basic roulette, he thought, red or black, odd or even, make your bet and watch the wheel spin.

"Disconnecting interphone," he told the pilot.

Service tucked the headset in a bin on the fuselage, pulled on a white wool balaclava and forced his helmet down over the top of it, dropped the face shield into place, and locked it. He looked up at Joe Flap who held up four fingers, meaning four minutes until he jumped. He hooked the equipment bag to both sides of his harness and swung his legs over the edge of the hatch. The aircraft had no internal cabin light except for the glow of flight instruments in front of Flap. The snow was racing sideways, a blur of small white arrows. Service stepped down to the right-wing strut facing aft and wedged his boot into the metal V. The wind was pushing the equipment bag against the back of his legs and making it difficult to stay on his perch, but he clung to the strut with his left glove and put his right hand on the D-ring of the parachute.

He seemed to be suspended in the frigid wind for hours until the engine power was pulled back and gunned, the signal for him to go. He tucked his chin to his chest and stepped aft off the strut, dropping straight down. As soon as he left his perch he pulled the ripcord and heard a sibilant *pfft* as the pilot chute came loose and began deploying the main chute. He relaxed, waiting for the parachute's opening shock, and told himself it was not quite as cold as he had anticipated. Adrenaline kept him focused on the things he had to do rather than on the elements.

When the air settled into the canopy, there was a sudden, violent yank at his crotch and he had the sensation of climbing as his weight settled under the silk. He looked up, saw the canopy above him, and immediately disconnected the equipment bag and lanyard so that the heavy bag would proceed downward ahead of him.

When the bag fully deployed, he felt a sharp tug below him and knew he had done all he could. He reached up both risers of the military chute and pulled with his right hand and pushed with his left to shift his body sideways to the wind, as close to forty-five degrees as he could manage. His mind was empty, his only focus the direction of the wind and relaxing himself for impact.

He had no idea how long he had been dropping, but he guessed the ground was close. He looked straight ahead toward an imaginary horizon, reached up the risers with his gloves, put his feet together, and relaxed his knees for impact. He felt no fear, only an urge to get on the ground as he popped loose the cover of the right riser release.

At the instant he felt contact, he let himself roll to his left side, and when he plowed into deep snow with his body, he released the right riser and the chute collapsed partway, and stopped dragging him. He instinctively rolled onto his belly and up to his knees, freed the second riser, and began yanking the shroud lines and silk canopy toward him. When the canopy was bunched around him, he used the lanyard to pull the equipment bag to him, unzipped it, got out his white camo parka cover, took off the parachute harness, stuffed his helmet, the harness, and parachute into the equipment bag, and finally allowed himself to pause and take a deep breath. Time to assess. First thought: Jesus, this wind is goddamn cold.

How long since he had stepped off the strut? Two minutes? He listened but couldn't hear the Beaver. The wind was growling and screaming, roiling fresh snow into a swirling white wall. You asked for shit weather.

No lights in evidence. Good. If he was on the drop zone there should be a tree line due south of him. First order of business: Get into the trees, relax, have a smoke, and evaluate the terrain and his situation.

He slid the equipment bag straps over his shoulders, cinched them as tight as he could over his bulky clothes, and trudged off into the fluffy, knee-deep snow, the wind coming over his left shoulder, his heart still racing from the suddenness of the jump and the landing. He had no idea how Joe had navigated to the drop zone, but he had. He hoped.

He thought he heard unmuffled engines moving toward him from his right and froze in place. What the hell? He dropped to one knee. The wind velocity had picked up, and the snow was still moving parallel to the ground as falling snow mixed with snow being whipped up from the surface. It also felt like the snow's consistency had changed from fluff to ice pellets, and he had no idea what that presaged for weather. The wind itself was a naked roar overhead, like a locomotive approaching, and somewhere below that sound, he could sense as much as hear engines coming closer. He went prone in the snow, knowing that the white gear bag would look like a snowdrift.

Snowmobiles came from the west, advancing steadily through the soft fresh snow, and passed twenty yards in front of him. He counted four, and wondered what fools would be out in this. People who knew the trails well enough not to worry about running into something, he knew.

When the machines were past, he got up and eased forward to where they had moved from his right to his left. He found the foot-wide track of the machines and stepped gingerly over it, rubbing out his own tracks once he was over. He moved into fresh drifts, knowing his tracks would soon be blown closed. If the locals were out tonight in near-zero visibility, he told himself, they could be out any time, anywhere. Keep that in mind while you're here. Planning for the worst was the only reasonable approach, he knew from experience. His old commander in Vietnam always insisted that the plan changed with first contact with the enemy, and he had no doubt that the Garden rats were his enemies as he marched south, wondering where the goddamn tree line was.

Ten minutes later the wind had shifted to directly behind him, and ahead he heard the clatter and rubbing of tree branches being whipped against each other. Soon he was at the edge of the tree line. He paused briefly, stepped inside, and felt around in the dark until he found a blowdown. He brushed away snow piled on the downed tree, used his boots to kick out a space beneath it, and got down into his hidey-hole. He dug into his equipment bag, took out a Snickers bar, and chewed it slowly. Sugar was quick energy, and energy equaled endurance.

He sat beneath the log reviewing preparations he had made with Lasurm. She would provide food and he would eat what she ate; she had started shopping after their last meeting, building up her stocks a little at a time so nobody would notice a change in her shopping habits. Batteries, cigarettes—she had a list of everything he needed. He had given her cash to pay for it. It wasn't clear how or if he would be reimbursed by the state.

Tonight Lasurm would have her outside lights on—one on the house, the other on her garage. She had been turning the two lights on for a while, again to make it look like her normal habit, but he told her if for some reason someone questioned this or got curious, she could turn on the garage light for one minute, at ten minutes after the hour, starting at 9 P.M. and continuing until 2 A.M. If he was not there by then, she should assume he was not coming, and await another ad in the Manistique paper.

Candy bar done, he got out of his hide, hoisted and adjusted his pack straps, and checked his compass. The tree line stretched east about a quarter mile, and he could make his way through the woods inside the cover and follow the elbow to where it bent to the south toward Lasurm's place. Or, he could cut directly through the woods to the next field and look for her lights and head directly for her house.

The wind was still making a racket in the trees, but the snow was not as heavy inside the cover with branches acting as an overhead filter. He chose to cut through on the direct line, and when he got to the outer edge, he stopped and searched south, looking for any sign of light. He found nothing but darkness flensed by blowing snow. He estimated he was about a third of a mile from her place. He checked his watch again. If her outside lights were out, she would not signal for another forty minutes.

If this was the right tree line.

A third of a mile would make a light shine like a beacon, but not in this weather. He needed to find the house, get in close, keep it in view, and wait. He checked his compass and began walking south into the open field, the wind still at his back and the temperature dropping. His brief stop had left him chilled. If he stopped again he would strip off his outer layer and put it on again when he moved. Dangerous to get sweaty in this kind of weather, he lectured himself. Hypothermia could settle in quickly. He moved slowly and deliberately to minimize perspiration, telling himself he would not stop again until he had the house in sight. This is a truly stupid idea, parachuting into hostile territory during a blizzard to see a one-legged woman who just wanted peace in the Garden.

PART III
NIGHT GARDENING

2 4

BURN'T BLUFF, FEBRUARY 14, 1976

The animal's fur was as coarse as a Brillo pad.

The snow paused just before 10 P.M. Service saw the darkened form of a house some two hundred yards ahead of him and walked toward it. It was the same house he had seen during the air recon with Joe Flap, a three-story box with a widow's walk on top, an old farmhouse with no trees close to it. The garage was unattached, thirty or forty feet south of the house. No lights, but he thought he saw the movement of smoke plumes from the chimney. There would be a ninety-degree turn in a county road several hundred feet south of the garage, and another east-west treeline, with Burn't Bluff at the western terminus.

He got next to the house, sniffed wood smoke, which reminded him of how badly he wanted another cigarette. When the garage light flashed on for one minute, and at 2201 went out, he breathed a heavy sigh of relief, circled to the south side of the building, stepped into the storm entry, and pounded twice on the door. If someone other than Lasurm answered, he would tell them he had run his car off the road and ask them to call the Delta County sheriff's department. It could be a hassle, but he would bull his way through, and let the county haul him out, knowing he would have to scrub the mission. *Be there,* he entreated as he waited.

The door opened three steps above him, and Lasurm's big blue eyes peered out into the darkness at him. She held the door open and he stepped up and past her onto a landing. Stairs led up and down from where they stood.

"Up to the kitchen," she said.

He shrugged off his pack and carried it upstairs into a kitchen with twelve-foot-high ceilings. The only light came from a few scented candles, and he smelled smoke from a fireplace.

164

"The lights," she said, hopping up to the kitchen behind him. She was not using her cane. "Word went around that people should keep their external lights off at night. You'd better get those wet clothes off. There's a fire."

He peeled down to his sweatpants, wool undershirt, and socks, and left his outer clothes in a pile on the kitchen floor.

She poked him in the lower back. "Straight ahead."

The only light in the room was from the fireplace. He felt around for something to sit on and eased into a stuffed chair.

She brought a bottle of Hartley's and two glasses and poured a generous brandy for each of them. "Why did they want the lights out?" he asked.

"People down here don't ask questions," she said.

"When did this happen?"

"A week ago," she said. "Are you thinking they anticipated someone like you might come?"

"Possibly," he said, but he didn't want to jump to conclusions; likewise, he didn't believe in coincidence.

"How *did* you get here?" she asked.

"I fell down a rabbit hole," he said. She didn't need to know the details.

She chuckled audibly in the darkness. "Does that make me the Queen of Hearts or the Mad Hatter?"

"That jury's still out," he said. He had an overpowering sense that he was being watched, but when he looked around he could see only the two of them.

"Hungry?" she asked.

"No thanks."

"Nonsense. I was so nervous all day I couldn't eat. When I saw the paper, I couldn't stop staring at the ad. Now you're here," she concluded, "and I'm starved."

Service followed her into the kitchen, watched her mix vanilla extract and heavy cream into pancake mix. When the pancakes were done she garnished them with orange peel and fresh mint, and he ate a couple and realized he was hungrier than he had admitted, and gobbled down six more.

He was reaching for syrup when he detected movement and heard a low snarl from the living room doorway. He instinctively looked without moving his head and felt his blood run cold.

The dog was the color of wet cement and splotched with black spikes of hair sticking up haphazardly. It had a long, pointed nose, its ears were flat against its head, and its intense yellow eyes were locked on Service. The dog's lip was curled back, showing a mouth full of menacing teeth.

Cecilia Lasurm said, "Miss Tillie, I see you've decided to join us." The animal crawled forward on its belly, keeping its eyes on Service. "She's paying homage to you," Lasurm said.

"It feels more like I'm being measured," he said. For a meal.

"Everything is fine, but please don't move until I tell you to," Lasurm said, adding, "She's never killed anything bigger than her."

He tried to force a smile, but failed. He didn't even nod as Lasurm got up from the table and came around to him, using the table edge for support. "Look at me," she ordered, and when Service turned his head she leaned down and kissed him on the mouth with a soft, lingering wet kiss. When she pulled away she looked down at the animal, which had gotten to its feet and was walking forward, wagging its stump tail. "Reach down with your hand," the woman said.

The hairs on his neck were electrified as he let his arm dangle.

The dog moved her head against his hand, and, summoning all the willpower he could, he rubbed once between her ears and let his arm dangle again. The animal's fur was as coarse as a Brillo pad.

"Miss Tillie is paying her respects," Lasurm said. "I'm afraid she's a bit overprotective."

The dog slunk back into the darkness of the living room.

"I found her on the highway ten years ago. She'd been shot several times with a pellet gun and she was starving, but she let me put her in my truck and take her to a veterinarian. She's been with me ever since. But she doesn't like guests, and all the locals know to stay away. Coffee or tea?"

"What the hell is going on?" he asked.

She said, "I've never allowed a man in here before. I had to find a way to let her know you were okay, so I kissed you."

"You knew that would work." Was her mind all there?

"I didn't know it wouldn't," she said sheepishly.

"It was *my* arm hanging there."

"She didn't bite," Lasurm said. "Dogs make you uncomfortable?"

He nodded, did not want to talk about it. Dogs scared the shit out of him, and he had been petrified of them as long as he could remember—all sizes, all breeds, all temperaments. He would willingly approach a criminal with a gun or endure a close encounter with a sow bear and her cubs, but when he confronted a dog, he was always in danger of falling apart.

"Let's be clear on this: The kiss was strictly for Miss Tillie," Lasurm said. "Am I making sense?"

"No," he said. "Yes." He had no idea. She was an odd woman in all ways, and his stomach knotted as he considered that coming here was a mistake— potentially a big one.

She sat down across from him. "You'll have all day tomorrow to get acquainted with Miss Tillie. She'll alert you if anyone gets within a hundred yards of the house, and if they get to the door she will be there to greet them. All you need to do to settle her and have her back off is to say, 'Gentle.'"

"Gentle," he repeated. "I won't be answering doors."

"Some females like to please," Lasurm said. "Will you go out tomorrow night?"

He nodded. *Some females like to please?* What the hell had he gotten himself into?

"Do you want me to drop you various places? I routinely visit some of my students at night."

"No, I'll do better on my own."

"All right, then, let me show you something." She went into another room and came back in faded, stained Carharts with one leg folded up. She had gotten her crutch and carried a small flashlight.

She led him into the basement where there were two furnaces. One of them was ancient, and she fiddled with something on the side and opened it like a door. "Strictly a facade," she said, switching on her flashlight. "It's level in here, but sometimes it can get a little icy."

He followed her down the dark tunnel, bending over to keep from bumping his head. The tunnel was less than six feet high and a little more than three feet wide. They walked for five minutes before entering a wide area. She found a switch and turned on a light. "My great-great-grandfather built the house in 1890. This was the storehouse. The tunnel allowed my grandmother to get to their supplies when they were snowed in. I've added heat, which vents all the way back to my chimney at the house. If you have to make yourself scarce, you'll be comfortable enough down here."

She left the light on and continued down the tunnel. He glanced at the compass pinned to his jacket and saw they were walking almost directly west. They walked for another fifteen minutes and came to a smaller underground room. There were some steps leading upward and boulders piled against the west wall. She patted one of the boulders. "Behind here there's a natural cave that leads all the way out to the bluff's face," she said. "When I was a kid I played down here all the time, and my mother insisted my father block off the cave to keep me out. Burn't Bluff is a honeycomb," she said.

"Limestone," he said.

She smiled. "Above us there's a small stone structure that looks like a pump house. The door is steel and bolted from the inside, with a padlock on the outside." She handed him a shoelace with a key dangling from it. "That will get you in. When you come back each night, coming in this way will make it easier for you."

"There will be signs where I've opened the door," he pointed out.

"It's winter," she said. "You're going to leave signs wherever you go, but this is set back in the woods and it's nasty, cluttered footing with a lot of windfalls. In summer people sometimes drift through here, but not in winter."

He followed her back to the other room in the tunnel, and she showed him how to work the heat before they trekked back to the house.

She led him through the kitchen to the front of the house, told him to grab his bag, and took him upstairs to a small bedroom. "It's an old house," she said, "but it's warm. We have to share a bathroom, but that shouldn't be a problem."

The room was narrow with a single bed and an old dresser. The floors were wood, with two faded throw rugs.

"You know if they find you here, you could get hurt," she said.

He nodded as she turned on a light and used the rheostat to lower the brightness. The house might be old, but it had been modernized.

"I'll be awake at six-thirty," she said. "I have to be at school by eight-thirty. If you want breakfast, it will be ready at seven-fifteen. If not, you're on your own."

He nodded dumbly, and she paused at the door and looked back. "I invited you here to do something positive," Lasurm said. "I hope you don't disappoint me." Miss Tillie glared at him with her yellow eyes and followed Lasurm.

"Fucking dog," he mumbled, but his mind was already shifting more to the mission than the threat of the animal. The next two weeks threatened to take him into a state of weirdness, but he was sure he was ready for whatever got thrown at him. Lasurm was strange and so was her ugly dog, but if the mission went the way he expected it to, he would not have to see much of either of them over the next two weeks.

25

THE GARDEN PENINSULA: FIRST RECON,
FEBRUARY 15, 1976

He needed not just to out-rat the rats, but to temporarily become one.

The outside door of the fake pump house was jammed by snow and ice, but Service managed to wedge it open with a shoulder. He was glad to be free of the house, despite it being warm and comfortable. Miss Tillie had followed him around all day, growling and snarling and making various sounds, none of which sounded particularly amicable. He had said the word *gentle* to her so many times, it was stuck in his mind like what Germans called an earworm.

When he got up to have breakfast with Lasurm, he had reviewed the list of names she had provided at the last meeting, and sat with her and his plat books making pencil marks by the homes and hangouts of the Garden rats. Before coming to the Garden he had contacted Lansing and gotten the registration numbers for snowmobiles, boats, and wheeled vehicles for the people on the list. If he encountered them during his travels, he would have some notion of whom he might be dealing with.

The weather had improved, but not significantly. The temperature had gotten up to eight during the day, and snow continued to fall, but the sun had not come out to melt and form a thin surface crust on the snow.

Lasurm would not be home for an hour. They agreed last night that she should maintain her regular routine during his time with her. It was 5:30 P.M. when he crawled out of the well house, cinched up the ruck he had carried in his equipment bag, and began his trek northward. He intended to skirt the edge of Burn't Bluff going north and veer inland toward the village of Garden, coming up on it from the south and inland. Lasurm said a lot of the troublemakers hung out at Roadie's Bar at night—the same place where he had been attacked by rock throwers.

The village was ten miles north of her place, and at his normal walking pace he could do ten-minute miles almost endlessly; but there was fifteen inches of fresh snow and deeper drifts, unfamiliar rolling terrain, fences and roads to cross. He would have to make numerous stops to make sure he was not seen. Because of all this, he decided to figure on a conservative rate of thirty minutes per mile. This meant he would need five hours to get to the village and five hours to get back. If he gave himself two hours in the village itself, he could still be comfortably back by zero five thirty, well before morning twilight. If something held him up in the village, there was high ground east of South River Bay, and no well-traveled roads for almost a square mile. Lasurm had shown him where an abandoned sawmill was located, and if he ran out of time and night, this would be his layover destination for the next day.

Knowing how far he had to walk and the pace he wanted to maintain, he wore long johns under his snowmobile suit and carried the rest of his layers in his ruck to put on when he stopped for breaks.

Once clear of Lasurm's tunnel, he crawled and walked northward through the slash for the first mile before aiming northeast to skirt Sand Bay, his mind lost in thought, and relying on his instincts to watch for any potential contact with others. Law enforcement was being used as an instrument in a state plan to eliminate commercial fishing in Lake Michigan in favor of sportfishermen and their wallets. Most of the conservation officers risking their asses in the Garden probably didn't have a clue about what was really going on, and this thought put him in a nasty mood. To counter his temper, he kept repeating the goals of his mission: identify the rat leaders and their followers; determine how and where they stage their operations; observe their landside tactics, where they meet, and how they behave. Overall: observe and learn. Most of all, do not act and do not enforce—observe only. He and Tree had gone on many missions in Vietnam that were similar to this. More often than not they went into the jungle to find and watch the enemy, not to kill them. *This is* not *Vietnam,* he reminded himself as he pushed through the deep snow. *Your Vietnam was eight years ago. Your Vietnam is history—finished.*

South of Fayette he angled through the woods east of the Port Bar and increased his walking speed, the wind hard out of the north. Initially his eyes had been filled with tears from the wind, but now that was finished. His balaclava seemed to protect his face as he walked on, not dwelling on the conditions. His job kept him outside year-round, making the weather largely irrelevant.

Why the hell did he keep thinking about Vietnam? He remembered meeting an air force master sergeant at the NCO club at Danang one night. The KC-135 boom operator had been in the Strategic Air Command during the Cuban missile crisis, and had told him how all of SAC's bomber and tanker crews had been briefed before being put on the highest alert level. They were told that President Kennedy was going to give the Soviets an ultimatum: Get your missiles out, or we'll take them out. Every airman understood that such an attack could lead to a nuclear exchange, but back then, every fighting man understood the stakes and his duty. The boomer couldn't understand how one president could trust fighting men with such a secret, while the troops being killed in Vietnam knew little or nothing about what the national intent was. They were losing the war through attrition and lack of national will.

The mess in the Garden felt too much like Vietnam, Service decided. Lansing was not leveling with the troops on the ground about what their actual objectives were, and as a result, conservation officers were left trying to enforce a toothless law for goals that might be specious at best. Lasurm had explained the economics of sportfishing versus commercial fishing, and Fahey had confirmed this in Lansing, which left him feeling somewhere between anxious and ambivalent.

The rats were waging a guerrilla war—an insurgency for personal economic reasons. Yes, insurgency was the right term, he thought as he walked north. The rats were insurgents, pure and simple, conducting what his old commander Major Teddy Gates called a low-intensity conflict. Gates had taught his marines how to think about—and, more importantly, how to think *like*—the enemy. As a result, they had enjoyed many more successes than failures compared to other American units fighting against NVA troops. Insurgents in Vietnam, he remembered, attacked police in small units, using speed, surprise, and terrain to shock the government and force them to concentrate their troops and expend more resources. The more the government did this, the more impotent it looked.

Nobody was getting killed in the Garden, he knew, but Lasurm made it clear that intimidation of residents surely was taking place. Evidence: In an area with almost one thousand people, you might expect more than one person to step forward and complain, but so far only Lasurm had shown the requisite gumption, which reinforced how effective intimidation was in keeping the locals in line for the rats. Lasurm's actual motivation remained in doubt. She had given him reasons, which sounded good but didn't bite. And how did her daughter fit into this? The woman was in jail, Odd Hegstrom was her lawyer, and Lasurm denied that her motives grew out of her daughter's situation. Replaying this information, he concluded that the less contact he had with Lasurm, the better for both of them.

The situation here was perplexing. The DNR and police authorities had so far reacted classically: COs no longer conducted solo patrols. Delta County deputies and the Troops made no routine patrols at all, and came into the Garden only when there was a reported emergency or a formal complaint. Even in these circumstances they tended to drag their feet in responding. In essence, the lawless had gained control of the peninsula, and Service had seen firsthand their harassment tactics.

The longer he considered all the angles, the more he was certain that this was a sort of domestic Vietnam; if someone didn't get the insurgents on their heels—and soon—they would continue to increase their confidence, and eventually somebody would get killed. This realization was a real-life Yogism of déjà vu all over again, and the more he thought about it, the angrier he got—not with the sort of white-hot anger that made him want to strike out immediately and blindly, but with the blue rage that Teddy Gates had taught them: To get the enemy off your back, put the bastards on their heels.

His old commanding officer used to say, "Don't get mad: Get even." Gates was an adherent of Sun Tzu, the Chinese general who was the first to codify rules of warfare around 500 B.C., and whose work was unknown in Europe until just prior to the French Revolution. Sun Tzu's lessons were based on having professional soldiers, good leadership, and common sense. As he walked, Service began to think about the lessons Teddy Gates and Sun Tzu had taught.

The closer he got to the town, the more certain he was that while the DNR needed accurate, timely intelligence, it also needed to treat this as the kind of conflict it had become. Their primary target should be the mind of the enemy leader. Lasurm said Pete Peletier was the top rat. If true, who was he, and what was his hold over the others? You couldn't attack the mind of a leader unless you had some idea of who you were dealing with. Don't wallow in doubt, he told himself as he marched on.

Less than a mile from the village Service stopped walking, found cover in a small aspen stand, and lit a cigarette. He got out a small iron grate he carried in his pack, pried the lid off a Sterno can, placed it under the grill, and lit the wick. He poured tea from a thermos borrowed from Lasurm into a cup and set it on the grill over the tiny flame. His plan, he realized, had been no plan at all; it was Attalienti's wish list. The trick had been to get into the Garden undetected, which he had done. Now what? Fulfill the wish list and split? No, he told himself. Not enough. You have to rethink the deal, top to bottom. Initially, he was disgusted by his shortsightedness, but this mood quickly shifted to a certainty that his gut was right: He was here for two weeks, and when it came time to withdraw, he somehow needed to leave confusion and mistrust among the rats about their leader. At the moment he was not sure how to accomplish what he wanted, but he had the germ of some ideas to ruminate on during the hike back to Lasurm's. Reconnaissance of the village would have to wait.

En route he detoured to the Port Bar, which was just outside the south gate of Fayette State Park, and stopped long enough to write down the registration numbers of snowmobiles, and descriptions and license numbers of trucks and automobiles parked around the bar.

As he headed into the final two and a half miles to the house, two things were clear in his mind. First, if Pete Peletier was the actual rat leader, his followers needed to begin to doubt him and wonder if he was representing them, or using them for his own ends. Second, to do the things he needed to do, he needed not just to out-rat the rats, but to temporarily become one.

"You aren't there to act," Attalienti had told him. But Attalienti wasn't here, and his views were based on his place in the DNR's shameful history here. No, Attalienti was wrong; he couldn't enforce the law here, but he could do more than just gather information. The bastards here needed to feel the isolation and uncertainty that the marines had felt in Vietnam.

When Cecilia Lasurm came down for breakfast, coffee was already brewing and Service was making eggs and toast. "Good morning," she greeted him with a quizzical look.

"There's a list of things I need," he said, placing a plate of scrambled eggs in front of her.

She studied the note he had left on the table and looked up at him. "Five vise grips, two screwdrivers, a funnel, eight rolls of duct tape, twenty pounds of sugar in two-pound bags, green spray paint, ten pounds of small potatoes . . . What in the world is going on?"

"You'd best shop in Escanaba," he said, placing two hundred-dollar bills in front of her. "I'm trying to think like a Chinaman," he whispered.

"At large or institutionalized?" she asked, making him laugh.

26

GARDEN PENINSULA, FEBRUARY 21, 1976

"All this turns you on—just like the rats."

For three consecutive nights he had explored the edges of roads and recon-noitered the layout around the houses of the rats on his list. Along the way he found five road-killed deer, cut out their hearts, and impaled them on some sticks he cut. They were frozen so there was no blood trail to worry about. They were now stockpiled inside the door of the pump house.

Tonight he had watched the Port Bar and its cheesy lighthouse facade. Five snowmobiles and two trucks on his list were parked nearby. Through frosted glass he saw people moving around inside. Once a man came out a side door and pissed in the snow, laughing like he had just cinched an Olympic gold medal.

When it was quiet Service poured a pound of sugar into the gas tanks of the snowmobiles. Sugar would take an hour or more to work, but then the machines would die and be unstartable until the owners pulled the carburetors, gas tanks, and fuel lines, and flushed everything. He slithered underneath the truck, used a vise grip to pinch off the fuel line near the gas tank, where it went from metal to rubber, and used duct tape to fasten the vise grip to the chassis. No matter what the driver did, the engine would not start with the line crimped, and the cause could not be discovered until somebody got underneath with a light.

Each night he carefully varied his routes, and tonight when he returned to Lasurm's, they drank coffee in silence. He showered and went to bed, only to be awakened from deep sleep by a heavy weight flopping on the end of the bed. He pulled the pillow off his head and saw Miss Tillie at his feet. She curled her lips when she saw him, and he tried to go back to sleep, telling himself not to move.

"Stop terrorizing the poor man," Cecilia Lasurm chided the dog, which immediately jumped off the bed. Service heard the animal's claws and feet on the wood floors and he rolled over.

"What time is it?" he asked sleepily.

"Noonish," she said. "You've got everybody spooked," she said. "And angry."

When he didn't respond, she added, "I'm on my way to a home visit. I'll be back early."

"Did they notice?" he asked.

"Notice what?"

"That Peletier's truck was left alone."

She shot him a quizzical look and walked out, the rubber tip of her crutch squeaking against the stairs as she descended.

During a dinner of bowtie pasta and meatballs, Lasurm poured red wine for herself and looked at him. "You're addicted to risk," she said. "If there was no risk, you wouldn't be a cop. All this turns you on—just like the rats."

He loaded his fork with pasta and shrugged. She was probably right, but he doubted she truly understood the difference between calculated and spontaneous risk. What he was doing now was calculated, he told himself.

"Is work all you think about?" she asked, dropping her fork onto her plate.

It suddenly felt like he was talking to Bathsheba, and the thought jarred him. He rinsed his plate in the sink, left it, and went into the tunnel to get ready for the night. Jesus, what was *her* problem?

27

THE GARDEN MISSION, FEBRUARY 24, 1976

"We don't need another damn cowboy here."

He had visited every known rat's house at least once during his nightly for-
ays. One night, he had sat on Middle Bluff watching the rats pull their nets
to collect fish, the nets basically in the same location of those he'd helped to
seize, which meant the poachers had already replaced them. Where did that
much money come from? He had followed them from the Port Bar as they
eased their snow machines through the state park's historic ruins, across
Snail Shell Harbor, and out onto the thick ice of Big Bay de Noc.

Snowmobiles provided excellent transportation in winter. Soon after
their introduction in the late sixties, sales had unexpectedly soared, and now
the houses and trailers of even the poorest U.P. residents sported TV antennas
and at least one snowmobile out front. Since the machines ran easier on
packed, hard trails than in deep, fresh snow, most drivers opted for the path
of least resistance and followed the same routes to their various destinations.
What appeared unpredictable before now began to take on a pattern as he
penciled the rat routes into his notebook. This was information that could
be used against the rats when his mission was done. He had sabotaged
vehicles on only three occasions, but figured he had three or four days left,
and decided it was time to step up pressure in his self-declared psychological
war. As a precaution, he wrapped and taped cloth over his boots to blur the
pattern and size of his tracks.

Ranse Renard lived directly across Garden Road from Pete Peletier, both
houses about a mile north of Fairport, six miles south of Lasurm's. Tonight
he had watched both houses since 10 P.M. Renard had pulled into Peletier's
driveway just before midnight, shouting and pounding on Peletier's front

door. The door had opened and the two men had disappeared inside. Renard emerged around 3 A.M., drove across the street to his house, got out, walked to the front door, turned around, and walked back to his truck, muttering under his breath. He took a flashlight out of the truck, got on his back, and wriggled underneath the truck to check his fuel line.

What was the man *thinking?* He'd just driven the truck across the road. Drunk *and* paranoid, Service told himself. He fought back a smile as he waited for Renard to settle inside the house before he approached the man's truck, popped the hood, pried off the distributor cap, jimmied the rotor loose and took it out, replacing the cap. He threw the rotor into the deep snow on the angled roof of the man's house. When Renard tried to start his truck again, he'd probably assume the problem was underneath and crawl under the truck, only to find that the fuel line was unimpaired. Service jammed a small potato deep into the exhaust pipe. *Give the man two problems to deal with,* Service thought as he got ready to leave—only to see a string of snowmobile lights coming south on Garden Road. Six machines pulled into Peletier's driveway. Their drivers dismounted and began shouting, "Pete—Pete!"

Peletier came to the front door and shouted, "Shut up, boys! My kids are sleepin'!"

Service watched him usher them inside, gave them fifteen minutes, crossed the road, quickly dumped sugar into all six machines, and made a fast tactical withdrawal into the woods.

A quarter-mile south of Lasurm's, he was working his way north through a tree line a hundred yards west of Garden Road as a half-dozen trucks came racing south. He wondered if a rat rally was getting under way. It began to snow as he opened the steel door of the pump house and disappeared into Lasurm's tunnel.

He dumped his pack and outer gear in the storeroom and turned toward the tunnel to the house to find Miss Tillie snarling at him. "Gentle," he said softly, "you four-legged pile of shit."

Lasurm was awake and waiting in the kitchen. He looked at his watch. It was not yet 4:30 A.M. "What're you doing awake?"

"Worrying, fretting, stewing—take your pick," she said. "You came down here to make peace, but now you're doing anything but that, and they're suspicious. They think an outsider is out to get them, and they're talking about trying to trap him. They're going to travel only in groups now," she said.

This confirmed what he had seen tonight. "It won't do them any good," he said.

"I would think a little fear would be a healthy thing," she said.

Fear and caution were not synonymous. He refused to defend or explain himself. "I'm gonna need more sugar."

She sighed. "I doubt a truckload of sugar would take the edge off the likes of you."

"I don't have an edge."

She sneered, "Any sharper and you could walk through walls."

"Talk about an edge," he countered.

She got up, snapped her crutch onto her wrist, and pushed the rubber tip against his chest like a sword. "Grady, it's your job to uphold the law. I don't approve of violence. God knows we've had plenty of that down here. I don't mean to tell you how to do your job, but you've gone over the line."

"Stay out of this," he said, immediately regretting it. She had opened her home to him and probably was taking more risk than him. He wasn't in the mood for this claptrap.

"I *can't* stay out of this!" she said sharply. "I'm in the middle of it, and the DNR is coming today," she said.

"Says who?" Why would Attalienti schedule a patrol while he was here? To maintain the appearance of normal DNR operations, he concluded, which made some sense, normalcy and routine the best covers for secrecy.

"Word's out. They always seem to know, don't they?" she said.

"They didn't know about me," he told her.

"They made everybody turn off their lights before you came."

There had to be another reason, he had already decided, there being no real trail to track him or his plan. Until tonight he'd seen no real caution from them—certainly nothing to suggest they were doing anything but operating confidently on their own ground.

He headed for the cellar stairs, Lasurm following close behind. "Where do you think you're going?"

"Out," he said.

"You just came in! You don't have enough night left."

"I'll have to make do," he said.

"You're letting your testosterone lead you! I wanted a smart, tough game warden, tough being secondary," Lasurm hissed at him. "We don't need another damn cowboy here."

He turned around and looked up at her, knowing she was right. He had come to the Garden with a mission, and had gathered the information Attalienti wanted. Would it help in the future? He didn't know. But his gut had driven him to step over the line and violate the captain's directive against action, and now if COs were coming down today, they might encounter more anger than usual—anger he had created by sabotaging rat equipment. Daylight be damned; he had to go out and support his people any way he could. "Don't forget the sugar," he reminded Lasurm, avoiding her eyes.

28

GARDEN PENINSULA, FEBRUARY 24, 1976

One thing was for sure: None of them walked alone.

The only on-ice net activity he had seen had been off the state park, and based on this he headed north from Lasurm's, hoping to get into position on Middle Bluff. To keep himself hidden he kept to the woods as much as he could, eventually climbing out to an overlook on the bluff where he saw seven snowmobiles and Stone's green truck and another DNR vehicle on the ice. It was now 8:30 A.M.; it had taken only two hours to get to the bluff from Lasurm's house.

Where were the rats? If this thing was about money, they couldn't afford to lose more nets, could they?

He sat watching his DNR pals until around noon when he saw men with ski masks filtering their way on foot through the woods along a buttonhook peninsula on the south side of Snail Shell Harbor. He saw no snowmobiles, but eventually a truck drove out across the harbor ice and made its way toward the DNR men. He could see through his binoculars that it was Ranse Renard's truck. Why weren't the others with him? Renard drove forward slowly, almost like a man with a white flag. Where was Peletier?

As he watched he heard grunting in the snowy woods just north of him. He immediately ducked into the trees to try to locate the source.

A man in a tan-and-white snowmobile suit was working his way down the crest of the bluff toward the cliff. He was carrying an uncased rifle with a scope. *Shit.* He couldn't just sit and watch the man take a shot at the officers. But he didn't want to show himself.

The man reached the lip of the bluff and knelt by a broken birch tree not more than thirty yards away. The winter sun was low and in their faces, the sky gray with hints of pink.

Service took off his pack, got down on his belly, and crawled through the trees behind the man, who had taken out a pint bottle, poured something, took a drink, and held up a sandwich, obviously in no hurry. Service could see lettuce hanging out the sides of the bread. The man took several hits from the bottle while he ate. Nervous, Service told himself, keyed up.

The rifle was standing against a fallen tree, the black barrel silhouetted against the surrounding white. The area was strewn with boulders, including several directly behind the man, most of them sunk into a depression. Service was within five yards, the man slightly above him, and he still hadn't decided what to do.

The man picked up the rifle, worked the bolt, and said, "Shit!" He immediately put down the gun and charged east along the path he had followed across Middle Bluff. Service had no idea what had set the man off, and he didn't care. He waited until he was out of sight, crawled upward through a seam in the rocks, and grabbed the rifle, a Remington bolt-action with a Weaver K4 scope. He retracted the bolt: no shell ejected. He checked the magazine: empty. The man had forgotten ammo! Service used the barrel to helicopter the weapon over the edge and retreated to his position, quickly hiding his tracks as he went.

The man was back in fifteen minutes. Service saw him use binoculars to watch Renard out on the ice. A figure in black was standing next to the truck. Probably Stone. The other officers kept working.

When Renard's truck turned around and headed back toward land, the would-be shooter began cursing and stomping around the rocks, kicking clods of ice and snow.

Service crawled south and saw the men on the opposite peninsula walk out of the woods to meet Renard, who stopped to let several men climb into the bed of the truck before continuing across the frozen harbor. Other men in the woods began to withdraw on foot in twos and threes. Renard had six men in his truck. Was this the core group? If so, what role did the others have—active sympathizers or merely curious observers? One thing was for sure: None of them walked alone. But where was their leader?

The shooter stopped cursing, snatched up his gear, and departed at a clumsy jog. Service trailed him across the bluff to a road, where a dirty pickup truck was snugged nose-first against a snowbank. He used his binoculars to get the license number, wrote it down, and waited for the vehicle to leave. The truck was dirty and slush-covered, but something about it seemed familiar.

He suspected the man would return with help to search for his rifle, which meant Service needed to vacate the area.

There were several possible routes, but he decided on one through the thickest woods to cover himself while daylight remained. When he got close to the Port Bar, he saw there were no vehicles; he hiked farther south another half-mile and found a place under some logs. He scooped out an opening and settled in to wait for darkness. Waiting patiently and alone was what game wardens did best.

While he waited he thought about what he had seen. Even on foot the rats were clinging to each other, and the fact that they came in on foot suggested he had crippled enough machines to make them wary. He had not gotten to all that many machines, which further suggested the rats were not as numerous as the DNR had suspected. He also knew that each time he struck, he was costing them time and money—and each time Peletier went untouched, his followers had to wonder why he was exempt.

Lasurm looked at him warily when he wrote down a telephone number and told her what he wanted her to do. "You want me to call Attalienti and tell him there's a rifle on the rocks at the base of Middle Bluff?"

Service held her coat out to her and nodded. "You have a party line here," he said. "Best use a pay phone."

She slammed the door on her way out. He felt bad about the way he ordered her around, but she was beginning to challenge him, and he didn't need complications right now. Attalienti was going to be pissed that he'd taken the man's rifle—but what was he supposed to have done? Let him shoot, or jump him before he could get off a round? This solution was a compromise that had allowed him to remove the threat and maintain his anonymity. To fight a rat you sometimes had to act like one.

29

GARDEN PENINSULA, FEBRUARY 26, 1976

"Even Napoleon didn't fight every day."

Service awoke with achy muscles and a windburned face, swung his legs to the floor, and checked his watch: 3 P.M. He rolled back onto the bed and went back to sleep.

Lasurm awoke him two hours later. "Aren't you going out tonight?"

"Did you make the call?" he asked, checking his watch again. What day was this? It was all starting to run together.

She was sitting on the side of the bed and smelled of alcohol. "The sugar is downstairs."

"Did you make the call?" he asked again.

"Do you *ever* lighten up?" she said. "The DNR pulled more nets yesterday. Renard and his people went out to talk to them, but there was no confrontation. He lodged a protest—told them someone is vandalizing fishermen on the peninsula. He thinks it's the DNR, and that he's the victim." Service knew that Renard had talked alone to Stone; his people had not been with him. The report of what he had said was Renard's version.

"Did you make the call?" he repeated.

"Yesterday, from Rapid River," she said. "Attalienti said he'd take care of it."

"That's all he said?"

"It's what you wanted, right?" She held up a glass of wine and took a drink. "Oh, I guess he also asked when you're coming out."

"You guess?"

"He asked," she said. "Don't be so damn literal, and stop being surly. I think you're feeling guilty about what you've done here. And you're exhausted. You've slept for nearly twenty-four hours."

"And you said?"

"My God," she said. "Do you *ever* break focus? I said I don't know, but it's soon, right?" She stared at him waiting for a reply.

"Am I cramping your style?" he asked

She took another drink and grimaced. "You haven't even seen my style." She saluted him with the glass. "I need another drink."

She drained her glass and went downstairs with Service following. Here we go again, he thought.

The wine bottle on the kitchen table was nearly empty, and she was fumbling with the cork of a new bottle.

"Are you sure you want to do that?" he asked.

She rolled her eyes and continued her efforts. He took it away from her and opened it.

"You going to warn me against the sin of overindulgence?"

"Sermons are your specialty," he shot back.

She wagged a finger at him. "You're a naughty bastard," she said. "Even Napoleon didn't fight every day. Do you think the Great Lombardi thought about football when he was making love to his wife?"

"Maybe *she* did," Service said. Lombardi had died in 1970. Now what the hell was she talking about?

Lasurm dribbled red wine down her chin and laughed out loud. "That's actually funny! Do you think it's a coincidence that the great general and the great coach each had a Marie in his life?" Her eyes were cloudy and she looked pouty. "When you look at me, what do you see?"

He shrugged, knowing there was no right answer.

"Exactly," she said. "Nothing. I'm nothing, the invisible woman."

"I . . . ," he said.

"Shut up! Did you not pick up on the fact that I've never allowed another man in this house? Did I not make that clear?" she added. "No, don't answer that either. You pick up on everything that fits what you want to hear."

"You make me sound like an asshole."

"You tell me what it makes you. You came down here to gather information and now you're acting just like them. The end justifies the means, an eye for an eye, all that biblical shit."

"I thought you were a good Christian."

She sneered. "Don't confuse spiritual with religious. What we each believe, even *if* we believe, has nothing whatsoever to do with any of this," she said wagging a finger at him, taking another drink.

"Any of what?" he asked.

"Don't play games," she said. "You're perpetuating the cycle you're supposed to be ending. I asked for you because I wanted to break the cycle here, clear the air, but you can't break laws to uphold laws. I didn't ask for Attila the Hun," she lamented. "And I did my homework on you, too: Responsible, smart, courageous, energetic, thoughtful, tireless, fair, loyal, but you're just like the rest of them."

All men, all COs, or all men on the Garden? He wasn't sure what she was talking about.

"It's one thing to mess with somebody's mind," she said, "but you can't beat them up."

"I haven't laid a hand on anybody."

She sneered. "Now *that's* a fact—but the word is somebody beat the hell out of Moe Lapalme yesterday and threatened him with his own rifle."

So that was the man's name. Service stared at her. "I took a man's rifle while he was gone getting ammunition and slung it over the bluff. He wasn't there at that moment. Remember, you called Attalienti to tell him where it is? I never touched anyone. If this guy is claiming otherwise, he's lying because he forgot his ammo and left his rifle unattended to go fetch it. He doesn't want to look like a fuckup."

She looked at him for a long minute, evaluating. "There are people who believe what Moe Lapalme says."

"Are you one of them?"

She said, "No, I don't believe most of what Moe says, but he can be very persuasive. He's the kind who could understand being beaten up, but he'd never admit to screwing up. Never. Nothing that goes wrong is ever Moe's fault."

What was she getting at with this Lapalme? His name had not come up in the original list of rats. "I never touched him, Cecilia," Service said. "But the Marquis of Queensbury Rules were for sport, not real life," he said, adding, "One leg." *Why had he said that?*

"Yes, of course; you see one leg or two, black or white, crippled or whole," she said, emptying her glass. "If you were the one with one leg, would you be a different person?"

"I wouldn't be doing this job."

Her blue eyes flared. "Meaning your job defines you?"

"That's not what I said—and what the hell is this conversation supposed to accomplish?"

"You *see!*" she said, "You see? Not everything has to lead to an accomplishment. A conversation is just that—an exchange. It doesn't have to *lead* somewhere, or even *anywhere*. Life is not about keeping score!"

"Naughty or nice, we all go to Heaven?" he said.

"There you go again," she said. "Heaven—a goal, the ultimate destination, only those with the highest scores get admitted—like MIT or something," she added. "That is so much *crap!*" she said with a disparaging laugh.

"Three days," he said wearily. "Three more days and I'll be out of your hair."

She tried to pour another glass of wine for herself, holding the bottle over the glass. Only a few drops came out of the opening. She plopped the bottle on the table and looked him in the eyes. "You haven't even gotten *into* my hair," she whispered. "Get me drunk and don't even take advantage of me. Man and woman this close together for two weeks, and all he does is nothing, sees one leg is all. I'm almost forty, you know . . . "

She was talking to herself now.

"'Nuther bottle," she said, slurring her words.

"You're way past last call," he said.

She nodded once, pursed her lips, and fumbled to get her crutch on her wrist. "Help me," she said. It was a plea, not an order.

He helped her to her feet, but she began to tilt and he picked her up in his arms. She weighed next to nothing. "Drunk crip," she mumbled. "I won't tell if you won't." She began to giggle as he carried her up the stairs, her crutch hanging off her wrist and banging along.

Service heard the dog behind them, and Lasurm said sharply over his shoulder, "Leave us *alone*, Tillie!" The animal stopped and retreated.

"Know what?" Lasurm asked when he set her on the bed. "I'm a Marie too. Cecilia Marie Lasurm." She had an arm hooked over his shoulder. "You getting me ready to bed?" she asked, and immediately began to giggle and whispered, "Meant ready *for* bed, not *to* bed." He ignored her.

"Undress me," she said.

"You're fine the way you are."

"Even one leg?" she said. She lifted it and wiggled her foot. "It's a nice leg," she said.

"Yes?"

"Yes, a great leg. Sleep," he said.

"Really? A great leg?"

"Yes, great."

"You're not goin' out tonight?"

"Not tonight."

"Promise?"

"Promise," he said.

"Shame," she said.

"What?" he asked, but her head was on the pillow and she was asleep.

He stood in the shower early the next morning, relishing the needles of hot water on sore muscles. His job frequently took him out of his vehicle, but this was a lot more walking than he was used to, and all of it through snow without benefit of skis or snowshoes. He could feel it every afternoon when he awoke for the next night's patrol.

A sound brought him out of his reverie and he saw the shower curtain sliding back; he immediately pivoted away, but Lasurm reached into the stream of water and touched him. "Scars," she whispered, her hand tracing lines on his chest and arm. She took the palm of his hand and put it under her robe. He felt scars where breasts should have been. "We both understand pain and decisions," she said. "You didn't pull your hand back." She patted his arm and backed away.

He stepped out of the shower, picked up a towel, and walked to her bedroom door. There were no lights. "I'm here," she said softly. "The invisible scars are the ones we feel the most," she added.

He lay down beside her and felt the warmth of her skin against his, and began his recitation. The women he had known seemed to always want to know about his wounds. "Left ab, Vietnam, rocket fragment. Right ab, AK-forty-seven round, also Vietnam, and it hurt like hell. Left forearm, a fifteen-year-old squirrel hunter accidentally potshot me with a twenty-two. Upper right thorax, Vietnam, grenade." The other scar had come when he stepped in front of his grandmother's 410 shotgun. He didn't count that one because it had been his own fault.

Later she lay beside him, whispering, "My grandmother died of breast cancer. Then my aunt and my mother. And my oldest sister. The doctors insisted I shouldn't assume their fate would be mine. One doctor actually told me that if a coin flip comes up heads one hundred times in a row, the odds of heads on the next toss remains fifty-fifty. I listened to what the doctors said and told them to take them off, get rid of them. I was twenty-three. My own doctor refused. I had to go all the way to Houston to find a surgeon who would do it." She nibbled Service's neck and whispered, "We're a lot alike. We loathe passivity. Faced with a problem, we look for solutions, for action."

"You said I'm perpetuating the cycle here."

"You're here because I asked specifically for you," she said. "But what you've done won't stop this thing."

"Not in the short term," he said, remembering Teddy Gates talking about Sun Tzu: Attack the mind of the leader, create doubt, undercut trust.

"Long term doesn't interest me," she said. "In September my doctor diagnosed ovarian cancer. He talked of surgery, radiation, chemotherapy, all of that. But I told him no, just let it be. I've already lost my breasts. They're not taking the rest, and if I die—well, we all die, don't we?"

"You can't just do nothing," he said.

"I would expect that response from you. I'm not doing nothing. Sometimes thinking and watching are doing a lot. I called you and the DNR in to do something about the Garden. If I can't live, I can at least leave a legacy." She rolled over and faced him. "I told my principal I wouldn't be in today. He assumes it's the cancer. I want to spend the day right here."

"I have to go out tonight," he said. "Cecilia."

She smiled. "You'll always have to go out there."

"Tell me about Moe Lapalme," he said.

"We have all day," she said, pulling him toward her. "Say my name again. Please?"

"Cecilia," he whispered.

GARDEN PENINSULA, FEBRUARY 27, 1976

"I've probably worn out my welcome."

The effigy hung from a wire strung across Garden Road where it crossed Garden Creek at the north end of the village common area. The figure was suspended by an oversize noose, draped in a gray uniform shirt, and had a German army helmet on top with DNR painted on the sides of the helmet. A sign on the body said FISH NAZI, the letters in bright red. Service was wedged between a cluster of buildings that overlooked Garden Creek, and he stood in the shadows, irked beyond words. He wanted to cut it down, but knew there wasn't enough time. He had another idea for getting back at the rats. Lasurm was right. He had gone over the line, but he knew he couldn't pull back now. Not yet.

He spent the day making signs and rigging his surprise, and when Lasurm got home from school, she came down to the storeroom looking for him, saw what he was doing, and said, "Creepy."

"It's a going-away gift," he said, admiring his work.

"Going away when?" she asked.

He detected concern in her voice. "Tomorrow night. I want you to drop me east of Garden after dark, and I'll take it from there."

"This is your last night?"

"I've probably worn out my welcome."

"Not with me," she said, putting her hand on his shoulder. "Moe Lapalme is making a lot of noise about why Peletier's equipment never gets touched," she added.

"He's trying to deflect attention," Service said, hoping Attalienti had recovered the rifle.

"That's Moe," she said, "first in line for glory and a no-show when things don't go right."

"You use a certain tone when you say his name," Service said.

"Are you sure you want me to drop you off?" she asked, evading his question.

"I'll be under a tarp in back of your truck," he said.

"And tonight?"

"Things to do. I wouldn't want to leave you with all that sugar. Waste not, want not."

She smiled and shook her head. "There's going to be a meeting tonight at Lapalme's house."

This was interesting. "Guess I'd better put Moe on the itinerary."

"They'll have guards on their vehicles," she said.

"Heavy snow coming in tonight," he told her. "Do you know how hard it is to watch something when you're cold?"

"You seem to do all right," she said.

"I do it every day. Where does Moe live?"

She told him that Lapalme lived in a small house just north of Garden, on a treeless lot packed with the hulks of abandoned trucks and cars.

"Just be careful," she said.

It was a long, exhausting ten miles to Lapalme's house, the snow swirling heavily out of the northeast. He found a hiding place among the derelict vehicles dumped on Lapalme's property and settled in. There were six pick-ups, two sedans, and several snowmobiles parked in Lapalme's driveway. No noise came from the house. He reconnoitered carefully and located the "guards" seated in lawn chairs in the garage with a small charcoal grill going. He got close enough to see a case of beer next to them. He watched them drinking and knew they were cold, focused on the hot coals and not paying attention.

The license numbers on the vehicles were not those of the ringleaders, except for Renard, but he had no intention of being selective tonight. Whoever was here would be Lapalme's pals, and that made them targets. He worked deliberately, moving from vehicle to vehicle, pouring a full two pounds of sugar into each tank. When he was done, he strung the sugar bags like clothes on a clothesline between two trees in the yard, and made his withdrawal.

One thing his two weeks had taught him: The rats were only modestly organized, and they only appeared to be more together than they were.

Cecilia Lasurm was in his bed when he got back.

"Your last day," she said from under the covers. "I called in sick again."

He undressed, showered, dried himself off, and got into bed next to her.

"Do you think your being here will change the situation?" she asked.

"I don't know."

"You can't even lie for my benefit?"

"Okay, it will change."

She laughed and kissed him tenderly. "You are not walking all the way up to the highway tonight," she said. "I don't think you're gonna have the energy for it."

GARDEN PENINSULA, FEBRUARY 28, 1976

"Don't look like youse broke nothin' important."

It was a Saturday night, and Lasurm had dropped him a mile east of Garden just after dark. From there, he had made his way toward town to a copse of trees along Garden Creek where he sat and watched Roadie's Bar. The parking lot was full, and stayed so until nearly 3 A.M., meaning the owners were probably violating state liquor laws. He made a mental note to pass this along. When the parking lot was finally empty, he crept onto the porch and quickly hung his message. Each frozen deer heart had a cardboard name tacked to it. All the hearts were skewered vertically on a long, thick willow branch. He used a rock to drive one nail into the main post in front of the bar. Above the deer hearts he left a sign that said SOON TO FALL. Peletier's name was not on the list; Renard's and Lapalme's were.

Service went from Roadie's to Lapalme's where he used lock grips to decommission both vehicles in Moe's driveway, dumped sugar in three snowmobiles, and left a note: "Run while you can."

Lasurm met him just north of Lapalme's at 5 A.M., drove him to Big Bay de Noc School, and parked in the faculty lot.

"They'll be watching your trailer," she said.

"I'll place an ad in the paper," he told her. They had already agreed to meet again, and he knew it would not be solely for DNR business. There was no parting kiss. They did not say good-bye. He got out of her truck, hoisted his unwieldy gear bag, and trudged northeast through the fields and woods toward US 2.

Joe Flap's pickup was backed into the drifted-over opening of a two-track, and the white-clad Service slid quietly out of the tree line, tossed his gear into the bed of the truck, and got into the passenger seat.

"Nice you could make it," Service said.

"I'm always where I promise ta be," the pilot said, grinning. "Don't look like youse broke nothin' important."

"Drive," Service said, wanting to put distance between himself and the peninsula he had haunted for two weeks. He'd broken laws. What was more important than that?

"People're wonderin' where youse've been," Flap said, doing a U-turn across US 2 to head west.

As they passed Foxy's Den at Garden Corners, Service saw a garbage truck turning south on Garden Road.

PART IV

FAITH IN LIGHT

32

MARQUETTE, MARCH 2, 1976

"You have an outlaw's heart."

Moe Lapalme's rifle was on a small table in Attalienti's office. "It took awhile, but Len managed to find it," the acting captain said. "No prints, and the serial number has been filed off. How'd it get to the bottom of the bluff?"

"Forgetfulness," Service said, piling his notebook and maps on Attalienti's table and explaining how he had found Lapalme setting up to shoot at officers on the ice off Fayette.

The acting captain nodded. "Too bad we don't have a round from the earlier shootings." Meaning, having the rifle was not adequate evidence. "But I guess it's one less long gun for the rats," Attalienti said.

There was something peculiar in the acting captain's demeanor. Wariness, maybe?

Attalienti said, "I have an idea how you got into the Garden, and I'm not happy about it. Joe Flap flew out of Marquette on Valentine's Day night, and the people over there called me to complain about our reckless ways. They assumed it was an official department flight."

Service decided to keep his mouth shut, to neither confirm nor deny.

Attalienti continued. "I told you before you went that the mission was strictly surveillance, no enforcement."

"I didn't do any law enforcement," Service said.

"You took a man's rifle."

"Was I supposed to let him take a shot at our guys?"

"You're clairvoyant? You *knew* he would shoot? We can't punish intent."

"It was clear to me what was going on." What was Attalienti driving at?

"Delta County has been getting a steady stream of complaints from the Garden—vandalism, harassment. That jerk, Ranse Renard, accused us of harassment." Attalienti paused and looked at Service. "All the complaints fall during the past two weeks. You wouldn't know anything about that, right?"

Service didn't answer.

"If one of my men turned vigilante, I would be forced to deal harshly with him."

"Do you want my report, sir?" Service asked.

Attalienti nodded, and Service launched into a forty-five-minute verbal recounting of what he had seen, including names and addresses of all the rats, where they met, how they operated, how their trails and meeting places worked. He had delivered everything the captain had asked for—everything but his understanding that Lansing's unspoken goals would undercut anything law enforcement tried in the Garden. "The real force down there is Pete Peletier," Service concluded, "and he's smart enough to keep separated from everything. We'll have one hell of a time nailing him."

The acting captain said gruffly, "Those are the same names as the complainants."

Service put a check mark next to six houses on the plat maps. All the houses were along Garden Road, spread out over five miles. "That's the crow line," Service said. Lasurm had identified these during his first night with her.

Attalienti looked at the map. "Difficult to evade," he said, "strung out that far."

"Have to run dark at night, in unmarkeds by day."

"Running dark on Garden Road is dangerous. It's not some two-track back in the bush."

"They operate at night," Service said. "We have to be out there when they're out there. Maybe the phone company could switch off the lines for a brief period."

"That would work once," Attalienti said sarcastically.

"Or maybe the phones could suffer a spontaneous malfunction."

Attalienti glared at him. "You have an outlaw's heart. We will not break laws to enforce laws."

"I was thinking more along the lines of an act of God," Service lied. "Do you know Sun Tzu?"

"The Chinese restaurant in Ishpeming?"

Before Service could reply, the other man said, "Peletier isn't on the list of complainants?"

Service said, "His recent luck seems to have been better than the rest of them, which probably has them wondering why."

Attalienti shook his head disapprovingly and held up his hands. "Delta County won't respond to the complaints. They've asked the Troops to handle them."

"When?"

"Tomorrow or the next day. I asked them to hold off until I knew you were back and safe."

"I'd like to go with them."

"That's your basic stupid idea. You're going back to the Mosquito and you're going to stay there."

"I thought I was part of the Garden team."

"Not anymore."

"I want to help."

"And I want to keep a good warden employed."

"I'm out?"

"Out of the Garden."

When he had returned to his trailer, Service had been forced to crawl through snowbanks six feet deep. He and Joe Flap had dug out the door so he could get inside to turn on the heat and water. Now as he drove up to the trailer, he saw that the area had been freshly plowed. Len Stone was sitting in a truck with an oversize plow on the front. Service invited him in and the acting lieutenant put a bottle of Jack Daniel's on the table in the kitchen area, peeled off his parka, and sat down.

"I ain't here," Stone said, uncapping the bottle and holding it out to the young officer. "Deano ream your ass?"

"He said I'm off the Garden team."

"Dat's just cap'n talk. He's gotta protect his own ass, eh? But da Garden's mine, and I choose who I want wit' me. You don't gotta say anyting. I figure Joe Flap flew you down dere and you used a parachute, which is about da craziest bloody ting I ever heard," Stone said with a wide grin. "Deano suspects da same, but I don't tink he can make up his mind ta say parachute. He sent me ta talk ta Joe Flap, but Joe, he's one of us. All he said was he wanted ta fly dat night."

Service took a slug of whiskey and passed it back to Stone, who said, "Youse got da rats whinin' like a buncha babies!"

"They already replaced the nets we took," Service said.

"I told youse, dis is about money. You messed wit' dere trucks and snowbugs and dat was good, but you can't be doin' dat stuff no more. You make your report to Deano?"

Service nodded. "He said I have the heart of an outlaw."

Stone laughed and nodded. "Can't be good at dis job if you don't!"

"I want back in," Service said.

Stone held up his hands. "Take 'er easy an' hold da horses. Not right away. For now youse concentrate on keepin' yer nose clean. Bottom line, you stole dat man's rifle, an' I don't want to know what else. If it come out it was youse, dere'd be trouble, and I'm tellin' youse, Lansing would let yer ass swing in the wind. So youse just take care of da Mosquito, and when it's time ta come back, I'll let youse know. Ask me, dis ting is gonna go on for a long time."

Service explained much of what he had seen, and after a couple of hours, Stone put on his coat and stuck out his hand. "I can't say what you done down dere is right, but everybody's been in dis job has had ta make da same kinda decisions. Maybe you wandered off da legal reservation, but I hope youse did it for good reasons, Grady."

When Stone was gone, Grady Service couldn't sleep. What he had done in the Garden was wrong, and so were his reasons. This wasn't Vietnam. It wasn't even a real war. He had sworn to uphold the law, and had stepped over the line for spurious reasons. He vowed that from here on, as long as his career lasted, he would go to the line, but no further. Shuck Gorley was right: An officer's mind was what counted. He had acted like his old man would have acted. Never again: It was time to be himself, not the shadow of his father. His last thought of the night was that he would bust Pete Peletier—no matter how long it took.

33

MARQUETTE, MARCH 15, 1976

"You fight dirty."

Cecilia Lasurm was waiting for him on the sidewalk in front of the Marquette County Jail. The snowbanks along the street were six feet high and smudged gray from vehicle exhaust. Snow was falling and would soon lighten the dreary gray. Lasurm was wrapped tight in an ankle-length parka. Her call had taken him by surprise.

"I need to talk to you," she had said, and he agreed. March was the dead month for most game wardens, a time between seasons; a time to repair and replace gear, and wait for the snowmelt when the action would start up again and the poachers would be on the big lake after spawners. He was still tired from his sojourn in the Garden, glad for the respite, glad to be home in his Mosquito.

She looked small, with lines etched around her eyes. Her face was red from the cold wind. "Thank you for coming," she greeted him.

"We could've talked elsewhere."

"Trust me," she said, taking his hand and leading him into the building.

They signed in and walked down to an interrogation room. Inside, a white-haired man sat at a table with the girl who had stabbed Gumby.

Lasurm said, "Her father and I never married. She was born when we were both sixteen. He joined the Coast Guard after high school and never came back. I can't blame him. Anise was headstrong from the beginning. When she was sixteen she got mixed up with the wrong people. She always thought of herself as a pathfinder and rebel, but she wasn't. She was easily led. Three years ago she fell in with Moe Lapalme—she was nineteen. I threw her out. She lived with Moe for awhile, drifted on, and took her father's name."

Lapalme had to be twice the girl's age, and Service suddenly saw the blue pickup truck racing by the Fishdam boat access, the girl with the long blond hair, and it all fell into place. "You knew she was back," he said.

"Word goes around the Garden," she said with a shrug.

"All that stuff you told me," he said, "about your reasons."

"I meant it all. My daughter just makes it more personal."

"You might have mentioned this before," he said.

"Would it have changed anything?"

He shook his head. "You called me up here to tell me this?"

"And to talk to Odd Hegstrom."

Service stared into the room. The man was talking to the girl, pushed back in his chair looking passive. "Her attorney," Service said.

"He would like to talk to you," she said, opening the door.

"Are you coming in?" he asked her.

"I can't," Lasurm said as he stepped into the room.

The young woman's hair was clean and untangled, but her eyes remained blank. She looked only a little like her mother.

Hegstrom pulled out a chair. "Thank you for coming, Officer Service. I believe you've met Anise Aucoin."

"Briefly," Service said, not looking at her. "Should there be a DNR lawyer here, or somebody from the prosecutor's office?"

Hegstrom's gaunt cheeks puffed. "What do you think?"

"I don't really know," Service admitted.

"How about if we make this off the record?"

"Is there such a thing?"

"There is with me. Did you actually see my client wield a knife?" Hegstrom asked. "Or any weapon?"

"She was in another room, in the dark. Everything is in my report."

"Yes or no?"

"No, but she was the only other person in the room."

"We're not in court, Officer Service, and you're not an attorney arguing a case. I'm just trying to understand what happened. If you couldn't see inside the room, you can't be certain what transpired. Would you agree?"

"The victim came out, the lights went on, the woman was the only person in there," Service said. What was Hegstrom after?

"Did you look under the bed, in the closets, outside the window? Was there an attic?"

Service said, "No, no, no, and I don't know. You can play this ludicrous game, but a jury won't buy it. There were deputies with me. It's their crime to investigate."

"Persuading a jury is like writing a pop hit," Hegstrom said. "The chords are all the same. You just have to find the most appealing order."

"My job is apprehension. Others handle prosecution."

"Did you read my client her rights?"

This caught him off guard. He assumed the deputies had done this. "I personally didn't Mirandize her."

Hegstrom rubbed his chin. "What was my client's demeanor when you entered the room?"

"She had concealed weapons."

"Bolts are weapons even without the crossbow to propel them?"

"She had just stabbed a man. The crossbow was close by."

"You allege."

"She had bolts by her leg, under the covers. They have sharp points. What're we doing here, counselor?"

"How did my client react when you entered the room?"

"She didn't."

"Did she threaten you in any way?"

"No."

"Are you saying she was unresponsive?"

"No. She asked if I wanted to see her breasts."

The woman smiled, the first sign that she was mentally present.

"What did you think?" Hegstrom asked.

"I didn't. The first priority was to clear the room of weapons."

"Where was the knife?"

"Stuck in the victim's back."

"I see," Hegstrom said thoughtfully. "And where is that weapon now?"

"In evidence with the county."

"You personally secured it?"

"No, the deputies did."

"Has the integrity of the chain of custody been maintained?"

"You'll have to take that up with the county."

"My client's prints were not on the knife. Did you know that? How do you explain that, given the charges against her?"

No prints? Nobody had told him this. Had Detective Kobera tried to call him about this while he was in the Garden? He kept quiet.

Hegstrom continued. "No fingerprints, Officer Service. Again, what was your impression of my client's emotional state when you entered the room?"

"I thought she was out of it."

"Unresponsive?"

"Out of it," Service said. "Jacked up—on a long flight with no ETA."

"Is that a medical diagnosis?"

"It's a professional observation."

"You have no medical or psychiatric training." It was not a question.

"Obviously not. Is this a deposition?"

"Do you see a recorder here? This is off the record, Officer. What we hear you saying is that you never personally witnessed the alleged stabbing, and you did not read Miss Aucoin her rights, or secure the evidence. You also appear to be unaware that no prints were recovered."

"You're oversimplifying everything," Service said.

"Facts *are* simple by definition," Hegstrom countered. "It's the array and interplay of facts, the interpolation and interpretation that render them complex."

"Are we done?"

"I didn't mean to irritate you," the lawyer said.

"I'm not good at mind games," Service said.

Hegstrom tilted his head and smiled. "I would think a game warden would be especially adept at such games. I've never met a police officer who hasn't bent the rules or occasionally broken them to make a case."

Service got to his feet. Was Hegstrom signaling that he knew he had been in the Garden? Had Lasurm told him? He left the room with a sense of dread and immediately began to try to replay the events of the stabbing. Who had removed the knife? Ambulance personnel? More likely it was someone in the emergency room. He hadn't read Aucoin her rights because that fell to the deputies who had actually made the arrest. In the future, he told himself, he would make sure he did this and not depend on others. How could the knife have no prints? Hegstrom had asked if they had checked the window or closet, and whether there was an attic—why was he asking such questions? Most importantly, had Cecilia Lasurm betrayed him for the sake of her daughter?

Hegstrom looked at him. "To paraphrase something, Grady—remember that faith in light is admirable at night."

Lasurm was not in the area of the room when he emerged. He found her out on the sidewalk, looking cold. "You want to let me in on what's going on?" he demanded, barely containing his growing rage.

"My daughter's a junkie," she said.

"That excuses her behavior?" he shot back at her.

"Don't be ridiculous. A substance abuser is responsible under the law."

"Do you doubt she did it?" he challenged.

"It's Hegstrom's job to find out."

"No," he said angrily. "The police determine that. Hegstrom's job is to make sure we've done our jobs fair and square, and that his client gets a fair trial."

"That *client* is my daughter."

"Hegstrom intimated that he knew I was on the Garden."

"I don't think for him," she said. "He didn't hear any such thing from me."

Service stared at her. "How far would you go to save your daughter?"

"I resent that question," she snapped at him.

"Answer me."

"She deserves the best defense, but I would never betray a confidence. I thought you understood that."

"You don't exactly have forever to let this thing run its course."

She bristled and furrowed her brows. "I'm well aware of my circumstances. You fight *dirty*."

"I have a dirty job."

"Which you chose to make dirtier in the Garden," she said with a hiss. "I have no idea what Hegstrom is thinking, or what he said to you, or why. He's got a job to do and, like you, he'll do whatever he thinks he needs to do to win. If this sounds like a sermon, so be it. Anise is an adult, and if she's guilty, she'll pay. If I wanted to set you up, Grady, I could have told Hegstrom about you and let him spring it at trial to destroy your credibility."

"Unless you told him and he's trying to steer my testimony and work a deal to avoid trial."

"I did not tell him, and I did not ask Odd Hegstrom to take my daughter's case," she said. "I understand you're angry, but I don't deserve to bear the brunt of your frustration. You tried to spread paranoia in the Garden. Maybe it's getting to you instead."

He sighed in frustration. "I'd better go," he said, wanting to avoid further escalation. He needed time and space to think and try to understand what this was about.

34

TRENARY, MARCH 16, 1976

"Connie, she takes care of mosta dat."

"Joe, did you tell anybody about the flight?"

Joe Flap squinted at him. "Da cap'n called me 'cause da airport people called him an' complained. Dey assumed it was a department flight, and dey said it was stupid and dangerous. Dey're a buncha pussies."

"Did you file a flight plan?"

"Bare bones, basic VFR, out and back."

"The visibility was terrible that night."

"Remember what I said, if I could see my prop it was visual? Dat's da pilot's call."

"Did you list a passenger?"

"Didn't have none ta list, did I?" Flap said, obviously pleased with himself.

"Stone figured it out," Service said.

"Len's a smart guy. He knows youse, he knows me, an' he knew your old man. It don't take an Einstein to add two plus two."

Hegstrom was also smart. How could he know about such a flight, and, if he knew, how could he figure out what it meant?

"You want a beer?" Flap asked.

"No thanks. What does the airport do with flight plans?"

"Dey twix 'em off to Air Traffic Control and send a copy down ta da District."

"The DNR district?"

"Yeah, Escanaba."

"Why?"

"Back a few years, dere was a budget crunch downstate, and Lansing cut pilots, planes, and flight hours. Da district believed da air patrols were cost effective, and asked for flight plans to be used in puttin' together dere arguments wit' da Lansing eyeshades."

"What's in a flight plan that could be useful?"

"Not a damn ting; I told 'em it was stupid, eh, but dey ignored me."

"They still do this?" The value of air patrols had long since been established and had become standard procedure at certain times of the year.

"Far as I know. I told Cosmo and Edey about it, but bot' of dem give me da brush-off."

Service called Len Stone from Flap's house. "Do you get copies of DNR flight plans?"

"I'm not da best inside guy, eh? Connie, she takes care of mosta dat. Why?"

"I'm not sure yet."

35

ESCANABA, MARCH 16, 1976

"I'm a trashy kinda guy."

"Been a while," Connie Leppo greeted him when he walked into the district office. "Your family situation okay?" As the district's dispatcher-secretary, she took it on herself to monitor what was going on among district personnel.

"All taken care of. And I got my equipment replaced. Thanks for asking."

"Youse gonna make da party at Sheila's tomorrow night?"

Party? His expression must have shown his confusion. "Saint Paddy's Day," Leppo said. "Tomorrow?"

If he'd ever known, he had forgotten. "Sheila?"

"Sheila Halloran, a Troop secretary over to Gladstone post. Her boyfriend's Al Eagle, da district fish biologist."

He hadn't met either of them. "I guess I missed the invitation."

She rolled her eyes. "It's posted in da coffee room. Da party's out to Al's camp up da Tacoosh."

The Tacoosh was a fast, rock-bottom river that flowed into Little Bay de Noc near Rapid River.

"Dere's a map on da board too," Leppo added. "You enjoy my mom's bakery?"

Connie talked a lot. "Great," he said, trying to recall what he had done with the baked goods she had given him. "Len said I should talk to you about paperwork."

Leppo grinned. "Da poor man slouches like a prisoner when he's gotta sit behind dat desk."

"What determines which papers get filed or thrown away?" he asked.

"It's called da file retention schedule. Lansing lawyers tell us what we gotta save and for how long. Anyting dey don't classify we can decide what ta do wit."

"What about DNR flight schedules?"

She looked up at him. "Ah, dose. Dey're local, an' we pitch 'em."

"After somebody looks at them?"

"Nope, I plunk 'em right in da circular file. We got enough paper in dis place, we don't need more, eh. Somebody way back got da bright idea to have 'em sent here, but nobody looks at 'em, so I toss 'em."

"Edey didn't look at them?"

"Nor da guy before him. We get a new boss, I always ask, and dey always say toss it."

"What else gets tossed?"

"Records Lansing says can go. We flag files, and on certain dates each year we clean 'em out or send 'em ta storage. An da wastebaskets, da janitor takes dose to da Dumpster every night."

"Do you cut the paper up or do anything to it before you toss it?"

She looked puzzled. "Sometime we bag 'em and take 'em to da Dumpster. Why would we cut stuff up? It's trash."

"The city picks up our trash?"

"Nope—Bay de Noc Trash Haulers. Dere on contract wit' city an' county. Dis way city an' county can keep down payrolls wit' benefits and all dat. Times're tough, eh."

"How often do they pick it up?"

"Couple times a week."

"On a set schedule?"

"Usually on Tuesdays and Fridays."

"At a specific time?"

"Seems to me I see Gary in da mornings. Sometimes he comes in for a cuppa coffee. What's dis about?"

"Gary?"

"Gary Aho. He's a good guy, eh?"

"I saw a BDN truck over by Garden Corners," he said.

"Probably Gary on da way home. Dey got a big operation, offices in Manistique, Gladstone, Escanaba, Menominee."

"Gary lives near Garden Corners?" He had seen the truck in the early morning.

"Cooks, just north of dere," she said.

Cooks, Lasurm had told him, was part of the consolidated school district that included Garden. This made Aho an area resident. The hair bristled on the back of his neck.

"The drivers take their trucks home?"

"Way I understand it, da drivers lease dere trucks from da company. Da company does sales, negotiates contracts, and handles da bookkeeping an' billing. Drivers have to take care of da trucks and pay for maintenance."

"Sounds like it would be hard for a driver to make any money."

"Gary says he does okay. He's a bachelor, eh."

Service glanced at the calendar. Tomorrow was a pickup day. "Where does the trash get dumped?"

"County landfill, I tink, but I'm not sure. Can't just dump garbage anywhere, right?"

"Do we have a copy of the contract?"

"You betcha," the secretary said.

"Can you make a copy for me?"

"If you watch phones while I run da copier."

"Deal."

When she brought him his copy, he asked her another question. "Gary comes in for coffee?"

"He doesn't come in every time, but he's a regular vendor, and dey're like part of da family, right? Is everything okay?" Her eyes showed concern.

"Sure; I'm just trying to understand how we do things here."

She laughed. "Never had an officer worry about da trash before."

"I'm a trashy kinda guy," he said with a wink.

He took the contract and a cup of coffee into the district conference room and sat down to read. The contract had been renewed by Edey last July, and would come up for renewal again this summer. It called for two ten-yard trash bins and one weekly pickup. Service looked into the parking lot. There was only one bin.

He walked out to Leppo's desk. "The contract calls for one pickup a week," he said.

"Yah, but Gary said da company is shorta bins right now, so dey brought us one and he makes two pickups a week. I told you he's a good guy. He takes good care of us, and he says we got da best coffee and bakery on his route."

"Have you watched him make his pickups?"

"Sure. He usually loads, den takes da truck down da alley and stops dere for ten, fifteen minutes before he pulls on. Not sure if dat's procedure or a timing thing," she said.

Or something more insidious, Service thought as he scribbled a note in red ink on the copy of the contract, and dropped it into Leppo's wastebasket when she stepped away from her desk.

36

"It's bait."

"You wrote *what* on the contract?" Len Stone asked.

"'Cancel: July seventy-six. Connie, please file.' I used your initials," Service confessed. "It's bait. I also threw in a copy of the weekly schedule for all officers."

Stone grinned. "Youse really want me to go along wit' dis? We could look pretty stupid, eh?"

"We could," Service agreed.

"All dis 'cause youse seen a trash truck over to Garden Corners?"

"Not just that. Aho lives in Cooks. He violated the contract. He's in and out of our office whenever he wants, which makes him invisible. How many times have you done surveillance and come up empty?"

"Goes wit' da territory."

"That's my point," Service said. "Knowing it might yield nothing, you still went."

Stone contemplated this briefly. "How do youse want to play it?"

"We wait in the alley and see what happens. We leave your unmarked on the street. If he doesn't stop in the alley, we jump in the unmarked and follow him."

"All da way ta da dump?"

"If that's how it works out," Service said. "I'll talk to Connie. If he goes into the building, she'll bump us on the radio when he's leaving."

The green truck pulled into the lot at 10:42 A.M. and backed up to the bin. The driver wore green coveralls, jumped down from the cab of his truck, and went into the district office. He came back out fifteen minutes later with a clear plastic bag, dumped it in the bin, and began hydraulically lifting the bin to dump the contents into the metal thorax of the truck.

Connie Leppo called them on the brick radio. "Three one hundred, Elvis has left da building."

Stone smirked. "She tinks dis is a game."

The driver climbed back into his truck.

"He's coming," Service said as the driver backed up. It wasn't Connie's job to detect security problems.

"I got eyes," Stone said. "Hair's too long for Elvis."

"And he's too skinny," Service added as they stepped into the door of the DNR garage that flanked one side of the alley.

The truck stopped in the alley twenty feet beyond them. The driver hopped down, climbed up the side, and dropped out of sight.

"He's carrying a gym bag," Service said.

"I seen," Stone said. "Move."

The two officers waited at the rear of the truck on the side opposite where the man had disappeared. When they heard him beginning to climb out they moved around the truck, and when the man's boots hit the slush, Service clutched his arm. "How's business?"

The startled man froze, but recovered with a sheepish grin. "How's she goin', guys?"

"What's in da bag?" Stone asked.

"Trash," the driver said.

"I thought trash belonged in da truck," Stone said.

"I needed ta sort it out."

"Youse mind if we see what's in da bag?"

The man shrugged, unzipped the bag, and held it open. "*Playboys*," he said.

"From the district office?" Service asked.

The man grimaced. "No, man; I saw 'em earlier, thought I'd fish 'em out before I dumped da load."

"You like da articles?" Stone asked facetiously.

The man looked confused. "No man, da tits."

Service snatched the bag from the man, turned it upside down, and shook it vigorously. The magazines landed with a plop in gray slush, and papers fluttered down behind the magazines. The contract lay faceup, the red note from Service's hand visible. Ink from the marker was smeared pink by moisture.

"Geez, dose musta gotten stuck to da magazines," the driver said too quickly.

"Let's go back to da office," Stone said, holding the man's arm.

"Do we gotta?" the man protested weakly, but he went along with them without further protest.

Connie Leppo shot them a worried look as they escorted the driver past her station into the district conference room. Service stepped back out to her. "Call the trash company, Connie. Ask them how many bins and pickups we're supposed to have, and ask them if they ever run short of bins for customers."

She reached for the phone as Service went into the room. "Coffee, Gary?" he asked the driver.

"You know my name?"

Service shrugged. "You're our regular guy, right?"

"Three years," Aho said. "You guys got da great bakery here."

Service stopped at Leppo's desk, but she was still on the phone. He went into the canteen, filled three mugs with coffee, used a Sears catalog for a tray, and returned to Leppo's station.

She looked up at him. "We're s'pposed ta have two bins," she said. "And one pickup a week. Dey do run short once in awhile, but never for more den twenty-four hours, and never for state agencies. Our contract is too valuable."

"Did you tell them we have only one?"

"I did just what youse asked," Leppo said, looking perplexed.

"Thanks, Connie. Relax."

"Youse comin' to Sheila's party?"

"Probably not."

"Too bad. She'll be a blast," she said.

Sheila or the party? Service wondered as he set a mug in front of the driver. "Black okay?"

"For java, not for broads," Aho tried to joke.

Service made a point to stand beside the man, forcing him to look up. Stone sat across the table. "Gary, why are our papers in your bag?" Service asked.

"I told youse, dey musta gotten stuck to the magazines, eh?"

Stone grinned. "Dat's bullshit, son."

"I don't get dis," Aho said. "It's trash. You're trowin' it out, right?"

"It's trash when it arrives at the dump," Service said. "Under the contract, you are the agent of transfer. It remains our property until it arrives at the dump; then it's theirs."

"Most people don't mind somebody picks up somepin' dey don't want."

"We mind," Stone said coolly.

"What's da big deal?" Aho asked.

"You don't get to take trash for personal use, and if you do, it's theft," Service said. "You're stealing government property." He had no idea if this was legally correct and didn't really care. He wanted to find out what Aho was doing and why.

"Man," Aho said, shaking his head disconsolately.

"What do youse do wit' da papers, son?" Stone asked.

"I told you, da magazines're for me."

"Dat's fine; an' da papers?" Stone pressed.

"I just wanted the *Playboys*."

Service said, "Gary, we called your company. The contract calls for two bins and one weekly pickup."

The man raised his hands in a gesture of peace. "Right, right. We ran short. I did it dis way as a favor ta you guys."

"Don't lie!" Service said sharply. "The company says it has never shorted the state and wouldn't because our contract is too important."

"You musta talked to da new girl at da office," Aho offered.

Service picked up the conference room telephone. "Connie, please get the head man at BDN on the phone." He looked over at Aho, who motioned for him to hang up. Service said, "Thanks, never mind, Connie."

Stone said, "Youse got to level wit' us, son, spit 'er all out. Whatever youse tell us, we're gonna check it out closer'n a fourteen-year-old comin' home from her first date. Youse got no wiggle room."

Gary Aho looked to Service to be in his late twenties. He had long black hair tied back in a ponytail and a wispy goatee. "What's with the papers?" Service asked, hovering over the man.

"It's a favor, okay?"

"A favor?" Stone said.

"For my uncle."

"What's dis uncle's name?" Stone asked.

"Pete Peletier, my mother's big brother."

Service had to swallow a smile. "The Peletier who lives down to Fairport?" Service asked.

"You know Pete?" Aho asked.

"Heard about him," Service said. "You're sayin' you go through our trash and pass it along to your uncle."

"I don't look at nuttin', man. I give it all to him," Aho said. "It ain't for me, eh?"

"What's your uncle do wit' it?" Stone asked.

"I don't know, man. Can I go now?" Aho asked.

"No, Gary," Stone said. "Youse'll give us da whole story or youse're going to jail."

"Jesus," Aho said. "I'll lose my job!"

"Da whole story," Stone reiterated.

"How long have you been doing this?" Service asked.

"Since I took da route."

"What did you do before that?"

"Twisted wrenches over ta Manistique."

"You lease your truck from BDN," Service said. "You must've saved up a bundle for that up front."

"Uncle Pete took care of it."

"He loaned youse da cash?" Stone asked.

"No man, it was a gift."

"In exchange for taking DNR trash," Service said.

"He said it was no big deal," Aho said defensively. "Just trash."

"He was wrong," Stone said.

"When do you take the paperwork to him?" Service asked.

"On da way home."

"To Cooks?"

Aho looked alarmed. "Man, you guys know where I *live?* You been spyin' on me?"

"No, Gary, some people over your way have loose lips. We heard about what you were doing for your uncle."

"I never told nobody, man," Aho said. Aho's expression went from suspicious to morose.

"You deliver the papers to your uncle's house?" Service continued.

"Yeah," Aho said, nodding lethargically.

"Do you call ahead?"

"I just show up and give 'em ta him."

"What time?"

"When I get dere—six, seven?"

"In the morning?" Service asked. He had seen a truck in the morning.

Aho grimaced. "No man, at night. I got a day route."

"Do you pick up trash in the Garden?" Service asked.

"No man. Another guy's got dat route."

He'd seen the other driver, Service told himself. Not Aho.

"You drive da big truck to your uncle's?" Stone asked.

Aho grinned. "No big deal—it's da U.P., eh."

Service understood. Yoopers parked bulldozers, dump trucks, logging rigs, and eighteen-wheelers in the driveways of their homes.

"How about we take a ride?" Service said.

"C'mon, man, you can't do dis ta me. I got my route ta finish."

"Youse prefer a room at da graybar hotel?" Stone asked.

"No," Aho said.

"Okay, den. We'll sit here today and dis afternoon, we take a ride, eh? Da route can wait."

"What do I get out of dis?"

"Maybe you don't get busted," Service said. "But you'll be a material witness and give us a statement. When the case comes to trial, you'll testify."

"Against my uncle? He'll want his money back."

Aho looked wrecked, but Service got the feeling some of this was for show. He couldn't really pinpoint his sense of unease, but it gnawed at him. "One lie and we bust you, Gary."

"Dere ain't no free bakery today," Stone added.

"Dis is so much bullshit," Aho whined.

Service got a pad of legal paper and a couple of pencils and put them in front of the man. "Write," he said.

"Okay I print?"

Stone nodded.

Service and his lieutenant stepped into the lobby. Stone said, "We gotta make sure we grab Peletier wit' da bag before we nail da SOB."

"Minus the one-handers," Service added. "We don't want to give him any outs."

"Da prosecutor may not back us up on dis," Stone said.

"You want to let it drop here?" Service asked.

"No, let's play 'er out, see where she goes."

"I'll ride in the trash truck. You use the unmarked?"

Stone said, "I'll borrow somepin' dey don't know over dere."

It was dark when Aho eased the nose of the big truck into the driveway of Peletier's house just outside Fairport. Service clambered out of the back, dropped down the far side, and moved quickly to the garage. He reeked of trash and he was cold. Aho went directly to the front door and knocked.

Pete Peletier came to the door and looked past Aho at the nose of the big truck. "What's goin' on, Gar?"

Aho held out the bag.

The man ignored it. "What's dat?"

"You know," Aho said, jiggling the bag.

Again, Peletier ignored the offering. "Where's your pickup?"

"I had ta use da big truck tonight," Aho said, still holding out the bag.

"Had to?" Peletier said.

Aho jiggled the bag again and his uncle snapped at him, "Stop shaking dat damn ting. I never seen dat bag in my life. Now get da hell outta here. I got tings ta do!"

Service knew they'd been busted. Peletier was acting like the bag contained plague. He knew something was up. No way Peletier could have seen him dismount from the truck. All he could see from the house was the nose of the trash hauler in the driveway. Stone was a mile back, waiting for a radio call. *Shit!* Peletier had asked Aho where his pickup was. Son of a bitch: Aho had snookered them. He normally came in his personal truck, not the trash hauler. The big truck had tipped off his uncle. Bastards, Service thought as he stepped out beside Aho and said, "DNR."

Peletier looked amused. "Dis like *Hawaii Five-O?*" the man asked. "Youse lost, Officer?" He pointed southwest. "Last I heard, da Big Island and Dano were dat way."

"Gary Aho, you are under arrest for theft of government papers." Service recited the man's rights and asked him to put his right hand behind his back, where he cuffed it.

Aho said, "You said it would be okay. This is a fuck job!"

Peletier said sharply, "Put a cork in it, Gary."

"You promised," Aho whined at Service as he cuffed the man's hands behind his back and held the cuffs to control him.

"Nazis," Peletier said with a growl.

Service picked up the bag with his right hand. "I'll be back for you, Pete," he said to the man.

"You got nothing, asshole," Peletier said. "*Nothing.*"

Service lifted Aho's cuffed hands. "We've got him, and there are always fingerprints," he added, holding the bag out.

Peletier didn't look particularly upset, but he shook a finger at his nephew. "Youse keep dat big mouth shut until da lawyer comes ta see youse."

"He's already made a statement," Service said as he engaged the radio and called Stone in to pick them up.

Service heard the door slam as he shoved Aho into the front passenger seat and got in behind him. "Hit it. I think we're gonna have company."

As Service would have done, Stone immediately shut off all lights, inside and out, and fishtailed onto Garden Road as he accelerated. It was several miles before an oncoming vehicle lit them up and swerved as it passed, the driver obviously startled. Running without lights was a good way to stay hidden, if you didn't hit anything.

"You guys are nuts!" Aho said, holding his cuffed hands in front of his face.

Service used the brick to call the Manistique Troop dispatcher and asked for assistance and an escort from the nearest unit. A state police officer immediately responded that he was westbound on US 2, a mile east of Garden Corners.

Service radioed, "Unit Eight Six, we're running dark, heading north in an unmarked. Light it up and start your music. We'll flash lights twice when we have you in sight."

Stone slowed for the ninety-degree turn just south of the village and accelerated straight through town. Service saw vehicle lights coming to life in Roadie's parking lot as they flashed by.

"Eight Six, we're clear of Garden. What's our speed?" Service asked Stone.

"Eighty," the lieutenant said matter-of-factly.

"Eight Six, we're northbound at eighty mike-paul-henry, running dark."

"Eight Six is southbound on Garden Road, all lit up."

Service did a quick mental calculation. "Intersect, four minutes max," he radioed. "Probable pursuit."

"Roger, Eight Six will swing in behind and follow you up to US 2."

Another state police vehicle reported on the radio that he was also headed for Garden Corners, ETA in one minute from the west on US 2.

"Do we stop an' circle da wagons?" Stone asked, concentrating on the road.

"We'll let the state transport the prisoner," Service said as he spotted an oncoming emergency vehicle's flashing lights.

Stone flashed his headlights twice and the trooper wheeled a tight one-eighty and fell in behind them.

Moments later they skidded into the gas station at Garden Corners. A state police cruiser was already there, emergency lights blinking.

A half-dozen trucks and vans roared up behind their escort and men tumbled out and immediately began to throw rocks.

Service jerked Aho out of the sedan, pushed him into the backseat of the waiting cruiser, and told the trooper to take the prisoner to Escanaba. The officer didn't question him.

Stone had his revolver out of his holster and was pointing it at the rock throwers, who had left their headlights on, flooding the COs and using the lights as a blinding shield. "Next one gets a round!" Stone shouted.

"Nail the Nazi fucker!" somebody shrieked.

"Next one!" Stone roared.

Service knew it was a bluff. They were trained and expected to shoot at a specific target, not wildly and blindly, and rocks at this range did not equate to lethal force.

The men swore and called them names and began to slam doors. The trucks backed out quickly and raced south on Garden Road, honking their horns.

Stone holstered his revolver and patted the shoulder of the first trooper who had come to their assistance. "Youse ever want to transfer, youse let me know," he told the Troop, who started laughing out loud.

En route to Escanaba, Service said, "Peletier knew something was up. He played dumb over the bag. Arriving in the big truck was a prearranged signal." He knew it had been his fault for not anticipating this.

After a lull, Stone said, "Ya know, sometimes I seen dat trash hauler parked at a house down by Garden. I shoulda said somepin."

"He probably swaps the big truck for his pickup," Service said, disgusted by his failure to nail the secretive rat leader. So close—and it was his fault they'd missed.

Stone looked over at him. "Buck up, boy. Youse stopped da leak been right dere in front of us for years. Youse figured it out. None a' us did. Dat alone is one helluva day of police work."

"I'll drop the bag at the Troop lab in Ishpeming tomorrow," Service told his lieutenant. "Peletier's prints will be on the bag."

"Don't waste da time," Stone said. "His lawyer will claim he give da bag to his nephew as a gift and why wouldn't his prints be on it, eh? An' he won't know nuttin' about no papers. We could try for a search warrant for Pete's house, but dere won't be shit to find by den." Stone looked over at him. "We're in dis for da long haul. We plugged da leak. We'll take dat for now."

Service lit a cigarette.

Stone said, "You got an extra one?"

"You smoke?"

"Tonight I do."

37

BIG BAY DE NOC PATROL, MAY 6-7, 1976

The only sharks out here were in boats.

The average date for ice-out on Big Bay de Noc was April 20, but not this year, when it was eight days late because of the hard winter and late spring. Service had not been back to the Garden since the confrontation with Peletier and Aho two months before. Aho, after his arrest, initially had been fired from his company, but was rehired when the prosecutor withdrew the charges, saying he didn't think a jury would find Aho guilty. This made it not worth the cost to the county, especially after Lansing also passed on taking the lead in the case. Service was unhappy about the developments, but Stone once again pointed out that they had stopped the leak, and told him it was time for him to come back into the Garden fray.

Stone and Attalienti had been busy in the Garden since ice-out in the bay. Stone and a marine patrol had gotten lucky two days after ice-out when they forced two rat boats onto boulders and ice berms on the shore of Ansels Point. The rats had abandoned their craft and scrambled into the woods. Within an hour the owner of the two boats called the state police to report them stolen. Stone towed the boats back to Escanaba, started condemnation proceedings in district court, and had his men clean up the craft and put them in working order, including blue flashers on six-foot-high metal posts and yelper sirens. Finally, the DNR had a couple of boats that could keep up with the rats, and Stone planned to use them until the court said otherwise.

This morning the fifty-foot PB-4 was to come across the bay to Burn't Bluff from Escanaba and grapple for nets southward. Service and Homes had put in at Thompson Creek, on the northeast extreme of the Garden Peninsula, and were running south checking out some of the shoals and bays along the east coast. Homes told him sometimes the perch spawned on the east side, but most of the action was on the west. Because soft ice preceded ice-out and made it impossible to run their ice-netting operations, and because ice-out was late, the rats were almost into the legal fishing dates. This meant they had lost money because of the weather conditions and that, out of desperation to take fish before legal fishing began, they could be anywhere.

Service and Homes were in one of the captured boats, a sixteen-footer with a two-hundred-horsepower Mercury outboard. Homes had renamed the boat *Little Rat*. The other confiscated craft was a twenty-footer, also with a two-hundred-horse motor; it would launch today from the Fishdam site as *Fat Rat*.

Service and Homes were to patrol south past Point Detour, continue past Summer Island, and move north through the cut between Poverty and Little Summer. *Fat Rat* was coming south from the Fishdam, and the two DNR Glastrons would be coming over from Ogontz. The PB-4 would come east from Escanaba.

They would all rendezvous mid-afternoon off Sac Bay, where Stone planned to grapple for nets. Attalienti and three other patrol cars were on the peninsula to provide land cover. Service had to admit that this patrol seemed more organized, with more resources and force committed than he had seen previously. A state trooper was parked at the Port Bar acting as a visible deterrent, and Service guessed that the information he had brought out was being used by Attalienti in planning Garden operations. Joe Flap would be overhead all afternoon and into the early evening.

Homes piloted the *Little Rat* like A.J. Foyt, putting the stripped-down sixteen-footer on the plane and running it wide open, throwing up a ten-foot roostertail as they raced southward, the hull slamming against the waves. Service had never been particularly comfortable in boats, and thought about telling Homes they were wasting fuel as a way of slowing him down, but they had two extra tanks of fuel on board. He clutched his seat, let the spray sting his face, kept his mouth shut, and endured.

|||||||||||||||||||||

They ran around the south shore of Summer Island and turned north. Homes finally slowed down to creep their way through the shoals that stuck up in places like a broken atoll. When they reached Sac Bay, they found the PB-4 thirty yards off the ice-packed shore. Someone was in the fourteen-foot aluminum deck boat, close to shore, throwing the grapple rope and dragging it across the bottom, hoping to snag illegal nets—either those that had sunk when the ice went out, or new ones they had just set by boat.

Homes eased the *Little Rat* alongside the PB-4, pulled the throttle to idle, and had Service toss out the sea anchor. There was a slight breeze and a small chop. Stone leaned over the rail of the PB-4. "Dere's a heap a' perch up to Ansels Point," he told them as they bobbed beside the mother ship.

"Nets in the water there?" Homes asked.

"Haven't checked," Stone said. "Buncha fish on gravel next ta shore down here, so dey'll be against shore all da way up to da Chicken Farm. Da rats know our schedule 'cause I been keepin' us pretty regular since we took dose two boats. Dey got somebody on shore watchin' us right now, and dey know how long our shifts been runnin'. Pretty soon dere gonna come out wit' dere short nets and see what dey can grab. Youse boys run up between Stoney Point and Ansels and anchor up. We'll give youse a bump on da radio when we start for home, but we'll anchor between Round Island and Chippewa Point and see what happens. Da rats only got a week till dey can net legally, and da dirty ones will want to get into da fish before dat." Stone looked down at Service from the larger boat and winked. "Since Feb-u-ary da rats been real nervous. Somepin' musta shook 'em up good."

"Bingo!" the man in the deck boat yelled. "Not marked," he added, as he began to pull the net hand over hand toward his boat. Stone flung his grapple into the water and began hauling to see if there were nets closer to the big boat. Service saw Ed Moody working the front of the PB-4, and waved as Homes ordered the sea anchor up. When Service hauled it into the boat, they blasted off northward.

||||||||||||||||||||||

They were anchored about halfway between Stoney and Ansels Points, bobbing in three-foot chop, the wind picking up from the north. The sky was overcast, no moon, no stars. The PB-4 had reported leaving its station, and since then, the radio had been silent.

Service and Homes ate ham and cheese sandwiches and drank coffee as they waited. It seemed to Service that as a conservation officer, he was always waiting.

"Who was working with Moody and Stone?" Service asked.

"Name's Moomaw, from downstate. Len's runnin' guys up here from all over, givin' 'em a week ta ten days in da Garden and shipping 'em home. Da more guys we give experience up here, da more support we'll have around da state. You fucking anybody dese days?"

"Just your wife," Service said.

Homes laughed out loud. "She's more fun den my mum, eh!"

"What's a short net?" Service asked.

"Hundred, two hundred feet with small mesh. Easier ta trow and recover den da longer gangs, best for shallow water work. We're gonna sit here and wait. Eleven or so, we'll start putt-putting toward Ansels, see what we can see. Want a candy bar?" Homes held it out. "Keep da energy up out here, eh."

Service chewed mechanically, not paying attention to the taste or the sugar.

"Da rats will run dark," Homes said, "but sometimes dey need to flip on dere flashlights ta handle dere nets. We'll look for dat, an' if we see anyting, we'll charge dere sorry asses."

"Without lights?"

"Just like on land. We want ta surprise da bastards."

"What about support?" Service wanted to know.

"Da rats will try to run ta Garden, I'm thinking. Attalienti and da boys will be land-side, strung out along da coast. Got three trucks ready to head south to where we need 'em, and Troops on standby in da wings. Attalienti says he has a pretty good idea where ta find and intercept da rats. How he knows, I don't know, and I ain't askin'. Our job is ta cut da rats off from Garden and hope dey run north. If dey do, dis time we got da boats dat can keep up; dis time, we got darkness and speed on our side. *Fat Rat* will wait out near Ogontz, and the PB-4 and the Glastrons will be south of us, so we'll have plenty of backup, just not close. Don't worry," Homes said.

"What's the Chicken Farm?" Service asked. Attalienti was definitely using his information, and it was filtering down to the officers.

"Dis Twenty Questions? It's a shoal north of Kates Bay. My wife any good?" he added with a chuckle.

"Below average," Service said.

"Man," Homes said, and guffawed. "You *have* been wit' her!"

The wind continued to rise, and with it came increased wave action. By ten the waves were regularly at five feet, some higher, and their anchor had come loose. They had drifted before Homes started the engine and began burrowing slowly over the peaks, the motor gurgling and chortling like an emphysemic gasping for air.

Service sat just in front of Homes with his binoculars sweeping the horizon ahead of them. It was almost too rough to see. A couple of times he had to grab hold to avoid being bucked out of the boat. Going overboard, he decided, could be lethal if help wasn't close by.

It was almost eleven when Homes tapped him on the shoulder. "We're about a mile out." Service felt Homes's binoculars over his right shoulder.

The engine shut off suddenly.

"What?" Service asked.

"North wind reduces wave action along da shore. Let's try ta listen for a while."

Service thought he heard something.

"What is it?" Homes asked.

"Sounded like metal against metal."

"Where?"

Service pointed a little left of their bow.

"Dat's Ansels," Homes said. A minute went by. "Okay, I heard it too. Dey tink dey're safe, making so much noise. Dey tink we all went home . . . dis will be *fun!*"

Fun wasn't the word Service had in mind, but Homes seemed to relish any action that entailed risk.

"Scalded dog!" Homes said before Service could ask what was next. "I'm gonna run full out. You keep your glasses ahead. When we have visual, I'll turn on da lights and da yelper."

The engine went from a growl to a high-pitched whine, the nose popped up, they bounced over a few waves, and began skimming the tops like a skipped rock, wave tops continuing to hammer the metal hull. Service checked his flashlight to make sure it was tethered to his life preserver. Likewise, he had attached a lanyard from his PFD to the trigger guard of his revolver. He wished there was more light and less wind.

Service tried to concentrate on the view through his binoculars, but the ride was too rough, the spray blasting from the bow. Even so, he thought he detected a blink of a light.

"There," he called to Homes, "a light."

Homes leaned forward. "Where?"

"Ten o'clock."

"Yes," Homes shouted. "I see the motherfuckers!"

The blue light began to rotate and the yelper began its eerie warble as they raced toward the target.

"Hundred yards," Homes yelled at Service. "I'm gonna put us alongside. You jump over an' shut dere motor off!"

The other craft was less than fifty yards away when Service saw light-colored froth erupt behind it.

Homes yelled, "Dey're runnin'!" Service thought he sounded almost happy about the prospect.

"Make sure you get dere bloody motor shut off!" Homes repeated as the quarry began to flee, holding the interval between them. Service knew his job was critical, that both men would board to make the arrest and prevent evidence from being cast over the sides.

Homes seemed to find more power, and as the distance closed, the other boat immediately began a series of abrupt right and left turns. No matter what they tried, Homes stayed with them. He seemed to anticipate each maneuver and they were closing steadily. Service saw piles of shore ice passing precariously close, and hoped Homes was paying attention.

Amazingly, the other boat seemed to gain some space with a double left turn when Homes was cutting right, and when they turned back, the other boat was moving away. Homes soon had them closing, and instead of north, the other boat was running due west into the main bay.

Service felt a sense of foreboding. Homes made it seem like the rats would throw up their hands, or if forced to run, try for the north. So far they hadn't done anything Homes had predicted. Not a good sign, he told himself, but Homes had gained on the other craft and was almost beside it now.

"Ready?" Homes called out.

Service moved forward to the bow in a low crouch, braced himself, put a foot on the gunwale and waited, his heart pounding. Stepping out of an airplane was a lot easier than this shit.

The distance between the two craft decreased steadily, and whenever the quarry tried to turn, Homes was ahead of their moves and drawing ever closer—like he had radar, or a sixth sense. Finally, they were within six feet, and Homes cut sharply into the other craft and grazed it gently. Service saw a man in dark oilers standing there, and aiming at the figure, he launched himself over the side into the other boat.

As his feet hit the deck, something struck him on the forehead, and he found himself on his knees. He tried to get up, propping a leg against a gunwale, but another blow came, this time to the back of his head. He had the sudden impression of time suspended, and of levitating before smacking the water face-first, and skipping before sinking and bobbing quickly back to the surface, gasping for air like he was at death's door, so focused on the cold and getting air that he had no idea where the boats had gone.

Fucked was the first word that came into his mind. Then, calm down, assess the problem, focus on what you have, not on what you don't have. He had his light and his pistol. Marine flares? No flares! Why didn't they issue marine flares? *Focus on what you've got,* his mind repeated. Thoughts coming in clusters, no order. Water temperature: What was the water temperature? He had taken a reading near Sac Bay. Thirty-eight there, or forty-eight? No, take the worst case. Warmer out here? No, assume same. Worst case. *Don't fight,* his mind said. Don't struggle. You're in the water and you can't change that. Conserve heat. You're in good shape, adapted to the cold, perhaps more this year than at any other time in your life. Big bodies cool slower than small bodies. Fifteen to thirty minutes before the lights go out, he told himself. *Stay alive.*

He pulled himself into a cannonball position, which lifted his head up enough so he could see, but the waves immediately pushed his face under and he had to go through the contortion again, trying to make his body as tight as he could to reduce exertion and keep heat in. Slow down, relax; don't swim—float! He eventually learned to take a breath before the waves dumped him, even to look around. No sound of the boats, no lights. All alone. *Fucking rats!* he thought. He needed to see a light, any light. Why the hell were game wardens boarding boats like pirates? This was the sort of shit frustration caused.

No idea how much time had passed. Too much? No, still alive. Too cold to be dead yet. He had heard an instructor in winter survival training say, "You're not dead until you're warm and dead." Where the hell was Homes? Body cold, but no shivering yet. That's good. Glass half full. He had wool under nylon, under an insulated jumpsuit. Thank God for wool. Not great for swimming, but he wasn't swimming tonight, just floating, trying to take one breath at a time, and not going anywhere except where the wind wanted him to go. *Don't think,* he warned himself, *Stay calm—no matter what.* Taste in his mouth: Salt. Blood? Forget it. The only sharks out here were in boats.

At some point he heard a sound, or imagined it. He uncurled his body and fumbled to get his finger into the trigger guard of the revolver, which was attached to his preserver by a lanyard. Stay calm, control breathing. Okay, finger set. He closed his eyes, tried to substitute hearing for sight. The crests of the waves seemed higher than five feet now. Eyes closed. There, yes. Sound for sure. A motor running hard. He lifted his arm as high as he could, fired a round, found himself temporarily blinded by the intensity of the muzzle flash. Had anyone ever calculated the candlepower of that? *Stay in the fucking game,* his old man's voice, the familiar refrain no matter what was happening. More sound. He lifted his arm, fired two rounds in succession; he ignored the muzzle flashes this time, his ears ringing. He hoped the rounds would land on some rat's head. Then: Wait, don't fire again too soon. How many shots left? Not counting, not paying attention. *Dummy!* No, wrong attitude. Okay, no problem. Not like he was going to reload out here. He laughed out loud, closed his eyes. Yes, a motor drawing toward him; he lifted his arm, fired another round, got dunked by a huge wave, came up coughing and choking on water. Christ, his lungs were going to fill with ice. How many rounds left? Never mind. Save it until nothing left. Under the water again, choking more, he bobbed to the surface and said out loud, "This ain't good."

A female voice: "If I was Florence Nightingale I'd strip and get under da blankets wit' youse."

"Is this a topless beach?" he asked, no idea why. He felt pressure near his rectum. "What's that?"

"We need your body temperature."

"Ninety-eight point six is normal," he said.

"You're not normal," the voice said.

"That smarts."

"Truth always does," the voice said. "Haven't lost the sense of humor, eh?"

"Damn," he said, flinching at the feel of the thermometer.

"I used Vaseline," the voice said.

"It feels like a baseball bat."

"I didn't feel a thing," the nurse said. "Everything's a little constricted," she said. "Ninety-four point eight. It's coming up."

"It?" he asked.

"You're not *that* warm yet," she quipped.

"That's not what the mermaid said."

"Mermaid?"

"Can modern science measure the buoyancy of breasts?" he asked.

"Say again?"

"Never mind. You wouldn't understand." Neither did he. His mouth was launching words unvetted by his mind. He felt heat on his forehead and neck.

"Drink," the voice said. "Tea and sugar."

"No candy," he said. "Bad luck."

"Tea," she said, trying to reassure him. "Tepid, not hot."

He sipped and spit it out.

"Too hot?" she sounded concerned.

"My lips don't work so good."

"Try again?" she asked softly.

"Okay."

This time he got it down. "Where am I?"

"Hospital," the voice said. "Escanaba."

"Where's Homes?"

"Right here, partner."

"I'm sorry about your wife."

Homes laughed. "She isn't."

"Rats?"

"I finally got control of da assholes, called for emergency help, turned da boat around, an' come looking for youse. Len had an ambulance waiting for us at Ogontz, and da county was dere to transport da prisoners. Da *Little Rat* drifted away and got lost. The Glastrons went ta search for it."

Service said, "Another drink?"

The nurse said, "You want to try to hold the cup?"

"Okay."

She helped prop him up against his pillow and put the cup in his hands.

"You're not so blue anymore."

"That's good, right?"

"That's very good."

"Did I pass out?"

"I don't know," Homes said, "but you looked *dead,* man. We got you on da deck and you started babbling some weird shit about mermaids wit' big tits."

"Can we talk about this later?" Service said, turning away from Homes.

The man in the white lab coat was short with a prominent nose, a perpetual smile, and dark hair combed back. "You Otter?"

"Service, not Otter."

"Sorry, your guys called you Otter. Cop humor, I guess. You'd think I'd learn. I'm a doctor."

Service let his eyes scan the room. Light was seeping through the shades.

"Warm enough?" the doctor asked.

"Head hurts."

"It should. I put six stitches in your forehead, eleven in back."

"Tasted salt."

"From the cuts. You're either damn lucky or Superman."

"Sir?"

"You've got a concussion, not a mild one, and you could use a neurologist, but we don't have one in town. I'm an internist. Your brain's internal, right, so that makes it my territory. You feel dizzy, nauseous?"

"Just sore, thirsty."

"We've got you on an IV for fluids. Body temp's normal now. You were in the water almost an hour. Most people wouldn't have lasted nearly that long. I'm not sure why you did."

"How long have I been here?"

The man looked at his watch. "About twelve hours. We're gonna keep you tonight, release you tomorrow if everything goes okay."

"Can I get up, walk around?"

"Later, maybe. There's a buzzer by your right hand. Use it if you need anything or feel dizzy. By the way, I'm Vince Vilardo."

"Grady."

"Not Otter."

"Not Otter—Grady Service," Service repeated. "Did we get the rats?"

"Rats?" the doctor named Vince said. "Don't worry about that. Right now you're gonna go to sleep."

"How can you know that?"

Vince smiled and held up a syringe. "I'm your doctor."

"You really ought to clean up the place. It gives the Garden a bad name."

Service peered into the room where Moe Lapalme sat with two black eyes and a bandage across his nose. Learning that it had been Lapalme in the boat had not been surprising. Moe might not be one of the leaders in the Garden, but he was in the thick of it. During his two-week recon he had not encountered Lapalme until he saw him with a rifle at Middle Bluff. Where had he been before that?

Colt Homes stood next to Service. "He's da one."

"Never know it by me," Service said. "All I saw were dark oilers. Too dark and too fast to see a face. Did he look like that when I left the boat?"

"It was kinda close quarters," Homes said sheepishly. "I went over right behind you and jumped da driver. Dere was some wrestling, and when I got 'em settled down, you were gone, and I about shit my pants. Neither of da bastards wanted ta turn da boat around."

Homes explained that he had threatened to shoot both men if they didn't calm down and do what he ordered. The scuffle in the boat had taken them way off course, and by the time Homes got the situation under control, he had no idea where Service was. Only the sound and muzzle flashes of his revolver had enabled them to find him and fish him out. "By den," Homes said, "I was wondering if we had a funeral on our hands. Lapalme thought da whole thing was kinda funny."

"Not now, I'd guess."

"It was close," Homes said seriously. "*Too* bloody close."

"We get their nets?"

"Yesterday morning. Unmarked, but in da area where you dropped the buoy. Found da *Little Rat* south of da Stonington. Joe Flap spotted it from above."

"Lapalme, of course, knows nothing about the nets."

"Never seen 'em before. Dey was just out for a boat ride when we come roarin' up on 'em and scared 'em, which was why dey bolted."

"Blood tests?"

"Both blotto and change," Homes said.

Meaning they had been over the blood alcohol level for legally operating a vehicle—on land or water. "At least we have that."

"An' some blood on Lapalme's oilers. He denies touching you."

"Probably the truth. It felt like a club, not fists."

"Three-pound fish bat to be precise," Homes said. "Your blood type was on da bat and it matched da type on da oilers. Neither Lapalme, nor da other guy, have your blood type. 'Course, dey say it was a pal who cut himself earlier. Dey've been arraigned for attempted murder, assaulting police officers, resisting arrest, fleeing, fishing in a closed zone during a closed period, driving while intoxicated, and more charges are going ta be added. We got dere boat, dere's no registration, and da VIN is missing."

"Does Murray think he has a case?" Murray was Delta County's prosecuting attorney.

"He says it will come down to da jury."

"Same old story." Juries were notorious for siding with poachers and lawbreakers in the U.P. "Did Lapalme lawyer up?"

"Young worm outta Negaunee named Tavolacci. We've bumped heads wit' him in several counties. He's one of da first lawyers da bad guys call."

"Is he good enough to get them off?"

"Can't rule it out, but if Murray and his people get dere shit together, Tavolacci will plead it out. Dat okay by you?"

"No," Service said, "but it would take two rats out of the pack. I'd like to talk to Lapalme, alone."

"Bad idea."

"Colt."

"Okay, okay. We'd better let Tavolacci know. He'll go ballistic if he ain't at da party."

"It's not about the other night."

Homes cocked his head. "You want a tape recorder?"

"Yes, but if it's okay with you, I'll hang on to the tape." Homes shrugged and handed the device to him.

"You know," Service said, pausing near the door to the room, "I never saw his face. I was in the water almoast immediately." He didn't tell Homes he had previously seen Lapalme in the Garden.

"Don't worry," Homes said. "I told you I jumped da other guy."

"Who is he?"

"Duperow."

"Regular rat?" This was a new name to Service.

"Fringe type—sort of an apprentice," Homes said with a grin.

"He wasn't on the fringe the other night."

"As he is now so painfully aware," Homes said. "If he decides ta get his own lawyer, he'll turn on Moe. You sure you don't want me ta sit in wit' you?"

"Thanks, I'll be fine."

"Da yak-shack's all yours."

"Yak-shack?"

Homes pointed, enunciated, "Interview room."

Lapalme sat across the table from Service.

"I guess we both had a rough night," Service said.

"I never touched you, man."

"You know me?"

"Seen you around."

"Really?" Service said. "Where?"

"How I'm supposed to remember. Your face looks familiar."

"How do you know I'm the one who got thrown out of the boat?"

Lapalme stared at him. "Because I helped fish your waterlogged ass out of the lake."

"Thanks," Service said. "I appreciate that."

Lapalme shrugged.

"Looks like you had some problems," Service said, nodding at the man's injuries.

"That fucking Homes," Lapalme said. "I tried to help Dupe and he beat the shit outta me."

"Homes jumped Duperow?"

Lapalme stared at the wall. "I want my lawyer."

"This isn't about the other night, Moe."

"No?"

"You know Anise Aucoin?"

Lapalme sneered. "That psycho bitch. What did she tell you?"

Service delayed answering, let silence eat at Lapalme's attempt at nonchalance. "What do you think she told me?"

"I—no! I want my lawyer."

"You've seen her since she got back," Service said, a statement rather than a question.

"I dropped that scag years ago, man."

"I don't believe you."

"What're you trying to pull, man?"

Service lit a cigarette and offered the pack to Lapalme. "I'm sure I saw you and her in your truck a couple of months back."

Lapalme leaned away from the table. "She told you that?"

"You're not listening, Moe. I said I *saw* you up on US Two by the Fishdam."

"You'da seen me that day, you'da come visiting," Lapalme said.

"Blue pickup, home just north of Garden. It looks like a junkyard, Moe. You really ought to clean up the place. It gives the Garden a bad name."

"What is this shit, man!"

"You were with her."

"Like I give a shit what you think."

"You like venison, Moe?"

Lapalme got up from the table and knocked over his chair. "You're as crazy as that cunt. I want my fucking lawyer!"

Homes was waiting outside the room. "What was all dat about?"

"Keeping my head in the game."

"You need ta call it a day, pal. Your concussion's showing."

"You're probably right." In fact, he had a headache that seemed to be getting worse rather than better. But he was sure now it had been Lapalme driving the truck with Aucoin as his passenger. Lapalme had slipped up and said "that day," as much as admitting he had made the drive-by at the Fishdam. He needed to talk to Lasurm's daughter, and he needed to talk to her without Hegstrom running interference. But before that, he knew he needed to go back to Show-Titties Pond. Hegstrom had asked some questions he couldn't answer, and before he went off on a tangent he wanted to know what Hegstrom thought he knew.

39

SLIPPERY CREEK, MAY 9–10, 1976

"You're a lout, Service!"

On the way back from the jail, Service stopped at the district office. Connie Leppo gave him a look. "Len said you're s'pposed ta be off for a few days."

"I'm working on it," he said on his way to the evidence locker, where he had left the two slugs recovered from the deer parts at the pond. It took thirty minutes to find the plastic bag with the slugs, and he cursed himself for not having a better memory.

On the drive home he found the afternoon light almost blinding; he put on his sunglasses, which helped, but his eyes continued to tear up and he felt a headache starting.

He had just walked into the Airstream when the trailer door burst open behind him.

"There you are, you scoundrel!"

Brigid Mehegen's diminutive grandfather stood in the doorway, his face flushed, brandishing a shotgun. He wore a pith helmet with a Civil Defense logo on the front. "You broke my grandbaby's heart!"

Service slapped the barrel of the shotgun aside and wrenched it away from the man. "Get out of my house." The ache in his head was sharper.

"This ain't no house. I gotta hurt you bad. It's the code."

Mehegen came in behind her grandfather, spun him around, and got in his face. "The same code says I fight my own fights," she growled.

"I'm upholding your honor," her grandfather said. "Not that you got all that much left."

Mehegen turned him around and ushered him out the door, slamming it behind him.

She looked at the cut on Service's head.

"Are you two a traveling tag team?" he asked.

"That's right: Make funny, Mr. Macho. Every cop in the U.P. is talking about your swim—*Otter*." She sat down at the table. "Don't mind that old man. The fact is, neither of you understand the concept of a fuck-buddy." She paused to let her words sink in. "There can't be any sex when the fuck-buddy disappears for a mysterious *and* undefined family emergency, and doesn't bother to call when he gets back to town. You're a lout, Service!"

Lout . . . scoundrel? He was being skewered with nineteenth-century vocabulary.

"I came here tonight to officially dissolve our fuck-buddyship," Mehegen said. "Do you care to offer a defense?"

"I forgot?" he said. His head was pounding now; he was cold again, and beginning to feel nauseous.

"That's it! You *forgot?* That does wonders for my ego!"

He waved his hand at her, felt the gorge rising in his throat.

"You're . . . *dismissing* me?"

"Unless you want—" He vomited on the floor and her boots and grabbed the edge of the table to maintain his balance.

"I'm getting help!" Mehegen said, her eyes wide.

He grabbed her wrist. "No."

She peeled his hand away and went outside. Moments later her grandfather came through the door. "He's a doctor," Mehegen announced.

"What kind?" Service mumbled.

"It matters, you puking all over?" the grandfather replied. "I was an OB/GYN before I retired."

Service vomited again and started to fall. His guests caught him and helped him back to the toilet.

He awoke in bed, his head still hurting, but the pain somewhat diminished. Mehegen's grandfather was standing by the bed.

"Feeling better?"

"I think I'm done throwing up."

"You got nothing left to expel but organs," the old man said. "You really let loose."

"You're actually a doctor?"

"Until liability and malpractice insurance got so bad it drove me out."

"High?"

"Probably more than you'll ever make in a year, but it wasn't just the money. I got tired of being sued, and my insurance company kept wanting to settle; and of course, my premiums kept going up," he explained. "I wasn't a bad doctor, or a perfect one. My problem was that I was the only OB/GYN for sixty miles, and I was outnumbered by lawyers. One day I just said to hell with it and moved up here. You've had a pretty good concussion. Did a neurologist look at you?"

"There wasn't one."

"That's the U.P. for you. When did you get the whacks on the head?"

"Two nights ago, more or less."

The retired doctor nodded ponderously. "Symptoms coming on this late aren't good. You need to get back to your doctor. He tell you it could take weeks for the symptoms to clear?"

Service tried to shake his head, but couldn't. "No." Actually, he had ignored what the doctor, Vince Vilardo, had told him. Ignored or forgotten. The way he had felt, either was possible.

Mehegen came into the room, kissed her grandfather's cheek, and after he was gone, sat on the end of the bed. "Cops are making a joke out of what you went through," she said. "I don't see the humor in it, and I'm spending the night right here."

Service started to protest but she held up her hand. "Tonight we'll focus on the buddy part. People with concussions are supposed to be watched," she said. "Why'd they let you out anyway?"

"Work," he said.

She rolled her eyes, growled "*Cops,*" and went to the front of the trailer, leaving him alone, but he followed her. "That night when you babysat Ivan Rhino, did he say anything when you were alone with him?"

She looked at him. "Not really."

"Nothing at all?"

"I can't believe you want to talk about *that!* He said two words: 'Right on.'"

"When was this?"

"You were inside with the deputies."

"Right on?"

"I thought his synapses were misfiring."

Maybe not, Service thought.

40

LITTLE LAKE, MAY 11, 1976

"He can smell a fart in a tornado."

Service stopped at the Escanaba district office, and Leppo immediately began to yip, "Outta here! Youse're s'pposed to be resting."

He opened the evidence locker and started searching for the slugs he had stored there. He gave up after an hour. He knew he'd put them there. Hadn't he?

Connie Leppo said, "I thought youse got what you needed from the evidence locker the other day?"

He had been here? Leppo held up an evidence custody form. It listed two rifle slugs, caliber unknown. He had signed for them May 9. *Shit,* he thought.

"Okay to use the phone?" he asked. Connie Leppo rolled her eyes and left her desk. He called the Marquette County sheriff's office and got the names of the two deputies who had responded to his call that night at STP. He left before Leppo could come back and scold him for being there. He sat in his Plymouth trying to recall picking up the evidence. He couldn't.

The deputies were Harry Wayne and Maurice Shelby. He called Wayne from a pay phone and asked if they could meet. Wayne agreed, and said he'd call Shelby.

It was fifty-three degrees, the snowpack melting quickly, leaving the side roads slippery with mud and slush on top and a substrate of holdover ice that had been packed down by vehicles over the long winter. He knew the warm-up wouldn't last. It would take heavy spring rains to really take the snow, and even then turquoise-blue ice patches would persist in the dark nooks of cedar roots until well into July. Fifties today, it could be below twenty tomorrow, but spring and summer were coming on.

The two deputies were waiting at Harry Wayne's small log house on Little Lake. There were patches of snow and ice stacked up on the south shore, opposite the cabin. The two men were in their late twenties, and both had been on the job for three years.

Wayne invited him in and offered him coffee. "She got a little wet down to the bay, eh?"

Service nodded. The deputy's comment was a way of acknowledging that a brother cop had gone over the edge and inexplicably come back. It wouldn't be mentioned again in his presence unless he brought it up, a subtle recognition that each officer who survived a close call needed to work out the aftermath in his own time and in his own way.

He got right to the point. "You guys up for a visit to STP?"

"Why?" Shelby asked immediately. "Any DNR violations were secondary to the felonies."

"I'm not questioning that," he said, "and I'm not trying to butt in. I just want to take a walk-through for a little peace of mind. It got pretty confusing that night."

The men looked at each other, and Wayne said, "What the hell."

"How's Eugene?" Service asked.

"They moved him from the hospital to lockup. They have him segregated."

"Because of a threat?"

"Because he's as simple as a brick. Even his lawyer's having a hard time understanding him."

"Did Hegstrom take him on?"

"Nope, just the girl. Chomsky and Rhino have their own court-appointeds. Rhino refused to share."

Service expected the camp road to be drifted over with snow and was surprised to see it freshly plowed.

There was a black New Yorker parked next to the camp building where the stabbing took place. Service pulled in behind the Chrysler and waited for the deputies to arrive. The Chrysler was sparkling by U.P. spring standards, almost no salt scabs or sand buildups on the bumpers.

The deputies picked their way through the mud to his patrol car. "When did the county release this place as a crime site?"

"Mid-April?" Shelby asked Wayne, who nodded in agreement. "Would have been earlier, but Hegstrom wanted to keep it roped off."

Why would Hegstrom want that? Service wondered.

Service knocked on the door and, after a long delay, an elderly man opened the door a crack and peered out. "I thought the police were done with this place."

"Mr. Agosti?" Service said.

"Who else would it be, more hoodlums?"

"I'm Conservation Officer Service," he said, turning to the other men. "Deputies Wayne and Shelby. We're sorry if we've interrupted you."

The man said, "What is it this time?"

"I beg your pardon," Service said. The old man was unexpectedly gruff.

"I wanted to come up in January before Angie and I left for Florida, but the detective said no. So I asked him to call me when the place was released and we headed on down to Florida. You think he'd have the courtesy to call? Not a chance. I had to call long-distance to find out. Angie and I worked hard for what we've got. We saved. We don't throw money around."

Talk about a non sequitur soliloquy, Service thought. No money to throw around? The man owned two camps on a nice piece of property, drove a nearly new automobile, and he and the wife spent at least part of the winter in Florida. "Did you build these places?" Service asked. There had been no camps in the area years ago when he'd been here.

"With my own two hands," the old man said.

"Can we come in?" Service asked.

"Why?" Agosti challenged. "So you can trash the camp again?"

Service glanced at Wayne, who arched an eyebrow. "Is this a bad time? Did we catch you on the way out?" Service asked.

"Just don't have time is all," Agosti said. "Come back tomorrow. I got things to do, and Angie's still in Florida."

"Did you drive up from Florida?" Deputy Wayne asked.

"Four days," the old man said, holding up three fingers. "Rain all the way."

Service looked back and saw Shelby peering into the vehicle and trying a door handle.

"What's all the stuff in the car?" Shelby yelled out as he walked toward the cabin.

"Stuff the wife wants," the old man said.

"For Florida?" Shelby asked.

"That's right, for Florida," the man said.

"Cross-country skis for Florida?" Shelby asked.

"'Course not; those I got to drop to my granddaughter in Chicago."

Deputy Shelby said, "Can you show us some ID, Mr. Agosti?"

"You guys come trash my camps and now I'm the criminal?"

The old man's reactions from the start had not been normal, Service told himself.

"Your car's locked," Shelby said.

"What, I'm supposed to leave it open? A body can't be too careful."

"Identification, sir?"

The old man opened the door slightly and patted at his trousers. "Guess I left it in the other room," he said and started to close the door, but Harry Wayne stuck his boot in to block it. Service heard the old man go scuttling away, moving with amazing alacrity.

They pushed the door open and went inside. "Some look-see this is," Shelby said. "Mr. Agosti?" he called out.

No answer.

Service wandered into the kitchen. It had not been cleaned up. As soon as it warmed up, the dried blood would attract flies and other insects. What was the old man doing here?

Shelby called out again. "Mr. Agosti?"

Wayne looked at Service. "He's gone."

"No way," Service said.

"Beam me up, Scotty?" Shelby said with a grin.

"He's here," Service said. "He was out of sight ten seconds max. He's not Houdini."

"Neither was Houdini," Shelby said.

"What?"

"Houdini's real name was Erik Weisz."

"Get serious," Service said, rolling his eyes.

"I am serious, that was his name," Shelby insisted.

"Let's open the Chrysler," Wayne said.

"You got a key?" Service wanted to know.

The deputies laughed.

"Illegal search," Service said.

Wayne said, "He couldn't or wouldn't identify himself. He's got to be a hundred and forty years old, and he's got cross-country skis and an uncased rifle in the backseat of his vehicle. Leave this to us, woods cop."

"You never said anything about a rifle," Service said.

"Up here everybody has a rifle."

"Uncased?"

"That too."

Service looked at Harry Wayne for support, but got none.

"There's a *Milwaukee Journal* on the front seat," Shelby said.

"You can buy them at Benny's in Gladstone," Service said. "Daily. Sometimes I even buy one."

"Game wardens can read?" Shelby asked.

"No jokes, guys. Something stinks here."

"We should call Sniffer," Harry Wayne said to Shelby.

"Who?" Service wanted to know.

Harry Wayne said, "Kharlamov. He's our new guy. He moved up from Pontiac. He was a tunnel rat in Vietnam. He can smell a fart in a tornado."

"He claims," Shelby added.

"We'll give him a test," Wayne said.

The banter of the two deputies was beginning to annoy him. "Call him," Service said, sitting down at the dining room table and rubbing his head. It was beginning to ache again. *Where the hell had the old man disappeared to?*

He was dozing when he sensed someone nearby, and awoke to find a craggy-faced man with a shaved head. "You're Service?" the stranger whispered. "Marines, right?"

Service nodded.

The man said, "I heard. I'm Alex Kharlamov, Highlands, K-nine and tunnels."

Kharlamov was short with powerful shoulders and a thick neck. "Where're the guys?"

"I told them to stay outside. They talk too much. Laurel and Hardy told me what happened," Kharlamov said. "There's got to be a hidey-hole."

Service was impressed with the new man's presence. He spoke so softly, his words barely above a whisper. "Did you search?" the new deputy asked.

"Not really."

"Good," the man said. "Ten seconds was the lag time?"

"About."

Kharlamov sat down Indian-style on the floor. "You fish for trout?"

"When I get the chance." Which had not been often enough.

Kharlamov smiled. "I came up here for the trout. Fewer, smaller fish mean fewer people. I like to fish alone."

"You've come to the right place," Service said.

"Could afford it, I'd be a hermit," the man said. "You fish hatches or attractors?"

"Whatever it takes."

"Me, I'm a hatch man. It's like surveillance. Sometimes conditions seem right and the bugs don't show. The key is to be in the right place at the right time, and to wait. Most people aren't patient enough." Kharlamov looked over at Service. "We're gonna have a hatch here."

"You get that from tea leaves or chicken guts?" Service asked.

Kharlamov smiled. "There's a vent grate in the roof overhang. Is there a basement?"

"Not that we could see. Foundation's poured, but it looks like a slab. The furnace is in a closet off the kitchen."

"Crawl space in the ceiling," Kharlamov said, "too shallow for an attic, and the grate's too large for the overhang. When you're sight-fishing, what do you look for?"

"Shadows first, parts of a fish next—never the whole thing."

The deputy grunted softly, slid a metal flask out of his jacket pocket, and held it out to Service. "Pepper vodka?"

Service took the flask. It was inscribed with the words standard bet in an ornate script. He took a drink and handed it back. "Special meaning?"

"Not anymore," Kharlamov said. "You're the one took the swim in the big water?"

"Yeah."

Service got up and watched Wayne and Shelby start their vehicles and drive away. He had no idea where Kharlamov had parked. Only the Chrysler remained by the cabin.

No more words were spoken for more than two hours. Kharlamov sat with his hand flat against the drywall, his eyes staring into a void.

Just over two hours after the other deputies drove away, Kharlamov raised his hand and showed one finger, then two, nodding to make sure Service had seen.

Service was behind the deputy, who had edged to the door of the bedroom where the stabbing had taken place. Service saw the barrel of a revolver poke into view and just as quickly, Kharlamov had the weapon in hand and the old man pinned by the throat against the wall, his face turning red and eyes bulging.

Another figure came darting into the room, not looking left or right. Service shouted, "Police—*freeze!*" but the figure kept going through the front door. He followed to find Deputy Shelby on top of a struggling figure in the snow and mud. The deputies had dumped the vehicle and come back on foot to wait outside.

They checked the two for identification. The old man had no wallet. The other prisoner was a young girl, twelve or thirteen, and she stared at them with hatred, refusing to talk. Shelby read them their rights, cuffed them, and put them in the back of Kharlamov's patrol car, which Harry Wayne brought up to the cabin.

Wayne stayed in the vehicle with the prisoners and radioed his sergeant.

Service went back into the cabin and found Kharlamov in the bedroom the two had bolted from. The floor in the closet was propped open. The deputy handed him a flashlight and motioned for him to climb down.

There was a sturdy ladder down to a landing and another ladder going straight up. Three wooden steps led down into a cellar, which was cold. Service shone the light around, saw rifles and clothes and chain saws and tools. "Looks like Laurel and Hardy missed the jackpot last time they were here," Kharlamov said, a simple statement, no sarcasm.

Service found it difficult to focus his thoughts, and when he finally managed to corral them, they were not on the mysterious goods, but on the trapdoor into the bedroom, Hegstrom's questions, and Gumby's blathering about "him-her."

41

MARQUETTE, MAY 13, 1976

"If not the girl, who?"

Joe Flap agreed to let Service have his place in Trenary for the night, and a quick telephone call to Nikki-Jo Jokola secured her agreement to place another ad in the Manistique paper. He promised Nikki-Jo this would be the last one.

Acting captain Dean Attalienti looked frazzled as Service stood in his doorway, waiting to be waved in. "You are supposed to be recuperating," Attalienti said.

"I am."

"We had another incident last night—three shots fired at the PB-4 off Garden. One of the rounds went through the cabin and missed Len by a couple of feet. He got out of rifle range, and two of our patrol units went through the village and came up empty-handed. This thing just keeps going on and on," the acting captain lamented. "What do you want?"

"The rifle from Middle Bluff."

"For what?"

"Ballistic tests." *If* he could find the missing slugs.

Attalienti looked exasperated. "It was never fired at us."

That day. "Different case, sir."

The regional law boss said, "Don't patronize me. It's in the evidence locker. Sign a chain-of-custody form and leave it with Fern. You're resting, right?"

"Yessir."

He still had not located the slugs, but he delivered the rifle to the state police lab in Negaunee. The intake tech stared at him. "What're we supposed to compare?"

"I'm working on that," Service said, feeling like a fool.

Service got to the Marquette County Jail around 12:30 P.M.

Eugene Chomsky's lawyer had a new briefcase and a stiffness that suggested she was either new on the job, or not happy about this assignment. She didn't smile when Marquette County Detective Kobera and Service walked into the interview room.

"Emily Linton," Kobera said. "Grady Service, DNR."

Service looked at a grinning Eugene Chomsky. "Hey, Grady!"

"Hey, Gumby."

"Hey, Grady," the boy repeated.

"My client has nothing to say," Linton said officiously.

"Relax, Counselor. This won't hurt your client," Service said.

"Sidebar outside the room," Linton said.

"We're not in a courtroom," Kobera told her. "Chill out, Emily."

Chomsky stared at Service. "Where badge?"

"On my uniform," Service said.

"Like badge," Chomsky said.

Service glanced at Kobera. "Do you think we could get a badge for Gumby?"

"You bet," the detective said, leaving the room.

"How are you feeling, Gumby?"

"Okay."

"Have you seen Ivan?"

"Got my own place," the boy said proudly.

"This is ludicrous," Emily Linton said. "The boy can't comprehend *any* of this."

"*Grady,*" Chomsky told her, pointing at Service. "Grady nice."

Service ignored her. "Can you help me with something, Gumby?"

"Okay."

"Stand up."

"Eugene, remain where you are," Linton ordered. To Service: "What do you think you're doing?"

"Not *Eugene,*" the boy said. "Gumby." He stood up. His lawyer looked at the ceiling in exasperation.

Kobera came back into the room and stood next to Linton.

Service positioned the boy near the end of the table on the side opposite the door into the room. "You like to play pretend, Gumby?"

The boy grinned. "Uh-huh."

"Can we pretend the table is a bed and you're at the door of the bedroom? You remember that night, right? Remember, you stepped inside to turn on the lights?"

"No," the boy said with a tight jaw.

"You don't remember?"

"Door there," the boy said, pointing at the other side of the room.

Service smiled. "Right you are." The boy remembered. He looked at Kobera as he walked the boy to the other end of the room. "The table's the pretend bed, okay?"

"Okay."

"You went into the bedroom to turn on the light."

"Uh-huh."

"Okay, this is just pretend. I want you to step into the room like you did that night, okay?"

The boy sucked in a deep breath. "Okay," he said, stepping forward and turning to the right.

"Where's the light switch, Gumby?"

The boy put his arm out. "Pretend?"

"Right, pretend. Show me where it is."

"There," the boy said, pointing to his right.

"Good," Service said. "That's good. Now I want you to pretend to turn on the light and say 'ouch' when you get pretend-stabbed."

"I won't stand for this," Linton said, trying to rise.

Kobera kept her pinned in her seat with his hand on her shoulder.

"Pretend, right?" the boy asked Service, concern on his face.

"Pretend. Nobody will hurt you. Turn on the light."

The boy took a half-step right, reached out with his right hand, made a small downward motion, turned to his left and said, "Ouch." There was no emotion in his voice.

Service sat on the table and asked Kobera to stand to the boy's right. Service pushed himself back on the table. "This is about where she was," he said. "Kneel," he told the detective.

Kobera nodded, got down on his knees, and made a couple of swipes with his arm, like he was stabbing at someone.

"Good," Service said. "Let's do it again, and let Jimmy pretend too."

"Jimmy," the boy said. "Okay. Him there," he added, looking down at Kobera.

"Detective Kobera is helping us. He wants to play pretend."

"Not him-her, him-*Cap'n,*" Chomsky said.

"Jimmy won't hurt you." Service held out his hand and Kobera tossed the badge to him. Service pinned it on the boy's shirt and the boy stared down at it, beaming with pride. *Him-Cap'n*? They were close to something, he could feel it. But what? The boy had something firmly in his mind, but how could he get it out of him?

"Badge."

"Gumby?"

"Yeah."

"Pretend one more time?"

"Okay."

They went through it again, and his lawyer declared, "That's enough, Eugene!"

Chomsky glared at her and said defiantly, "*Gumby!*" He tapped his chest. "Badge."

Linton's head dropped.

"Thanks, Gumby. You did great," Kobera said.

Service patted the boy's massive shoulders. "You see where we are?" he asked Kobera.

"If this reenactment is even halfway close, there's no way Anise Aucoin stabbed him."

"Do I get an explanation?" Linton asked.

"When we have one, Counselor," Detective Kobera said.

"Badge mine?" Gumby interrupted.

"Yes, you earned it," Kobera told the boy. "Thanks."

"Let's talk to the surgeon who patched him up," Service said when they were outside the room.

"I've got all the medical reports."

"I want to hear the words come out of his mouth."

The surgeon met them in the doctor's lounge and immediately lit a cigarette. There was dried blood on his scrubs and his hair was greasy. "Jimmy," the doctor said.

Kobera said, "Dr. Guild, Grady Service of the DNR."

"It's Fred," the doctor said, shaking hands. "What can I do you guys for?"

The man had a powerful grip. Service reminded him of the case.

"I remember," the surgeon said. "It's all in the medical records."

"I just wanted to hear it from you."

"Sure. The stab wounds were upward and from the boy's right."

"Based on?"

"My eyes and ten years in Detroit Receiving Emergency. They like blades down there almost as much as guns."

"Why didn't the blade hit something vital?" Service asked.

"The third wound was more parallel than the other two. It was still slightly upward, but basically parallel. Up a little bit more and the kid would have had serious problems."

"Parallel to the floor?" Service asked.

"Or the ceiling—take your pick."

Service got down on his knees and feigned two quick thrusts into Kobera's buttocks; then he extended slightly upward and struck again.

Dr. Guild said, "I think that looks pretty close to what happened. The third blow was meant to go deep. The assailant probably lifted a little to get additional leverage."

They thanked the surgeon and walked outside. "You got somebody in mind?" Kobera asked.

"You agree it couldn't have been Aucoin?"

"Theoretically. The assailant was in the closet. If not the girl, who?"

"I'm working on that," he said.

"You going to tell Hegstrom?" Kobera asked.

"In time," Service said. *Where the hell had he put the damn rifle slugs?*

42

TRENARY, MAY 16, 1976

"Who's the 'Cap'n'?"

Joe Flap had vacated his house for the night to visit a friend in Ishpeming.

Cecilia Lasurm arrived around 8 P.M. and stood in the dining room, shaking her rain hat like a wet dog. "U.P. weather," she said.

"It rains everywhere," he reminded her.

"Not in the Gobi Desert," she said, tilting her head back to kiss him. "I was beginning to think our time had passed," she said, hugging him gently, and after they lingered in the embrace, she turned away and sat down at the dining room table. "You pushed it too close out there on the lake," she said.

"Thanks to Moe," he said.

"Word is he never touched you."

"Not with his hands. He tried to give me the last rites with a weighted priest."

Lasurm's eyes were locked on him. "That's Moe. I've been visiting Anise," she added. "I do most of the talking. Near as I can tell, she's been on junk since she left."

"How're you?" he asked.

"My diagnosis is the kind that doesn't change. I'm coping."

"Anise didn't stab the boy that night," he said. "I think I have proof."

"Actual evidence?" Her eyes were intense.

"The detective on the case buys it," he told her.

"She refuses to talk about it," Lasurm said. "Odd had a psychologist talk to her. He thinks she was too high to remember any of it."

Service remembered the blank look on the girl's face that night. "Maybe she will now."

"Have you told Odd?" Lasurm asked.

"Not yet. We know Eugene didn't stab himself. We know Ivan Rhino was in custody in the patrol car at the time, and we're pretty sure Anise didn't do it. All we know for certain is that the boy got stabbed."

"You're not boosting my confidence," she said. "Nobody else was there."

"Who's the 'Cap'n'?" he asked. Gumby and Ivan Rhino had been involved with Anise Aucoin, who was a Garden woman, and Gumby was now talking about "him-Cap'n." It was a stretch, Service knew, but maybe there was another Garden link—and who would know better than Cecilia?

Lasurm lowered her eyes. "The army ranger captain or the fishing boat captain?"

"There's two of them?" *Shit,* he thought.

"Just one. For a while he claimed he served as a ranger in Vietnam, but I knew he was a cook with a habit and he never made it to Vietnam. They booted him out on a general discharge."

"A step above dishonorable," the said.

"I suppose," she said. "When he got into fishing with the rats, he insisted whoever worked with him address him as captain. It's Moe," she said. "Moe is the Cap'n."

"Moe Lapalme?" Service said.

"Moe Lapalme," she echoed. "What's Moe got to do with this?"

"Everything," Service said. If he could find the damn slugs and get a match.

43

MOSQUITO WILDERNESS, MAY 17, 1976

"Aren't we a little young for brain farts?"

It was cold again, in the mid-forties and raining, and Service spent the day looking for trout fishermen, but few were out. Most native trout-chasers preferred live bait or spinners, and wouldn't get serious about their fishing until after July 4 when the rivers would be down and clear again.

John Voelker, the former state supreme court judge turned writer, was a legend in the fly-fishing community, but locals thought of him as eccentric and still clung to their old ways. Too bad for them. Just after noon there was a two-hour hatch of dark Hendricksons over a riffle in the Mosquito, and just downstream in a long run the surface was alive with feeding fish catching emergers and cripples. On the walk back to his vehicle he saw a sow bear and three cubs. She woofed and sent them up a tree before loping away. He knew she would be close and watching him, but it just proved that not every mother bear turned psycho when people came near her cubs.

He was still taking heavy doses of ibuprofen, and the headaches were finally more or less under control. The bug hatch had gotten him in the mood to fish, but the fly rod he usually kept in the trunk of the Plymouth Fury wasn't there. His memory was just not working. This morning he could not find his boots, and was forced to wear the old pair that pinched his feet. He already felt a blister building on one of his heels, and told himself it was his own damn fault.

There were two worm-dunkers working Lilah Creek just north of the wilderness. Service watched them while Hendricksons came off, the men oblivious to the hatch and rising fish. Once people got locked into a method, they were blind to other possibilities. Everyone had blind spots. He wondered how many he had.

Service knocked off at five. The fishermen could have the rivers tonight. His feet hurt, and the missing slugs were still eating at him.

Mehegen's truck was parked by the Airstream and she was sitting on his stoop. She wore boots, tight jeans, a hooded gray sweatshirt, and a faded Detroit Tigers ball cap.

"Hey sailor, buy a girl a beer?" Her grin disappeared as he approached. "You don't look well at all."

"I'm better," he said.

"Than what?"

He opened the door and let her in. "Couple of beers in the fridge," he told her. He sat down and took off his old boots and peeled down one sock. There was a puffy redness the size of a dime on his heel, a blister for sure.

"Grady?" Mehegen said. She was holding the fridge door open, looking inside. "What's this all about?"

She pulled out his boots and held them up. She was smiling.

"Is there also an evidence bag in there?" he asked, joking.

She leaned over, looked around, and pulled out a plastic bag. It dangled from her hand. "Aren't we a little young for brain farts?"

4 4

BOAT-EATER SHOALS, MAY 19, 1976

"You ready ta get your feet wet again?"

Sergeant Blake Garwood was silent as he steered the twenty-foot *Fat Rat* out of Gladstone, across from Squaw Point marine navigation light, and headed south toward Little Bay de Noc. Grady Service adjusted the straps on his life preserver and grimaced in the icy mist. Yesterday he had taken the slugs up to the state police lab in Negaunee, and met with Detective Kobera to share his thinking—that Moe Lapalme had been in the room with Anise Aucoin and was the one who stabbed Gumby. If the slugs from the poached deer in the cabin matched Lapalme's rifle, they had a good shot at tying Moe to Aucoin and Ivan Rhino, and the prosecutor could use this information to work a deal with Rhino—in return for evidence against Lapalme. He was headed out onto the big lake again for another marine patrol, but his mind was behind him, on land, when Garwood interrupted his thinking. "Coast Guard reports a trawler on Boat-Eater Shoals," the sergeant said.

"Long way from the Garden," Service said. "For rats." From what he had seen, the rats tended to cling to the waters off the Garden Peninsula. The Boat-Eater Shoals were a few miles off the Stonington Peninsula and just northeast of Minneapolis Shoals. As usual, Stone had called the night before and asked him to go with Garwood.

"You ready ta get your feet wet again?" Stone had asked.

"Not literally," Service told his LT.

"Blake's solid," Stone added.

"Good," Service told the man. He was still having headaches, but they were lessening in their severity, and work was work. You couldn't do the work only when you felt okay.

He had thought it would be a routine patrol until the Coasties called in to give them a heads-up. The icy drizzle and a growing wind didn't help.

"Doubt it's rats," Garwood said. "We've had some reports of unlicensed Wisconsin boats working our waters. They probably figure we're so busy over to the Garden that they can slip in and pick up a couple of bonus loads. Should be easier than a rat patrol," he added. "You okay with this?"

Service nodded.

Garwood throttled back to idle a couple of miles from the shoals and let the boat drift, pushed by a steady north wind. "We won't be able to turn a trawler if we have to chase," the sergeant said. "And they won't be able to out-fast us if we catch them pulling nets, so we're just gonna take 'er easy, work our way in slowly, and look for their lights."

"Then what?" Service asked, thinking about the botched assault on Moe Lapalme's boat.

"Depends on what we see," Garwood said with a shrug.

Why was this stuff so unplanned, so off-the-cuff? The department needed more people for marine patrols, and more and better boats to do the job. At least tonight they had the rat boat to give them some speed. What hurt most was a strong sense that Lansing didn't really care: In time, commercial fishermen would be bought out, and only tribals and sportfishermen would remain. All this effort and risk was for nothing but principle. But at least he had found the slugs. That was a definite plus for today.

"Lights to port," Garwood said. It was a few minutes before midnight, and the drizzle had turned into a blustery rain with variable winds going from soft breezes to powerful gusts.

Garwood had his binoculars up. "Barely moving, but their stern is lit. I think we got lucky. They're lifting nets. We can board her."

Service cringed at the words, asked, "Numbers?"

"Boat that size, three, maybe four total crew. We'll try to come in quiet, run dark and silent, tie up to them, and go aboard."

This sounded better than a high-speed chase and the Errol Flynn approach. "What's the layout?"

"Forty-footer. They bring nets up along the transom and over the starboard gunwale. Power and controls are forward. I'll angle us in and slide over. You go first and make straight for the helmsman forward. I'll take the crew aft."

"And if they cut their nets and run?"

"Not likely—nets cost too much. Remember, they're all about the money."

Service had his doubts, but Garwood was in charge, and not all keyed up like Colt Homes had been the other time.

As they drifted in, their sounds were masked by the sound of winches in the trawler, which was shaped like a double-decker baguette. When their nose rubbed the wooden planks of the larger boat, Service went over the gunwale into the opening. Two men on the opposite side were peeling fish from green nylon netting. Two other men were standing forward at the controls.

The eyes of the two men ahead of him widened and one of them shouted, "Oh shit!" Before Service could announce himself, Blake Garwood came vaulting across, bumped him, and stumbled forward into the two men working the net. Service watched as Blake suddenly lifted up and went sprawling over the gunwale of the other side—and was gone. The two men with the nets stood up and looked at him and at the men up front, and nobody seemed to know what had happened or what to do.

"Drop nets!" bellowed one of the men up front as he slammed the twin throttles forward and the boat surged. The two aft crewmen started doing something to the nets.

"Michigan Department of Natural Resources!" Service screamed. "DNR! Stop the fucking boat!"

"Don't stop, boys!" the man at the throttles shouted over the roaring engines.

Service went forward, pulled out his revolver, and ordered, "Stop!" He fired two rounds through the roof. The captain immediately pulled the throttles back and the boat lurched as it lost momentum and gave way to the waves coming onto the bow.

Jesus, Service thought, *Where was Blake?* They had to get him. Fast. The men stared at him and he stared back. No sound. Shit—the jerk had cut the engines off completely. "Start her up again," Service ordered, the revolver still in hand. "You'd better hope my sergeant is all right, or you are in deep fucking shit."

"We never touched him," one of the men in back said.

"You got spotlights?" Service asked.

"Somewhere," the captain said. He was small with a ratty white beard tinged red in the low cabin light. "Find them and get this thing turned around. Take her slow and easy." He could picture the stinking tub running over Garwood.

Ten minutes later a green flare shot up into the night sky and fizzled.

Service saw the origin and had the captain steer toward it. Since firing the shots, the crew had been cooperative. They soon spotted Blake Garwood and hauled him in, placing a blanket over his shoulders.

"Nobody touched me," the sergeant said sheepishly. "I slipped on something, caught my foot, and went over the side. I heard shots."

"I needed to get their attention," Service said.

"You two scared the bejeezus outta us," the captain said. "We come for fish, not to hurt nobody."

"Why'd you run?" Service asked.

"Reflex," the captain said, avoiding eye contact.

Garwood had managed to secure the *Fat Rat* to the trawler before making his dramatic entrance—and exit. Now they headed north to Escanaba, towing the smaller boat. The captain was not happy, but resigned himself to having his trawler impounded until he could post a bond and get a lawyer to work out the return. He made coffee for Garwood, and Service sat smoking and studying the layout. There was a door in the center of the deck. "What's that?"

"We call it the kiddie hole," the captain said. "Guy owned the boat before me used to take his kids out and pull up on shallow shoals and open that door and let his kids dip smelt with nets."

As they approached Escanaba, Service said to his sergeant, "You had marine flares."

"No shit," Garwood said. "I had nightmares since you took your swim, and figured I'd add a little insurance. I bought 'em myself. I got two years until retirement," he added. "Then I'm moving to the mountains in Tennessee and I don't ever want to see another bloody boat."

45

ESCANABA, MAY 26, 1976

"You're dead when I get out."

Serverino "Sandy" Tavolacci was standing outside the Delta County Jail chewing a cigar stump. He was short and wide and built like a wrestler. It was fifty degrees and overcast, but he wore dark sunglasses and a black trench coat with the collar turned up. His hair was brushed straight back and glistened. Tavolacci, Service had learned, was becoming the mouthpiece of choice for major poachers in the central and western Upper Peninsula.

Gar Murray, Delta County's prosecuting attorney, was standing with the defense lawyer. Last year Murray had written a controversial letter to Lansing, declaring that the Garden situation was on the verge of being out of control, and if Director Curry didn't improve support for DNR officers charged with patrolling the peninsula, Murray would publicly disclaim any responsibility for the death or injury to an officer on patrol in the Garden. Further, he would ask the state attorney general to release him from the obligation of enforcing commercial fish laws in any prosecution stemming from a death or injury to DNR personnel. Murray's letter had created a minor furor in Lansing, with lesser lights calling it an act of cowardice; but Len Stone told Service that Murray had written the letter as a friend and supporter of law enforcement. Murray had been trying to force Lansing to do a better job of supporting the same people they were putting at risk. Good goal, lousy tactic.

Service had never met either man.

Murray had hair the color of a female cardinal and eyes that made him look like a predator on a constant lookout for food. Service introduced himself to both men, but Tavolacci immediately turned away and went inside.

Service noticed he walked with mincing steps, like something was jammed up his behind.

"Gar Murray," the red-haired man said, shaking Service's hand. "Don't mind Sandy. He's just an asshole."

"By birth or training?" Service shot back.

Murray laughed. "That's pretty good. You feel that way about all lawyers?"

"Only the ones not on my side."

"A true professional," Murray said, clapping him on the back and holding the door open for him. "Shall we?"

Tavolacci was already in the interview room with Moe Lapalme. Both of them looked agitated. "What da deuce is goin' on, eh?" The lawyer asked when Service and Murray walked into the room.

Murray put his briefcase on the table. "Save the Finnglish today, Sandy."

"Let's expedite. I've got other meetings on my docket," the defense attorney said, no trace of Yooperese in his language or pronunciation.

Detective Kobera was twenty minutes late. Lapalme and Tavolacci carried on an extended hushed conversation while they waited, and Service and Murray stepped outside the room.

Kobera arrived, breathing hard, and handed a large envelope to Murray. "Sorry I'm late," he said.

Service looked at the detective. "We get a match?"

"Damn straight," Kobera said. "You want to do the honors?"

"I'm just a game warden."

Murray looked like his mind was elsewhere, but he said, "Sandy's gonna scream for the evidence. Fuck him," Murray added. "I'll mail it to him."

"I'm gonna read Lapalme the charges and his rights," Kobera said.

"We'll arraign in two hours," Murray said. "I've already talked to the judge."

The three men filed into the room. Lapalme looked cocky. Tavolacci looked wary.

Kobera charged Lapalme with attempted murder, grand theft, breaking and entering, conspiracy to commit theft, and fifty-eight other counts involving stolen goods.

Tavolacci said nothing.

Formalities done, the three men got up and walked to the door, where Service stopped and made eye contact with Lapalme. "Nice seein' you, Cap'n."

Lapalme tried to come up out of his chair, but Tavolacci held him down.

"You're dead when I get out," Lapalme said with a low growl.

Kobera looked at Murray. "Threatening an officer of the law?"

"I'll add it," the prosecuting attorney said.

Service said to Lapalme, "I'll be waiting for you."

46

GARDEN PENINSULA, FEBRUARY 14, 1977

"When you least expect it, when you think you're safe, I'll be there."

The parking lot of Bay de Noc High School was jammed with vehicles. Service waited to arrive until fifteen minutes after the scheduled start of the memorial ceremony, and double-parked as near to the entrance as he could get.

A couple of teenage boys saw him get out of his truck and began to follow him.

He walked into the gymnasium and stopped. The casket was at the end of an aisle created by two banks of metal folding chairs. There was a portable lectern in front of the casket where a priest was reading. When the man looked up and saw Service, he stopped and stared.

Grady Service wore his class-A green uniform, his wheel hat tucked under his left arm. He marched forward, looking neither right nor left. He could smell wet wool and ripe bodies packed too close together, but there was no sound and the air felt heavy.

The priest moved aside as Service stepped to the lectern.

Pete Peletier was sitting near the front, on the right side of the aisle. Service locked his eyes on to Peletier's and began. "My name is Grady Service and I am here to say good-bye to my friend, Cecilia Lasurm."

He felt sweat under his arms and began to question his judgment, but continued. "Cecilia was everybody's friend, and the teacher of many of you. That's why you're here—to honor her memory and the contributions she made to all of our lives. Cecilia believed that the actions of a few selfish people should not be allowed to destroy the reputations of all the good people who surround them." He paused to let his words settle in. There was still no sound.

"Cecilia learned a year ago that she was dying," he said. "When she got the diagnosis, she evaluated her situation and decided she would die on her own terms. She refused pain medication, and she kept doing her job: teaching the children of this school, and coming to your homes to help those children who couldn't get here." Another pause. "Cecilia believed that no matter the obstacle, you should keep doing what you think is right. She hated the conflict between people like me and some of you. Her only dream was that we would settle it so that children here could grow up without cringing every time they saw a police car. I came today to say good-bye to my friend, and to tell you that I know many of you share her dream. Will it happen? I don't know. It's in your hands, not mine. And not theirs."

Service looked at Peletier and said, "Pete." All the heads in the gym turned to look at Peletier. "Pete, thank you for the courtesy of inviting me here today. As you and I have discussed many times, we have more in common than we have differences."

The crowd began to murmur as Service did a crisp about-face, walked to the head of the open casket, leaned down, and kissed Cecilia Lasurm on the lips. He straightened up, put on his hat, saluted her, turned sharply, and marched out of the gymnasium in silence.

Peletier caught him by the elbow halfway to his truck and tried to spin him around.

The rat leader's face was flushed. "You cocksucker—I never invited you. It was you," Peletier stammered. "You tried to turn 'em against me. You think getting Moe will change anything? We'll never change, do you understand? Never."

Service looked at the man. "I understand, Pete. I'm counting on that—and that's why I'll be back. When you least expect it, when you think you're safe, I'll be there. You and I aren't done."

Service got into his Plymouth and started to pull away as a dozen young men came running toward him, their arms cocked to throw things, but Peletier held up his hands and they immediately dropped their missiles. The last thing he saw was a red-faced Peletier extending his middle finger.

That night he heard that Cecilia Lasurm's house had been torched and destroyed.

PART V

COLD VENGEANCE

MARQUETTE-GLADSTONE, APRIL 22, 2004

"Red rats."

Service hated shopping, especially in sprawling chain stores, but Nantz wanted to stop at Kmart in Marquette. She was trying to secure a shopping cart by shouldering her way through shoppers mingling just inside the entrance, when a huge man lumbered out of the crowd, wrapped Grady Service in a bear hug, and lifted his feet off the ground, swinging him around. "Grady, Grady!"

"Put me down, Gumby!"

"Eugene," the man said calmly. "Eugene." He gently lowered Service, opened one side of his blue vest, said, "Badge," and beamed proudly before trundling off to greet another customer.

As usual, Nantz shopped with the focus of a programmed android.

En route to Gladstone she said, "Are you going to tell me what was up with that back there?"

"That what?"

"Don't play thick, Service. The man who lifted you like you were made of Styrofoam."

Service grinned. "Eugene Chomsky."

When no more was said, Nantz said, "Dinner on the twenty-fifth with Vince and Rose, Lorelei and Whit." Vince Vilardo, the doctor who had treated him after his near-death experience in Big Bay de Noc; they had been friends ever since.

Lorelei Timms was the state's new governor, and Whit was her longtime husband. Through a series of serendipitous events, Lorelei Timms had taken a shine to Service, and now the governor and Maridly were fast friends.

"Walter and Karylanne will be there," Nantz added.

This brightened him. Walter was his son, a son he'd known nothing about until last summer. His ex-wife, Bathsheba, had been pregnant when they'd separated and never bothered to tell him. She had died in an aircraft in Pennsylvania during the 9/11 disaster and only afterward did Service learn he was a father, a role he was still trying to adapt to. He and Walter had been through some rough early going as they tested each other, but things were settling down and he liked the boy and enjoyed his company. Karylanne was his Canadian girlfriend, and Nantz was convinced she was "the one." Walter was not yet seventeen and in his third semester at Michigan Tech University in Houghton and was taking spring and summer classes so he could lighten the load for next fall and winter, when he would have a full athletic scholarship and officially join the varsity hockey team he now skated with on an unofficial basis.

"That's good," he said. He was looking forward to watching his son play college hockey.

"You'll be nice to Lorelei," she said in a tone that wasn't a request.

"I'm always nice to the governor."

"Just don't be so damn blunt. Remember, she actually *listens* to you."

"And you don't?"

"When there's something worth hearing."

He put away the groceries while Nantz poured oil into the deep fryer. Yesterday Simon del Olmo, the young CO in Crystal Falls, had dropped by with a box of fresh smelt he had bought from the retail fish house in Stephenson.

"Be fun to go smelting," Nantz said as she began to roll the tiny fish in flour.

"They don't much run up the rivers anymore," he said.

She rolled her eyes. "They gotta have sex somewhere, Service. We all do." She held up one of the six-inch-long silvery fish by the tail. "Sex makes more of these."

"They spawn on reefs off creek mouths now," he said.

"You're making that up," she said skeptically.

"One of the fish biologists told me. It's supposed to be a secret."

Nantz rolled her eyes. "Be good to see Walter," Nantz said. "He hasn't been home in weeks."

"I'm going back to the Garden tomorrow," he said. "Fish runs are starting." Because of personnel shortages, he was doubling his duties as a detective with routine game warden patrols.

As a conservation officer for more than twenty years he had spent most of his time policing the Mosquito Wilderness area, where he was like a neighborhood beat cop. Since his promotion to detective his job had changed and instead of patrolling, he took tips directly from both informants and other officers and plunged into cases, covering most of the Upper Peninsula. But the state was short on money and DNR law enforcement was short on people and since January, sergeants and detectives had been doing double duty—their own work, plus covering regular patrols. Part of him was glad to again be doing the job he had done for so long.

"How long has it been?" she asked.

"My last time there was in seventy-six." He omitted Cecilia Lasurm's memorial service the following year.

"You've never said much about the Garden. And who is Eugene Chomsky?"

He opened an inexpensive bottle of Malbec, and started taking the smelt out of the oil with tongs while Nantz put new ones in.

"I swear," she said. "Getting you to open up is like pulling teeth. Eugene Chomsky? He treated you like a long-lost brother."

Service kissed her and stepped back. "This is a really long story."

"You know what the Chinese say," she said.

"A journey of a thousand miles starts with a single step?"

"I was thinking a good fuck starts with a single stroke."

"Are you always horny?"

"Right now I'm curious. Talk, Service. No talk, no sex—*capisce?*"

Grady Service talked all night and Maridly Nantz listened, seldom interrupting.

It was after midnight before he finished. He got up from the table to stretch and make more coffee.

"When COs talk about the Garden, they always cringe," she said. "They didn't tell us any of this down at the academy."

"Because it's mostly ancient history," he said. Nantz had been in the DNR academy the year before. She was scheduled to enter the academy again this year—if it was held, which right now seemed iffy because of the state budgetary crisis brought on by the policies of former governor Samuel "Clearcut" Bozian.

"How much longer did it go on after you were out of it?" she asked.

"In May of eighty-three some of our guys got shot at off Ansels Point, and in December of that year, two of our guys tried to bring some illegal nets ashore at Fairport and got jumped by a mob of forty to fifty people, most of them wearing ski masks. It was about two in the afternoon. They were driving up the pressure ridge on shore when the mob came out of nowhere. Rocks got thrown, punches exchanged. Our guys had to pull their weapons to back off the crowd.

"They immediately called the Manistique Troop post for reinforcements, and they sent down three squads with six guys. The mob turned on them, destroyed one of their radios, slashed a tire. They also wrecked one of our snowmobiles and stole the other one, the one with the sled loaded with nets. We never saw the machine, the sled, or the nets again. The Troops took our guys in and tried to retreat, but the rats had cut trees down to block them, and they had to run out through the snow to get around and out. It was a classic ambush. The rats waited until our guys were nearly ashore before they attacked, and after the Troops arrived, they tried to cut them off. Two arrests were made a couple of days later."

"That was seven years after you were involved," she said.

"Hegstrom told them he could buy them ten years, and he pretty much did. The state began buyouts in seventy-nine. Stone and Attalienti had a good plan, but marginal support and no understanding of the realities on the ground from Lansing. We were pretty much on our own, and everybody knew it—especially the rats."

"The conflict went on," she said.

"It did. State money eventually went to those few commercial fishermen who managed to meet the requirements of Order Seventeen. Some of them got almost sixty grand to hand over their nets and give up fishing. Most got a lot less."

"Sixty grand was a lot of money back then."

"The Garden was always about money," he said with a nod, "not a way of life or resisting authority on principle. About six weeks after the so-called Garden Riot, the director decided to attend a public meeting with Garden people. He went up there with an NRC commissioner. The director wasn't a bad guy, but he had less than six months on the job, and went without telling anyone in the U.P. what he was doing. A crowd of two hundred verbally ripped him a new asshole and put him on the defensive, and he told the people that his officers had been overzealous and maybe too hard-nosed, and that some personnel changes might have to be made. He claimed later that all he wanted to do was defuse the situation. Apparently he was thoroughly briefed and backgrounded by the chief, but being told about it and seeing it are two different things. The meeting was news all over the state: 'DNR Director Criticizes Game Wardens,' that sort of headline. Our guys went apeshit, and we damn near had a revolt. The director grudgingly drove back up to Escanaba and spent an entire day with law enforcement and fisheries personnel. Naturally, he limited it to the district, not understanding that our people from all over the state had done time up here."

"You were at the meeting?" she asked.

"I asked him to give us one specific example of when we had been too hard-nosed, and he had to admit he couldn't. I think he thought he was doing the right thing, meeting with people in the Garden, but it was a major faux pas. The meeting was like Vietnam all over again, the troops getting trashed for the failings of civilian leadership. The director tried to make nice, but nobody wanted to listen."

"Did he take action?"

Service shook his head. "He didn't dare. He had promised the Garden people a plan, but he never delivered it. Our guys knew what had to be done and they kept doing it. Our big mistake was not being hard-nosed enough," he added. "Without the discipline and training of our guys, people could have gotten killed."

Then he told her what he had done, omitting nothing, including his intimacy with Cecilia Lasurm.

"You broke the law?" she asked.

"I'm not proud of it, but Attalienti and Stone protected me. If we totaled up damage on both sides, it would have been a push," he said.

"You're rationalizing," she said.

"I should have been fired," he admitted. "It took until seventy-nine to get some court rulings to uphold our right to seize under Order Seventeen. After that the courts began to routinely condemn seized equipment."

"What did you accomplish?"

"I got a better idea of how they operated and who was involved, but all I did was put them on their heels for a bit. They were breaking laws before I got there and they kept doing it after I left, but more locals finally began to come forward; we used a lot of undercovers, and we began to squeeze them hard."

"The court rulings were a major development," she said.

"Yes and no," he said. "Remember what I said about sportfishermen and state policy?

After that infamous meeting with the director, a lot of people turned their anger on the Indians, and they started getting what we had been getting from the rats. When violence turned that way, the whole deal got classified as civil rights violations. The feds tried to move in and clean it up, but they didn't handle it as well as we had. Once the Indian issue arose, the violence wasn't just in the U.P. Some of the nastiest stuff took place down around Traverse City and Ludington, but the battles there were sportfishing groups against Indian commercial netters. It wasn't as nasty or sustained as the Garden had been, but because it happened below the bridge, it got a lot more media attention."

"Only the players changed," Nantz said.

"All but us," he said. "About a year after the Garden meeting, a U.S. district court judge signed a consent form for a negotiated settlement among the tribes, who were fighting each other in addition to the sportfishermen. The order closed all gill netting below the forty-fifth parallel, and gave the tribes exclusive rights to northern Lakes Michigan and Huron, and eastern Superior. The problem is that the Indians are human, and just like the rats, they wanted more. Both Bay de Nocs remained closed at the same times and for the same methods as before, so the tribals began to become rats."

"Red rats," she said.

"Yeah," he said with a smile, "and some of the old white rats worked for or with them."

Nantz studied him. "This is what you have to go back to?"

"In some ways it's even more frustrating now. Every tribal member is entitled to take a hundred pounds of fish a day on a subsistence card the tribe issues. Who eats a hundred pounds of fish a year, much less a day? Lake Michigan fish are filled with PCBs and other crap, but the tribals get their take, and our people check their cards and find them taking spawning perch along with walleyes in areas open to them—and there isn't a damn thing we can do to stop it. When we find them in violation, we write citations and send the tickets to the tribal courts for disposition. Meanwhile, the fish they take finds its way down to Chicago and as far away as New York City. We can apprehend and cite, but the tribal courts decide the penalties."

"The tribal courts don't cooperate?"

"Some do and some don't. Some of the magistrates think their brothers are entitled to all the fish in the lake in payment for injustices done two centuries ago. Some magistrates also believe that tribal members have a right to do whatever they want to do outdoors, and the state has no say in it."

He stopped talking and drank some coffee.

Nantz said, "Did Moe Lapalme come after you?"

"Moe spent four years inside, got paroled, broke parole his first week, and disappeared. He got killed in a fight with a commercial fisherman in Cordova, Alaska, in 1990."

"What about the rat leaders?"

"A couple of them branched out into growing dope—Garden Green—and went to prison in the eighties. There's still dope down there, but we have drug teams on top of it most of the time. A couple of the rat leaders moved out of state and got into trouble in other states. A couple are still down there, acting like exalted senior citizens."

"Cecilia Lasurm," Nantz said. "You knew I was going to ask about her."

"She died in 1977," Service said.

"Cancer?"

"Car wreck," he said.

"You didn't say accident."

"She was in a world of hurt and refusing pain meds, and I think she didn't want to go on."

"Where did she die?"

"She obliterated a telephone pole at the bottom of the M-Twenty-Eight hill south of Munising."

Nantz said, "And?"

"The Troops calculated her speed at over a hundred."

"Were there skid marks?"

He nodded. "Enough to allow them to conclude she had tried to stop."

"You don't think she did."

"I think she wanted her daughter to get her insurance. The brake marks were there to prove she didn't want to die." He didn't tell Nantz that Cecilia had talked to him about this a month before she died. She had sworn him to secrecy forever.

"She was decisive to the end," Nantz said.

"The insurance company fought it, but in the end they paid."

"Her daughter got the money?"

Service nodded. "She was sentenced to time in a rehab center and they cleaned her up, but it didn't take. She moved to Minneapolis, blew through the money, overdosed in St. Paul, and died."

"Did you love Cecilia?" Nantz asked quietly.

He didn't answer right away. "No," he said finally. "I admired her courage."

"Do you really think it takes courage to kill yourself?"

"It takes a kind of courage to make the decision. The act is simple once you're committed. It comes down to facing what's best for you and the people you care about."

"That's bullshit," she said. "Suicide is the ultimate selfish act. What happened to Brigid Mehegen?"

"She's a Troop lieutenant now, in Berrien Springs or somewhere down in the southwest corner of the state. Are you jealous?" he asked.

"Are you jealous of all the men I slept with before you?"

"Not until you put it that way," he said.

She smiled with self-satisfaction. "Can we go back to Eugene?"

"Criminal charges were dropped. He's mentally retarded."

"He burned animals alive," Nantz countered.

"Put a ten-year-old's emotions with Ivan Rhino and that's what you can get. Eugene's actually very kind and, in the right company, he does fine. Attalienti hired him to do odd jobs out of the regional office and paid for it out of his own pocket. When Captain Grant came in, he put Eugene on the payroll so he'd have health benefits, and he found a place for him to live near his place on the Dead River."

"When Kmart came to town, Eugene applied for and got the greeter's job all on his own, full-time, with benefits."

"What was that deal with the vest?" she asked.

"When he first started at Kmart, he spotted a shoplifter, flashed the badge we'd given him, challenged him, and ended up throwing the guy through a plate-glass window. He takes his job seriously. The guy was a Cat dealer, high as a hawk in a thermal. The cops came, found a portable lab in the guy's car, and busted him. The guy tried to sue the store from prison, but the case got thrown out. Eugene got to keep his job, but he has to wear his badge inside the vest and show it only to law officers."

"I'm surprised the corporation didn't fire him."

"Every cop in the county went to bat for him. The store manager got the message."

"About that fuck-buddy of yours," she said, but he covered her mouth and hugged her close, and she settled in and let it go.

"She married a Troop lieutenant. They've got two kids," he whispered.

48

WILSEY BAY CREEK, APRIL 23, 2004

" . . . Far out, dude."

He and Nantz had exercised before sunrise, and then had breakfast. She was talking about this and that, but he wasn't paying close attention. His mind was on the day's work.

Ice-out had been late again this spring, but northerns were moving up the streams to marshy areas to spawn, and walleyes had been congregated in the mouths of rivers and creeks for more than a week. They would soon surge upstream looking for spawning gravel where they would remain for several days. While congregated for spawning, the fish were extremely vulnerable to poaching.

This afternoon he had scouted the upper Tacoosh and found walleyes collected in some rapids. He drove from the Tacoosh to the Whitefish, hid his truck in some trees, and hiked a third of a mile west to the river. There were even more fish here than in the Tacoosh, but the Whitefish's cedar floodplain was still pocked with runoff, and he had to island-hop his way in and out. Scouting finished, he climbed up a small rise on all fours and sat down in the grass to have a cigarette. The team wouldn't meet until four. He had lots of time to sit and enjoy the solace and the sounds of the swollen river below him.

A doe wandered into the open from some aspens to his right. He made a whoosh sound to see her react. Her head snapped toward him, ears alert, but immediately looked back the other way. Something over there interested her more than him. She finally turned and bolted away, her flag high.

He leaned over to lower his profile in the grass and watched. After a few minutes he saw the silhouettes of two men moving through the cedars. Now and then one of them splashed in one of the pools. He took out his binoculars and zeroed in on the movement. Too dark to make out real detail, but one of the men had a stick on his right side. Spear? In the middle of the afternoon? This would be too easy! He crawled a little closer to the lip of the hill. Poachers didn't linger long when they were spearing and netting in rivers. They'd get in, get their fish, and get out.

Fifteen minutes later he heard the men coming back. A game trail led along the bottom of the hill, following the contour. He let them reach the trail, stood up, and slid down. "DNR!"

The men froze. A small brown-and-white mongrel with floppy ears lowered its head and began barking.

"Quiet, Oliver," one of the men told the dog.

"How's it going, guys?" Service asked.

"Lookin' for steelhead," one of the men said. Both men were carrying unassembled spinning rods. One man had a net over his shoulder. It was too small for steelhead.

"No steelies here," Service said. "You've got to go upriver about a mile. There's good spawning gravel up that way."

"We drove down from Marquette," the man said. "Runs up there are lousy so far this spring."

"Our first time for steelhead," the other man said. "There's all kinds of big bass in the river down there." The man looked over his shoulder.

They were walleyes, not bass, but he didn't correct them. "You guys weren't in there long."

"No steelhead. You saw us?"

He did not tell them he'd mistaken their rods for spears.

"How far upstream did you say?" the man asked again. "For the steelies?"

Service told them how to drive up to it. "Too far to hike."

The little dog kept jumping against his leg and licking him, his tail wagging.

He poured coffee when he got back to the truck. Fishing rods as spears? This was not the way to start a patrol, and he wondered if he was starting to lose his edge.

He knew both rivers would provide good hunting for the next few nights, but when he got to the team meeting at the new Escanaba district office near the Mead Plant, Eddie "Gutpile" Moody and Grant Ebony reported to the others that they had pinched three tribal spearing crews at Wilsey Bay Creek last night at the bottom of the Stonington Peninsula. Tonight Moody and Ebony were headed south of Escanaba to Chigger Creek and the Cedar River, but they thought someone should hit Wilsey again, certain that poachers would not expect the DNR two nights in a row in the same location.

"You can make book the word's out today that we were there last night," Ebony concluded. "They won't be expecting more company."

Candace McCants was down from the Mosquito, which was her turf now. Another six officers had come in from the western counties where there were no fish runs.

"I'll take Wilsey," McCants said. "Grady, you want to partner up?"

He agreed, and they sat with Moody and Ebony getting briefed on Wilsey Bay. Service wasn't paying attention, knowing the Korean-born McCants would absorb what they needed. He was feeling some anxiety about going to the Stonington instead of the Garden, but duty was duty, and there was always tomorrow night. He had not thought much about Cecilia Lasurm in years, or even the Garden, for that matter, but last night's talk with Nantz had conjured a flood of memories—of how pensive some of the officers were before patrols, of Homes cowboying across the ice, his swim and rescue, Garwood's swim and the Wisconsin poachers, rocks pounding the sides of their vehicles during land runs, the wild ride with Stone in his truck, the lifting shed being crunched by the rat truck—all of it. Stone, Homes, and Garwood were retired now, Homes just three years ago, and like Stone, still living in the U.P. Garwood had moved to the hills of Tennessee, just as he'd said he would.

Attalienti had been a good captain, but when Cosmo Metrovich finished his run as acting chief, Metrovich had retired, and Attalienti had been sent south to be captain of the southern law zone. Another captain had been assigned in his place, and when he retired, was replaced by Captain Ware Grant. Only during the past couple of years had he gotten close to Captain Grant, who for the past two years had faced some health issues. Sooner or later Grant had to retire, and Service knew eventually he would also have to face the same decision. He had put in way more time than he needed to retire with full benefits right now, but he had recently been promoted to detective—and though the promotion initially had been unwanted and unsettling, he was getting accustomed to the job and finding it a challenge. Even his paranoia about giving up the Mosquito Wilderness had abated. McCants had taken it over from him, and he had total confidence in her ability.

A horseblanket named Surdy had once told him to keep doing the job as long as he was physically able and it was still interesting and fun, which meant he didn't have to think too hard about retiring anytime soon.

"You're creeping me out tonight," McCants said as they walked out to her truck through the rain.

"Just tonight?"

She jabbed him in the ribs with an elbow.

It had rained all day and was supposed to last another twenty-four hours. There were flood warnings for the western counties. He checked the digital thermometer in her truck: thirty-eight. The water wouldn't be much better, and he was glad he was dressed for it: nylon-wool underwear, a second layer of wool, wool socks and uniform pants, wool shirt, bulletproof vest, parka, insulated rain bibs, 400 mg Thinsulate boots. He'd be wet, but he wouldn't freeze. When he first began his career, he had barely noticed the cold. Now he fretted continuously about dressing properly. Age, he thought grimly.

"They'll be out tonight," McCants said as they pulled into the Shell station in Gladstone. She began filling their tank on a state credit card. "The weather sucks. Why do the assholes think we don't work in crappy weather or off the beaten path?"

He left her and went inside and bought a half-dozen candy bars, two large bags of Fritos, and filled their thermoses with hot coffee. They'd need caffeine, carbs, and sugar in this weather.

"You know Wilsey?" she asked as they passed through Rapid River.

"Not really," he said. "You?"

"Never been there before. Did you hear what Grant and Gutpile said about the culvert?"

He had not paid attention. "A *culvert?*" He hated culverts because they pinched down streams, and when the melt was on, pushed the waters up. "We could have used a daytime recon down there," he complained. "I checked the upper Tacoosh and Whitefish this afternoon. There were herds of eyes in both."

"You want to hit one of them instead?" she asked.

"No, they're expecting us to cover Wilsey."

She said, "Five Thirteen south to K-Twenty-four and east till we cross the creek." She grinned. "It sounds like the route to the Emerald City."

"Yeah—follow the yellow mud road."

"Grant said they hid their truck west of the creek. He said there were some northerns up, but not a lot. With this weather they might be in or they might not. Let's cross the creek and see if they're in. If not, we can double back to Squaw Creek."

Squaw Creek was eight miles north of Wilsey Bay, and they would cross it on their way south.

"Pike come up the Squaw?" he asked.

"Mostly eyes."

"Sounds like a plan," he said.

"I've got a thermal imager," she said. "You bring your generation-three?"

"We have a thermal imager now?"

"I borrowed it from a Troop. It's a video unit, but it'll do the job for us—especially in this soup."

The department issued a certain number of infrared binoculars to each district, but they were second-generation and depended on ambient light. Service had bought a set of generation-threes from the Cabela's catalog. His featured an internal light source, which made them effective in total darkness.

"Aren't we the techies," McCants said with a laugh. "There's a small issue down here. Tribals can spear below the annual average waterline, but not above it."

Service looked at her. "What brain surgeon came up with that?"

She shrugged. "Does it matter?"

"Hell yes, it matters. We've got heavy runoff. How the hell do we determine the average annual waterline or floodplain in these conditions?"

"Don't get bent out of shape. Grant said they checked it out yesterday afternoon. The line's about fifty yards below the culvert. He stuck a six-foot pole in the bank to mark the limit."

"How big's the culvert?"

"Five- or six-foot diameter," she said.

"Average annual waterline," he complained. "This is bullshit."

McCants chuckled. "You'd hate it if this job was cut and dried."

"I must be a happy man."

"You are; just cranky."

When they turned east on K-24, McCants turned off all their lights to run dark. The culvert ran under a steep earthen berm and the road crossed over the top. McCants stopped on the berm and Service flashed the external spotlight down into the water.

"It's cooking like Niagara," he said, "and all stirred up. I can't see shit down there."

"I'll find a place to turn around. We'll stash the truck west of the creek and walk down to take a closer look."

They drove east nearly a half-mile before McCants found a driveway into a camp built back in a ragged line of cedar trees. As she turned left into the driveway, Service glanced back down the road over her shoulder. "Lights on the road behind us," he said.

"Damn," McCants said, cutting the truck past the cabin and nosing it close to the building's north wall.

Service quickly walked to the southeast corner of the building, looked west, and saw that the lights were still coming. "They stopped for a sec and then came on," he said. "At the crick, maybe."

"They use a light?" she asked as they went back to the north side of the building and stood between the wall and her truck.

"Couldn't tell," he said. Visibility was terrible.

The lights turned into the camp driveway thirty feet from where they stood, stopped, backed up, and went back to the west.

"Did they see our tire tracks?" she asked as they jogged out into the road to watch what the vehicle did.

The vehicle's brake lights blinked, a couple of small spotlights came on, and then the vehicle moved on.

"They're definitely looking," McCants said. "Let's saddle up. We might as well work from here."

They fetched their packs, flashlights, thermoses, and equipment, and began to jog down the south side of the muddy road, Service following behind her. "I can't believe they didn't see our tracks," McCants said over her shoulder.

He answered, "Like the boys said, they aren't expecting the DNR two nights in a row."

"I don't see the lights anymore," McCants reported.

The rain was suddenly heavier, and it was so dark that Service could barely see her even though she was no more than six feet ahead.

"Grant said there are some boulders and hummocks of hard ground in the marsh grass south of the road," she said.

"You get the tickets tonight," he said as they picked their way along through the rocks in knee-deep water. The marsh grass came up to his thighs, and several times he barked his leg against rocks he didn't see.

"You just don't want the paperwork," McCants said. "Still no lights," she added. "Maybe they decided to move on."

"How close are we to the creek?" Service asked.

"About a hundred yards. Can't you see it?"

He couldn't, but despite the sound of the downpour, he thought he could make out the the roar of water boiling out of the culvert.

McCants picked her way along like she had X-ray vision, and eventually stopped. "Light," was all she said. They were still in knee-deep water. "There," she said, "two o'clock. Let's set up here," she added.

Service bent over and groped around, felt a hump of firm ground. He got on his side on the east side of the cover, slid off his pack, and got out his night scope.

"See it?" she asked.

"The rubber eyepiece fell off this damn thing," he grumbled. It did that a lot.

"Two flashlights moving just left of us," she said. "They have them pointed at the ground. Branching off now, one to our left, one to our right, headed upstream toward the culvert."

"Are they in the water?" His night vision used to be exceptional. No longer.

"I can't tell," she said.

Neither could he. How could she see at all? She was curled up an arm's length away and he couldn't see her through the wall of rain.

She clicked on the thermal imager, which threw out backlight, and lowered the device to just behind the top of the rock.

"They just took a fish," she said. "Look."

He scootched over to her and saw red, yellow, and green outlines of two people. One held the light, the other held a slender black straight line in front. "The dark line's a spear?" he asked. He'd already misread one silhouette today. Suddenly the man made a downward thrust and stumbled around.

"I think he just nailed another one," he said, releasing the device and sliding to his right to escape the glare. Now he was completely blind. "Goddamn thing blasted my night vision," he said. "How far from the road are we, and are they above the marker?"

"The road's just over to our right, and I think they're well above the marker," she said as the rain pounded them, making a steady *whooshing* sound. "I think the other guy just got a fish. The lights are converging."

He saw nothing.

"Move on them?" she asked.

"Let them take another," he said, his eyes beginning to readjust, but not fast enough.

"Got another," she said. "They're together and one of the lights is flickering. I think the battery's going bad. Let's leave the gear and move!" she whispered as she got up and bolted ahead into the rain and black.

He followed, but stopped after a few steps. Where the hell was she? He could hear the rush of the creek ahead. Had she veered left from their hide or gone straight ahead? Probably the latter: Candi always went right to the heart of things, taking all problems head-on.

He felt stupid standing still and began to ease forward. Had she cut through the creek or gone over the berm road? He had no idea. He stopped and listened to see if he could hear her boots, but there was only the rain and creek pouring through the culvert. She probably kicked it in gear, trying to intercept the poachers before they got to their vehicle. *You don't have to run,* he told himself. Let her young legs do the hard work. *Where the hell was the road?* He stopped again, moved his eyes while keeping his head still, trying to get his rods and cones working. No good. He had angled right from the hide, right? Not sure. *Shit.* The creek was ahead. He could hear it. Slow down, you can't catch up now. She's too damn fast. Move deliberately, be ready to help when she yells. He chuckled involuntarily. She had bolted like a deer. *You used to do that,* he told himself. Get the lead out and stop walking like Sandy Tavolacci, he admonished himself. He took one stride confidently and the ground felt solid and smooth. *Okay, go!* He took another stride.

There was a moment when he imagined he was flying, until gravity took hold, his right thigh struck something hard and sharp, and he was underwater and pulling instinctively with his arms to surface. He came up gasping, his chest heaving from the shock of the cold and the surprise. *Jesus Christ!* The current was spinning him counterclockwise. He tried to do a couple of breaststrokes against it, but immediately knew it was too strong, the force too concentrated near the culvert opening. The culvert! *Fuck!* He looked, saw the opening, black and gaping, and realized he was going to go down headfirst. Desperately he kicked and stroked and managed to turn his body around, and then he was inside, on his back, racing boots first down the black tube, rocks and debris banging the back of his head and back. Ahead he saw a gray circle, light at the end of the tunnel. He almost laughed. You are in the fucking water, you clumsy fucking moron!

The water shot him out of the tube like a bullet and the outfall swallowed him as he smacked his right thigh against another large rock, the impact turning him clockwise onto his stomach. He tried to swim up and get onto his back, and looked up to catch a glimpse of a light shining at him before momentum and current swept him downstream into the night.

He tried to swim with the current, and as he did, he accelerated, making his body ride higher so that a couple of kicks and backstrokes enabled him to get on his back, his feet facing Lake Michigan. He considered yelling out, but decided to keep quiet. He had no idea where Candi was, or if she had approached the suspects yet. *Don't fuck it up for her,* he told himself. It's bad enough to stumble into the river, asshole. Don't fuck up the patrol.

Think, he told himself. How far out to the big lake? Two hundred, three hundred yards? The creek was up and fast, but no way it can carry you that far.

Could it? Put out your arms, Christ on the cross going down the river. Wait for obstacles. When you feel something, catch it with your arm, kick your legs, scissor out of the main current into a side eddy.

He missed the first four or five rocks, but managed to stay relaxed and focused, closing his eyes to concentrate on feeling rather than sight. Ow! *Damn!* A large rock bashed the end of his elbow and he missed grabbing hold as he recoiled from the pain. Okay, you survived the big lake. This pissant creek isn't going to win this thing. Get your head in the game. He missed two more rocks before he caught a third one with his left arm, and violently twisted his body left and kicked his right leg over and felt himself drop out of the main current into smoother water. He was still moving downstream, but with less speed. He put both arms down and felt for the bottom and found only cobble, some of the rocks sharp. He jammed his gloved fingers between the rocks like a rock climber and started pulling himself to the left, toward shore.

His face was in pea gravel and sand, his lower body still in water. Hypothermia, he told himself. Replay evolution, crawl out of the slime, get to your feet, *move it.* Motion is life, rest is death.

He got his knees beneath him, put one foot out, used his fist as a prop on the gravel, and pushed up. Hell of a ride, he thought, not wanting to think about all the things that might have happened, all of them negative. Move, don't stand, stop gawking.

A flashlight was shining about seventy-five yards to the north and above him. Was the rain letting up? He could see the berm and the creamy gray froth of water being expelled from the culvert.

"Ca-di?"

"Up here," she called down to him.

He stumbled forward, his clothes heavy with water. He was cold. He got to the bottom of the steep berm and started to scramble up but lost his grip, hit his face in the mud, and slid down. He immediately started back up and kept scrambling until he was facedown on the road.

"We've got them," McCants said. "They went east toward the dead end. They have to come back this way."

"I-wa-in-wa-tah," he said, thinking he sounded like Eugene.

"I know," she said, "we have them."

"Don-un-stan," he said. Why couldn't he talk normally?

"Grady?" Concern in her voice.

"Wen-true-cul-ver," he said, trying to enunciate.

"Oh Jesus!" she said. "Are you okay?"

He felt her hands on him. "Okay," he said. "Okay."

"Are you hurt?"

"Cold," he said, his teeth chattering.

"Here they come," she said.

He looked up, saw headlights approaching, reached for his flashlight. Not there. The lanyard had ripped off during his swim.

McCants lit up the vehicle, a Japanese model. "DNR," she said, letting her light sweep inside. He saw three people, two up front, one in back.

"Dee-en-ah," Service parroted, knowing it came out convoluted. He tried to take a step but tripped on something, bent down, and clawed at it with both hands. A broom? He worked to lift it.

McCants said, "Their spear. They must've dumped it."

She ordered the driver out of the vehicle. His face was pale under her light beam, his eyes wide with fear as he stared at Service. Why wasn't the man squinting?

"Get the truck, Grady."

"Okay."

Safer to keep moving. Her extra keys were in the thigh pocket of his bibs. He stopped, took off his waterlogged gloves, dropped them on the ground, and groped with numb fingers in the pocket. He heard the keys jingle, clawed them out, and held them in both hands, manipulating them until he got a key between the first two fingers of his right hand. He picked up the gloves, stuffed them in the left thigh bib pocket, and began walking down the middle of the road, not caring about prints now, his boots squishing with each step. Face and hands frozen and numb, feet warming up—*A good sign,* he told himself. Visibility not good but better, his legs stiff, clothes heavy. He squinted into the rain and tried to move steadily if not quickly.

Finally at the truck, the fucking thing parked almost flush against the cabin wall. Jesus, Candi! Go through the passenger side. No, computer and commo console are in middle. Too easy to get hung up. Squeeze through here, think skinny. He held the key in his right hand, groped an inside pocket for his lighter, found one of the four he carried. Lighter in left hand, he tried it, but got only a raspy sound. *Shit.* Again, go slow. This time it ignited briefly and went out, but he saw the lock. Okay, again. You can do this. Candi's alone with three poachers. Got to get back to her. He fumbled to get the key against the lock with his right hand, tried the lighter again, and got only a brief flame and light, but it was enough. He pushed the key in, turned it right, and felt the lock give way with a soft *pop.*

He hit his chin trying to squeeze into the driver's seat, but finally made it. He got the engine started, put it in gear, touched the gas. No movement. What now? Think it through. He sat still. She had turned left. Wheels still that way? Yes. He straightened them out, tried the gas. Still stuck. Okay, reverse. Tried that, moved a little, felt another thump. What the hell? Okay, back to drive, cut wheel slightly right, accelerator. This time the truck surged forward. He turned on his headlights. *Shit.* There was a windrow of small trees in front of him. Tired of obstacles and blockages, he floored the accelerator, crashed over and through the trees, bounced wildly into a rock field and fishtailed, cutting the wheel hard left and back to the right when he saw the muddy road.

McCants had the driver outside the car. Service pulled up behind them, lit them with his headlights, and got out. The man stared at him as he grasped his arm and ushered him around the truck and pushed him into the passenger seat. He stood outside, shuffling his feet and shivering while McCants interviewed the three people, one at a time, the poachers in the passenger seat, Service standing outside in the rain, shivering.

Tickets written and all three released, McCants searched the creek bank and recovered four dead pike while Service stumbled back into the marsh grass and retrieved their packs.

"Open beers in the car," she said as they headed west to leave the Stonington.

"You write them?"

"All three are nineteen. They were really polite," she said.

"Turn on the goddamn heater!" he grumbled.

"It's on full," she said, stopping the truck, digging her thermos out of her pack and filling the cup with coffee for him. "They swear their tribal magistrate told them anything below the culvert is fair."

"Which magistrate?"

"Etta, in Manistique."

"She wouldn't tell them that," Service said.

"Well, the rule is confusing."

"Out of our hands," he said. "If she told them that, she'll dump the tickets. If not, she'll nail them. You write MIP?"

"No. You could barely talk when you came up on the berm," she said. "Are you sure you're okay?"

"Fine. Some bumps, cold."

She began to laugh.

"What?"

"After you went for the truck, the driver asked me if you had been hiding in the culvert."

"You said?"

"Yeah, he's got a special suit! He said, 'Far out, dude . . .'"

They both laughed. McCants said, "Every poacher in the U.P. is gonna be checking culverts from this night forward. How does it feel to create a legend?"

"Bite me," he said.

"You're lucky the culvert wasn't blocked with debris," she said. "Why didn't you yell for help?"

"I didn't want to mess up your tickets."

"*Jesus,* Grady! There will be other tickets! Been me, you'da heard me twenty miles away. I want to be like you when I grow up, Grady Service."

"I stumbled into the fucking river," he said. "How many of you have done that?'

"But you had on your special suit," she said.

He laughed, but he was also thinking that the poachers had seen him come tumbling out of the culvert, and if he had been in serious trouble, or injured, he would have drowned or died of exposure because they had fled. It was a sobering thought.

49

"You want me to make some finger Jell-O too?"

He got as far as the living room, his joints aching, dropped his wet clothes in a pile, and curled up on the couch under a fleece blanket. Cat immediately jumped onto his hip and kneaded the blanket to make a nest. Usually her claws dug in and he batted her away, but tonight he was too tired and numb to care, much less feel. He had found the animal years before in a bag of kittens that somebody had drowned. Why this one had survived was beyond him, but it had turned into a feline misanthrope, which made her an animal he could relate to.

Later Newf came down and slobbered in his face. "Leave me alone!" he growled at the 130-pound female Canary Island mastiff. A former girlfriend, a veterinarian, had given the animal to him, and Newf's presence over the past couple of years had finally begun to erode his fear of dogs. He shoved the animal's massive back away, and she plopped on the floor beside the couch and began to snore.

"You reek!" Nantz said, brushing her fingers over his forehead.

Service opened his eyes, felt stiffness and pain.

"Wanna start the day off right?" Nantz asked.

"Oh God," he said, covering his face with his arm.

She cupped her hand behind her ear. "Grady Service refusing sex? Did I hear right?"

"Help me up," he said, extending his hand.

"Honey!" she said when the blanket dropped away from him. "Your thighs!"

He stared down at reddish-blue bruises the size of silver dollars.

"Your face," she added.

"Windburn," he said, trying his legs.

"It looks like you toweled off with sandpaper."

He touched his jaw. No feeling. He hobbled on up to the shower and stood a long time, letting the hot water cascade off him. He didn't want to think about last night.

He started to brush his teeth and stopped when he felt the top two teeth move. What the hell? He leaned toward the mirror, opened his mouth, and probed with his fingers. The slightest pressure pushed the teeth back to almost ninety degrees. He jiggled each of them and felt that they were barely connected, that it wasn't so much the teeth as the gums that had given way. "Just fucking great," he said. His mouth wasn't sore, and there was no mark. When had the teeth come loose?

Nantz was in the kitchen. He got coffee and sat down.

"We need to call Vince," she said.

"We're not calling anyone," he spat back at her.

She tilted her head, put small bowls on the table in front of each of their places, and went back to pour orange juice.

He looked down at the bowl, a poached egg atop a slice of Brie, both on a thick slice of sweet onion and tomato. The egg had been peppered, and a dollop of Tabasco sauce lay on the membrane over the yolk. He broke open the egg with the tine of his fork, put some in his mouth, heard the loose teeth click and move, and put down the fork.

"What's wrong?" Nantz asked. "You love this breakfast."

He sighed, opened his mouth, and wiggled the teeth.

It took a moment for her to understand. "I'm calling Owie," she said.

Owen Joe was their dentist, but everyone called him Owie.

"No," he said with such force she didn't try to argue.

He was too sore and stiff to run, ride the stationary bike, or lift weights, but he sat with Nantz while she went through her workout, and felt his tongue involuntarily poking at the loose teeth.

"The Garden last night?" she asked as she dried sweat off her face and shoulders with a towel.

"Stonington," he said. "With Candi." He offered no further information.

"You can't work tonight. You can hardly move."

"Leave it alone, Mar. I'm going." He had been waiting for this night for a long, long time.

He warmed canned chicken soup for lunch. Neither hot nor cold liquids seemed to affect the loose teeth. At least he could have his coffee.

"*Canned* soup?" Nantz asked disapprovingly. "You want me to make some finger Jell-O too?"

"Can you load it with carbs?" he asked.

"You need a dentist and a shrink," she said.

He packed his gear bag and ruck after lunch and took a one-hour nap. He got dressed and was ready to leave at 3 P.M.

Nantz walked out to the patrol truck with him and handed him his thermos of coffee. "You're going to the Garden," she said. It wasn't a question. "Remember, we have dinner with Lori tomorrow night."

"You had to remind me," he groused. He put the vehicle into reverse and backed up. He saw Nantz standing by the driveway staring at him, hands on her hips, a sure sign that she was unhappy.

50

GARDEN PATROL, APRIL 24–25, 2004

"Buy us a beer, Pete?"

McCants approached him before the group meeting. "Partners tonight?"

He shook his head, and when it was his turn to talk during the meeting, he said, "Garden Creek," and eyebrows bobbed all over the room.

Sergeant Phil Callow said, "You know policy. No solos to the Garden." Callow had been promoted to sergeant in January from the Newberry district. His old friend, Lisette McKower, now the lieutenant in Newberry, told him that Callow was a good man, and would make a good sergeant once he lost some of his anal ways over regulations. She pleaded with Service to give him time.

"I'm not your report," Service said. "This one is my call." Could the others hear his teeth clicking when he talked?

McCants frowned across the table at him.

"Garden Creek?" the sergeant said.

"Eyes," Service said.

"Yeah," Gutpile Moody, the longtime Schoolcraft County officer chimed in, nodding his head. The other COs all nodded in support.

"I don't like this solo deal," Callow said, not wanting to give in so easily to what could be interpreted as a one-man mutiny.

"I've got my eight-hundred if I need help," Service said. U.P. conservation officers had gotten the 800-megahertz radio system less than a year before; game wardens below the bridge had gotten it a year earlier, and state police throughout the state had been on the system for nearly three years. The state police had intended that it remain their dedicated system, but a state congressman from the U.P., his son a CO, had fought to get the DNR on the same system, and had succeeded. The 800 allowed someone on the system to talk to and monitor any other officer in the state.

"Think I'll take a run down to Poodle Pete," Moody said.

"I don't know that one," Callow said.

"Poodle Pete Creek," Moody said. "It's four miles east of Garden."

"Walleyes?" Callow asked.

"Eyes," Moody said, nodding.

"Okay," the sergeant said, finally relenting. "At least somebody will be close to the Lone Ranger."

Moody stood beside Service after the meeting and Service asked, "Walleyes in Poodle Pete?"

Moody shrugged. "Sounded good to me," he said. "For all I know it's barren, but if I look tonight, then we'll know, right?"

McCants joined them. "I'll be with Gut tonight. You want to borrow my floaties?"

"Bite me," Service said.

"Garden Creek—for real?" she asked.

"For real," he said.

"Eyes?"

"Would I bullshit you?" They were for real. After Lasurm's memorial service, three Garden citizens had contacted him and told him they supported Lasurm. One of them was a teacher. They had been providing information since late 1977, and some of it he passed on to the department. But his special interest was Pete Peletier, and over the years he had discovered that Pete had a weakness. The buildings over Garden Creek had stumped him until the night when he and Blake Garwood caught the Wisconsin trawler and he saw the "kiddie hole." It had taken some time to confirm his suspicions, but eventually he had.

The informant who had tracked Peletier closest was gone to Green Bay for a few days. She had left her garage unlocked for him. It was two blocks from the village center, and thirty feet from Garden Creek.

Service ran dark more than twelve miles toward town before going off-road three miles north of the village and eventually working his way to the town's edge from the east and into the woman's garage.

Peletier no longer led rat fishermen on the Peninsula. Some of the old rats had lasted to collect state payoffs, and now most of them were gone. But the fish still spawned every April in huge numbers, and there was money yet to be made. The new rats were younger, many of them coming from other areas of the U.P. to poach the Garden's rich spawning grounds. Locals still partook, but not in the numbers they had years before. Peletier had been the rat leader and the smartest of the group, staying out of the limelight, but he had never stopped poaching. Only his tactics had changed.

Service had considered making the grab years before, but by then he was no longer part of the core Garden team, and at the time, the equipment was not up to what he needed. Only in recent years had equipment for COs dramatically improved. Service got his exposure suit out of his bag and slid into it. The suit afforded both insulation and flotation, and was designed for prolonged exposure to extreme cold. Such suits and shorter float coats were now standard wear for lake patrols. The only drawback was color: electric orange. He got around this by wearing black coveralls over the suit. He waited in the garage until midnight before moving stealthily down to Garden Creek, sliding into the water, and letting the current carry him downstream feet first. He had taken 800 milligrams of ibuprofen with some peanut butter crackers an hour before, careful to chew on the sides of his mouth. Though he was still stiff from last night, some of the pain from his body had relented. Like most officers he used a lot of ibuprofen. If ever there was a blue-collar magic drug, this was it.

Years before he had stood in the opening between buildings north of Roadie's and gotten angry over the effigy suspended over Garden Road. The effigy had rotted away over the years, though a fragment of rope still dangled from the overhead wire as a reminder. As the creek carried him beneath the first set of buildings, he put up his gloved hand and used the heel of his hand to retard his speed and progress until he was almost into the gap; from there he propelled himself over to the rocks. It was no more than three feet from the floor above him to the surface of the creek. It was entirely black behind the buildings. Light from the street filtered through openings in the structures, but illuminated nothing underneath.

He moved into the rocks, took off his pack, got out his thermos while he waited, and watched beneath the buildings thirty feet to the north of him. The creek passed under them and then swung southwest under Garden Road. According to his informant, Peletier, having been dropped off by one of his grandchildren, would already be inside. The rat leader had purchased the building in 1990 under the name of one of his children, and had installed a sign in front that indicated it was a cabinet shop. No such work went on inside, and the informant said it was not unusual for Peletier to take a hundred pounds of walleyes each night until the spawning run was complete. He gave away most of the fish to friends, his poaching not intended to feed himself or generate cash, but to simply keep doing what he had always done, and to spit in the eye of the DNR. It was the strangest poaching setup he had ever seen, and typical of Peletier's penchant for secrecy.

Service used his infrareds to scan the black water. The internal beam made dozens of white goggle eyes litter the green scope. The fish were packed into the stream. He checked his watch, stashed his pack and scope deeper in the rocks, and slid back into the water to let the current sweep him down to the next set of ancient wooden buildings. As he slid under the floor he got hold of a joist and stopped. He stabilized himself, squatting on the cobble bottom, felt around for the seams in the floor above him, and pushed back against a greasy black post to wait.

The door opened about thirty minutes after he got into position. There was only the slightest glow of light from above, and unless someone had been looking for it they would never have seen it. A long-handled net splashed into the water and swept around before being pulled upward. Even in the low light Service saw the flash of a fish in the net and heard it flopping on the floor above him.

The netting continued for more than an hour. After each round the fish tended to scatter away from the activity and the trapdoor closed, only to open again and resume when the fish had calmed. Service counted twenty-two fish. He could hear them on the wooden floor above, their muted flopping, the sound of many people brushing the heels of their hands over the tight skin of a kettle drum.

The next time the net came down, Service grabbed it with both hands, drove it upward into the hole, and followed it. Popping through the opening, he heard someone grunt and fall heavily to the floor.

Service emerged through the trapdoor, turned on his flashlight, and lit the man.

"Hey! What da hell!" Peletier shouted.

"I bet you thought I'd forgotten, Pete."

"Youse!"

"Buy us a beer, Pete?"

"My arm," the old man said.

"Are you okay?"

"Youse nearly give me a heart attack."

Service said, "Don't worry, Pete. If your arm doesn't work, I'll grab your wallet for you."

"Dis is trespass," Peletier protested.

"Stop whining, Pete," Service said, holding out his hand to help the man up. "Let's get that beer."

He cuffed his prisoner, gathered the fish in a burlap bag the poacher had brought, took the man's wallet out of his pocket, led him onto the street, and locked the building for him. "You've got some nice fish here," Service said, dragging the bag along. He guessed more than a hundred pounds, which at ten dollars a pound meant a fine of court costs plus more than a thousand dollars.

They went between the buildings and Service reached underneath and pulled out his pack before walking toward Roadie's two hundred yards away. He called Moody on the 800. "You guys wanna grab a beer?"

"For real?" Moody radioed back.

"Roadie's."

"Rolling," Moody said.

The patrol truck arrived with its blue lights flashing before Service and Peletier reached the tavern.

McCants looked at the bag of fish and said, "That's a real mess."

"Pete's," Service said, urging him up the stairs.

The blue lights had brought bar patrons to the front windows, but as the officers walked through the door, they retreated. Service headed directly for the bar where he put the sack of flopping fish on top, pulled out a stool for Peletier, climbed up on one next to him, and unlocked his cuffs.

"Four beers," Service told the bartender, who had a Rasputinish beard and eyes to match.

"Youse missed last call," the man said.

"You'll make an exception tonight," Service said, looking around. There were about a dozen people standing back in the shadows. "In fact, put a round up for everybody in the house."

The bartender hesitated.

Peletier nodded, "Do it, Al."

A roly-poly waitress helped the bartender set bottles on the bar top.

Service got out his ticket book, handed Peletier's wallet to him, and said, "Take out your license, please."

Service began writing and stopped. "You got a fishing license, right, Pete? You know you need a new one after March first."

Peletier shook his head. When the tickets were finished, Service tore off his copies and put the originals on the bar. "No license, fishing during the closed season, using illegal methods, and taking during the closed season. You don't have to appear at the court, Pete. You can call them and find out how much the fine is and mail it in. You have ten days to contact the court; otherwise, a warrant will be issued for your arrest."

Service turned to look at the others who were standing back from the bar. "Put a beer in your hand," he said.

The people moved slowly to the bar and lined up. Service removed Peletier's handcuffs.

Service lifted his bottle. "To the DNR."

Nobody drank, and Service chuckled. "Yeah, I can see how that would stick in your craws. C'mon boys, drink up and relax. No need to check for sugar in your gas tanks or pinched fuel lines tonight." Service looked at Peletier. "Long time coming, Pete, and it doesn't begin to make up for all you did, but something is better than nothing." Service paused. "The state pays me to do this job, but tonight I'd pay the state."

Peletier shook his head, rolled his eyes, and smiled. "Yeah, youse got me good, eh. But it took a long time."

Service picked up the bag of fish and headed for the door, flanked by Moody and McCants.

They dropped Service at the garage where his truck was hidden. "Sugar in gas tanks?" McCants asked.

"History," Service said, feeling as good as he had felt in a long time.

"You are unfuckingbelievable," McCants said.

Service looked her in the eye and grinned.

51

FORD RIVER, APRIL 25, 2004

"Every legend deserves a monument."

In preparation for retirement, Vince and Rose Vilardo had built a small log home on an oxbow in the Ford River. The house sat on a lump of high ground with river on three sides. Huge cedar trees leaned out over the water, in danger of falling in. As usual Service and Nantz were running late because of her. It didn't help their punctuality that the governor's personal security team had frisked them and put them through a metal detector before allowing them to walk up the muddy two-track driveway to the house. Along the way Service saw several black-clad state police officers positioned in the cedars along the river's edge—the governor's security detail.

Vince met them at the door with two glasses of Amarone.

The governor and her husband, Whit, were in the den, which had a picture window overlooking the dark river. Nantz and Lorelei Timms embraced as Service shook hands with Whit.

Service said, "So much security. Only three months as governor and she's already got people so yanked they want to whack her?" Service joked to the governor's husband.

"Looks like somebody already tried to get you," the governor shot back. "Where's Walter?"

"En route," Maridly said. "Allegedly."

"Late," Service said. "Karylanne is almost as bad as Mar. Have you figured out how to balance the state checkbook yet?"

Timms smiled. "If I eliminated everything in the state except health care, we still couldn't make up the deficit."

Service held up his glass. "Sam Bozian."

Governor Timms laughed. "He didn't do it all by himself, Grady."

Service was surprised when Odd Hegstrom walked into the room, leaning on a cane. He had to be in his mid-eighties now, and except for a limp, he had not changed much since the last time Service had seen him.

Rose brought Hegstrom a small glass of tomato juice and introduced him to Maridly. When she turned to Service, Hegstrom said, "Grady and I know each other." The distinguished-looking attorney looked over at him and added, "I hear you're still in the heart of the fray."

"I'm going to name Odd to take the remainder of Jeremy Vigo's term," Timms said. Vigo was a longtime member of the Natural Resources Commission, a hay farmer from Chippewa County. Commission members were appointed by the governor and as a group steered policy and other matters for the Department of Natural Resources. Vigo, who had died just before Christmas, had been a well-known champion of tribal causes, a position which often made him unpopular around the state.

Hegstrom seemed to guess what Service was thinking. "Contrary to popular belief," he said, "my firm has never had the tribes as clients for their casino interests. My involvement was strictly personal and pro bono to help with the feds and the treaty issues. I told Lori I'd take Jeremy's term to represent all constituencies, not a narrow few. We both know how legends grow once they start," Hegstrom concluded.

Legends. Service cringed at the word.

Hegstrom plucked a folded fifty-dollar bill out of his sport coat pocket and held it out with an unwavering hand. "Pete Peletier bet me in 1976 he would never be cited by the DNR. This morning he called me and told me about the tickets. He said his fifty was in the mail, so I thought you should have this now." Service did not reach for the money. "Pete can be obstinate, but he's also a man of his word, and I see, so too are you. Please take it."

"I don't want the jerk's money," Service said.

"It's not his, it's mine," Hegstrom said.

"Wiggle words," Service said.

Hegstrom bowed slightly. "Some professional habits are ingrained."

"It was your bet, Counselor, not mine. Besides, isn't there a statute of limitations on bets?"

Hegstrom smiled. "We're both gamblers, Detective, and I never thanked you for what you did for Anise Aucoin," he said, adding, "I was at Cecilia's memorial. That took courage on your part. It was audacious to put Pete on the spot like that. After that, mistrust spread like a virus, and a lot of the residents down there admired your being there—knowing it was a tremendous risk to you. I think things started to open up for your folks after that."

Service had never seen it that way, and changed the subject. "You knew Anise Aucoin was innocent and you knew Lapalme was involved. You asked me some questions that day in the interview room."

"Cecilia said you were aggressive and a man of integrity. I simply planted seeds and you took it from there."

"When it finally sank in," Service corrected him.

"Never discount luck in any undertaking," Hegstrom said, and when Service continued to ignore the money, he slid it back in his pocket and smiled. When Service sat down at the table, there was a dented metal thermos in front of him, crudely stenciled with the word SHUCK. Hegstrom looked at it deadpan, but Service knew it had been Hegstrom who had repatriated the thermos, probably from one of his Garden clients—perhaps even Peletier.

Vince had grilled a pork roast on a bed of apples and onions. The perfume rolling off the plate left Service salivating and wondering. The loose teeth had rattled in his mouth all day, and he wondered if he dared bite into it. The pork would be soft enough, probably, but the baked potatoes would have to be skinned. This tooth thing was a pain in the ass.

He was trying to decide what to do about the food when Walter and Karylanne rolled in. Vince said, "We were just sitting down, so sit. It's gettin' cold, eh?"

Walter was seventeen now but looked older. His time at Tech had already matured him, and Service approved of what he saw. Karylanne and Maridly both talked so fast their words thickened into verbal pudding.

"Hey, Pop," Walter said, eyeing his father's untouched food. "If you're not going to eat that, I can help you out."

Service pushed back from the table, folded his napkin by his plate, and glared at his son. "Touch it and you will become permanently left-handed."

He went to the bathroom, pulled some tissue paper out of a box, opened his mouth, and yanked the teeth one at a time. Both made a grinding, ripping sound, but came out. He rinsed his mouth with water until there was no more blood. He wrapped the teeth in tissue, stuffed them in his pocket, returned to the table, and attacked his dinner.

When he looked up he found everyone staring at him. "*What?*" he said.

Odd Hegstrom tapped his glass with his spoon and said, "Every legend deserves a monument."

Vince Vilardo hit a light switch and a grove of paper birches between the house and river flooded with light. Service stared at dozens of shiny yellow things dangling from the branches.

"Are those *floaties?*" Karylanne asked, giggling.

Service tried to act annoyed but ended up laughing as hard as the rest of them, and leaned over to Nantz and whispered, "McCants dies."

Maridly Nantz squeezed his arm and rested her head against his shoulder.

Grady Service felt content as he half-listened to table banter, but his mouth hurt and he still ached from his encounter in the culvert. The reality was that his body was failing him, no matter how hard he worked to stay in shape. How long could he keep doing this? He worried about Nantz and his son, but these were regular worries. Something deeper inside him was gnawing, a sense of dread growing, that despite all he had seen and gone through over the years, something even worse lay ahead.

AUTHOR'S NOTE

This book is not intended to be a history, but as a work of fiction I hope it captures the rancor, frustration, and nastiness inherent in the events of what I have chosen to call the Garden War, which began in the late 1960s and stretched on into the 1980s.

As wars go, it was relatively bloodless, and no one died. But the violence, tensions, and conflict were real and intense, and if the reputation of the Garden Peninsula and its residents continues to be one of lawlessness, it is the fault of a few, who willfully and repeatedly break laws. In talking to people it is clear that what went on was a form of domestic insurgency, and it was waged against conservation and other police officers who did not make the rules but were merely trying to enforce them.

To step out of the shadows of bullies and thugs takes a special kind of courage, but some courageous citizens of the Garden eventually did so.

In some ways I can understand the anger and frustrations of legitimate commercial fishermen who were threatened by politics and science, neither force in their favor, and both aimed at putting them out of business.

But I hold no sympathy for the rats.

The poaching of spawning fish continues in Big Bay de Noc and surrounding waters, and the illicit sale of illegally taken fish floods markets each spring and drives down prices set by legitimate businesspeople. Fish stolen from the citizens of Wisconsin and Michigan still find their way to Chicago and New York City fish markets.

Poaching is theft, driven by greed, and reveals a dark side of the human character. No race has exclusivity in this dirty business, and until it ends, game wardens and conservation officers will be out there to stop it—in conditions that defy description—with the support and understanding of their leadership in Lansing, and sometimes, when necessary, without it.

Conservation officers, unlike poachers, are rarely motivated by money. They work because they believe in and love what they do. Officers do not always agree with the rules and regulations they are asked to enforce, but enforce them they do.

I owe debts of gratitude to veterans of the Garden War who so selflessly and patiently gave of their time, sharing stories, memories, impressions, and yellowing clippings. Most of all, I thank the erudite late chief, Rick Asher, whose untimely death in 2003 touched us all. Others who tried their best to educate me include: Lieutenant John Wormwood (retired), Sergeant Ralph Bennett (retired), Officer Dave Vant Hof (retired), Lieutenant Tom Courchaine, Sergeant Darryl Shann, and officers Grant Emery (who introduced me to running dark, and took me on my first Garden patrol on an eighteen-degree "spring" night), and Steve Burton (who taught me the ins and outs of Wilsey Bay Creek).

I would also like to thank the DNR's media spokesperson, Brad Wurfel, who was helpful in countless ways (and whom I had the great pleasure of watching hook more than fifty king salmon with a fly rod in just one October day on the Muskegon River).

Others who have helped me gain a better understanding of the life and challenges of Michigan's Woods Cops include: Sergeant Tim Robson, Sergeant Mike Webster (retired), and officers Bobbi Bashore, John Huspen, Phil Wolbrink (retired), John Wenzel, Paul Higashi, Dave Painter, Ryan Aho, and Sergeant Gene Coulson (retired).

Any errors in the story are mine alone, a reflection of my failures as a student, not those of my teachers.

I sometimes worry that my stories of criminals and scofflaws in the Upper Peninsula will leave readers with the impression that the people who live in that harsh environment are all lawless and antisocial. They aren't. The majority of Yoopers are independent of spirit, passionate with opinions, adventurous, tough, loyal, and caring, and I am privileged to have so many as friends and fishing partners.

The mother of an old friend—a lifelong Yooper from St. Ignace—has taken exception to my calling the U.P. a wilderness. I told her I would happily refer to it differently if she would provide an alternate description. So far she hasn't produced, so I continue to say it is a wilderness that's easy to love, and I am glad we have it.

If nothing else, I hope these stories make people interested enough to take a look at the Upper Peninsula of Michigan and appreciate how lucky we are that its geography and people are a part of our state and culture.

I also thank my kids for putting up with my continual meanderings, and my agent Betsy Nolan and editor Lilly Golden for making me better than I am.

Joseph Heywood
Portage, Michigan
November 9, 2004

AFTERWORD

I have been privileged to patrol with Michigan Conservation officers for almost two decades, at a rate of about a month a year, which is a lot of butt-time in a truck in the woods. This has exposed me to the triumphs, heart-breaks, and frustrations of officers going about the difficult work of wildlife law enforcement, and it has led me to remarkable, enduring friendships, which I treasure.

Every citizen who takes an undersized or extra fish, or deer, is a thief. Such people steal from other citizens as surely as bank robbers.

But most miscreants are accidental, momentary transgressors, driven by an occasional surge of greed they can't easily fend off.

A small portion of the rest of such folks are not victims of momentary greed, but are driven by it. There are only a few such individuals, not linked by educational or socioeconomic status, but by an abiding intent which encompasses a mindset of I-will-do-what-I-want-and-nobody-can-make-me-do-otherwise. These folks, some of whom grow up in families which inculcate such values, and some who come to such crime on their own, commit themselves to large-scale theft and circumvention of rules and laws. They take what they want, when they want, how they want, from where they want and to hell with anyone who thinks they can stop them. These people do what they do to satisfy twisted egos and for financial gain. As a writer, these are the natural resource criminals who interest me most. My stories are about all transgressors in our natural resources world, but the last category assures that conservation officers (and writers) are likely to always have jobs that serve all of us, quietly, bravely, and largely unseen.

Joseph Heywood
Alberta, Michigan
August 20, 2018

Made in the USA
Monee, IL
26 October 2022

16564487R00194